Passed Over Master And Apprentice.

Brenn looked above him, expecting a wheeling bird or a thick rack of clouds. Instead, he saw that the stairs had extended themselves, spiralling around behind him and ascending to a narrow, shimmering landing on which a large door rested. It looked familiar somehow: thick, no doubt heavy, rough hewn of an especially sturdy-looking oak. It sat on a film of glittering air, as though it were afloat on a layer of extraordinarily clear ice.

Most striking of all, it seemed to lead to nowhere. Behind it lay an expanse of cloudless sky.

"Where does it lead to, Terrance?"

"It leads back home," the wizard answered cryptically, and not pausing for further questions, set foot on the first of the transparent stairs.

"Is this a vision, sir?" Brenn was giddy with the view. Or giddy with the height—he was not certain.

"You might call it that," Terrance mused. "That is, unless you're used to such scenery." Soon Terrance was four, five, six steps above him: if you turned your head just right, it seemed as though the wizard was standing on nothing.

He turned in the air and beckoned to Brenn . . .

A SORCERER'S APPRENTICE

MICHAEL WILLIAMS

POPULAR LIBRARY

An Imprint of Warner Books, Inc.

A Time Warner Company

For Teri, again.

POPULAR LIBRARY EDITION

Copyright © 1990 by Michael Williams

Popular Library®, the fanciful P design, and Questar®
are registered trademarks of Warner Books, Inc.

Cover illustration by Edwin Herdes
Cover design by Don Puckey

Popular Library books are published by
Warner Books, Inc.
666 Fifth Avenue
New York, N.Y. 10103

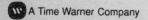 A Time Warner Company

Printed in the United States of America

First Printing: November, 1990

10 9 8 7 6 5 4 3 2 1

Acknowledgments

It's during the long hours of finishing a book that you become most grateful to those who helped you at various times in the process.

First of all, a long-standing thanks to Margaret Weis and to my agent, Scott Siegel, who believe my stories. Thanks also to Brian Thomsen, for giving me the chance to tell another one.

Special thanks to Peggy Leake for her guided herb lore tour and to Professor Thomas Van of the University of Louisville for pointing me toward helpful texts on medieval arms and warfare. Their assistance was invaluable: any mistakes regarding lance or plants proceed from my ignorance, not my ingratitude.

To Ruth Miller, Joan D'Antoni, Dick Humke, Anne Carter Mahaffey, and Steve Pike—my deepest thanks for their "many acts of kindness and of love." Also thanks to my parents, of course, for continued patience where impatience would be understandable.

Finally, of course, there is my wife Teri, who read the manuscript, proposed and discussed ideas, and helped guide the story from its inception, presenting suggestions and honest criticism that deepened and enriched both this book and the process of writing it.

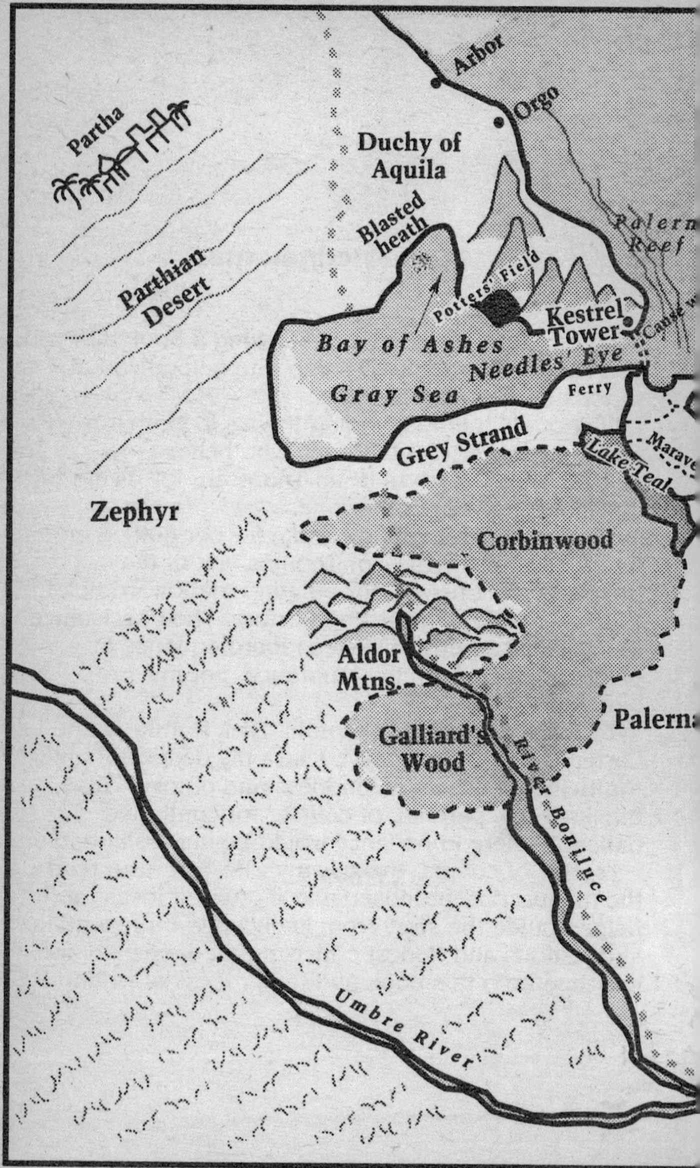
Arbor
Orgo
Partha
Duchy of Aquila
Blasted heath
Parthian Desert
Potters' Field
Kestrel Tower
Bay of Ashes
Needles' Eye
Gray Sea
Ferry
Grey Strand
Lake Teal
Zephyr
Corbinwood
Aldor Mtns.
Galliard's Wood
Palern
River Boniluce
Umbre River

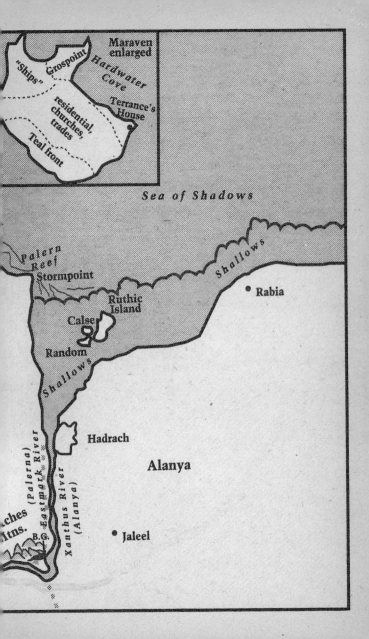

Maraven enlarged

"Ships"
Grospoint
Hardwater Cove
residential, churches, trades
Teal front
Terrance's House

Sea of Shadows

Palern Reef
Stormpoint
Shallows
Ruthic Island
• Rabia
Calse
Random
Shallows

(Palerna) Eastmark River
Xanthus River (Alanya)
Hadrach
Alanya
ches Mtns.
B.G.
• Jaleel

≺≺≺ **Prologue** ≻≻≻

In the topmost room of Kestrel Tower the woman murmured over the candles, her elegant, hawklike features uncommonly still. Around her a high humming sound filled the close air of the chamber, as though spirits or sirens wailed to her as she chanted.

The candlelight touched her pale skin with transparency, glittered in the gray wells of her eyes as she stared from one flame to the next, waiting for signs. At last her gaze rested on one, passing from the hot wavering air at its edges to the blue rim to the hottest fire encircling the wick, which burned yellow and white and yellow, then suddenly clear and silver like moonlight reflected off water.

"Ah," breathed the enchantress Ravenna, cupping her hands to the taper and continuing her chant, drawing closer, closer, until the gray of her eyes turned black, and the silver light at the heart of the flame seemed to be moonlight.

It was the calm sea she saw in the candle—the lulled, ashen waters of the Sea of Shadows as they appeared in the hushed hour before daybreak. A galley heaved into view around Stormpoint, its sails lowered and its crewmen poling their way through

1

the treacherous waters of Palern Reef. Its lanterns rocked slowly in the tranquil dark.

The ship was the *Constantin* out of Genoa, its cargo the customary cinnamon and saffron, and bolts of Cathayan silk. All hands were on the deck, the sailors vigilant in the monster-haunted, coral deadly waters. The captain was a Florentine, or so Ravenna guessed from the complex embroidery of flowers on his tabard. He was a gaunt man who looked to the prow and shivered as the city of Maraven lurched into view.

"*Grande città, pièna de duòlo e di torménto rio,*" he whispered to no one in particular, though the helmsman overheard and nodded grimly in agreement.

Ravenna frowned, straining to hear his words in the soft popping of the candle flame. What he was saying was elusive, and her Italian had never been good.

But it was something like "A great city, full of grief and of cruel torment."

"Florentines," the dark woman scoffed and, gracefully tying back her blue-black hair, peered into another candle.

In the last hour before the dawn, the docks were at their most silent, and even the most drunken of the sailors had returned to shipboard and hammock by now. A Venetian carrack rocked off the Grospoint. The ship had already unloaded its cargo, and now the captain dozed in his hammock, either braver or swifter to port than those Genoese still asail on the Sea of Shadows.

He was an older man who had sailed as far east as Sidon, west to Almaria, and beyond the Ice Latitudes northward, where the men are short-furred and tusked like oliphants. The city of Maraven and the surrounding lands of Palerna were unknown to him, though, hidden in his maps under drawings of dragons and leviathans, under compass roses and the bearded billowing faces of winds. He tossed in uneasy sleep, awash in the slow movement of tides and the mixed and cloying smell of spice and perfume and fish and rotting seaweed.

Ravenna peered closer into the candlelight where his image lay. " 'By each spot the most unholy,' " she began, " 'in each nook most melancholy . . .' " Intoning the words of the ancient chant until the veil of the captain's sleep parted before her expectant eyes and she looked into his dreams.

There the hangman's gibbets lined the causeway from Maraven to King Dragmond's Kestrel Tower, and black boils marbled the necks of the poor, and the dead were hauled forth in carts like cargo from the hold of an anchored ship, dropped unceremoniously in shallow boats, and rowed out onto the gray sea.

For after forty years of threat and rumor, of here an incident and there an outbreak, the Death had settled on Maraven to stay.

The enchantress smiled, and as she moved to yet another candle, a dark woman rode through the captain's imaginings on the back of an enormous raven.

In the new flame, she saw the Ships section of town, a district named when Maraven was little more than a harbor and a boatyard. Here the ships were built entirely outdoors, and by this hour of the night the square was empty except for the shells of galleons and pinnaces beached on their sides, masts stacked in alleys and sails hoisted atop houses as though the inhabitants awaited only prevailing winds to leave town altogether.

There were some, indeed, who would love to have ridden those ships away, into the farthest country. For since Dragmond had ascended the throne, beggars and unhoused laborers had filled Maraven, evicted from dwellings that were not much to begin with but were at least a roof and wall against November nights like this. Their houses given way to rows of monuments and statuary, the poor people flocked at night to the Street of the Boatwrights, to Tar Street and to Mizzen, where the ships lay half-formed, awaiting peg and hammer and pitch. There they crawled into boats and into the husks of boats, these outcasts, and sheltered themselves in the sweet, raw sawdust-smelling holds.

Three of them were dying of the plague that night, one of hunger. One, an older woman named Esperanza, of all things, simply fell asleep and refused to awaken in that mysterious and melancholy ending that some people, especially the old, seem bent on making in the hardest of times.

A boatwright's apprentice would find her near sunrise, a damp shawl around her shoulders and a little necklace of shells laced through her stiffening fingers. He would think of his own grandmother and close her hand about the necklace when the Watchmen came to cart her body out to the potter's field.

Along Hardwater Cove a sheer face of black rock descended to a black beach. At this hour all of it, beach and rock alike, was covered by the tide. Houses and storefronts towered over the gray water, little more than shabby outlines in the dense morning fog.

Torches bobbed between this sad array of buildings, casting a yellow light over the bleached and weather-beaten wood. A squadron of the Watch—"Dragmond's Inlaws," as the poor people called them in whispers—ambled down the Street of the Bookbinders on a less choice patrol. Moving wearily, cursing the night, each other, the chilly north wind off the water, the dozen men turned right onto Cove Road, an ancient, badly paved thoroughfare that followed the Hardwater Cove from Grospoint to the Eastern Gate.

Torchlight glistened on the red leather of the Watchmen's armor. Their shadows lengthened menacingly against the shop fronts. Now and then, it looked as though something darker moved along with them, afloat in the heart of those shadows.

Ravenna, breathing deeply, looked closer.

At the front of the patrol, the captain of the guard, a handsome, cold-eyed young man of about twenty or so, squinted as he watched elusive dipping lights—the lights of the *Constantin*, no doubt—weave through the Palern Reef, out where the Sea of Shadows stretched northward into the dark.

"On the job, boys," he ordered the uneasy lads behind him. "Be at your sharpest. We have the first ship of the morning. It's past the reef now, and we're past time for Wall Town."

"I say leave Wall Town to its own devices, Captain," one of the Watchmen called out, masked by the darkness and by those around him. "Why risk the Death or a knife in the ribs for a mess of outlanders and paupers?"

A grumble of agreement rose from the ranks.

The captain pretended not to hear. Instead, he steered his

company right onto the Hadrach Road, toward the middle of Wall Town, where each large stone house sheltered four, five, even six families, where the sores of the plague were beginning to spread of late, and where, in the last week alone, the first death cart had been sent to dine.

As the column turned its back on the shore and headed southward, each man wrapped his face with a silk scarf and slipped a clove into his mouth. This week the Venetians, who had lived with the Death for a century, were telling the Maravenians that the plague newly rising in their midst rode from victim to victim on the stench in the air.

"Of course," Ravenna observed with a smile, lifting her eyes from the candle and glancing around the chamber, where Dragmond's arms—a dragon displayed, clutching a globe in its talons—emblazoned a dozen shields hung high on the walls. "The Venetians have a surplus of clove and of silk."

She yawned, stretched sinuously. Soon she lost the Watchmen amid shack and signboard and narrowing street. At the edge of the candle another light arose—a light more fresh, more clear and healthy.

It would be an hour yet before the new light reached the city, cutting through fog and darkness and the silence of the alleys. But its presence in the candle marked the end of the search.

Quickly, deftly, the enchantress extinguished the flames, breathing the last words of the incantation as her eyes paled to their accustomed gray. She felt colder suddenly, as she always did when the circle of light dwindled around her.

Wrapping her dark blue robe tightly about her shoulders, Ravenna descended the stairs to her bedroom, where King Dragmond would be stirring, eager for intelligence.

Cove Road was still for only a moment after the Watch passed.
Something skittered in an alley. The swift sound of a wingbeat
rushed by overhead.

Then a muffled sound rose from somewhere in the face of the
rock.

It was scarcely solid, this natural stone wall at the north of
the city: it had been pocked and honeycombed and in some parts
hollowed by eons of water and the sporadic fires that had formed
it in the first place. There were caverns and tunnels riddling the
coast of Palerna—nothing large or even permanently dry, but if
you were watchful and tidewise, they were large enough and
dry enough.

Four small forms scrambled up the dark, spongy rocks onto
Cove Road. Slight, hooded, they brushed sand from themselves
and laughed quietly.

"Wonder what the Watch was after, Squab?" the tallest one
of them asked as the four stood together in midstreet. The tall
one wore the red leggings of a Watchman beneath the dark cloak,
but her accent—for it was a girl beneath cloak and leggings—
was certainly not the aristocratic brogue of the Teal Front.

"After the fact," the short, fat one said.

The other three laughed.

"The way I figure it," said a third, the smallest, "we've an hour or so afore the light breaks and the new Watch comes this way. Now where's this house you're so hot to rifle, Brennart?"

The fourth, the silent one, turned and walked east down Cove Road, and the others followed.

At the far northeast of the city, where the Maraven Wall finally ended at the waters of Hardwater Cove after skirting the entire eastern half of the town, there was a small stone house where wall and water met. Round and squat, it appeared to have started as a turret or a lighthouse before the builder had second thoughts somewhere in the midst of its third story. As a result, it looked as though some great shearing instrument had emerged from the sea and lopped off the top of it: the topmost windows suggested an attic or upper story scarcely tall enough for a man to stand in, and out of the roof a stairway rose, its steps spiraling up into nowhere. Around the yard of the place lay rubble, builder's stone, weathered wood.

"Are you sure it isn't abandoned, Brennart?" the tall one whispered as Squab broke from the others, assuming a post where Leeside Alley joined Cove Road a street or so from the house in question.

"Saw lights atop it yestere'en," Brennart answered curtly, pointing. "In that window there, I think. In one other, I don't remember which. Leastways, that's no sign of abandoned, the way I got it figured. Now . . . are we about our business, or must I talk you into this again and again?"

The tall one shrugged and moved gracefully toward the house. Brennart and the small one followed. The three of them reached the wall at the same time, slipping along it through shadow and moonlight like smoke in a brisk wind.

"Up on the roof, Dirk," Brennart ordered. "But you'll be taking my cloak with you, for the wind atop is a norther."

Quickly and wordlessly, as though the offer might be revoked at any moment, the small one snatched Brennart's cloak and scrambled up the side of the house like a spider up the frame of a window.

"Why, thankee, Brennart, for your kindness," Brennart muttered, his voice high and mocking and cynical.

With Squab down the street as a lookout, and Dirk perched nimbly on the eaves, Brennart and the tall girl slipped to the side door, where the Maraven Wall and the eaves of the house hid them from passersby. They paused there and listened.

"Reckon *he* lives here?" the girl asked.

"What difference does it make, Faye?" Brennart replied impatiently, crouched and attending to the lock at the door.

"What if he *does* live here, Brenn?" Faye whispered tauntingly. "What if he . . . changes you into an eel or something?"

Brenn snorted. Out of the dark came the rattle and scrape of metal against metal.

"I have heard that such changes take place regularly, Brenn," Faye persisted, her back to her busy friend. "Goniph says this'n is fond of the form of the rat, since he keeps an old dog fond of rattin'."

She stared westward down Cove Road. Squab crouched where they left him, dark in the light of the half moon.

"I have heard, for that matter, that a wizard is fond of . . . shrinking body parts boys don't care to have shrunk."

"Enough!" Brenn hissed. "Attend to the streets instead of the sport . . ."

"Locked as well, Brenn," Dirk called softly from overhead, leaning over the eaves like a dwarfish gargoyle, his warm cape snug at his shoulders.

"You can always gouge at the other if this one's past your skills," Faye observed. She smiled crookedly, her eyes still alertly scanning Cove Road.

"Do *you* want to try it, Faye?" Brennart asked, a little loudly and defensively, shivering as he held a thin, awllike tool up to the hooded girl above him. Then, more softly: "It's a simple lock, but for some reason I can't compass it. Bring a candle this way, so's I can get a look at it."

"Not on your life," Faye insisted. "No telling who's on watch for the likes of us."

Nonetheless, she fumbled in her cloak for a candle and tinderbox. For a moment, brief as a passing shadow—perhaps a bird overhead or a cloud passing rapidly below the moon, borne on a sudden and violent wind in the high skies—the door darkened further still, and she looked up.

The sky was clear above her. The Forest Lord was on the rise in the southern sky, three lonely stars at his belt.

What is this? Faye thought. *What is the rareness of this night, that I am thinking 'Watch closely, remember everything'?* Then there was a click in the darkness below her—a sound as brittle as breaking ice.

"Keep your light," Brennart announced triumphantly, setting his hand confidently to the latch.

Something's awry, Faye thought, her eyes racing over the alley and the roof and even over the timbers of the door. *Something's far awry, and I'll be kicking myself when it comes to me clear as the daylight and just as unwelcome.*

Above them, Dirk scrambled to the top of the half-finished stairwell, the highest point in the house, and signaled Squab with a brisk, dramatic wave. He paused: there was something about the air at that height, or the particular cloudiness of that evening, or the reflection of moonlight on the cove, he was not sure. Whatever it was, the city looked changed from atop the turret house. Wall Town seemed less urban and dingy, perhaps: the endless sequences of roof and spire and chimney Dirk knew firsthand gave way to open courtyards he did not remember ever having passed by or even heard about.

In the midst of these courtyards, though it was difficult to tell by night, there seemed to be groves of trees and spectacular fountains.

Dirk, however, was not one for marveling. He shrugged, signaled wildly to Squab, and scurried down the strange, broken platform, as Brennart slipped through the door below and Faye, pausing a moment to look behind her, followed him inside.

"What kind of room would you call this, Faye?" Brennart whispered.

"A study," she replied, at last lighting the candle. "A library."

The single taper bathed the room in a feeble light, wavering over a high-topped mahogany desk, its shelves and writing surface white with vellum and paper. The leather spines of a thousand books shone atop heavy shelves lining two of the walls: the shelving on the third rose around a squat, unlit fireplace, and the fourth wall was bare except for a hat rack, a lectern, an odd pair of skeletal, wooden wings discarded in the corner, and yet another door that seemed to lead back into the darkened house.

"Nothing but books and scrolls and manuscripts here," Faye pronounced. "And junk."

"And the books well used, damn it," Brenn added, standing in the center of the room while Faye moved immediately toward the secretary, rifling through its drawers and pigeonholes. "Goniph always says—"

"—'Leave be a house where the books are worn, for reading is a sign that a man has no money.' I know, Brenn. I know the Rule of Hand better than you do."

Faye frowned, held up something small and glittering to the candlelight, shrugged, and pocketed it. Brenn started to ask her what it was, but she interrupted.

"Fact is, we're in here: the lock lifted and the lookouts posted. Might as well see what we can find."

Brenn nodded, brushed back his hood, and moved toward the farthest shelf. Holding the books aloft in an awkward attempt to catch the candlelight, he whispered their titles. Faye shook her head each time he stumbled over longer words.

"Aquilan Con . . . Conj . . ."

"Conjury," Faye grunted as she scooted the secretary out from the wall, checking behind it for secret compartments. "Invoking, it means. Calling things up. Though if the Aquilans were ever any good at it, they'd fix up their mess of a country."

"I can't even start with this one." Brenn chuckled, holding up the spine of another book so that Faye, emerging from behind the desk, could read the title by the dim candlelight.

"Thaumaturgy."

Brenn looked at her in bafflement.

"Damned if I know, Brenn."

"The crafting of miracles," a small voice whispered, faint and high-pitched and insinuating. Brenn looked at Faye, who continued to stare curiously at the book, having said nothing. Then he shook his head, thinking that something—a flea perhaps, or a mosquito late in season—had crawled into his ear and made him hear things.

It was funny, but in the wake of that whisper he heard pipes and the sound of tumbling water.

Late had become early. No doubt he was tired.

"Well, I didn't come here to read, Faye," the boy pronounced, reaching for the book. "Let's see what's . . ."

Suddenly the room was awash in a bright green light. Faye bolted for the door, into the darkness almost before the dropped book of thaumaturgy struck the ground.

The air outside the house tasted of limes, as the silence of the night was broken by the slamming of the door.

Dirk was halfway down the wall as Faye passed him, his short legs whirling, three steps for her two, as he tried to keep up with her down Cove Road. Squab watched them approach, framed in the light of the circular house behind them, and grabbed Faye by the arm as she glided past him.

"Where's Brenn?" he hissed.

Dumbfounded, Faye and Dirk spun about.

"I thought . . ." Faye began.

"Well, it looks like you were thinkin' wrong," Squab said coldly. "Goniph will be *charmed* by this, I'm certain."

Faye started back for the house, but both of her friends restrained her.

"Leave him, Faye," Dirk whispered. "He's in the hands of Dame Fortune now."

"Or Dame Sorrow," Squab added ominously.

The three of them stood at the intersection, watching the green light in the house pass from one window to the next and back again, as though some small, luminous creature was trying to free itself.

"Reckon he's a crab or a squinchfly by now?" Squab asked maliciously. "Or quarry for the dog?"

Least experienced of the group when it came to burglary and inside theft, Brenn froze at the sudden rush of light over the books in front of him. In the fraction of a second before he realized he had been discovered, he thought he was caught at the edge of an explosion—of some terrible eruption where shock and sound followed the first flash of light—and he braced himself for the fire and concussion that did not come.

Instead, he heard the footsteps behind him, racing across the floor and onto the cobblestones outside.

He heard the door slam shut, and he whirled to face the center of the room.

Later he would recall that the night's weariness had left him altogether and that the room smelled of mown grass and juniper.

Brenn sank despairingly to the floor and covered his face, awaiting the growth of a pig's snout, or six legs and an exoskeleton. Meanwhile the shadows of table and secretary and book-laden shelves towered menacingly above him, deep violet-red against the green light of the room.

Suddenly the shadow of the hat rack in the far corner grew and lengthened, then broke away from the rack itself and coursed insanely up a far wall.

Though the boy could not tell by eye, ear, or any of the senses, he knew, as a thief knows by instinct on a crowded market day, that a set of watchful eyes was on him—someone else had come into the room. Slowly he spread his hands, peering through his fingers at the dodging shadows about him.

Brenn reached for his knife, and a voice tumbled from the shelves above.

"Last thing you should do. What good's a knife against shadows and air?"

Brenn gasped, sat back heavily against the door. Frantically he scanned the room for a foe more substantial than light or shade, and again the voice spoke to him, this time from the book of thaumaturgy Faye had dropped in her frightened getaway. It lay on its spine on the floor in front of him, its pages turning back and forth in a switching wind.

"What good are your eyes and your ears? As loyal to you as your friends?" the voice prompted.

Brenn turned, desperately rattling the latch of the door. It would not give, but spoke to him instead, the same voice rising from the palm of his hand.

"The first story is easy to enter, not so easy to leave," it said, and chuckled almost pleasantly, as the green light swirled around the door, around the astonished boy, who leapt backward into a shelf, dazing himself in a rain of vellum and pens and books.

Brenn sighed and turned back to face the center of the room and the changing shadows and whatever else awaited him, as another cluster of shadows thickened and darkened and took on form in the far doorway.

In the strange light filling the library the wizard looked imposing indeed, dark-robed and magnificent and green like a god of shipwrecks. His hair and beard were long, tangled like seaweed, and a white flame nestled in each of his lifted hands. He spread apart his fingers, the white light rushed to the ceiling . . .

And the room settled. Its corners became distinct and its glow faded into the ordinary light of a hurricane lamp and a half-dozen or so candles, one of which, Brennart noted with alarm, was anchored by its wax firmly atop a human skull, staring at him from the top of a large mahogany table littered with machinery and glassware.

In the candlelight the man's dark robes dwindled into a simple brown nightshirt. His long flowing hair and beard paled and silvered and took on a less intimidating length. Where before he had looked terrifying and masterful, now he was only sleepy and bemused—more like a schoolteacher than a sorcerer.

"I suppose I couldn't get you to forget this ever happened?" the boy asked weakly.

"I'm not good at forgetting things," the wizard replied with a quirky half smile. His accent was country Palernan, pronouncing his "not" as a strange down-country "notte."

Facing the tall man, who stooped and smiled like a benign old crane, Brennart backed toward the door by which he had entered this library, intent on trying it one last time.

"May Those Who Stand Up for Thieves grant me a safe

departure and a dark night," he entreated under his breath, and reached behind him, his hand coursing quickly to the latch.

It was still locked firmly and tightly, though now it had the decency not to speak.

"Damn!" Brennart spat, wishing dire punishment upon Faye and Dirk. Just as quickly he took the wish back, when he remembered the rusted works of the lock breaking neatly but a moment ago.

"Who *are* you?" he shouted at the man in front of him.

The old fellow shook his head and snorted, while settling onto a tall stool by a lectern covered with papers. His knees poked pale and knobby from beneath his long brown nightshirt: it would have been a funny sight, given less frightening circumstances.

"You have all the brass in Palerna, don't you, boy?" he asked in a deeper, more melodious voice than Brennart had expected.

"That was someone else, sir. I mainly pick locks."

"No, no. Not what I mean at all," the man said with a smile.

Brennart waited silently, hand still fixed to the latch of the door.

"It's just that where I come from," the man explained quietly, almost casually, "questions such as 'who are you?' or 'what are you doing here?' are more . . . proper from the burgled than the burglar."

"You *are* a sorcerer, aren't you?" Brennart asked, giving the door behind him a quick, secret tug. Where before there had been some give, some play, as though a stronger man might have yanked the damned thing open, now the door was resolute. It seemed like part of the wall.

So much for safe departure and dark nights.

"What if we begin anew? Are you a thief?" the man asked, rising from the stool and walking briskly to the contraption-littered mahogany table.

"'Tis a harsh word for what I do, sir."

"As is 'sorcerer,' lad, for my own work," the man replied, picking up something bronze and complicated from the mess in front of him. Half in the light of the skull candle, he turned away from Brenn, his hands busily adjusting the device.

"If not 'thief,' boy, how would you rather I call you?"

"I have come to prefer the term 'enterpriser,' sir," Brenn replied stiffly, backing toward the door and pushing so ardently at the latch that his fingers throbbed.

"And I the term 'counselor,' " the man replied. "By the way, you can pry at that thing all night if you choose to. It is firmly—and I might add, metaphysically—locked."

Brennart shouldered into the door one last, forlorn time, on the off chance that his captor was a liar. The latch had become a natural formation, as firm as the rock face on the cove outside, as solid as the Aquilan Mountains.

"What do you have in mind for me, Sir Counselor? Will you give me over to the Watch?"

"Please, please. Terrance will do, lad. We don't go all that much for titles around this house. For reasons you shall see," he added darkly.

"What do you have in mind for me, Terrance?"

Brennart scanned the room quickly for other doors, for windows—for anything leading from this library to the outside. Aside from the farfetched prospect of climbing up the fireplace and aside from the door through which Terrance had come, the room was airtight, like a cell or a mausoleum.

Cautiously Brenn looked back at the sorcerer—or counselor —who had set the bronze device back onto the table and was now fumbling through the folds of his robe, in search of something.

"If . . . if you're searching for a wand, sir, or a globe of transforming . . . perhaps we can discuss it for a moment before you go about changing me into something small and six-legged and repulsive that you can step on and sweep out the doorway tomorrow."

"What in blazes is a 'globe of transforming,' young man? Never heard of such a thing. Ah, here it is."

Terrance drew a roll of vellum out of the ragged brown cloth, and Brennart curled against the door in terror, thinking *Scroll! Scroll! This is my last night as a human!*

The wizard tossed the roll toward him. It struck the ground beside him, and he flinched, awaiting explosions or fire or other magical disasters.

"Oh . . . it's nothing nearly as dramatic as you have in mind, Brennart," Terrance said, seating himself again on the stool.

"Wait. Wait. How do you know my name?"

"It's right there on the document." The wizard smiled. "Step over by the fire. Warmer there. You're still shivering."

"What fire?" Brenn asked, glancing at the cold hearth.

Wordlessly the wizard extended his hand, and the charred and weathered logs at the back of the fireplace burst into flame and crackled cheerily, invitingly.

Brennart swallowed hard. Reluctantly he picked up the vellum and peered suspiciously at the elegant italic script that filled it.

Indeed, his name was written throughout. In a different hand and ink, to be sure, but his name, nonetheless.

"Oh," he said meekly, turning the vellum curiously in his hands and moving meekly toward the fireplace.

"A writ of indenture," Terrance explained.

"What's that?"

Again the wizard reached into his robe.

"A simple legal document. Read it if you like."

"How do you know my name?"

"Read."

Brennart sat back, scanning the formal script, the seals, the wizard's scrawled signature at the bottom of the sheet. His lips moved in silence, and with his finger he traced one line of script, then another. He frowned and held the document at arm's length.

"Bunch of double-talk. Like an Alanyan trade agreement, filled with whereases and parties of the second part. What does it mean?"

"Simple," Terrance declared, drawing a bottle, then a gourd, then a tiny short-tailed rodent, then finally a quill from the folds of his robe. "At last. Knew it was there.

"A writ of indenture makes formal the intention of two parties to work together. For a period of five years, you're my apprentice, doing various odd things around an odd house."

The wizard smiled ironically, eyes fixed on Brennart.

"What you're to do is sign—there at the bottom, by my signature."

Set lightly on the table, the rodent slipped into the eye of the skull, where it curled up happily and went to sleep beneath bone and tallow and fire.

"Why me?" the boy asked, holding the roll up to his nose.

"Your name on the writ, innit?" the wizard asked, his smile broadening as he extended the pen to Brennart.

"What if I don't sign?" Brennart challenged. "My guild-master told me never to sign nothing without him being there."

"Then it will be the . . . *sorcery*," Terrance pronounced dramatically and confidently, turning the feather in his hand, brushing the end delicately across the face of the skull, then through the tip of the candle flame. "Or the Watch. Your choice. All your choice."

There was a brief, foul-smelling burst as flame touched feather, and a menacing hiss as the wizard wetted his fingers and pinched the burning end of the quill.

"By your signature, you say?" Brennart quickly offered, reaching for the pen. Terrance produced a small inkhorn from the robe, ceremoniously handing it and the quill to the cowering boy by the door.

Brennart clumsily signed, his printed letters broken and awk-ward next to the cultivated script of the wizard.

What difference does a signature make, anyway? the boy thought, smiling as innocently as he could imagine as he offered it all—pen, horn, and document—back to Terrance, who ac-cepted it casually, almost offhandedly, as if it were every night of the week that a burglar broke into a house, only to sign away five years of his life to the very person he intended to burgle.

What difference does a signature make? If the old coot is foolish enough to take this as binding, I'll be halfway down Cove Road before the ink dries at the bottom of that page.

"There. That wasn't hard, now was it?" Terrance asked sooth-ingly. He looked at the document, frowned at Brennart's sig-nature, and stuffed it all—quill and inkhorn and vellum—back into the folds of his robe.

Where no doubt it would be eaten by moth or dormouse, Brenn thought. Or by the rodent who scrambled out of the cavernous eye of the skull and leapt through the candlelit air, flashing gray on silver on gray as it landed softly somewhere in Terrance's ragged brown pockets. The wizard folded his arms and stared calmly at the boy, his robe still churning and rustling from all the goings in and out.

Brennart cleared his throat.

"Now that we have transacted, sir, maybe you can tell me what all my service involves?"

So I can laugh about it with my friends tomorrow when I'm miles clear of this place.

Terrance rose slowly and picked up the bottle he had drawn from his robe. Full of something amber and inviting, it was.

Whiskey, no doubt, Brennart thought. *Good. The old man's a rum hound to boot. All the better should there be noise when I spring myself.*

But a rum hound Terrance apparently was not. He drained the bottle, but curled his lip disgustedly, as though its contents were something he was forced to take—medicinal, for sure, and perhaps even magical. Quickly he wiped his mouth, then shook his head.

"They can make a dragon out of smoke and conjury," he muttered, "and yet a good-tasting potion is beyond their power.

"But regardless of the taste," he sighed. "Drinking these things has just become necessary."

Setting down the bottle, Terrance turned to Brennart. For the first time since their sudden and accidental meeting, the old man's smile was warm, almost kindly. Pulling his robe close about him, he turned and walked from the room.

"Good night, Brennart," he called over his shoulder as around him the flames of the candles waned and dimmed and finally went out, leaving the room lit only by the glow of the hearth.

"How do you know my *name*?" Brennart called after him urgently, almost desperately.

The wizard stopped in the doorway.

"I rise with the sun—no later," he stated, reaching into his cloak and pulling out something shapeless that had apparently ignited in the dark folds of the cloth. He waved his hands dramatically, as though shaking off the fire, then smiled and winked at Brenn.

For a moment he looked older, more weary than Brenn had imagined him.

"By sunrise, the kitchen fire should be blazing, water heated, the rooms swept and dusted, and fresh rushes laid at the main entrance and through the front hall. That's what the writ says.''

"Absolutely, sir!" Brennart called out, stifling a laugh. Whatever door or window in this circular, godforsaken place had been left open or ajar or even unlocked, the boy was sure he would find it. There would be plenty of time to climb out and down to the street, to rejoin his companions and tell them the story, complete with a fanciful lie or two, before sunrise sent the lot of them into the cellars where the guild was quartered.

"Oh. The writ also says that you cannot escape," Terrance declared, looking over his shoulder and winking.

"I have no intention of doing so, sir."

"Neither here nor there," the wizard remarked. "You've signed on for the voyage."

The very moment Terrance was out of earshot on his way up the steps, Brenn sprang into action. Racing through the downstairs as though he had been set on fire, the boy crashed against the rough-hewn banister of the stairway, careened off it through the kitchen and into the corridor, and within a breath found himself in the solar—the enormous dining and receiving room at the front of the house.

The main door was not promising. It was locked with three locks, each of which would have been a night's work for a thief twice as skilled as Brennart to open or pick or dismantle. After a few minutes with his knife at the first of these, the boy sighed, slipped his weapon back into the pouch at his belt.

"Upstairs," he whispered, and scurried out into the corridor.

Halfway up the stairs Brenn stopped dead in his tracks, looked up into the green, waving light, and heard the sound of snoring, of wings beating, and of a strange, shrill song in a minor key. It was more dangerous, he knew. For that was where Terrance slept, evidently, and a wizard roused suddenly from sleep by the squeak of a floorboard or by something shifted or toppled on a shelf could change a boy into seaweed or imprison him in crystal.

Though Brenn was by no means a coward, the mystery of what lay above him, not to mention the menacing things his own imagination called up, caused him to turn on his heels and race back down the steps, slipping on the last one and somersaulting down the corridor, back into the entrance to the solar, where he lay for a dazed moment, rubbing his battered back.

There in Terrance's huge front room, propped where it belonged by the man-sized fireplace, a black iron poker nearly as tall as Brennart lay clean with disuse. The boy picked it up, turned it in his hands. The poker had a heft to it, a sturdiness.

Darker thoughts may have crossed his mind as he held the heavy iron tool. After all, the place was remote, at the easternmost end of town. Nobody—not even the thieves—was sure who did or didn't live here. There are few fourteen-year-old boys, brought up as Brennart had been brought up and trapped in the house of a strange and frightening old man, who would not have entertained thoughts of violence, even for a moment.

And yet, if those thoughts crossed the boy's mind, they crossed so quickly he had no time to recognize them. For he thought like a thief, not an assassin.

"We'll see how sturdy that grillwork is," he whispered, and scrambled onto the oaken table.

Had someone passed by Terrance's house in the darkest part of the morning, the lamplight that filtered through the iron latticework of the solar windows would have uncovered an odd scene indeed. A slight, wiry boy, having hooked one end of the fireplace poker through the iron grid of the kitchen window, now dangled desperately, with a slowly slipping grip, from the other end, hoping to use his weight as leverage to pull the ironwork from its moorings. Pots and cleavers and metal cups dangled in turn from his belt. In the deep and deceptive shadows of the ceiling, it might have looked for a moment as though Terrance had hanged a tinker.

The clatter when the boy fell was tremendous. Pots tumbled and broke across the floor, and there followed a brief silence. Then the whole downstairs was filled with the sound of small, skittering feet as the startled mice and grannars that had crept from the walls to scavenge took cover.

Brennart groaned and stood up, shedding saucepans and ladles, rubbing his backside. One sad tin cup that had remained tied to his belt swayed there, sad and wrinkled and mashed like a piece of bad armor.

"Designed by a damned engineer, *all* of them!" he hissed, and stomped back into the library. There, in the fading lamplight, he lifted volume after volume from the shelves, searching methodically behind them for secret passages, for the sudden shift or movement of a book that would set a wall spinning and reveal a tunnel or a stairway or something the books were there to hide.

All he found, though, were more books, then more books, then bare stone walls.

Seated on the topmost shelf of the library, Brennart looked down into the litter of books and manuscripts and scrolls. At first he had stacked them neatly on tables and lecterns. Then, as the hours wore on and he had climbed higher and higher up the shelves in search of that passageway to freedom, he had discarded them more randomly, more quickly and desperately.

Below him the covers of books lay open, the pages turning back and forth in the aftershock of their flight from topmost shelf to the library floor below. It looked like a landscape of paper and linen and vellum below him, as though it had snowed in the library.

Brennart sighed, climbed down the shelf, and stepped carefully through the book-littered room. He passed the cleaner kitchen floor, where through the big window the first sun rays of morning glimmered mockingly over metal. Heavy with fatigue and drowsiness, he wandered finally into the front room where he climbed atop the oaken table and, lying on his back, stared out the small grated window directly above him.

There the Forest Lord had risen to the height of the lightening sky, the bright stars in his belt paling overhead, the green unfixed star of Pytho dimly afloat in their midst. Brennart had heard the astrologers talk of this, and he had listened, for celestial sciences were the only ones that interested him. It was said that when the green star came to the belt of the Forest Lord, we should expect great changes—quiet at first, as great changes often are, but growing in weight and importance as the days progressed, long after Pytho had left for another quarter of the sky, in perpetual search of the home she would never find.

Sleepily the boy mused that whatever those changes were, it looked as though he would be stuck here, missing all the excitement while he stewed under some kind of magical house arrest.

"Why he would want me as apprentice is beyond my knowing," he thought aloud, folding his hands behind his head, his eyelids sinking drowsily. "But my name was all over that contract.

"Still, I've heard the merchants say paper and ink can dry and crumble. That they bind nothing more than good intentions. When I think of it, maybe even the intentions around here are not so good.

"The doors are locked. And the windows. But there's a way out of here, I'll warrant, if it takes a week or a month or a year to find it.

"And in the meanwhile, I guess I've never heard of an enterpriser who'd be hurt by knowing a little magic."

Brennart paused and closed his eyes.

"I suppose," he whispered to himself, resigned for the moment to his circumstances and tottering at the edge of sleep, "I'd better find the broom and get to work about this place."

So, bearing the best of intentions, he sank into sleep as the green star crept into the belt of the Forest Lord.

As Brennart drowsed, as the sun rose behind the Maraven Wall and the light from Pytho and from the Forest Lord dimmed and faded into the morning sky, Ravenna gave up her vigil, too.

She turned from the chamber window. Caught in the sunlight for a moment, that pale and flawless skin seemed stretched and fragile, the famous ebony hair lifeless and tired. To the mirror she walked, and as she gazed long and hard into her reflection, her face took on its old vigor and life, and the color returned to her countenance.

Behind her, on the huge royal bed, King Dragmond stirred toward wakefulness.

"Sleep now, my lord," the enchantress whispered, her eyes on Dragmond's reflection. "Sleep now, for the snake is in the forest, and a long night of wakefulness is coming."

Dragmond awoke to find her staring calmly into the mirror, her smile assured and fathomless and beautiful.

III

Brenn started from his sleep to find the alert face of the wizard poised above him. It seemed Terrance had been waiting there for some time, and winked when he saw that the boy was fully awake.

Groggy and a little alarmed at the prospect of a wizard craning over him, Brenn rolled away from the foxlike nose and the clear green eyes, dodging imagined thunderbolts, the infamous fireballs that transform the unlucky offenders of magicians into salamanders. Instead, he toppled to a very unmagical dirt floor and landed badly, his head ringing from solid contact with a capsized iron kettle.

"I think you have misread the writ, lad," Terrance explained casually.

Brenn felt he had dropped off the table into the midst of a conversation. He scrambled to his knees and rubbed his eyes.

"Or did you skip over Addendum B to the sixteenth clause?" Terrance asked solemnly, drawing writ and spectacles from the fresh blue robe he was wearing, donning the spectacles, and opening the writ.

"Which reads," he continued, squinting, " 'The party of the first part doth by no means fashion, understand, or fancy that the cleaning of a house involves removing item, material, or artifact from its proper and natural position and casting said item, material, or artifact, into a place determined by the party of the second part as *in the way*.' "

"Beg your pardon?" Brenn muttered, rising sluggishly to his feet.

"In short, it is not your job to disrupt things, but to put things back."

Brenn glanced quickly around the solar, finding to his surprise

24

that everything was returned to its place—everything, that is, except the offending kettle, which it almost seemed had been left there to emphasize his fall from the table.

"You . . . you've tidied the place while I slept," he observed.

Terrance rolled his eyes as he pulled a chair up to the table.

"Pots and pages so deep I got mad wading through them to breakfast. I had no choice but spellcraft."

Brenn ran his finger in disbelief across the immaculate surface of the table—dusted, apparently, while he lay sleeping atop it.

"Then why," he asked, "have you any need of me?"

"Who says *I* have need of *you*?" The old man laughed. "Now, if there's one thing I know of boys, it's that they require more breakfast than civilized people. Eggs?"

"Indeed, sir!" Brenn marveled, unable to remember the last time that it was more than a piece of dry bread and a cup of tea that carried him through the morning. He recalled Faye and Dirk crouched in the rocks by the seashore, over a faint fire and a scrawny sliver of fish.

"Fish jerky," Dirk would say. "Good for ye."

At least one good meal would follow the wreck of an evening. He'd have something to brag about when he got back to them.

"Climb the stairs," Terrance ordered, "and you'll find two rooms. Don't go in mine: the door's closed and should stay that way. The other is the guest room. At this time one of our guests is a setting hen by the name of Gallina. She'll no doubt object to your taking her eggs, but consider the process of taking them something to get you on your toes of a morning. I'll have no sluggishness once we waken."

Carefully, as if the wretched thing were made of porcelain or cut glass, the wizard lifted the iron kettle from the floor and placed it softly on a hook above the fireplace.

"Then, sir . . ." Brenn ventured, putting his hands into his pockets and backing toward the stairwell, "after breakfast? Do I have to begin my . . . lessons?"

Terrance crouched by the fireplace, using the bent and battered poker to stir the flames into life. Turning toward the boy, he smiled cryptically, half of his hawkish face bathed in firelight.

"Your lessons, Brennart, have already begun."

* * *

The boy ascended the stairs, muttering. At the second-floor landing he stopped, caught in the blue light of a tinted glass window.

There on the landing, egg basket in hand, he felt an icy wind pass through him and smelled the sharp, metallic odor that follows a spring rain. He stepped from the landing into the warm darkness of the upstairs corridor.

It was unusual—all this sunlight and color. It was even unsettling. Accustomed to burrowing into cellars like a rat or a mole by day, then emerging by night to be about his business, Brennart saw the world as a rule in blacks and whites and grays and silvers—in the muted tones of moonlight. He was not sure that he liked the reds and greens and blues of Terrance's house.

"While you're about the upstairs," the basket in his hand chirped, something in its voice metallic also, like the sound of chimes or of sleigh bells, "you might as well look about your quarters in the attic."

Brennart sighed, picked up the basket he had just dropped in astonishment, and walked toward the entrance to the guest room.

It was an incredible room to be taken over by chickens. Gallina had settled the threshold as her own, firm atop her nest, her red and white tail toward the center of the room. The rows of her neck feathers spread like a mane when Brennart approached, and she squawked threateningly, dipping her neck, then slowly, wickedly raising her sharp little beak as though she intended to gouge someone's underbelly.

It was hard to look beyond the likes of that. Brenn stepped back from the doorway, the vision of breakfast eggs fading into bread and tea and overcooked fish as the bird scolded and menaced. From a greater distance he could see beyond the bristling feather into the burnished interior of the room.

"Now *this* belongs in a wizard's house!" the boy exclaimed heartily. For the trunk of an enormous black tree passed through the center of Terrance's guest room.

Its roots were somewhere in the sandy ground outside and below, which was odd soil for a tree in the first place. But the oddness did not end there: some accident or wizardly design had guided the bole of the tree through the window—some years back, evidently, for the trunk had grown to fill the frame and indeed to stretch and crack the surrounding wall at several points.

Once in the window, the trunk bent to a horizontal, spanning the room and emerging through the other window, where no doubt it coursed up to fresh air and light. Six feet wide at least, it was. Brenn had never seen a tree that size, but being a city boy, marked it down to his own ignorance.

The trunk bristled with all kinds of smaller plant life. There were leaves growing out of notches and cracks in the bark—the boy recognized the smells of rosemary, of mint, of bay, and there were dozens of other odd plants he could neither smell nor name. Above this indoor herb garden a narrow bed had been made up, and beneath that bed a hollow in the trunk opened into a small cavity Terrance had appointed as a desk, complete with papers, pens, and an odd green fruit that glowed with a heatless light, sufficient to illuminate the room while leaving the rough bark of the trunk as undamaged and as rustic as it might have been down in the Corbinwood, or in any forest or copse far from the ravages of city life.

Branches snaked from the heavy trunk to net the room's ceiling in a tangle of wood and dried leaves. Brenn marveled over the squawking Gallina as the red light shone on bark, on wood, and on the broken, beautiful stone walls in the shadows.

"Wonder what *his* room is like?" the boy whispered, eggs having passed completely from his thoughts. He remembered the wizard's warning, however, and passed by the room, gazing curiously at its plain gray doorway as he climbed the steps to the place he would be quartered.

The attic was by no means glamorous or at all strange. Brenn's spirits sank to see how bare it was—a simple rush mattress and a lamp at one end of the long room, a stack of boxes and crates and chests at the other. It was as though Terrance had simply swept the storage aside, thrown down the first thing softer than the floor itself, and called it comfortable.

"I've slept in worse," Brenn said to himself, and kicked the mattress disconsolately.

"Except"—he paused, sitting heavily on the rushes—"it's like he expected me all along."

There was no time to ponder these arrangements. For when he sat, Brenn noticed the slant of light that issued out of the ceiling. Above him a trapdoor lay wide open, a rope ladder dangling from it down to the floor of the attic. Through the wide frame of the trapdoor, the November sky lay cloudy and pale.

"That leads to the roof," Brenn exclaimed dully. "Wonder why Dirk never—"

But all of this was too confusing right now. The boy set down the basket and reclined on the mattress, watching a distant bird—a hawk, perhaps, or a high-flying alcedo, the kind that the old women say steal human children and drop the poor babes in the sea—as it shrieked and turned in a tight circle above the house, then darted out to sea.

Or at least in the direction Brenn thought the sea lay. Despite its few rooms and many windows, this round house had the knack of turning about his sense of direction. Sometimes it seemed as though the place was spinning, the rooms shifting place in the house.

Even in the dark of the morning, while he tried to pry open the downstairs windows, Brenn could have sworn that the landscape outside was moving, shifting gradually before his eyes until, while he tugged one last desperate time at the window grating, he thought that Cove Road had vanished—that what lay out the window was rock and beach and water, as though the whole northern coast of Palerna had dropped into the Sea of Shadows.

Brenn closed his eyes, listened. The sounds arising from downstairs let him know that Terrance was rummaging about the library—or was it the kitchen?

The boy sat up, shook his head. Muttering to himself, he crossed the attic floor and scrambled up the ladder leading to the roof.

"I must get an outside look," he growled, "before I lose my bearings altogether."

Though the wind from the sea was cold, and rather strong from the rooftop, Brenn welcomed the fresh air. The roof around him composed an eerie landscape, littered with brick and stone and discarded, salt-rimed furniture. Aside from the half-finished stairwell he had seen from Cove Road the night before, Brenn found three rows of brick arranged neatly near the trapdoor, the foundation, no doubt, of yet another fireplace. He could imagine what the floor of the tower would have looked like had not its builder run out of energy or money or time.

Nonetheless, there were things less predictable, downright bizarre on the roof. Out of the guest-room window below, the black tree rose, coursing up the side of the tower wall until it spread its branches, bare now except for an occasional yellow leaf.

"Why didn't I notice that when I was watching the house?" Brenn whispered incredulously as he looked over the edge of the roof to where the trunk of the tree bellied out, then bent in a sharp right angle straight into the open window. "Better yet, why didn't Dirk say something last night?"

All of it was too perplexing.

Yet one thing seemed simple enough. If a boy was nimble enough—say, young and quick and of a thiefly nature—the climb down the bole of that tree and the short drop to the ground would be almost routine. From there, of course, the streets of Maraven awaited, and there were alleys and basements and sewer mains that would baffle the respectable likes of Terrance, no matter how learned or magical.

Brenn set one foot to the trunk of the tree. Then stopped.

He withdrew his foot and once again stood solidly on the roof, looking out toward Wall Town and southward.

"It'd be a good way for him to hand me over to the Watch," he concluded cynically, pacing nervously by the naked stairwell. "Or change me into a stinkbug, and still feel good about himself."

"Well," Brenn mused, his steps having taken him to the edge of the roof. "I expect I'll look for a better way out of here. After all, it's like the Goniph says: Sometimes the best trick is trust."

Pausing, the boy looked north over the roof to where the black beach slanted steeply into the water. Of a morning the Sea of Shadows lived up to its name, dappling with black and gray whatever the brightness of the sun.

Off to his left, Brenn saw a ship poling its way through the reef and out to sea. A carrack, he could tell from this distance, though he could not make out the colors it was flying. Behind the ship was lush green peninsula—the tip of Aquila—and in the midst of all that greenery Kestrel Tower loomed dark and ominous like a poison tree in a garden.

Brenn shuddered and looked beyond the Maraven Wall where Cove Road led out of town and dwindled into a wide dirt path on the eastern horizon. The old trade route was still the main road to Stormpoint and south to Hadrach beyond, but nowadays it was less traveled. Affections had cooled between Maraven and its southern neighbors, and the traffic on the once-crowded road could no longer support even a modestly ambitious high-wayman.

Nonetheless, folks in Maraven still said you were "up the Cove Road" if you were outlandish, or strange, or if there was a whiff of danger about you. Youngsters still watched the road for marvels, and legends still circulated that when the next great king came to Maraven on his way to the throne and a hundred years of justice and peace, he would come there by Cove Road, bringing the forest with him.

Brenn was pretty sure that by the time you were fourteen, you had seen most of the marvels you were going to see, and you'd caught on that most every legend had to do with a time you weren't living in. He laughed wearily as he looked eastward to where two riders approached the town.

"Here comes the great king now," he whispered ironically, seating himself precariously on a stack of bricks and watching as the riders skirted the end of the Maraven Wall, rejoining the road not a hundred yards east of the tower. As they drew even nearer, passing virtually underneath his nose as they followed Cove Road toward the heart of Maraven, Brenn could see that the one in charge was a handsome young Alanyan perched on a huge red stallion, followed by a quiet black child on a gray pony.

The Alanyan, of course, drew all Brenn's attention. His long robes were red and gold, so bright that had you seen him on the horizon at sunrise, you would be hard-pressed to tell which was the sun, which the traveler. He was about thirty years old, and blessed with the finest black moustache Brenn had ever seen. At his shoulder, drab against all that flash and glitter and color, a reciting owl roosted, its head lowered against the full bright morning sun.

The Alanyan looked up to the rooftop. His eyes met Brenn's calmly, quizzically. Then he pulled a gold-bound book from those glamorous robes and, lowering his eyes, began reading as the horse passed from view around the front of the house.

Next to him, the black child was virtually invisible. Brenn scarcely noticed little of the girl except the red headband she wore, striking against the dark brown of her skin and the gray of her clothing. Ruthic she was, Brenn knew by her skin color. From the big island in the Shallows, from a brilliant people famous for science and scholarship and for keeping to themselves. All the more surprising to see her here.

However, the girl seemed to find Maraven less exotic than it found her. Spurring her horse to a trot, murmuring something to the beast in a language Brenn had never heard, she followed the Alanyan around the corner of the house. When Brenn could see neither of them any longer, he crossed to the center of the roof, intent on descending down the rope ladder into the attic.

"Well, at least the house is at an interesting crossroads," he pronounced aloud, his foot hooking onto the first rung.

"Less interesting for our guests without their breakfast," a stern voice remarked from above him. Startled, Brenn tipped forward on the ladder, nearly losing his balance in the process.

Terrance sat at the top of the unfinished stairwell, a frying pan in his hand.

"Terrance!" Brenn exclaimed. "I didn't hear you . . ."

"Nor would you with all the gawking you were about," the wizard snapped sternly. "Now that you've reviewed our guests, why don't you go down that ladder and rifle Gallina for an egg or two so that they won't go hungry."

"You mean the Alanyan that just passed by . . ."

"Is at the kitchen table, awaiting my hospitality, the reputation for which is in jeopardy thanks to your dawdling about and gawking at the coastline and the maple."

And then, without fanfare, Terrance was gone.

It was an instant thing, his disappearance. None of the fading or crumbling to dust or vanishing in smoke Brenn had always imagined a wizard would prefer. Instead, he was simply there at one moment and gone at the next, so suddenly that Brenn blinked foolishly at the stairwell for some time afterward, until a voice from below boomed up something about delay and eggs and dire punishment.

Brenn had enough sense to don gloves when he returned to the guest room, but soon he wished for gauntlets. The hen parried his every maneuver toward the nest, cackling and spitting and lunging, tearing scraps of cloth from his sleeves, unseaming one glove with a deft stroke of her beak, until he remembered an old legend Faye had taught him: that if you drew a straight line on the ground in front of a chicken, you could hypnotize her.

Well, nothing else was working.

Inspired, Brenn hopped high over the nest and fumbled through the papers and pens in the tree hollow until he came up with the charcoal pencil he was looking for. Staring malevolently at the hen, he set the point of the pencil to the floor, as close to her as was prudent, then drew a straight line away from her, all the while muttering the little incantation Faye had taught him.

Slowly, curiously, the hen set her beak to the charcoal line and rested there a moment. Brenn waited, knowing hypnosis took time. Soon he took a quiet burglar's step toward the nest, but not quiet enough: Gallina cocked her head and trained one black and glittering eye on him.

Brenn jumped back, and squawking, the hen rose and straddled the nest, wings whirling. From his new vantage point atop the tree trunk, the boy watched her scratch the mark from the floor, stare up at him defiantly, and hop back onto her nest, where she settled like a toad, regarding him balefully.

Brenn had just about decided to call it a morning, to race downstairs and face whatever discipline awaited him. The hen was simply too smart, he concluded, but then he imagined with dread what the Alanyan and his companion would think were they to believe that the young apprentice to the great Mage Terrance had been outwitted by a chicken.

Terrance would probably transform him into a footstool.

Surely something else would avail. Brenn scanned the room

frantically, his eyes finally resting on the green-glowing fruit upon the desk.

If nothing else, it would make a good projectile.

It was surprisingly cool to the touch, firm and leathery. Its light shone eerily about the edges of his fingers, and the shadow of his hand coursed up the bole of the . . . maple, was it? onto the ceiling of the guest room. Gallina followed the shadow with those beady, malicious eyes, silent for the first time since he had entered the room.

Thoughts racing, Brenn moved his hand rapidly above the light. The shadow darted from wall to wall, and the hen tilted her head to track its movement.

Quickly, almost without thinking, Brenn twisted his hand, locking his thumb, notching his index finger. On the ceiling it cast the simplest of a child's shadow figures—the fox, the wolf, the big dog.

Squawking in terror, Gallina leapt from the nest, sprang for the door, and fell over, fainted dead away. Brenn stood above the nest triumphant and amused, lifting the paltry pair of eggs as Gallina stirred fitfully and mumbled. He was onto the landing before he stopped.

A red, dodging light raced through his memory. A cellar wall, a time before he could talk—perhaps before words or even the sound of his own name made sense. When a bright man with a red beard made shadows in a little room, and his mother was afraid.

Even now, in the pleasant blue light of the wizard's landing, much older and at least wise enough to outwit the chicken now rising dizzily to her feet in the guest room, he had trouble expressing just what it was he remembered.

An ordinary event, tumbled randomly from his memory? A portent or warning?

Or something to remember now that he was here—*because* he was here?

Brenn shook his head, baffled by options. He shrugged and descended the stairs.

≺≺≺ IV ≻≻≻

The Alanyan and the girl were seated at the oaken table when Brenn entered the solar, paltry takings in hand and a little the worse for wear from his encounter with the protective Gallina.

With scarcely a look in his direction, Terrance gestured, made introductions as the boy set the eggs on the table. Brenn took note of where he stood in the pecking order, which was not much better than he had stood with Gallina upstairs. Terrance introduced him first, withholding the name of the Alanyan and the Ruthican girl until he had given account of Brenn's relatively recent arrival and the less-than-honorable circumstances that had brought him to the job.

The Alanyan, a prominent alchemist named Ricardo, seemed amused by the whole business. He was an older man than Brenn had assumed from first glance. His dark hair, though, shone without a fleck of gray, tied in the triple Alanyan braid, in which the alchemist kept pins and feathers and one thick gold chain that looped through the braid several times, then lost itself in the red and golden robes.

Ricardo laughed as Terrance snorted and growled over Brenn's sudden arrival and frantic attempts to escape. All the while, the alchemist thumbed a deck of Parthian divining cards on the table in front of him. Since nobody outside of Partha believed in the soothsaying power of the cards, no doubt Ricardo had been trying to finagle Terrance into games of chance that, from the look of both men, might well end with the Alanyan owning the house if not most of the Maraven Wall.

Brenn wished earnestly that he could be Ricardo's apprentice instead.

Especially since the girl Delia, who had the job already, seemed neither charmed nor all that interested in what was going on in the wizard's solar. Quietly, almost drably, she hovered over bread and cheese, her eyes fixed on a distant point outside the window.

"Well, what brings you to Maraven this time, Ricardo?" the wizard asked, gesturing obscurely to Brenn.

"There's still a market, if nothing else, is there not?" Ricardo answered in fluent Palernan, spreading the cards before him and leaning back in his chair. The reciting owl at his shoulder started from sleep and shrieked out:

> *"But I shall put you in mind, sir, at pie-corner.*
> *Taking your meals of steeme in, from cookes stalls,*
> *Where like the father of hunger, you did walke*
> *Piteously costive, with your pinch'd-horne-nose,*
> *And your complexion, of the romane wash,*
> *Stuck full of black, and melancholique wormes,*
> *Like poulder-cornes, shot, at th'artillerie-yard."*

Brenn leapt back, having had enough of beaks and feathers to last him the morning. Ricardo only laughed, and Terrance addressed the alchemist in a tone of mock scolding.

"Is that the kind of thing you Alanyans listen to on the road nowadays?"

"Show the bird some charity, Terrance. It's hard being nocturnal this hour of the morning," Ricardo replied, and winked at Brenn. Then he glanced at his apprentice, whose nose had just buried itself into a book. He raised his eyebrows, his moustache hiding the hint of a smile.

"It takes your mind off of destinations, Terrance," he continued more soberly, and the wizard nodded.

"You'll get no argument from me, Ricardo. Right here's as far into Maraven as I myself relish going."

The alchemist reached for a teacup, his dark eyes resting on Delia, on Brenn, on the wizard, lighting rapidly and passing on, until he had scanned the entire room. Brenn recognized the look: he had seen it at the cockfights and the dicing dens over in Wall Town. He found it odd indeed in a scholar.

Then again, the boy told himself, why worry? After all, he was naturally suspicious, and his thoughts had been capsized by the disruptions of hens and strange memories. Far more interesting was this talk of the city, which was moving on to economics, to politics.

"I'm too young to remember it," Ricardo said, the owl hopping down his arm and onto the table, "but from what I hear I'd have liked the city better under your man Aurum."

"Gone to hell in a handcart, it has," Terrance snapped, snatching one of the eggs from Brenn and leaning his gray-maned head over the back of the chair in a bizarre attempt to balance the egg on his nose. "Near half the people poor, more and more of 'em plagued each day, and what's left over living off the misery of the sick and the starving."

"Still a market for the simple stuff, though," Ricardo conceded, breaking off a piece of bread and offering it to the owl, who stared at him wide-eyed for a moment, then snapped the crumbs from his hand. It strutted down the table, self-important and muttering poetry, perching finally upon the old brass doorknob that remained affixed to the table.

"Simple things like love philters, get-rich-quick lotion, and receiver salts," Ricardo said, shrugging. "They sell no matter who's king, regardless of how bad the times are."

"Don't you feel a little bit . . . dishonest?" Terrance asked. "Peddling your fly-by-night chemistry, especially to the poor?"

"It fills a gap in their yearning," Ricardo pronounced solemnly.

Brenn had seen this look before, too.

"That it does, indeed, Ricardo," Terrance conceded, handling the egg, staring at it as intently as a diviner might a crystal. "But is that good enough?"

Ricardo glanced once again at Delia, who looked up from her reading and frowned.

"I'm an alchemist, not a philosopher, Terrance," he replied brightly.

Brenn grinned, admiring his style. Neither Terrance nor Delia seemed altogether that impressed, though.

Idly, Terrance stirred his tea for a moment, his thoughts mingling with the steam and the faint hint of oranges that rose from the cup in front of him. All of a sudden, as though he were being jostled awake, he sat upright, eyes flickering to where Brenn stood listening to the conversation.

"Well?" he drawled impatiently, now staring directly at the boy.

Brenn swallowed hard, stuffed his hands into his tattered pockets.

"Sir?"

"Brennart, do you expect our guests to poke holes in the eggshells and suck out the yolks like weasels?"

Terrance paused dramatically, eyes fixed on his new apprentice.

"I suppose . . . I suppose I should . . . *prepare* them or something?" Brenn offered, stepping clumsily toward the table.

" 'Preparing' would be quite nice of you," Terrance agreed, tossing the egg, balanced and examined, back to the boy. "It is a process that generally requires a frying pan and butter and salt."

Brennart grumbled in the kitchen while the conversation continued in the solar. Beyond him, over the crackle and hiss of eggs in the pan, he heard voices rise and laughter burst forth, the musical laughter of the girl joining in with that of Ricardo and Terrance.

"Some apprentices, it seems, are better treated than others," he spat, lecturing the eggs as they stared back at him from their bed in the black iron skillet.

"Far as I can see, I'm here to bustle while the rest of 'em eat."

The talk of Maraven and King Dragmond and the Old King continued through breakfast, hearty and amusing to everyone but the boy, who was seated below the salt, up and down and back to the kitchen at the beck and call of everyone else at the table.

"Some more bread, lad," Terrance ordered, yellow yolk staining his unkempt white moustache.

"Perhaps more butter to put upon it?" Delia requested politely.

"And honey would be most welcome, if there's any in the house," Ricardo chimed in.

"Bring me a mouse, Brennart!" the owl called out as the boy

passed through the kitchen door, much to the amusement of everyone.

Everyone, that is, except Brenn. Who, red-faced and muttering even more nasty things than he had muttered before, rifled the pantry for bread and honey, stepping into the tiny cool cellar beneath the pantry to retrieve the butter and snatching a mouse from thunderstruck Gibb, the cat.

Before he returned to the company, he stopped at the table and pocketed a silver saltcellar that would draw good money from a fence in the Grospoint.

Still, as he passed through the kitchen with bread and butter and honey and half-eaten mouse destined for the plates of those seated and talking, Brenn was aware he was listening to the best of gossip.

Everybody, it seemed—even the young girl from a secluded people—knew more about Maraven than Brenn did. At least the Maraven of the high places, the country of kings and sorceresses and the Kestrel Tower.

"I've heard tell," Ricardo said, his voice lowered, "that he keeps her there at his whim. That indeed, she has done terrible, murderous things to be kept there."

Terrance sipped his tea, looked out the window.

"Do not underestimate Ravenna's intelligence," he warned. "Or Dragmond's stupidity."

Ricardo frowned, shook his head. He reached across the table, extending the index finger of his surprisingly small right hand. The owl hopped from the doorknob onto the finger. Then, scrambling up the alchemist's arm and perching on his shoulder, the bird swiveled its head about comically.

"This is where *you* underestimate, old friend," the Alanyan scolded. "You always have, you always will."

Ravenna, Brenn thought as the two men of science bickered over the last of the breakfast.

Ravenna. Dragmond's mistress.

It was all he really knew of the mysterious black-haired woman in the Kestrel Tower. Dirk had pointed her out once as the boys walked the Teal Front of an evening. She was afloat on the Teal Lake, borne on a gondola in a fleet of gondolas manned by Watchmen.

Her face was an extraordinary white—the white of new snow or of distant stars.

Dirk, of course, had something vulgar to say about her. But *Beautiful*, Brenn had thought at the time. *How lovely she is. And how beyond sorrow or care or even the dirt of the city.*

Again he thought of her, out where the moonlight spangled the dark lake. Where she glided dark and lovely on those waters like a beautiful black swan.

". . . always been your problem," Ricardo was lecturing, the gold rings on his hands flashing as he gestured to enforce his argument. "Just because Dragmond has someone else to do his magic doesn't mean he's a fool."

"All monarchs are fools," Terrance pronounced, folding his arms dramatically and finally. Something disturbed from sleep chattered and stirred excitedly in his robe, and Ricardo's owl swiveled its head hungrily at the sound.

"But, sir," Delia asked with caution, her eyes on Brenn, "would you have said the same of your . . . charge Aurum?"

She, too, would be lovely, Brenn thought, *were she not so quiet and daunted by it all.*

"Aurum?" Terrance snorted. "As big a fool as any, I'll warrant. Too much the skirt-chaser for a statesman, and too fond of hawking and games of chance."

Ricardo raised his eyebrows comically. The owl at his shoulder settled its head into a nest of feathers, closed its wide amber eyes.

"But better," Terrance continued, one bony finger pointed to the ceiling, green eyes flickering and intense, "better by far than that . . . villain of a half brother who sits on the Kestrel Throne in his absence.

"And you, Ricardo, would do well if you're bent on selling your wares, to simply go across the causeway to the tower— that is, if you can stand the smell from the gibbets. Perhaps you will be lucky: this is November, after all, when the hanging bodies reduce to the elements less quickly and with less fetor.

"Once across the Needle's Eye and onto the tower grounds, you'll find the business brisk. Dragmond has more money than he can count—even more than he can spend on that gang of prodigals and cutthroats he calls an army. You could sell him *all* those damnable . . . nostrums and potions!''

The wizard paused and gathered breath, glaring almost angrily at the Alanyan, who stared intently at Delia and then, all smiles and winks banished, spoke softly and seriously to Terrance.

''We—*I* am dreadfully sorry, Terrance. Do not think that we take your angers lightly.''

Quickly, almost dramatically, the old wizard softened. For a moment a look of profound weariness passed over him, as Brenn recalled it from the night before when Terrance had paused and wavered in the doorway to the library.

He is not well, Brenn thought.

''I know, Ricardo,'' the old man conceded, his voice almost a whisper. ''I know. Let us forgo politics for the day. You are, after all, my guests in Maraven, and welcome to stay the night. That is, if you have no lodging more worthy of you.''

'''Tis the worthiest lodging in Palerna, where we are right now,'' Ricardo pronounced graciously. The owl murmured at his shoulder, dreaming no doubt of the night, of poetry and of veiled philosophy.

Brenn sulked in the attic as the sunlight deepened and the afternoon passed toward evening.

At Terrance's instruction he had cleaned the guest room to spotlessness, dusting the walls and the tree and sweeping the dried leaves from the floor. After a brief struggle he had evicted Gallina, who, having lost her eggs and her courage to the shadows of foxes, was not nearly the fearsome opponent she had been that morning.

Then Brenn had ascended the stairs gloomily, in his hands a slim volume of poetry Terrance had ordered he take with him. Scarcely a minute or two of reading had told the boy that this was even more unattractive stuff than he had feared. Brenn traced his finger along the page as the words became more and more difficult, until he came to one that stopped him absolutely. Sighing, he lay back on the rush mattress, resigning himself to an afternoon with nothing to do.

For an hour or so he passed the time by rummaging through

boxes stored in his living quarters. And for an hour that was interesting enough business: he found a set of compasses, a dulcimer, a pendulum that when swinging back and forth caused the dust to stir around it on the attic floor but seemed to do nothing much else. He found a jar, half-filled with a powder that smelled of leaf and light and the faint whiff of juniper he remembered from the night before. It tasted of fresh water, and for a moment after he placed a pinch of the powder to his tongue, the attic wavered in a green light.

Brenn sighed again as the room returned to its everyday shape and color, the red light of late afternoon tumbling through the trapdoor onto the floor of the attic. In a far corner Gallina had already slipped her head beneath her wing and fallen asleep, where she scratched and scavenged in her dreams. An occasional muffled outcry was the only reminder that she was even there.

The house sounded empty as Brenn descended the steps onto the blue landing. Quietly Brenn moved to Terrance's door and peered through the keyhole.

He could see nothing.

Taking a deep breath, he knelt and reached into his pockets for tools.

"You're a curious boy, indeed," said a quiet, musical voice behind him.

Brenn spun about, fearing an angered Terrance or, given the strangeness of the house, something far worse.

Instead, Delia stood in front of him, mildly surprised herself. She had removed the startling red headband, and Brenn looked in astonishment at the sapphire that lay in the center of her forehead. It took him a moment to see that the stone was fixed there, as though her skin were a jeweler's setting.

Though he had heard her laugh before—that morning, when she sat in the solar and he sweated away in the kitchen—here on the blue landing was the first time Brenn saw her smile.

He had been right all along. She was truly lovely.

"It's hard," she said, "those first few days as an apprentice."

Brenn frowned and leaned back against Terrance's door.

"When you have no idea who the master is. Or about his disposition, or what is expected of you. I remember it well.

Indeed, I hid under my master's bed until he fell asleep, because there is an old superstition among my people that a man's character rises to his face only when he sleeps.''

"And what did you find out about Ricardo?" Brenn asked, wrapping his arms about his knees and curling into a tight ball.

Delia frowned.

"You are a fortunate boy," she pronounced. "More fortunate than you know. Your master is an odd one, I'll grant you, but he's kind. You may not see it right off—the kindness, that is —but that is oft the way with the great magicians.''

" 'The way,' Delia?"

She nodded vehemently, the sapphire glittering on her brow, catching the blue light of the landing until Brenn gathered his tunic about him, suddenly filled with a brisk winter cold.

"There is a saying among alchemists, Brennart, that the house of gold is the basest of metals.''

Brenn scoffed, stretched out in the hall.

"I guess there's a regular mine in Terrance, Delia. I don't know what it was like for you in the first days of your apprenticeship, but all I seem destined to be is a glorified houseboy— sweeping, laying rushes, cleaning up the messes I've made, preparing meals for company.''

Delia nodded solemnly as the boy in front of her rattled on.

"Look," Brenn said, his face suddenly sincere and guileless as he reach into his tunic and drew out a lovely little book, ribbed and bound in gold. Delia looked at it curiously as he placed it in her hands.

"*Elementa Alchemica*, it's called. That's Latin for basics of alchemy, you know. And inside it says, 'being a compendium of most needful knowledge for alchemists aspiring, would-be, and might have been.' It's a real how-to book, how-to being the only reading if you ask me, without all that poetry and philosophy to cloud the waters.''

Delia nodded and pursed her lips. Brenn was too intent in his bargaining to notice the hint of a smile at the corners of the girl's eyes.

"It's a prized addition to my library, but it's yours if you persuade Ricardo to take me with you when you go back to

Alanya. I'm eager to know what a real apprenticeship is like, Delia. I'm sure it's not all housekeeping and drudgery.''

"I'm sorry, Brenn," Delia said, handing the book back to him. "For even if Ricardo would take you, he couldn't. And even if he could, he wouldn't."

Brenn nodded disconsolately. Even after such a short time in the wizard's employ, he was becoming numb to contradictions.

"But this is such . . . such everyday business. For the life of me I thought I was here for magic!"

"Indeed you are, Brenn. You are," Delia interrupted, her gold eyes urgent, intense. "But magic . . . well, magic approaches you in its own time.

"As does alchemy," she sighed, turning slowly toward the guest room. "It approaches you slowly, until you have learned to approach it . . . by a side door."

"My book is always available," Brenn offered cheerfully. "I'll throw in a silver saltcellar."

Delia smiled again, this time a little crookedly, turning back to Brenn as she opened the door. Behind her, in the clear light of the guest room, some elaborate arrangement of beakers and retorts and alembic and tubing steamed and bubbled by the banked fire in the hearth. A dozen or so small open vials, each filled with an amber liquid, sat in a row on the desk, steam rising from their mouths.

"I've a long night of watchfulness ahead of me." Delia smiled. "After all, though, it is but one night—nothing compared to the long watch some are beginning."

She left him on the landing, there amid blue wind and shadows.

He lay back on his mattress in the attic. He could not recall ever wasting so much of a day in something as useless as thought.

Outside the afternoon had passed into evening, the attic into a slanting light that dwindled and dwindled until, through the trapdoor to the roof, one star emerged in the sky, faint and glittering like Delia's sapphire. Soon it was joined by another, and another, then the edge of the door took on a strange yellow light as the moon slipped into the boy's view.

Brenn stirred. Distant bells from the churches rang the first hour of the night. By this time he was usually prepared for business, out of the guild cellar in Wall Town and onto the streets of Maraven, where the gold lay ready for gathering.

He wondered what Dirk and Squab were up to. What Faye, especially, was doing, and whether the night would pass without her thinking of him and wondering what had befallen him.

He sighed, plucked the untuned strings of the dulcimer. And suddenly a blue light rose from the floor and the whole attic returned to its daylight shape in front of him. For a moment Brenn looked in astonishment at the dulcimer, then realized that the light was nothing but the opening of the door to the rooms below him.

Relieved, he chuckled a little. The dulcimer looked quite ordinary in this new light.

"For a moment I thought that when I touched the strings . . ." he began.

The sound of footsteps arose from below him as someone ascended to the attic.

Quickly Brenn shoveled rushes over the dulcimer, leaned back, tried to look calm and reflective and guilty of nothing more than quietness and good behavior.

It was, as he had expected, Terrance, back from whatever paths he and Ricardo had followed through the city. The wizard paused at the top of the steps, nodded gruffly at his apprentice.

"May I be of assistance, sir?" Brenn asked dryly. "Clean something up? *Prepare* something?"

Terrance snorted, climbed into the attic.

"You have cabin fever, boy. Being confined to quarters makes a lad jumpy and ironic. Like a professional scholar. I won't have that in my house."

"I have no choice in the matter, sir," Brenn responded. "Being taken against my will and all."

"Put the dulcimer back where you found it."

Brenn swallowed loudly. The rushes shifted and crackled beneath him as he sat up on the mattress.

"*How* did you—"

"Heard it from the bottom of the stairs," Terrance interrupted, a smile showing faintly in the wilderness of his beard.

The wizard walked to the center of the room, sitting atop an old sea chest that had been the object of Brenn's attentions earlier in the afternoon. Idly he looked at where he was sitting, as though he had just discovered that the trunk was there.

"There're scratch marks around the keyhole," he exclaimed in mock surprise, arching his eyebrow and looking directly at Brenn. "Fresh, as I make them out.

"You aren't all that cunning with a lock pick, are you . . . *enterpriser*?"

"Cunning enough to get into *this* place!" Brenn blurted out angrily. "I found the lock to the door outside easy enough for what you consider my limited skills . . . *counselor*."

From the folds of his robe Terrance drew forth another vial of the amber liquid and drank it down quickly, reluctantly.

"Did it ever occur to you that the lock was . . . *too* easy?" he asked with a chuckle. He smiled at the boy, arched an eyebrow.

"That's easy to say when it's after the fact!" Brenn began. "You're fixing the gate after the horse has run away!"

"How . . . charmingly rural of you, Brennart," the wizard said, laughing. "But as you can see, *my* horse didn't get away!"

Brenn settled into a dumbfounded silence. He remembered his name throughout the writ of indenture—a document drawn up and waiting for him before he broke into the house. Perhaps even before he had thought of robbing the place.

By now the attic was almost dark, lit only by the blue glow from downstairs, which seemed to be fading in turn, leaving the room in deep shadows.

Terrance cleared his throat.

"In the coming days," he began softly, "you will discover your home here, Brenn. I surely hope you do.

"But you must learn the city, too."

Brenn smirked. What could this bookish old coot tell *him* of the city?

"Tomorrow is for clear air and sunshine," Terrance announced. "For learning how to function by day rather than by night. When Ricardo and Delia head for town in the morning, we shall accompany them there. We shall make a day of it, you and I," he proposed like a benign grandfather.

Brenn squinted at him through the darkness, but it was no use: the old man's face was obscure, almost invisible at this late hour.

"Do we start my magic lessons tomorrow?" the boy asked eagerly.

Terrance chuckled mysteriously. "My goodness, no!" he exclaimed. "Magic would be dangerous in those clumsy hands. Tomorrow is a simple trip to the market."

"But when—" Brenn began in frustration, but the wizard was halfway out the door, framed briefly in the blue light before he vanished, the footsteps on the stairwell fading into silence below. Brenn lay back on the mattress, muttered something inaudible but probably obscene.

"Never!" he exclaimed aloud to the unsympathetic dark of the attic. "I have signed on as a lunatic's valet!"

Above the frustrated gaze of the boy, the planet Pytho, green as a dragon's eye, moved conspicuously through the belt of the Forest Lord, then behind a dark, gliding cloud.

<<< **V** >>>

Terrance showed him the writ again before they reached Leeside Alley, still within sight of their own front door.

"I trust that even with *your* letters, Brenn," the wizard warned, "you can read clause sixteen easily enough."

Brenn took the vellum roll and opened it. Somehow it felt larger and heavier in his hand. Squinting, trying to appear to understand the blur of long words and foreign phrases that littered the document, Brenn ran his finger down the margin in search of something familiar like his name, or a street name, or numbers.

Ricardo craned over the boy's shoulder to look at the document, but a strong, quiet tug at his robe by Delia reminded the Alanyan that the writ was none of his business. They walked farther down the road together, leaving Terrance and Brenn standing in the middle of the street, poring over the scroll.

"Here it is," Brenn pronounced after a long, uncomfortable silence. " 'The apprentice will not try to escape on market days or he will be in . . . in . . .' "

" 'In dire circumstance,' I believe the phrase is," Terrance said triumphantly, his eyes on the far northern horizon where the Palern Reef shone wickedly in the morning light. "I thought this might be a time to remind you of your obligations."

Brenn shook his head, rolled up the writ clumsily. It appeared and felt larger still as he handed it to the wizard, who held it to the light, then hid it at once in his bright blue robes. Together they lengthened their strides, slowly closing the distance between themselves and their companions, who were still some distance ahead of them on Cove Road. At that distance the alchemist and his assistant looked like creatures from another world, glass and tubings protruding from their packs and from the saddlebags of the horses they were leading.

"What makes you think I had designs on escape?" Brenn asked angrily.

"Why are you so fired and furied?" Terrance asked in return, his long strides lengthening still more until the boy beside him broke into a trot to keep pace. "Are you angry at my mistrust?" Suddenly the wizard turned and stopped at the Street of the Bookbinders. Smiling almost kindly at his new apprentice, he pulled the black, broad-brimmed hat down over his eyes.

"Or are you angry at yourself, that you've had no thoughts of escape?"

They continued together, sorcerer and apprentice, counselor and enterpriser. Terrance read from a small leather-bound volume he kept on a chain around his neck, while Brenn kept pace with him, muttering and growling. First Delia, then Ricardo stopped in the road ahead of them. Together, then, the party reunited, they traveled west down Cove Road until the soot-covered buildings of Grospoint shoved into view and they found themselves in the midst of the market district.

At this time in its history, Maraven was a city in decline.

Once a prominent port, drawing goods from Hadrach and

Partha, from Aquila and Calse and Random, the town had been a lively center of trade as the ships came east out of the Sea of Shadows from Genoa and Venice and Marseille, bringing wine and spice and silks from Cathay in their holds. Not two decades before, in the reign of the young King Aurum, Maraven had seemed a promising place indeed—no major city, at least not yet, but a muscular small city that would eventually put itself and the surrounding Palernan countryside on the maps of the greatest shipping companies of Europe.

Dragmond had seen to that.

For the past ten years or so, money drawn at great pains from the farms of Palerna and from Maraven, its capital city, had found its way to the king's hands and the king's hands alone. Dragmond, in turn, had invested fortunes in foreign shipping companies and in foreign markets, while less and less money returned to the Palernan shores.

The king grew fat while the country starved. Or so the people said.

The people were to blame, the king accused in return. Their crops were not as rich, their ships not as fast as those from abroad.

Whatever the argument and whoever was right, Maraven had dropped off a hundred maps. A new generation of navigators and ship's captains was on the rise, most of whom claimed that the City by the Gray Sea was legendary, the home of dragons and of manticores and of fathers who devoured their children. Fewer and fewer ships rested in the Maravenian harbors. Trade had dwindled until Palerna's only reliable trading partner was the small Duchy of Aquila to its north, where the produce from the rich volcanic coastal farmlands was brought to port by Dragmond's Northern Army, who closed the deal with broadsword and bow.

Grospoint, once the heart of the city's business, was a shabby district now, dealing primarily in trinkets and gossip and terribly expensive cure-alls that restored only the hopes of the buyers. Called "Gaunt" by the townspeople, it was a desperate and extravagant place, run like a besieged fortress rather than a market center. Booths were set up hurriedly and taken down in the same fashion, so that the streets resembled a camp filled with ramshackle lean-tos, tents, and places of business set up in the open air, where tradesmen sat bare-headed to the November wind and called out harsh slogans to passersby.

Dozens of storefronts were empty, the buildings having been abandoned, but the merchants dared not set up shop in any of them. Such places were owned by wealthier businessmen—some by King Dragmond himself—who charged exorbitant rent for their use or left them empty so that smaller businessmen would have less space in which to peddle their merchandise.

It was here that Ricardo and Delia took their leave. The dark-haired Alanyan shook hands solemnly with both Terrance and Brenn, thanking them in a roundabout Alanyan fashion for the hospitality and kindness of the night before. Delia stood back quietly, holding the reins of the horses, her gaze intent on Brenn until the boy felt uncomfortable and timid.

"I cannot believe we shall ever repay the kindness," Ricardo concluded, "but rest assured that within the hearts of two be-draggled travelers, your hospitality remains enshrined, perpetual unto a time that should the opportunity arise in which we might return your generosity . . ."

"Thank you, Terrance, Brenn," Delia said, her golden eyes sparkling. "I know we shall meet again."

With a long last look at the wizard's apprentice—a look that mystified the boy—Delia turned and led Ricardo onto the dirty and loud Point Square, where the alchemists and medicine men had set up residence, selling love philters and plague cures and hair restoratives, and the booths were abuzz with rhetoric and the ringing of coins on wooden tables.

For a moment Terrance stood at the mouth of the square, watching the glamorous Alanyan and his apprentice set up their booth, the reciting owl darting back and forth on Ricardo's shoulder, shrieking out a shop's invitation over the excitement of the milling crowd.

> *"If thou beest borne to strange sights,*
> *Things invisible to see,*
> *Ride ten thousand daies and night*
> *Till age snow white haires on thee . . ."*

Quickly the passersby, drawn by the owl's flutter and verse, gathered about Ricardo and Delia.

"Bless the girl," Terrance breathed, so softly that Brenn was not sure for a moment that he had heard the old man rightly. "Bless her in these hard, inscrutable times."

Turning to his apprentice as though rising out of sleep or enchantment, the wizard frowned.

"Well? Best be about our business!" he ordered, pushing the boy toward the Street of the Chemists, a wide avenue that had outgrown its name years ago when the farmers and bakers and vintners had set up shop in its midst.

Brenn knew the street well. His friends called it Duval's Alley, after the young man who leaned against a baker's stall and watched them approach.

Though his small purse contained only two silver coins, Brenn shifted it at once to the front of his belt. He and Faye had often laughed as the pigeons passed through—the merchants and Watch captains and moneylenders, who would come to do their own marketing for the gods knew what reason and would leave a purse light, halfway back to their homes in the wealthy Teal Front before they knew the difference.

Duval was sizing up Terrance, it was certain. Brenn tried to get the pickpocket's attention, to wave him away and about other business, but Duval paid the boy no notice after a brief, dismissive glance.

Terrance, meanwhile, his person jingling and pennies dropping from his sleeves, walked to an Umbrian vintner's stall, where racks of wines were displayed haphazardly. Obviously and innocently, the wizard rustled in his robes, fishing out two scrolls, an old shoe, a chattering grannar, and an empty phial before he came across his purse and opened it, displaying a handful of coins—both gold and silver—to anyone within a hundred feet of him.

Duval leaned forward against the baker's stall, his interest renewed. Brenn rushed over to join Terrance and, while the wizard bargained with the vintner, gathered the discarded things from the counter—all except the grannar, which scurried away and, its chipmunk coloring and big ears flickering amid the feet of the milling crowd, was soon lost somewhere up the street.

His hands full, Brenn looked desperately back toward the baker's stall. Duval, of course, was nowhere to be seen.

Meanwhile, Terrance was ready to be robbed by yet another inhabitant of the Street of the Chemists.

"Three silver pennies for a bottle of this wine, my good man?" Terrance asked merrily, setting the coins on the counter.

"Terrance," Brenn urged, tugging desperately at the wizard's robe. Umbrian wine was notoriously bad, the occasional good bottle a rare thing amid the spoiled, vinegary swill that the blond Umbrians hauled up through the Zephyrian grasslands and across the Boniluce into Palerna. An honest merchant and a buyer with sense would have dealt three bottles for a penny rather than three pennies for a bottle.

Unfortunately, the Umbrian vintner was a blue-eyed bandit, and Terrance . . . well, Brenn concluded that Terrance believed if somebody was selling it, it was worth something. With an enormous sigh, completely powerless in the transaction, the boy watched Terrance hold up the wine and the vintner hold up Terrance.

The wizard walked into the middle of the street, looking through the yellow swirl of the wine up into the cloudy sky. Brenn followed him, looking around alertly for Duval or any of Duval's Urchins—the half-dozen or so street children the cutpurse employed.

Brenn reached Terrance's side just as the wizard held the bottle at arm's length and chanted.

> "But that which most doth take my Muse and
>   mee
> Is a pure cup of rich Canary-wine,
> Which is the Mermaids, now, but shall be mine:
> Of which, had Horace, or Anacreon, tasted,
> Their lives, as doe their lines, till now had
>   lasted."

"I beg your pardon?" Brenn asked, sidling closer to Terrance, trying to catch the words of the chant.

"Simple, my lad." The wizard smiled, pocketing the bottle. "It's what I call investment."

"I don't understand."

"That Umbrian lad sold me the bottle with the claim that here was a three-penny wine. I am only assuring that he will be no liar when I open this over dinner tonight."

Brenn frowned as Terrance paced off toward the baker's stall, trotting to keep up with the wizard's lengthy strides. Terrance took only a few steps, turned, and faced his apprentice with a seriousness Brenn found unsettling.

"Where is the magic in what I have just done?" he asked, grabbing the boy by the arm and pointing a bony finger in his face.

"I beg your pardon?" Brenn asked nervously, stepping back.

"The magic, lad! The magic! What have you seen that is magical?"

Brenn looked to the ground, cleared his throat.

"Well, sir, I suspect that the wine in that bottle you carry is better now than it was but a moment ago."

Terrance snorted.

"It is," he proclaimed, "but the fact that you mention that shows how little feel you have for magic to begin with."

Angrily Brenn broke free of his master's grasp.

"If that is so," he blurted, "then why do you keep me here? Why the bars and grates on the damned solar windows? Why the clauses in the damned writ of indenture? Why the writ itself? Why, the whole thing's no more than imprisonment!"

Terrance laughed, tossing yet another penny into the hand of the baker and taking a loaf of bread in return.

"If you recall, Brennart, I said you had little feel for magic *to begin with*," he replied patiently. "Which you do.

"You're like an Umbrian wine, boy. Domestic and sour, with a much better opinion of yourself than you have a right to have. It's a common vintage.

"But tonight you shall have some Umbrian wine with me. Only half a glass, mind you: you're much too young for more. Only a taste to let you know something important about . . . wines and things."

"It's all the same to me," Brenn spat. "Just wizardly non-sense. You're trying to make me lose my bearings."

"Of course not," Terrance soothed. "You're here on the

Street of the Chemists. Behind you is Point Square, and yet another street over is Albright II's old armory. Come to think of it, you know the town as well, if not better than I do. Here. Hold the bread.''

"But I was not speaking of geography, sir," Brenn insisted, the warm loaf pleasant in his grasp, considering the brisk November air.

"Well, I am quite fond of geography of all sorts," Terrance replied, and stalked off through the marketplace, his long strides leaving the boy behind. Brenn followed anxiously, occasionally losing sight of the wizard in the crowd. At those moments all that lay before the boy was a landscape of legs and jostling bellies and loud foreign haggling.

They were frightening, those times, and it was only later that Brenn sat back, shook his head, and wondered why it was that, writ or no writ, he had not used one of those moments to escape, to lose himself among all those people. Later, he decided that either his brief stay at the wizard's house had dulled all his better instincts, or Terrance had put some vexing enchantment over him that had sapped him of all wisdom.

Whichever it was, at the time it felt like concern for the old man, wandering innocent and alone amid a generation of cutpurses, mountebanks, and confidence men, his money there for the taking. Needless to say, the boy was relieved when, time and again, the iron-gray hair of the wizard bobbed into view above a swarm of merchants and buyers. Then, wading through milling bodies with his street child's grace and know-how, Brenn would almost reach the man, only to lose him again.

"Impossible!" the boy spat, ducking under a cart filled with potatoes and ripe corn, then slipping from the hands of the vendor as, for some peculiar reason, an ear of the corn *just happened* to drop into his grasp. Terrance was lost again, no doubt beaten by thugs and moldering in some remote alley, or picked up by the Watch for questioning, beaten by uniformed thugs and moldering in some remote alley.

Slipping between two arguing brewers just before one of them—a fat woman with a pleasant face and the forearms of a longshoreman—drew a foot-long knife from behind her stall and opened a whole new round of negotiations, Brenn slipped along the side of an abandoned building, his back pressed to old stone and faded, chipped yellow paint. He caught a glimpse of Terrance at another booth, speaking merrily with a closed-faced vendor. Closer still, and the trouble he had dreaded began to unfold, only seconds away from coming to pass.

One of Duval's Urchins, a cocky, red-haired boy they called Eglon, had sidled behind Terrance and, his furtive, ratlike face scanning the crowd for witnesses, was moving closer and closer to the wizard until robe was brushing robe and hand, no doubt, was closing around the old man's purse.

Brenn started to call out, but stopped short in fascination. For Terrance had begun to sing, in a high, scarcely musical voice, a song about a piper's son the boy remembered vaguely from childhood.

> *"Tom, Tom, the piper's son,*
> *Stole a pig and away did run . . ."*

For a moment Brenn recalled firelight, a rain outside, the face of his mother. A tall old man, his back turned, walking out the door of the old house in Wall Town, out into night and rain. But the memory vanished when Eglon tumbled away from the wizard, skidding along the cobblestones with a squealing blur at his back.

For a moment Brenn thought of magical wind, of circles of protection. Then he realized that it was the largest pig he had seen in the market that year, its fat legs wheeling as it trod across Eglon's back in a frantic attempt to escape.

Eventually, boy and pig gained their footing, scurrying off in opposite directions as a dozen bystanders or so, their attention brought suddenly to the incident, laughed heartily, and the dumbstruck merchant reached under the counter for the jar of honey Terrance had come there to buy in the first place. Cautiously Brenn approached the wizard, looking all around him for approaching livestock. Terrance turned to him, smiled mischievously.

"Oh, *there* you are, Brennart!" he said as if pigs issuing from beneath his robes were natural occurrences, as ordinary as, say, a sudden change in the weather. "Won't this be delicious for breakfast with the bread we bought earlier?"

Brenn smiled weakly and nodded, only then reminded that in his haste to recover Terrance's trail through the crowd on the Street of the Chemists, he had set the loaf down somewhere . . . he hadn't the faintest memory just exactly where that was.

They returned to Terrance's house as the sun was setting, bearing honey and wine, fresh corn and another loaf of bread, their shadows lengthening on Cove Road in front of them. An evening wind, cold and forbidding, lifted off of the Sea of Shadows. A goodly way from shore, off at the edge of Brenn's sight, the white spindrift rose from the sea's dark water as the waves rushed over the submerged reef.

It was melancholy to return to the house by night. Ricardo and Delia were gone, of course, lodged in a part of town that was no doubt closer to their business, and Brenn did not relish the prospect of being the sole focus of Terrance's attentions. The wizard was much too haphazard, he had decided—filled with mysteries, with strange expectations, and most of all with ideas for chores and duties and projects that the boy had no interest in doing.

Should've done it while I had the chance today, Brenn thought silently. *But there will be other chances anon, and when they come, I'll do what I can to get out of this arrangement.*

He could not tell what Terrance was thinking. In a quiet, even a pensive mood, the wizard stopped where the Leeside Alley joined Cove Road, at the very spot where he had shown Brenn the writ that morning. Silently he stared out upon the dark, restive waters, sighed, and spoke to nobody in particular.

> *"Alas, so all things now do hold their peace,*
> *Heaven and earth disturbed in nothing;*
> *The beasts, the air, the birds their song do cease;*
> *The nighte's chair the stars about doth bring.*
> *Calm is the sea, the waves work less and less."*

Sure enough, the words were spoken and at once the sea calmed. Brenn wondered at the words and the waters, if Ter-

rance's speech had stilled the sea or if the stilling sea had called
up the words in the heart of the wizard.

"What difference does it make?" he asked himself wearily.
"I'll be gone the next time the old man looks the other way."
Yet, whether it was the newfound calmness of the night or the
hard day behind him, or whether it was something else entirely,
he somehow felt no urgent need to escape.

Let it wait a day or two. The chance would offer itself.

As for now, there was something inviting about a night's sleep.
About the prospect of breakfast, and about having done not much
of anything that would recommend him to the attention of the
Watch. He would stay a few days—no more than a week or
two—and then . . .

For now, though, he welcomed the glow of the banked fireplace in the solar. He relished the mulled Umbrian wine, which
was as delicious as Terrance had promised. Even the rush mattress in the attic was inviting as he ascended the steps from the
blue landing, and that night, pleasantly warm under blankets,
he awoke once to look up through the trapdoor to the roof, where
the stars swam dizzily in the black sky overhead.

"There are worse places," Brennart told himself, feeling suddenly alert and watchful. Something dark had brushed at the
edge of his dreams.

But the attic around him was familiar, Terrance's snoring
arising from downstairs and Gallina the hen rumbling in dreams
of her own over in the far corner. Calmly, his assurance restored,
the boy closed his eyes and slept again, his thoughts on honey
and bread for breakfast.

The king was not pleased with the omens.

The smoke had risen in the shape of a large bird, and when
Dragmond suggested to the visionary—an Alanyan dwarf with

a long white beard—that perhaps it was a kestrel or a raven, boding good tidings for the royal house, the terrible little man had smiled the gap-toothed, drugged smile of a visionary and shook his head patronizingly.

"'Tis a cowbird, sire," the Alanyan cackled. "A cowbird, who lays her eggs in another's nest."

Puzzled, the king had looked to the other signs. There were cards, of course, and crystals. The stone from the rocky Aquilan inland, broken by mallet and chisel and examined by the same visionary.

Who again cackled and saw cowbirds.

"Then you must lay *your* eggs in another nest," Dragmond had retorted and, summoning the Watch captain, had ordered the disrespectful seer back to Hadrach, robe, cap, and vatic root.

Now the king was seated in the throne room, ringed by candles. He stared into the bowl of water.

Aquamancy was the last resort of diviners.

The calm surface of the water reflected candle and shadow, his own pale eyes and the red carnelian at his throat. Deeper he looked, past the surface into the depths of the bowl, where light shifted and shone on the submerged white of the porcelain.

It was like it had been for a week, now. Instead of visions, a bowl full of water, nothing more.

Then the water clouded with blood.

Dragmond averted his eyes. His gloved hands shook as he set the bowl cautiously on the dark mahogany table where his crown and his sword lay.

Pytho in the belt of the Forest Lord. Strange birds in the smoke and the rock.

Blood in the water. And the dead on the road outside.

It had begun last summer. At sunset they dragged themselves north to the causeway, sometimes two or three, but on the hotter nights as many as half a dozen. Whatever their numbers and whatever the heat, they bundled in rags and blankets that also hid the enormous black sores that spread and festered and eventually swallowed each of them. The children were the most pitiful, but there were also sailors and shopkeepers, scholars and farmers, even the occasional unlucky trader or guardsman in the nightly march to the edge of the causeway.

They looked across the mile-long strip of land, across the Needle's Eye to the king's own grounds, where tame deer and peacocks roamed amid vine and moss and liana and pendulous pear trees.

As they stared desperately at the distant garden, afloat in water and mist and safety, the sufferers menaced the Watchmen by their very presence. They were more frightening than the poor souls on the gibbets, these strange and mottled harbingers of the plague, and the Watchmen lifted their pikes or nocked their bows because nobody knew how the plague spread—through breathing or touch or even an exchanged glance.

Assembled at the foot of the causeway, the dying would stare up into the windows of the tower itself. It was too far away for the king to make out their faces, their expressions, and most often they were silent. Then you could look away into the dark rooms of your quarters, admiring your silver and tapestries and ornamental armor. For a moment you could forget that terrible vigil on the Palernan coast.

Now and again, though, almost spontaneously, a song rose from among them.

> *Brightness falls from the air*
> *Queens have died young and fair*
> *Dust hath closed Helen's eye*
> *We are sick, we must die.*

Dragmond would cover his ears and call out the Watch, who covered their faces with scarves and walked among the dying, wielding spear and sword.

The poor creatures stood there and accepted their deaths. No doubt they preferred the edge of the sword to the lingering pain of the plague.

Whatever passed through their minds, they continued to gather and watch. One night in August, when the astrologers had come to the king with the bad tidings about Pytho, an illusionist found his way into the ranks of the dying and an image of King Drag-mond took shape in wavering light above the tower. Many in

Maraven thought that a fireworks master from Cathay was visiting the king, paying for his keep by showing his most glamorous work.

So they believed, watching and admiring the beautiful display until the flesh fell away from Dragmond's image, terrible red strips of fire falling away into the waters. Aglow amid the bright stars over the Sea of Shadows, a skeleton of lights danced in a crown and crimson robes.

And again the killings began.

Through that time the darkness was loud with songs and shouts and screaming, and the king did not sleep.

Now it was November, and with the cooler weather, the plague had again abated. But still Dragmond did not sleep. He paced the throne room manically, hollow-eyed. He lay on the cot they had set for him, but he found no rest. Sometimes he would nod, would doze for a fitful second in his chair, or standing at the window would suddenly realize he had been asleep for a moment. And yet, when he lay down, sleep was as distant, remote, and inviting as a lush garden across a mile of causeway.

"I shall be like Ravenna anon," he murmured to himself, pouring the water from the bowl onto the stone floor of the throne room. It swirled for a moment, oily in the candlelight, then trickled through cracks in the masonry.

Pensively Dragmond set the bowl back on the table and seated himself in the onyx throne. Leaning back against the cold stone, he looked out an eastern window into the heart of the winter stars.

"Like Ravenna anon, never sleeping."

Ravenna had told him not to worry. To sleep soundly, because she had seen the signs again and again through his fourteen years on the throne of Palerna.

After all, a star passing into a new region of the heavens meant nothing in itself. It happened every season, sometimes every week. Of course, it might bode something: a change in the weather, perhaps, or a shipwreck or a famine in a far region.

Pytho was the uneasiest of the moving stars. Just before Aurum, Dragmond's predecessor, had vanished mysteriously, the green light had come unmoored in the heavens and sailed into the constellation Harpax—the Sign of the Winged Women. And though it had passed through other constellations since—through the Scythe and the Fishes and the Drowned Man—nothing momentous had happened in the kingdom.

Yet each time the star moved, astrologers took note, and the king took readings of omens and signs.

"Leave the paths of birds and planets to me," Ravenna whispered softly, seductively, rubbing his tightened shoulders with her slim white hands. "Best you keep your eyes to the earth and the country around you.

"For when the heavens send danger to a king, oft they send it by expected hands."

If that was so, Dragmond thought, the message of Pytho was for someone else. His borders were safe, and the threats to the crown from neighbor and faction seemed weak, if there were threats at all.

To the west the Atheling of Zephyr had his hands full with the Parthians again, the two countries ablaze with desert skirmishes and grassland cavalry battles as everyone tried to establish a border disputed for five hundred years. Try as he might to marshal the skills of his brilliant cavalry, the atheling had yet to find a path over the Parthian desert that would allow him to strike at the heart of his perpetual rival.

Dragmond laughed cynically to himself. He was sure that neither Parthian nor Zephyrian would listen to reason. Their eyes averted from Palerna, they would kill one another forever.

To the east, Alanya was as large and as disjointed and as mad as ever. As any alchemist could tell you, merchant and scholar do not mix well, and neither can govern. Just when it seemed that the Alanyans had unified themselves enough that the loose confederation of counties and duchies and city-states might become something more than a market and storefront for the rest of the continent, a powerful merchant or a learned master at the University of Hadrach would propose a way to unify the whole country. But that was no threat, for the proposal would anger a duchy, which would in turn quarrel with a city-state and in the process offend some powerful coastal count who would cut off the sea routes to Hadrach and thereby infuriate the merchants and scholars, causing an outburst of poisonings in high places and mysterious disappearances of bards and merchants.

Nothing to worry about on that front, Dragmond concluded. Though the ruling powers to his east and south now clamored against him, their song would change with the weather. Indeed, when the seas grew treacherous in December and the overland routes became the only safe way to send goods westward, the Alanyans would forgive King Dragmond, no matter what they imagined he had done and no matter what he had done in fact. Again the markets of Maraven would be filled with hawkers and nostrum sellers and alchemists.

Dragmond smiled, closing his eyes.

Indeed, his only cause for alarm lay directly south, where the thick deciduous forest of the Corbinwood had reddened and yellowed and browned and the last of the leaves were falling. By December it would look like a thicket of brier and branch, stretching nearly fifty miles to the banks of the Boniluce.

Sometimes at night, when he rode in his gondola over the glassy face of Lake Teal, Dragmond would look off toward the Corbinwood, as though even in the dark and at great distance, he might catch a glimpse of Galliard.

"I will kill you yet, cousin," he whispered, his gloved hands stroking the stone arms of the chair. "Though you cannot, will not return, someday I shall travel those miles myself and set sword to your larcenous throat."

For now, Galliard was out of reach, very possibly in the grasslands of Zephyr or the Aldor Mountains, but most likely in the woods he ruled like a lord. There with a band of robbers and road agents—two dozen at most and ill supplied, to hear the country people tell it.

But then, the country people loved Galliard. It was probably more like a thousand.

Every time the green star shifted to new surroundings, the king looked south first, toward Galliard. For the exiled Duke of Aquila had a thin claim to the throne, and one never knew when he might try to make good on it. That was why General Helmar was stationed south of Lake Teal with two thousand infantry, five hundred cavalry, a dozen catapults, and as many ballistae.

King Dragmond had become cautious in all things.

So cautious, in fact, that he knew Ravenna was in the room at the very instant she stepped over the threshold.

"I have attended to my duties," he said, his face expressionless, his back to the dark woman.

Ravenna nodded as though he were watching. Gracefully and dramatically, she moved silently through a wash of candlelight to the mantel, where the banked coals glowed at her approach.

Dragmond rose, turned to face her.

She was beautiful in the red rising light, her black hair tied behind her and her black robes shimmering. Casually she lifted the yellowed skull of a Zephyrian cavalry officer from its place on the mantel. She looked intently into the vacant sockets with a distant, appraising stare that the king knew well.

He shivered, and not for the first time.

"I am sure you have, Dragmond," Ravenna replied with a sweep of her cape, her low voice filling the room as if the walls themselves whispered in a rich, melodic unison. The flames of the candles inclined toward her voice as though they listened.

"I am sure you have, but duties are oft not enough," she pronounced. "So you brood, and you play with the candles."

"And what does that mean, Ravenna?" the king snapped, striding toward the window. He clutched the sill and stared out onto the beach and the restless autumn sea, where the spindrift flickered white under the waxing moon.

"Only what I said. That duties are oft not enough, my dear," she replied calmly. Having warmed herself by the fire, she moved to the center of the room. There, encircled by candles, she sat on the throne. Daintily, almost primly, she folded her hands on her lap, turning her gray eyes to Dragmond.

"What would you have me do, then?" he asked, his back to her still.

She knew there were times he dreaded to look at her. Not that he found her unattractive—indeed, just the opposite.

And yet when he wanted direction—to be told what to do—he could not meet her gaze.

She smiled, rested her fire-warmed neck on the cool onyx.

"Oh . . . I do not know, Dragmond. I do not know yet. But the green star is prophetic this time. Of that I am sure."

"How—how do you know, Ravenna?" Dragmond asked, turning to face her. "Couldn't it be a drought? Something to do with Parthia or Hadrach?"

"It could be," Ravenna replied tauntingly. "Is that what your bowl told you?"

The king flushed, his bright eyes darting to the empty bowl on the table.

"Our augurers," Ravenna pronounced dramatically, "have told me otherwise."

"What have they told you?" Dragmond asked urgently, taking a sudden, aggressive step toward the sorceress, then catching himself in midstride. It would not do to rouse her anger with kingly strut and bluster.

Patiently he awaited her story. Casually, almost lazily, she passed her hand over the crown, the bowl, the sword.

"All of the aspects were present," she said, after a long, infuriating pause. "Pytho in the belt of the Forest Lord, the half moon tipped like a cup, and the sun hanging between the Scorpion and the Archer."

"I know, Ravenna," Dragmond interrupted. "By the gods, I know all that! Why do you think I've bounded myself with candles and spent the last fortnight watching the flight of birds and swirling water in a bowl?"

"Some there are," the sorceress pronounced, "who see into the heart of the water, into the dreams of birds."

Dragmond shuddered again. To him, all augury was a groping in the dark. In the countless times he had followed the wavering crescent of geese as they reeled southward toward the Notches, in the carafes of water that had passed through the porcelain bowl that lay on his mahogany table, the king had seen nothing but fowl and water. Yet he had heard of others who saw otherwise.

Ravenna knew them all.

Knew the exiled duchess who read cards and the facets of emeralds for the merchants living along the Teal Front so that they would know when to sell saffron or when the seas would be calm enough to send for oranges and spikenard and myrrh from Sidon.

Knew the old hag who wandered the Hardwater Cove, reading portents in the arrangements of refuse that the tides left in the thin strip of black sand.

Knew those who read stars, stones, and tea leaves, those who saw the future in what the fisherman's net brought forth and those down in Wall Town who read darker things—things that even soldiers such as Dragmond blanched to imagine someone reading.

"I have called upon those seers," Ravenna pronounced. "And last night, five of them offered to help us."

"Show them in," Dragmond replied quietly, but the sorceress shook her head.

"They and I have transacted. We transacted, we spoke in the deep hours, and all of us concurred that a pretender is among us."

"A pretender?"

"Yes, dear," Ravenna answered dryly, condescendingly. "One who, if the time and the place and the knowledge are right, may have designs on this very chair in which I sit."

"You seem very calm about that," Dragmond accused. "I should suspect that if I were no longer king, you would no longer be . . . whatever it is *you* are."

"Then again," Ravenna observed, picking up the bowl from the table, "you have seen only water in this."

And blood! the king almost cried out. *I have seen blood, too, Ravenna!* But he held his peace, out of mistrust or embarrassment—which one he was not sure—and the dark woman continued, turning the pale bowl in her pale hand.

"As you well know by now, nephew, I have resources beyond my visions." She bit her lip and looked directly, alluringly at Dragmond.

The king's heart lurched, and his face felt hot.

"Chances are that I'd be a welcome advisor in *any* man's court," Ravenna observed, hooking one languid finger in the rim of the bowl and dangling it precariously at arm's length. "But then, I do hate change. The sudden falls from power of the high and mighty tend to . . . unsettle me."

Casually, as though smoothing her hair or shading her eyes against a sudden rising light, she let the bowl drop, let it shatter on the stone floor still wet from the water it once contained.

"That is why I transacted with them," she explained, reaching to the table once more, this time lifting from it the gold, emerald-studded crown of Palerna.

"We had a long . . . conversation. From which I have freshly returned.

"I invited Captain Lightborn. Whose opinion I know you respect in matters political."

Dragmond's eyes narrowed.

Lightborn. The scarpines. The broken glass and the hot oil.

"By the end of our conversation," Ravenna continued serenely, eyes fixed on the largest emerald in the crown, "the augurers were eager to read for us. Indeed, each of them saw this pretender in the future of the city. Oh, some saw him as little more than a mild threat some years down the road—a Galliard, plying his discontent in a far-flung region of the continent. Others saw him as more immediate, more dangerous, especially if we could not find him quickly."

"Then again," Dragmond interrupted, trying to silence his rising dread with jests and false bravery, "this pretender could be a week of heavy rain."

"Oh, I think not, m'lord. I think not," Ravenna drawled. "For there is one certain way to tell whether an augurer speaks the truth."

Dragmond stared at her, thunderstruck.

"All of their bodies fell northward when they died," the sorceress announced coldly, tossing the crown back onto the table and rising from the chair.

As she had tossed away the lives of five augurers.

"Then . . . then why *five* of them, Ravenna?" Dragmond stammered. "Wouldn't the death of *one* have told us what we needed?"

"Perhaps," she answered, walking to the window and taking Dragmond by the arm. "But then we would have had four witnesses, four mouths to tell that the throne of Palerna was again contested. And four possible enemies, if any of them believed that the pretender, whoever he is, had half a chance to seize your throne.

"Never trust an augurer, Dragmond," she announced with a false solemnity, her lips brushing the neck of the speechless king.

Dragmond swallowed, wavering between fear and desire.

"I cannot believe you, Ravenna," he said, intending to shout but finding himself murmuring. "Is there any humanity lost in all that darkness and beauty?"

"Tell that to the dead on the causeway," she said with a smile, encircling his neck with her pale, serpentine arms.

VII

In the weeks that followed his first uncertain nights as an apprentice, Brenn took up poetry himself. He was hardly convinced that the words and the lines the wizard had recited in the marketplace had anything to do with the remarkable events that happened there, and yet there was no explanation for stampeding pigs, or for good Umbrian wine, for that matter.

So Brenn looked more closely at the volume Terrance had loaned him during that first day at the wizard's house. For the first time the boy cursed his earlier laziness—his refusal, despite the Goniph's and Faye's urgings, to devote much time to reading anything more than the practical manuals and popular romances that had been his fare through his short career of thievery. Most of the poems blurred beneath his untutored stare, and he caught himself thumbing the pages despondently, looking for one stanza of verse that was suitably large and dramatic and at the same time composed only of words he understood and could pronounce. For Brenn had read—no doubt in one of those romances—that the conjurer who stumbled in his conjury or missed a subtle meaning in a line or phrase would sometimes fall through a hole in the earth or burst into flames before he had even finished speaking.

And yet . . . it offered temptation. It might be something to take with him from this wretched place: a book of memorized charms, of particularly *practical* poems. He had heard someone say that some verses could even open locks.

But none of the helpful poems seemed to be here.

Brenn was almost through the volume before he found one that suited him. Anxiously he had looked that night at the few pages remaining, then, turning the second-to-last page, came across something grand and yet orderly. Slowly, he passed his finger over each word.

> *Her eyes the Glow-worme lend thee,*
> *The Shooting Starres attend thee;*
> *And the Elves also,*
> *Whose little eyes glow,*
> *Like the sparks of fire, befriend thee.*

> *No Will-o'-th'-Wispe mis-light thee;*
> *Nor Snake, or Slow-worme bite thee:*
> *But on, on thy way*
> *Not making a stay,*
> *Since Ghost ther's none to affright thee.*

> *Let not the darke thee cumber;*
> *What though the Moon do's slumber?*
> *The Starres of the night*
> *Will lend thee their light,*
> *Like Tapers cleare without number.*

Brenn looked up from the page. The attic around him had sunk into darkness at the edge of his candlelight. Through the open trapdoor a dark bank of clouds covered the moon and settled, as though it were ready to wait out the night.

"That's it!" he whispered softly into the cluttered room. Gallina, her head tucked under her wing, stirred slightly and clucked.

"Let's shed some light on this place," Brenn pronounced calmly, scanning the text once more. Then slowly, his mind a swirl of images and memories and long imaginings as to just what would happen when the whole of the poem had been said, he began to recite, quietly and cautiously at first, but picking up confidence and volume as he went along, until the part about the stars sounded like first-rate chanting indeed to his apprentice's ears, and was loud enough to wake Gallina, who rustled on her nest with a squawk.

Brenn took a deep breath and sat back on his mattress, awaiting wonders. But nothing happened. The attic was still cluttered with boxes and dappled with candlelight and shadow, and aside from Gallina's uneasy stirring, everything seemed to be more or less in the spot that he left it.

The sky above the trapdoor was midnight blue and cloudy, just as it had been before all this poetry and nonsense, and below him Brenn heard a faint, high chuckle—no doubt Terrance laughing in his sleep or two grannars in a contest over a scrap of bread in the kitchen.

Brenn stood up, set down the book, and walked toward the attic steps in disappointment. It was then that something seemed odd about the shadows. The boy stopped, took stock of the situation.

The shadows were blurred and doubled. It took Brenn only a second to realize that they were cast by *two* sources of light. Turning quickly, looking up at the trapdoor, he saw the city sky from a new angle and noticed a shimmering light on the northern horizon, bright and wavering as though something was on fire.

"By the gods, it worked!" the boy exclaimed to nobody in particular, and eagerly, curiously, set foot to the lowest rung of the ladder that led to the roof.

Suddenly the attic exploded in shrill laughter, and all around him Brenn saw the glow of small green eyes. He froze on the ladder, awaiting the worst.

The boy had never seen elves before. In this, of course, he was not alone. Though there were probably hundreds of the little creatures in Maraven alone, hidden in attics and sewers, safe within the hollow trees of the parks down by the Teal Front, and deep within the recesses of the porous rock along Hardwater Cove, it was the rare person indeed who had seen one.

Everyone, however, had heard legends. In all of the stories, the elves were a tragic and glorious people, tall and pale and beautiful, all of them bearing a thousand years of sorrow and of wisdom in their eyes.

Perhaps the elves *had* been such a people once and had fallen onto hard times. Or perhaps the legends were the wishes of storytellers or just plain mistaken information.

For they were hardly things of beauty. Short, flop-eared, and hairy, they looked like house pets gone terribly wrong. Two of them scurried into the moon-bathed center of the floor and waited there, the pale light catching the sharp, glittering blades they carried.

One was dressed only in a bat skin, its membranous wings draped ominously over his shoulders. The other was covered with a man-sized wool stocking cap, hairy snout, oversize ears, elven arms and legs all protruding from holes worried into the weave of the thing.

Brenn froze on the ladder, unable to climb or descend.

Below him the armed visitors exchanged words in a guttural, undecipherable language. They raised their swords and scurried to the foot of the ladder.

Punctured by knee-high hooligans, the boy thought. *That's what I get for conjuring*. On the edge of panic, he lifted himself to the next highest rung.

But neither of the elves seemed up to skewering. Quickly they crouched in defensive postures that would have been funny were it not for the vicious looks they gave the boy—not to mention the razored edges of their blades. The two were a guard of sorts, watching the enemy, it seemed, while their companions took on the business of the night.

Gallina squawked as they dragged her from the nest, down into the darkness, where there was yet another squawk and the hysterical sound of elven laughter.

A young elf, shorter and more rounded than the others, dirty with cobwebs and guano, scurried out of the dark and onto the nest. Drawing his sword, he swiftly gouged a hole in the base of the egg. While Brenn looked on in bafflement, the unsanitary-looking creature lifted the egg in both hands, tipped it to his lips, and eagerly sucked the contents from the shell. Then, staring directly at Brenn with a green, contented look, he belched loudly, dribbling egg white from his hairy chin, and scrambled back into the darkness.

"Damn!" Brenn exclaimed. "They're a messy business! I wish I'd never unleashed 'em!"

Through the night he repeated those words, or ones very much like them, for when one vicious little creature was deflected from rifling the pantry for cheeses, another would take its place, swimming in beer, stealing Terrance's bright handkerchiefs, or finally, just before sunrise, breaking the middle of the three solar windows with a well-hurled andiron.

Brenn sat down in the rubble and shouted the vilest, most unrepeatable thief's curse he knew.

His companions covered their hairy ears and laughed.

A floor above the beleaguered boy, Terrance turned on his cot and chuckled softly.

"Easy to call up, lad, but a damnable nuisance to get rid of!" he observed, turning his eyes to the window, where the moonlight shone through the iron latticework, checkering the bedroom floor with shadow and light. Rising from bed, Terrance approached the window and looked down onto the water, northwest to Grospoint, now settled in shadow. Beyond the business district, the wizard could see nothing but shadow and the faintest of lights that seemed to rise out of the foothills of the Aquilan Mountains.

That would be Kestrel Tower.

"I should know," he whispered wearily, staring at the distant light. "I'm a damnable nuisance myself."

He smiled mischievously and turned from the window. The room he faced was twice as small and nearly as spare as that of his apprentice in the attic. A solitary cot sat in the center of the room, beside it a nightstand upon which sat a lamp and a basin. Except for a single mahogany wardrobe, the rest of the room was empty. All in all it looked as though someone were in the process of moving, having settled all but the heaviest furniture elsewhere and awaiting another day, another time to come back for the last items.

Robes and books and manuscripts littered the floor: though Terrance was meticulously neat throughout the rest of his house, he let his sleeping quarters flourish with a kind of benign neglect. Moving back toward the bed, the wizard stooped, began to lift one of the larger volumes lying on the floor. He winced, clutched at his back.

"I suppose that one's down there permanently." He chuckled glumly, reaching for a smaller volume.

"Just as well," he proclaimed, reading the title by the dim lamplight. "*The Geography of Zephyr*. If the lad is the one, we may need this anon.

"Then again," he conceded, thumbing through the slim volume in his hands, "the time is coming when we will need to know all volumes, because we cannot know which ones we will need."

Heavily he sat on the bed, his eyes fixed once again on the window, his thoughts on the distant tower he could no longer see from where he sat.

"Twice before, Ravenna," he whispered calmly. "Twice before it has come to this. Come to a reckoning between the two of us. Both times you have won, old girl.

"Which is why you are up there, looking out. And I am down here, beneath your notice if I am lucky."

Terrance smiled again, setting the book on the nightstand and extinguishing the lamp.

"Right now I would have it no other way."

For a long moment the old man sat motionless in the dark. Then slowly, only faintly visible in the fractured moonlight of the room, he reclined onto the cot for a long and dreamless night.

"Must get my sleep," he concluded. "Tomorrow there will be elves to clean up after."

Over in Grospoint, right off the Street of the Chemists, a window had been left ajar in one of the older, more established storefronts, whether by accident or by some mischievous design. The night air weaved through the oilcloth-covered grating and returned out the window itself, smelling of spices.

Faye and Dirk stood by the window in shadows, the large man crouched beside them. Quickly the girl locked the fingers of both hands together, making a stirrup of sorts for Dirk, who, given only a little boost, was up to the windowsill where, setting his shoulder against the grating, he slowly forced the iron latticework inward.

For a brief, uncertain moment the thieves held their breath, listening for the scrape of metal on stone, the high-piercing sound of rusty hinges.

"Ah," breathed the Goniph in relief as Dirk opened the window silently. Then the big man stepped forward. Gracefully he lifted Faye to the sill, where the nimble girl stepped through the window and joined her friend in the storage room of the spice shop. The Goniph sat with his back to the storefront wall, sighed deeply, scratched his beard, and waited for his apprentices to finish the work.

He lifted his eyes to the tipped cup of the half moon, as the light tangled in the wild shock of his curly brown hair and glinted off the silver ring of his nose. To someone passing by the spice shop at that moment, it might have seemed as though the burly man sitting below the window was in the midst of some transformation into a large animal—that instead of waiting for the full moon to change him, he had ventured out a fortnight early and was caught by the light of the half moon in a strange country halfway between man and beast.

In the last few years the master thief had outgrown his profession, as he liked to say. He remained the Goniph, as he would be until he retired or left the art by a less fortunate path, and he continued to carry the title well. His real name had been lost twenty years before in the clouded memory of the Maravenian streets, where pickpocket and cutpurse and second-story man and even the highwaymen on Cove Road or Gray Strand had gradually forgotten that he had ever been called anything but the Goniph.

As the Goniph, his reputation had flourished. Most of his company remembered no other master, and many of them believed he was the Goniph who the oldest thieves spoke about with reverence—that, indeed, the big man had been alive and filching and ruling the Maravenian Thieves' Guild back to the time that the city's foundations had been laid six centuries ago. Perhaps, it was whispered, he was here before the city, when all there was along the Palernan coast were volcanoes and gray water.

Larger and larger he grew in the imaginings of the city's underworld. But he also had grown larger and larger in fact. Three hundred sixty pounds was too much to hoist through a window or slip through a narrow chute or trapdoor, so now the Goniph delegated those pursuits, reserving for himself the task of gathering information. He lifted knowledge from the shop-keepers, filched rumors from Dragmond's Watch and the ships' captains, and, on rare occasions, pilfered state secrets from those in Kestrel Tower.

The Goniph had found King Dragmond an interesting mark. Street-clever, perhaps, but not nearly as intelligent as public proclamation made him out to be.

But tonight was not a night for captains or merchants or kings. It had been one of Duval's Urchins, a little girl of ten or eleven, who had let it slip to the big guild master that young Cathelle the spice merchant had been inattentive with his storeroom windows of late. Spice, of course, was expensive—the most valuable of valuables in Grospoint.

Spice demanded the Goniph's presence.

He had brought Faye and Dirk along with him. A week ago it would have been Faye and Brenn, for a spice run was a favored assignment, a venture that demanded the best in the guild. Since then, Brenn had vanished in the house of the wizard, no doubt transformed into rat or bird or six-legged vermin, and Dirk had taken his place as the Goniph's second apprentice.

First apprentice, of course, was always Faye.

The big man had taken to her early. A spunky, dark-haired girl with the wits of an alchemist, she had come to him at the age of six—or five, or seven, he could not be sure—had her letters and numbers within a month, and moved on to poetry, philosophy, and the dangerous readings that made her give half her own takings to the poor of Wall Town and refuse to steal within the borders of that wronged and wronging district.

She would be at him to give his worldly goods to the hospitals, the Goniph thought in frustration. And yet he seldom could hide an enterprise from her watchfulness—certainly never one of this

. . . magnitude. Though this adventure was easy—uncannily easy, with the shipment fresh in and the window to the storeroom left ajar—it still demanded procedure, for the best apprentices sulked and grew restless when left behind on a spice venture.

Silently the big man waited, still crouched in the shadows by the window. In a minute or two he would hear the call of a nightingale, rare in the smoky streets of the city—rare enough, in fact, that the trilling *tereu* of the bird could serve as a signal among thieves.

He closed his eyes as an eager rumble rose from deep in his throat. Closed his eyes and, filled with a late and plentiful supper, must have nodded into sleep for a moment, for when he opened his eyes again, the eastern horizon was filled with light.

"What in the name of . . ." he began, looking around him frantically. Then cupping his beefy hands in front of his mouth, he let sound the call of the nightingale. Inside the spice shop there was silence for a moment, a gasp of disbelief from Faye. Then Dirk's face appeared at the window, a mask of puzzlement and shock.

"Get out of there, and bring Faye with you!" the Goniph hissed, his eyes on the brightening cobblestones in the Street of the Chemists. "I'll be damned if I know how, but I've botched the hour!"

Dutifully the apprentices scrambled through the window, their eyes scanning the street for movement, for arriving merchants, for Dragmond's Watch. Steadily, the hulking shape of the master leading them, the trio slipped through Point Square and down the Gaunt Alley, where they caught the East Road into Wall Town.

It was only when they were back to their cell, when the Goniph stood at the alley doorway until his apprentices crossed the threshold, that he noticed a strange darkening in the sky as the eastern light faded. Quickly, as though the night had turned itself around, the darkness returned to the streets, the outlines of buildings blended into one another, and to the north the glow of the lighthouses and the more distant light from Kestrel Tower stood out once more against the darkness.

Dawn, it seemed, was still several hours away. The Goniph shook his head, plunged into his own perplexing darkness.

"Came from over toward the East Wall," he whispered to himself. "Over where I lost the boy some nights back.

"Bears looking into," he muttered angrily, closing the door behind him. At the very same moment back in Grospoint, the spice merchant, roused by the light from a fitful sleep in which he dreamt he had forgotten something small but dreadfully important, stood in his storeroom and thanked his lucky stars that nobody had discovered the window he had left ajar.

Not only thieves and merchants noticed the light in the eastern sky. In the gardens of Kestrel Tower the larks took up song and a solitary rooster arched its back and crowed, awaking a dozing Watchman on the battlements who, thinking his shift was nearly over, tried to appear even more vigilant to impress the guard who came to relieve him.

More watchful than these, the dark woman in the tower turned east, her gray eyes urgent and intent.

Sometimes, in the top rooms of Kestrel Tower, the candles burned so brightly that inexperienced helmsmen, straying off course out in the Sea of Shadows, were shipwrecked when they took the glow for the beacon of a distant lighthouse and followed it into the reef. But tonight the light to the east was the rival of any torch or candle. For a moment, when it shone on Ravenna's pale face, her skin seemed dry and stretched, as though she were three times as old as the beautiful woman who plotted and peered over oracles in the rich Maravenian night.

"Terrance!" she murmured. It was almost a curse, the way she said the wizard's name. Her eyes still fixed on the mysterious eastern light, she moved quickly to the center of the tower room and, turning her back to the false sunrise, walked to the westernmost point of the room, where she cupped her hands over a light blue candle that stood in a wide pool of wax, formed by a long, curious vigil some years back. The wick flashed suddenly with a low blue flame, and Ravenna stared across flickering miles into the dreams of the wizard.

Terrance dreamt of food and wine that night: hams and pies stacked on a sagging table, a barrel of whiskey tapped in a cool moist corner.

Like the whiskey, his dreams were amber.

Ravenna shrugged, reached to extinguish the candle. But there was another intelligence in the house—alert, darting from object to object like a bird in a rising swarm of flies. Ravenna sat back, waited patiently for this intelligence to sleep, to open its dreams to her.

At last, the flame of the candle low and guttering in the rising circle of watery wax, the image appeared in the fire. Ravenna brushed back her hair and leaned forth hungrily.

It began with whiskey, though it was not the wizard's dream. Then the fire revealed a weaving image of eggs. A saucer of sour milk. Something dark in the gutters of the house itself, and a strange rushing movement from dark into light back into dark. Cobweb and cheese.

Ravenna leaned back and laughed viciously. Then, wetting her fingers, she pinched the hissing wick and plunged the tower room into darkness.

"Elves!" she said aloud, her voice almost singing in its malign delight. "The senile old fool's botched a spell and conjured up elves!

"The hair on the furniture alone will be enough to keep him busy for the rest of his miserable life!"

Calmly Ravenna walked to the window and breathed in the gray, salt-smelling morning air. Still laughing, she looked down onto the causeway, where the guardsmen were hoisting a blanket-covered body into a rocking rowboat.

"Who could have foreseen it?" she asked to no one in particular.

≺≺≺ VIII ≻≻≻

That winter it was alchemy, when the north wind swept off the Sea of Shadows and left the inhabitants of Hardwater Cove sniffling and bundling and cursing the powers that be.

"It isn't all turning base metals to gold, Brenn," Terrance

warned as the two of them set up the alchemist's apparatus of tubing and wire and bottle and alembic. Apparently the subject had not interested the wizard for some time, for the materials were deep among the boxes of the attic, and to get to them Brenn had to clear away a decade of old robes and scatter a long-abandoned mouse's nest. Finally, the alembic in sight, he had to fend off a pair of aggressive elves armed with dinner forks, who skewered the boy's hands and arms several times before they dove shrieking behind a sea chest, leaving a trail of guano and feathers behind them and the air astir with dust.

Coughing, Brenn had hauled the whole damned machinery out into the open part of the attic. He dusted it until the rag grew heavy with lint and dirt, then picked up another rag and then a third, which finally finished the job.

Wheezing, sniffling, he stood in the center of the floor, copper tubing in hand.

"After I've gone through this? Braved dust and mouse and waylaying elf, only to have you tell me there's no gold in this?"

Terrance frowned, holding a metal beaker under his bespectacled nose, the better to inspect it for dents and holes and rendings. "I said that gold wasn't the *only* thing. In fact, the business of changing base metal to noble is a terribly hard transaction. If it were so easy," he added, staring curiously at his apprentice, "why would Ricardo ever have to leave home? He could stay in Hadrach or Jaleel or whatever loud Alanyan city he hails from and make gold the livelong day."

It made sense to Brenn, who had concluded some months back that Ricardo was a bad alchemist. After all, it was clear from their brief stay with Terrance last November that Delia did all the work.

"Then what do *I* have to make, Terrance? I mean, if not gold."

With that air of mystery and mischief that by now could be counted on to anger his apprentice, the wizard lifted one of the capsized boxes and drew from it an old brown woolen robe. He wrapped the ratty thing tightly about his shoulders and shivered a moment in the brisk air of the attic. Brenn waited, at first with eagerness and then with rising irritation.

"I've been making gold for some time, Brennart. Indeed, I am constantly making gold."

"And just what is *that* supposed to mean?" Brenn asked angrily, handing a loop of copper tubing to the wizard, who slipped each end of it into the mouth of a curious, toad-shaped vessel.

Terrance whistled an old Umbrian drinking song and did not answer. Nonetheless Brenn's anger faded quickly, his curiosity rising as he noticed that some device was indeed taking shape on the floor in front of him.

It resembled the elaborate machine he had seen in the guest room that night he had opened the door on Delia. But it was more reckless, more haphazard, as though the elves that still infested this attic had designed and assembled it.

Five, six, seven containers there were, from head-sized beakers to a single, thumb-sized phial at the end of a long brass tube. The apparatus was still empty, all wires and bottles, but already there was something official-looking, if sloppy, in the space it occupied on the floor.

Silently, smiling that curious smile that generally meant Brenn was in for an afternoon of perplexity and mistakes, Terrance bent the copper tubing into the shape of a duck's head, drew a piece of ribbon from the sleeve of the ratty robe he had just donned, and swiftly, daintily, tied a bow about his handiwork. Then, making duck noises, he rose and descended the steps to the second floor.

Brenn sat on his mattress, clutching a tripod and a tinderbox, and listened to the sound of rummaging rising from below him.

"It's a fool I'm with," he whispered into the dusty attic, startling an elf who had come from hiding to explore the premises. Chittering with fright, the vile little thing plunged into a maze of crates and sea chests in the northwest corner, leaving a faint smell of rotten eggs in the air.

"But no doubt the fool is after chemicals. Things like sulfur. Like quicksilver and electrum and that phosphorus that glows in vials though it be absolute dark all about."

Brennart liked to think of these things. He had heard the Goniph talk of the wonders an alchemist could do with a pinch of gypsum and a vial of nitre, and something or other else that together went into the making of that black firepowder from Cathay—the stuff that made the pictures of the king up by the tower last August. And though the boy had never seen an alchemist do all that much beyond making simple foul-tasting tonics and the occasional poison or two, he was convinced that this stage of his studies held more promise than the gauzy, backfiring poems he had memorized and recited through the long autumn and into the turn of the new year.

Here was the meat of magic: something with formulas and components and directions.

The noise resumed on the steps, as Terrance descended yet another flight to the library, the kitchen, the solar. He was down there quite a while, as Brennart had nodded off to sleep by the time he returned to the attic, his mouth agape and snoring, his head propped uncomfortably on the iron tripod. Terrance took the last flight of steps slowly, so the two elves who were in the process of relieving Brenn of his shoes managed to take one of them and scramble to safety before Terrance came back into view, his arms laden with a dozen bags, boxes, and bottles.

"Be alert, boy!" the wizard boomed. "A lad can't sleep on paraphernalia!"

Brenn snorted and scrambled to his feet, discovering in the process that one of them was missing its shoe. He cursed loudly and inventively, raising the tinderbox over his head as if to hurl it into the midst of the precariously stacked boxes at the far end of the attic.

Where, he hoped fiercely, it would ignite itself and the attic and the whole house, as long as it burned elves in the process.

"Now, now, boy!" Terrance soothed. "There's at least one shoe missing for every elf on these premises, I'll wager. Extraordinarily fond of human footwear, they are, though they don't have an earthly use for any of it they might make off with.

"It surprises me," he continued, the infuriating smile returning, "that you of all people would take larceny so hard. Especially since you can go among those boxes and find another shoe."

"But it won't be mine, I'll wager," Brenn argued glumly, his anger again beginning to subside.

"But *I* shall wager it will be a serviceable shoe, natheless," the wizard replied merrily, drawing a mortar and pestle from the folds of his robe. "Folks set too much stock on things matching, on pairs looking like pairs and families like families. What's needed are a few more distinguishing marks, if you ask me."

"What are we going to make, Terrance?" Brenn asked, changing the subject before his temper took over. Despite himself, the boy found his curiosity rising again as the wizard drew two, three, four little porcelain boxes out of those bottomless robes, setting them on the floor in front of him and staring at them intently, as though a pea or a penny lay under one of them and it was his task to guess which one.

"A case in point," he murmured, his eyes never leaving the four almost identical boxes arranged in a row. They were hand-sized, oval, and reddish brown. Each had a black dragon embossed on its lid.

"Had I followed my own philosophy," Terrance explained bemusedly, scratching his beard, "I'd know exactly which one of these to open."

"What . . . harm would there be in opening the wrong one?" Brenn asked cautiously, backing away from the apparatus, the visions of the house in flames still fresh in his imaginings.

"You never know," Terrance declared ominously, picking up the closest of the boxes and shaking it by his ear, to Brenn's great alarm. "Elixirs and extracts can be most volatile stuff. I heard of a merchant family on Teal Front that mixed *flammagloriae* in with their wine at supper—must have fallen from the shelf or something—and all six of them exploded. Found remnants and fragments from Ships to Wall Town.

"I'm not entirely convinced it was an accident," Terrance added with a frown. "Trade families have been detonating one another down in Hadrach for nigh on two centuries."

Brenn started to laugh, but a severe look from the wizard checked him. Terrance shook the box once more, set it down, then, getting on hands and knees, sniffed at two others.

"Had a friend once, an alchemist in Partha, made a man pee blue for a month."

"What?" Brenn almost shouted in astonishment.

"Pee. You know, urinate. Make water."

"I *know* that, Terrance," Brenn sputtered. "What I don't see is what practical good that might serve."

"Oh, absolutely none," Terrance declared serenely, picking up the fourth box—the only one that remained unshaken or unsniffed. "Done as a joke. A slow-acting sugar that hit the poor fool's urinary tract about a year after his trip to Partha. They put the man in hospital in Venice. Bled him until he almost died. Might have killed him outright were it not that the alchemist in question had a cousin in the college of surgeons there who knew the trick himself.

"The same fellow—this . . . *friend* of mine—worked closer to home," Terrance continued, holding the fourth box up to the light. He stared in long silence, then nodded confidently.

"What is it, Terrance?" Brenn asked.

"What this fellow did," Terrance continued, "was give a potion to a poet. Was supposed to make the man rhyme accidentally, continually, and felicitously.

"Instead, it struck him blind on the thirtieth of each month. He'd go to sleep the night of the twenty-ninth and not see a thing until he wakened on the thirty-first. Or the first, depending on the calendar.

"Came in handy when my alchemist friend decided to take up with the poet's wife. They set their rendezvous for the thirtieth of each month, when the husband in question was sightless and knocking against furniture.

"Things went well for them. Until February, that is."

The wizard smiled maliciously.

"He was always a terrible man. The poet dispatched him with a powerful potion, bought from a more powerful alchemist, that rendered the adulterer transparent.

"It also rendered him dead, of course. And afterward the poet wrote a long and impassioned ode that defamed his rival for posterity."

He pointed at Brenn.

"Which should be a lesson for you."

"Never court another man's wife, sir?"

"Oh, yes! I had forgotten *that* lesson, though it is a good one. I was thinking of 'Befriend all poets.' A lesson that will come in handy for you through the years."

Again the mysterious smile. Sick of all the veiled knowledge, Brenn itched to throw the wizard down and interrogate him, to ask him what exactly he had in store for apprentices and why it demanded all this cloak and dagger, then rifle those robes himself, extract anything worthwhile, and march out the front door back to Wall Town.

To try strong-arm tactics would be folly, though. Brenn had seen enough of Terrance at work to know that the wizard was not about to be daunted by physical threat or even by a straightforward show of muscle. Furthermore, though Terrance was pushing seventy, Brenn could tell by his lean, gristly frame that it would take more than one teenaged boy to wrestle the old man down.

"What . . . what are *we* up to with our alchemy, Terrance?"

"I beg your pardon?" The wizard opened the porcelain box ever so slightly, sniffed the underside of its lid with a furtive, quick movement of his nose, as though he were doing something dangerous or even illegal.

"Ah, this is the one!" He smiled. As he opened the box, the smell of juniper filled the room once more, and a green light spread from the box throughout the attic, illuminating dark cobwebbed corners and a leaded window Brenn had never noticed before. The music of harp and flute filled the room.

Over by the northernmost wall of the house, the light struck two crouching elves, armed with dinner forks, who sniffed the air eagerly and uttered little shrieks of delight. Out of hiding they rushed, straight toward Terrance, but caught themselves after only a few frantic steps. Reluctantly, as if a strong binding cord tugged them toward the wizard, the elves turned and scrambled back toward hiding, moving more slowly and heavily with each step they took until it looked as though they were trying to run underwater. Finally, panting with exertion, they crawled on all fours into a crate, pulling an old robe in behind them, no doubt to stop the music and the light and the smells.

"What is that?" Brenn exclaimed, his eyes still on the crated pests.

"Juniper mash," the wizard replied with a chuckle. "That's what our alchemy is all about."

"I don't understand, Terrance."

"Zephyrian gin. We're making gin, Brennart."

Slowly, pouring the juniper mash into a cucurbit, the gourd-shaped beaker that formed the body of the alembic, Terrance whistled a minor-keyed Alanyan tune. Then he set the cucurbit upon the iron tripod, capped it with the tubed head of the device, and explained his strategy as the elves cooed and sang from the obscurity of boxes and sea chests.

"It is the one known substance on the planet that stirs an elf without fail," he announced, steadying the alembic. "The tinderbox, please."

The boy fumbled in his pockets until he remembered that the box was where he had cast it, lying on its side in the middle of the rush mattress. He fetched it, handed it to the wizard, who lit a fire beneath the cucurbit without a pause in history.

"It's been known to send them migrating, to change the right of succession in one royal elven house, and to have started three of their last four wars—at least the wars we have records of."

As the gin mash bubbled, the cooing of the elves became a fierce, joyous wail. A short fat one, sniffing with greedy ecstasy—no doubt the one fond of dear departed Gallina's eggs—rushed from behind a broken concertina and craned over the alembic where the vapors escaped through a narrow leak. Chirruping like a quarreling squirrel, the portly little creature rolled his eyes and fainted dead away, jostling the tripod and singeing his hairy ears as he tumbled facefirst onto the attic floor.

"So it begins," Terrance announced triumphantly. "Now, when the gin is distilled, we fill bowls and saucers and set the things around the house, just as you'd spread poison for rats. The elves love it, cannot get enough of its smell and texture and taste, but by the gods, they can't hold it. Takes them hours to sleep it off.

"So it's a simple process. You set down the saucers, and when morning comes, you go through the house and gather up elves."

Terrance looked at the boy with stern amusement.

"Someday, Brenn, if you don't turn yourself into a grannar or a squinchfly with all that poetry you're abusing, you'll realize the truth about magic."

"And what is that, Terrance?" Knowing he was on the verge

of a scolding, Brenn ceased to be interested in anything the wizard had to say.

"That it's a lot like lying."

Brenn fondled the porcelain box, his eye on the burning lamp beneath the alembic.

"One spell, one conjury," Terrance continued, "takes two, three, sometimes even four to be undone. What's more, when you go about picking the edges on the fabric of things, you might as well expect a little . . . unraveling.

"Ah. Even now it's beginning. Not a slow gin, this Zephyrian stuff."

The wizard laughed as the clear receiver took the first several drops of the distilled liquor.

"It's like lying, because folks can magick and magick until they forget what is their doing and what things were like to begin with. That is when disaster comes riding in."

By now Brenn was entranced by the flickering lamp, scarcely attending when his master spoke quietly, almost sadly.

"Magic should be used only as a last resort, as I always say. Sometimes I think that the greatest magic-user is the one who does not use his art at all."

Silently the two alchemists sat in the round, curious attic, watching the gin rise in the vial.

The Zephyrian gin worked, as Terrance had promised. On the first morning after setting out the saucers, Brennart found one elf. On the next morning he found two.

And slowly, gradually, the wretched little creatures were dumped unceremoniously on the beach, where they awoke in the noon light, rubbed their eyes, heads, backs, and nether parts uncomfortably. Then grumbling and coughing, they found their way into the dark recesses of the porous rocks, where no doubt they spent the rest of the winter in hibernation or the haze of hangovers.

By the middle of February almost all of the elves had been flushed from hiding and driven from the house. Brenn still heard one or two of them scratching around the premises at night, and the occasional egg or jar of olives ended up missing from the larder, but by that time in the winter, Brennart's attention had turned sharply elsewhere.

For the prospects of alchemy were in his blood and in his imaginings.

Of course he remembered the wizard's warning—something about magic and lies. However, it had been a long month since Terrance had said those words, and Brenn was hard-pressed to remember just what magic had to do with lies, or vice versa. And after all, the wizard had spoken only of magic.

Alchemy, on the other hand, was science.

So it came to pass that the young budding scientist found himself in Terrance's library, poring over alchemical texts. Most of them were dense, unreadable—more obscure than the most punishing poetry—and Brenn set those aside at once. Yet unlike the philosophical double-talk he had suffered before the turn of the year, even the worst of the alchemical texts had a certain useful fascination. Brenn promised himself that someday, when his knowledge improved, that these would be the first books he would come back to master.

That is, after those on thaumaturgy.

That long and puzzling word made him think of Faye. He thought of her quite often, and for some strange reason found himself imagining her on Lake Teal at night, riding in a gondola and dressed in a long blue silk robe.

The thought unsettled him. It made descriptions of even the most interesting alchemical experiments downright impossible for a boy to follow. So Brenn thought of Dirk, which was easier, because his thoughts of Dirk were never all that long or hard to begin with.

Then Squab came to mind, the little taunting fat boy who had made Brenn's last autumn in the guild a misery from the first leaf fall to that night when the door refused to give. With Squab on his thoughts, the boy thumbed through the book with renewed vigor.

Perhaps he could find the Parthian recipe for "Blind on the Thirtieth."

One day, then two passed in the library. Terrance had complained that the alembic was still set up in the attic when all the gin had been distilled and poured and all the evictable elves evicted. Brenn put him off with a nod and a wave, and the wizard, pleased to see his apprentice at last taking an interest in reading *something*, decided to let it go a while longer.

"Blind on the Thirtieth" never showed up. But the Blue Water potion did.

Brenn crowed with delight when he came to the page and found the directions, which were, outside of a word or two, simple to read. He thumbed through the formula eagerly, copied it down in his blurred, ragged hand, and rifled the cupboards and larder until he found all the ingredients he needed. Or at least, all he could read.

Someday—maybe even someday soon—he would ask Terrance what "volatile" meant.

He was surprised how much the substance smelled like Zephyrian gin. Perhaps it was because he had not cleaned the alembic all that well.

He should have expected that smell and the steam and the bubbling would draw elves.

One of them—a burly little sort who, if Brenn recalled correctly, had something to do with stealing Gallina—sneaked out from somewhere in the attic when the elixir had reached full boil in the open beaker. Elves were nothing if not stealthy, and the dusty creature had crossed the floor of the attic and was standing tiptoe by the tripod, breathing in the fumes, before Brenn even noticed that anything was out of the ordinary.

"No!" he shouted, and stomped his foot, trying to roust the nasty little thing with noise and bravado. Instead, he stomped too hard, shaking the old hardwood attic floor. Though the tripod held steady, the beaker atop it was tilted by a leaning elf. It tipped over, pouring boiling elixir on the screaming creature, who toppled over backward and lay still, moaning.

Brenn didn't know what to do. Red flesh blistered on the poor hairy thing, cooking it in its rags and raising enormous blisters on its tortured face. The elf cried out once, weakly, then split the air of the attic with a long, terrible shriek.

The house was unbelievably silent afterward. Outside, Brenn heard the distant cry of a gull.

Then nearer, from right below him, the stumbling sound of Terrance rushing up the stairs.

The sight that greeted the wizard was a ghastly one. His apprentice cowered in a corner of the attic, torn between pity and fear at the sight of the damaged elf near the toppled alembic. Trembling, trying to rise, the creature wailed to its companions, who answered loudly from the surrounding walls but dared not come to its rescue.

Terrance did not pause for amenities. Moving urgently and quickly, as though he were on fire himself, the wizard swooped to the side of the elf and picked up the writhing thing. The elf screamed at his touch, at the sudden movement.

Lifting the elf on high, Terrance closed his eyes and steadied himself. It was as though he was sleeping or entranced. Above his head the elf moved one scalded hand pathetically, then lay still.

I've killed it, Brenn thought, tottering at the edge of tears. *Called it a nuisance and a filthy thing, then killed it through my damned carelessness. The gods know it never deserved this.*

Silently he set his face in his hands.

There was a long moment in which Brenn expected the worst. He would look up, find the elf dead, lying limp in the hands of an unforgiving, angry Terrance. So it was a chastened boy who lifted his gaze and discovered, to his great surprise, that the blisters had receded from the unconscious elf. Its hair, only a moment ago matted and falling out from the onslaught of the boiling water, seemed somehow drier, healthier, less damaged.

The creature whistled, stirred in Terrance's arms, and began to snore merrily. The wizard smiled, and despite himself, Brenn smiled, too.

They continued to smile until their eyes met. Then deep in the back of Terrance's stare Brenn saw a harsh, flinty anger.

"You do not listen, do you, boy?" the mage spat, setting the elf gently onto the attic floor. Brenn noticed Terrance's hands were red and white with blisters and that his brow was beaded with smaller blisters and with sweat. The wizard turned and was across the floor in a stride, towering over the terrified Brenn and handing him a solid cuff on the ears.

"All my talk about *not* doing this is never good enough for the likes of you, is it? No! You'd rather be a chemist like Ricardo or a wizard like me than what you are!"

He cuffed Brenn again, this time less soundly, then stepped back clutching his blistered hand.

Behind them, the elf cooed and rolled over, awakening to find itself alarmingly exposed in the presence of the two large humans. It squawked and scrambled onto the junk pile and then, with a healthy athletic leap, lost itself in the dark of the rafters.

Terrance grabbed Brenn by the shirtfront and pulled him to his feet. He winced, stepped back again.

"I keep forgetting these damned hands!" he shouted, his raised voice sparking excitement in the beams and the walls of the attic. A solitary elf flashed from behind a broken lectern and vanished down the steps to the second floor, trailing grape skins and a spool of thread behind it.

Calmly, as cold and as precise as mathematics, the wizard instructed his apprentice.

"The time has come, Brenn, for kindly Terrance to give way to Terrance the taskmaster. From this day forth you will not experiment with arts scientific or magical without my knowing, and failure to keep your end of this bargain will result in your dismissal. Or worse, if I choose to exercise worse.

"Then again," Terrance added, staring directly at the boy. "Those are the terms under which you signed on, now aren't they?"

"I beg your pardon, sir," Brenn sniffed, his remorse and fear changing quickly to anger as the wizard lectured him. "I don't recollect having signed to permit your fingers in everything I do!"

"Read the fine print, urchin!" Terrance snapped, drawing the writ from his robe and shoving it into the boy's face. "Clause sixteen covers it, if I'm not mistaken."

Squinting, his lips moving, the boy read the clause aloud.

> *"Henceforth the party of the first part will not experiment with arts scientific or magical without the*

*knowledge of the party of the second part. Failure to
hold troth resulteth in the dismissal of the apprentice.
Or worse, if the master chooseth to exercise worse.*

*"And NEVER, NEVER do high-temperature alchemy
in the presence of elves. The master cannot unscald
the lot of them."*

Stupidly Brenn looked from the document to the wizard, from
the wizard to the document.

"T-Terrance!" he whispered, setting the writ down as though
it were boiling in a cucurbit. "How did you . . ."

"Divination, lad," the wizard replied, much more softly this
time and again with the hint of a smile. "You'll learn about it
this spring—when the elves leave and divining things blossom
and the birds come back. As for now, rest assured that what you
do under this roof has been foreseen and provided for through
generations, by powers larger than my own."

An hour later, when the elf had been set free by the beach, Brenn
sat upstairs, mending the canvas sack he had used to transport
the elf to the beach. The old stitching had finally given way
under the creature's nails and teeth, and one of Brenn's gloves
had followed. Halfway on his journey coastward, the boy had
set aside every ounce of pity he had carried for the elf not an
hour earlier and, opening the bag, had kicked the damnable thing
down the rock face to the soft black sand. The little monster had
risen to its feet, sputtered, and hissed malevolently at Brenn
before it vanished into the porous seawall.

Both master and apprentice were on the mend. Brenn used
the last of the gin to cleanse the tooth marks in his thumb. A
floor below him, Terrance at last dropped into his afternoon nap,
his blistered hands bandaged and his temper soothed with a dose
of the strange amber potion.

It was only then that the apprentice mulled over clauses and
numbers and came up even more suspicious.

"But the last time I looked," he said to himself, mending
needle poised over the bag in his hand, "clause sixteen had
something to do with town. And nothing with chemistry and
elves."

Thinking these thoughts, the apprentice accidentally sewed the bag to his sleeve.

The change of the seasons in Terrance's house was swift and absolute. One morning in the middle of March, the wizard went to the center solar window, stared out the hole made by elf and andiron six weeks before, and, turning back to his apprentice, smiled and made the announcement.

"It is spring, Brennart. Time for divinations."

The boy's spirit leapt at the prospect. Somewhere within him, the seasons had changed, too.

Slowly, after the mending of the elf, the boy felt a gratitude to Terrance—felt something that bordered on respect for the wizard. He was like the Goniph, this Terrance—full of the smarts and the know-how to get a boy by in a ravenous city. And even though wizardry was not Brenn's calling, at least he knew a good deal when he saw it: a roof, three meals a day, and a chance to learn enough magic to line his pockets—and the Goniph's pockets, of course—when he went back to thieving later.

So for now, the guild beckoned a little less strongly than it had before. Brenn missed Faye, he trusted she could take care of herself, and there would be plenty of time to see her again.

Plenty of time later.

Brenn had kept prudently out of the wizard's path for the last month, his attentions on housework and gardening and ridding the place of what few elves still hovered about causing trouble. All in all it had been a peaceful time—a time devoted to soothing Terrance's ire and grumpiness.

But for a boy of his nature, peace such as this did not wear well. Boredom and routine made this new promise of divination all that more welcome, and he eagerly ransacked the house for all the prophetic items the wizard requested: Alanyan fortune cards, an ancient ephemeris that showed the places of fixed and movable stars through the houses of the heavens, three feathers from a phoenix, a bag of tea leaves, two crystals, a fishnet, and a lamp.

The divining things assembled on the solar table, Brenn leaned forward eagerly, thumbing the pages of the ephemeris as Terrance approached merrily, his eyes filled with a playful, mocking laughter.

"Divination is easy, lad," he pronounced, picking up one of the crystals and gazing through it. "There is just one rule to the whole business."

The crystal caught and splintered the sunlight, as the ceiling of the solar blossomed in a wide rainbow cast by the light on the stone. Terrance tilted the stone and sighed with a profound melancholy, as if the rainbow itself had saddened him somehow.

"Sir?" Brenn closed the ephemeris and waited expectantly.

"Just one rule," Terrance repeated. "And that is 'Don't you believe it.' "

"I—I—" Brenn stammered. "I don't understand."

"Nor does anyone who divines," Terrance said. "Imagine reading the inside of a rock to find the futures of empires."

He laughed musically, tossed the crystal back on the table.

"Doesn't it, sir?"

"Beg your pardon?"

"Doesn't the inside of the rock hold the futures of empires?"

"Certes it does. But it's not going to tell you."

"I don't understand."

"Come with me," Terrance said, nodding toward the stairwell. Together, master and apprentice climbed the steps to the attic.

"Let's start with a big one," Terrance offered. "One that has been the talk of Maraven since late last year."

"The presence of Pytho in the belt of the Forest Lord."

"There. You know as much as any astrologer. Pytho entered the belt as November ended and December began—"

"About the time I came here."

Terrance shrugged.

"Pytho would have done what Pytho would have done had you gone to Cathay instead. What do you make of it?"

"Sir?"

"Pytho in the Belt. It's generally held to be an omen of great portent—this Pytho moving into another house of the heaven. What do you make of it?"

"Something momentous is about to happen?"

"Exactly!" the wizard exclaimed. "Brilliant! Especially since something momentous happens every day. Up the ladder to the roof, now."

Brenn scrambled up to the roof of the house, followed by Terrance, who puffed and gasped a little at the last two rungs of the ladder. There in the spring sunlight, among the first warblings of birds and the faint smell of greenery rising from the south and from inland, Brenn was struck at how old the master looked—how harried.

It's like he's holding off something, Brenn thought. *For all of his jokes and philosophy he is tired, like he alone is propping up a sagging wall.*

Surprised by his thoughts, the boy willed himself back to sunlight and breezes and the fresh, seaweedy smell of the beach below them. Off the coast between beach and reef a pelican sailed low over the water, folded in its wings, and dropped as though a distant archer had fixed it with an arrow. A second later the bird was in flight again, the tail of a fish dangling from its long hamper of a mouth.

"Feed their young with their own blood, the pelicans do," Terrance said. "What else have you heard about them?"

"When they roost in the black caverns along Hardwater Cove, there's a storm in the offing on the Sea of Shadows," Brenn said, reciting what the Goniph had told him.

"That's one you can prove or disprove. You and your old companions used to frequent those caverns, Brenn. When you saw pelicans there . . ."

"A storm would always follow, sir," Brenn proclaimed.

Or was that true? *Always?* The boy searched his memory.

"Then *that* is divination!" Terrance proclaimed. "It's good for one thing and one thing only—so that fools such as you and

I might know the weather the next day. Lean no further on divination than the next day. Or the weather.''

"Why, then?" the boy asked, bewildered. "Why take the time and the trouble to teach it?"

"In Alanya," Terrance began, gliding gracefully away from Brenn's question, "they tell stories about the Oracle of the Notches. A hundred kings and queens have consulted it over the centuries, climbing through the narrow mountain passage to the steaming fissure that overlooks the source of three rivers— the Umbre, the Boniluce, and the Eastmark. There, they ask the Cloudreader to interpret the rising vapors—to find shapes in them as you would find shapes in a cloud bank on a lazy day. Those shapes, it seems, contain the future.''

Brenn nodded. The wizard set his foot on the half-finished stairwell and looked over his shoulder.

"It's all dreadfully symbolic, to hear the Alanyans tell it. For the steam comes from the waters that mingle under the oracle, and the Eastmark is said to represent the past, the Boniluce the present, and the Umbre the future. Whatever that means. Come along, now.''

Terrance set foot on the second step. Brenn moved to the foot of the stairwell and stopped there, baffled.

" 'Come along' where?"

"The Alanyans are quite the philosophers, you see. They know that in the confluence and the steam the waters of the rivers are so intermingled that no mortal could tell one from the other.''

"I'm sorry, sir," Brenn interrupted, still at the foot of the stairwell as Terrance took yet another step. "I'm afraid I don't follow that philosophy.''

"Well . . .'' Terrance began, turning and sitting on the third step, his gaze settling somewhere far away. "I have this friend who consulted the oracle once.''

"You always have *friends* who try the wondrous," Brenn needled, stifling a grin. "Don't tell me *you've* never divined.''

"This *friend*," Terrance continued, "was about your age when we traveled south together, down Hadrach Road and beyond toward the Notches. Son of a king, this fellow was.''

"That would be King Aurum?" Brenn asked. "The one Ricardo talked about? The one before Dragmond?''

"The very same." Terrance nodded, his eyes turning suddenly to Brenn. "What a lad of fifteen had to do with oracles was beyond me, but Aurum persuaded me to go, saying he was no ordinary lad, but one destined for the throne of Palerna and therefore one who should know a little of past, present, and future, and how they were woven together.

"I must admit," Terrance added, a little sadly, "it seemed like sound reasoning at the time.

"So there we were. We rode on horseback from Stormpoint all the way down to Hadrach—a five-day journey on a good mount—then three more days by boat up the Eastmark to its source in the heart of the Notches.

"The Cloudreader was dressed like a mystic, to be sure. But he had the eyes of a shoplifter. I pointed this out to the prince, who laughed at me and trusted the man at once, as he trusted every stranger. Together, the three of us climbed through a narrow mountain pass, following the strange blossoming of steam from the rocks above us. It was deathly hot there, though it was early spring—much this time of year—and we were high in the mountains by the time we stopped to read the oracle.

"What the prince saw I am still not completely sure. But the sunlight pierced the rising steam, and a rainbow spread across the vaporous face of the mountain behind the crevasse, and Prince Aurum gasped, and I gasped at the look on his face, and the Alanyan gasped when he saw we were both gasping, and a sensible passerby might well have thought we were short of breath from the altitude and the steam. But the Cloudreader gasped for money, and I because the prince had the Lock, and the prince—well, you had to take his word for what he saw."

"What's this 'Lock,' Terrance?" Brenn asked. Visions fascinated him, mainly because he had none of his own to ponder, and imagined that those of others must be glamorous and specific indeed, with skies opening and voices descending and birds and cascading flowers and rivers of light.

Those were the tales that the sailors told, at any rate. This business of Locks and of gasping at rainbows was confusing, but it seemed like heady stuff indeed. Terrance paused, rubbed his eyes wearily, and continued.

"The Lock is the moment of certainty, in which visionary and vision are one. When the visionary sees a scene from the future or a symbol of that future and *knows* for sure that he is looking into things to come. It is when, as the Alanyans say, he looks down the Umbre and knows the current.''

"What I wouldn't give for a moment like that!" Brenn exclaimed. Suddenly stargazing and bird following, aquamancy and aestumancy and retemancy seemed the most glamorous things a boy could possibly do. He could imagine the thiefly advantage of reading a bowl of water or a fisherman's net or the outgoing tide for prospects and omens.

He could even imagine giving up theft for such visions.

"What you wouldn't give!" Terrance exclaimed, snapping the boy's reverie. "The price of the Lock is oft everything. And oft it isn't worth much once you have it.

"For I said the visionary *knows*. I did not say that he knows *correctly*."

Curious, Brenn sat on the bottommost step and listened as the wizard explained.

"You see, divination oft grants you a fragment of the future—an image or a scene or a symbol. *That* is a fact. But it is not the truth. Indeed, when somebody Locks on a vision or prophecy, you should always assume that they are somehow wrong, and wrong in a grave, unruly way."

"I don't understand," Brenn said, resting his elbows on his knees.

"Neither did Aurum," Terrance conceded. "I tried to explain by telling him the story Mardonius told me the night before he was put to death for treason."

"Mardonius?"

"The Duke of Aquila for all of a fortnight. Mardonius was Duke Danton's son, and Danton was King Albright's cousin, certes. Which made Mardonius second cousin to Aurum. Or first cousin once removed—I never have understood all those firsts and seconds and removals."

"But about Mardonius, sir?"

"Mardonius!" Terrance nodded, as though he had just found something deep in a closet. "Mardonius had come to the Notches before, some years before Aurum made the journey, before the boy was even born, for that matter. He consulted the oracle, and

Locked on an image of himself in his ancestral home up in Aquila, drawing an ancient sword out of the stone floor of his great-grandfather's meditation room—a sword that had been lodged there for years. The family had forgotten the meaning of its presence, but rumors were still abroad that it had something to do with the duchy—with succession and with rightful heirs —and that Great-Grandfather Aquila, for whom the duchy was named, had planted it there 'unto a time it would show its purpose.'

"Then, for reasons nobody knew, the old man closed off the room, warned his own sons away from chamber and sword, and what he knew of the weapon's portent and purpose he took with him to his place in the High Tombs along the Aquilan coast."

"That, and a ceremony. As each Duke of Aquila ascended the throne of the duchy, he and the seven viziers—the intellectual and spiritual advisors to ruler and land—would enter the room of meditation. They would emerge later—sometimes hours, sometimes only minutes.

"And each time the new duke was a changed man: somber and, in some indescribable way, defeated.

"Certes, Mardonius had heard the legends from the north. How a king, obscure in origin and humble in appearance, had confirmed his right to the throne by drawing a sword from a stone in the presence of the assembled knights and nobles. No doubt Mardonius had fallen into a story of the same weave, or so he believed. Half sleeping in the saddle on the ride from Hadrach to Maraven—a ride that took a week in that time, because the country was wilder then, the road an unkempt horse trail through marsh and thicket—he pondered the mystery.

"The most famous legend, the one he and his brothers had heard as they grew to manhood, was that the sword *singled out the crown of the line*. What the phrase meant was obscure: Julian, the eldest brother, believed it was simply that whoever drew the sword from the floor would be the greatest duke in the history of Aquila. Then again, Julian was always the least ambitious, for ambition was less necessary when you were your father's first heir.

"The middle son, Osprey, was more bright and bitter. He was

cast in the mold of the old rebel lords who refused a foreign king. He had maintained that the man who drew out the sword would lead Aquila to independence from oppressive Palerna and 'the great whore Maraven.' ''

Terrance stopped and smiled. ''His phrase, not my own.''

Brenn sniffed impatiently, eager that the story continue.

''Osprey was sure that 'crown of the line' meant nothing other than that the chosen man would wear a crown—would be no longer a tributary duke, but the genuine King of Aquila.

''Mardonius did not know what he thought on the matter. As the third son, he was sure that whatever came to pass in the meditation room would have nothing to do with him. That, certes, was before he traveled to the Notches and Locked on the vision.

''As the steam from the fissure rose and covered his vision, Mardonius's first obstacle was apparent. After all, he was the *third* son of the duke, and two brothers stood between him and the duchy—two healthy, young fellows, neither of whom would delight all that much in stepping aside.

''So he hastened the process. The night after his father Danton died, Mardonius set the machinery in motion. He hired assassins to dispatch Julian and took care of Osprey himself with poison. The two tragedies fell within a fortnight and, as you might imagine, aroused the curiosity of Aquila's neighbor and liege to the south.''

''King Aurum?'' Brenn asked as the wizard paused again.

''King *Albright*! Your schooling is weak, boy, and if you learn nothing from divining or prophecy or foretelling, at least you should have some *history* by the time I'm done with this!

''Albright came north himself, along with a bodyguard of a thousand crack Palernan infantry. At the time, Albright claimed that the soldiers were there to assure that Mardonius did not meet the fate of his brothers before he could ascend the ducal throne.

''There were some of us who guessed that his reasons were darker, more secretive.

''Imagine, if you will, Mardonius's discomfort when he heard that Albright himself would join with the seven viziers in the secret ceremony, locked in the room with the new duke and the old sword and the history that embraced all of them. But what was he to do? After all, he was Albright's vassal, and the king had every right to witness the mystery.''

The air around the wizard and the boy was still. The winds that rushed perpetually onto the cove from the northern sea died down, as though Aquila to the north of them was holding its breath, waiting as the rest of its story was told.

''So Mardonius did not draw out the sword after all?'' Brenn asked.

''Certes, he did,'' Terrance corrected. ''It was a fact that the oracle gave him south of here in the Notches. A fact, but not the truth.

''The nine of them assembled—king, duke, and the seven viziers—standing about the sword in a loose, informal circle. Albright was the one who described the weapon to me. That was sometime later, and by then he was very ill and his memory not so good.

''Natheless, he said that it was the most promising of swords, its blade half-embedded in stone. The hilt was of gold and onyx, the cross guard cunningly wrought to resemble the balanced arms of a scale, the pommel a figure of a blindfolded maiden.''

''Divine Justice,'' Brennart exclaimed, his eyes fixed on the wizard.

''Indeed,'' Terrance acknowledged, ''and it consoles me that you recognize her image.''

Brenn nodded reverently. He did not say he had learned the image from the jailhouse wall, on the several occasions when he went with the Goniph to see to Dirk's or Squab's release.

''Mardonius recognized her at any rate,'' the wizard said, taking up his story once more. ''And a great misgiving passed through him.

''For the eyes on the pommel seemed to stare into him when, at the instruction of King Albright, the doors closed behind him and he entered the circle of viziers and set hand on the hilt of the sword.

''Easily and steadily he drew the sword from the stone floor. The sound of metal grating against rock filled the room for a brief moment, and two of the wise men covered their ears. But the blade came forth cleanly, as though it had been lodged in the earth or in soft wood only.

"And the sword's legend was inscribed on the blade, in printing so ancient that it seemed to hover between letter and rune. *Libra potestatis sum*, it read, and three of the viziers bowed down to Mardonius."

"*Libra* . . ." Brenn began, then frowned.

"*Libra potestatis sum*. 'I am the balance of power.' "

"So Mardonius held the balance of power," Brenn declared. He was strangely disappointed by the story, having hoped dearly for more glamour and lights and explosions, a farfetched, dramatic end for the villain Mardonius.

Terrance smiled. "That is just about what Mardonius claimed. He raised the sword above his head and shouted, 'I hold the scales of justice!' The blade whistled as he turned it in his hand, and in that brief moment he stepped into his glory."

"Funny thing, Terrance," Brenn mused. "From the way you were telling this, what with all the murdered brothers and seized inheritances and whatnot, I expected things would turn out bad for this Mardonius. I expected—"

Impatiently the wizard raised his hand, waving it at the boy as if he were swatting flies. "Enough of your expecting!" he growled. "As if the story were over!

"For only three of the viziers bowed down. The other four were wiser wise men, you might say. At least on that occasion.

"Albright turned to one of them, a native Palernan who had joined Danton's court as a lad of sixteen, studied in Hadrach, lectured in Partha, and ended up back in Aquila for the gods knew what reasons—a roundabout scholar to say the least—and asked him why he did not bow.

" 'I was waiting to see what the king would do,' the scholar said, his eyes on the blade of the sword.

"King Albright laughed, delighted at the man's honest roguery. 'You do know,' he insisted, his brown eyes sparkling, 'that the King of Palerna bows to no man.'

" 'I also know that the king says when the story is over,' the scholar added. He did not know at the time that his clever flattery—which Albright knew was flattery, as the scholar knew that Albright knew . . .''

"Go on, Terrance!" Brenn interrupted in exasperation, slapping the stair with the flat of his hand.

"He *didn't* know," Terrance insisted, as if it were somehow the most important point of his story. "Albright turned to his cousin and spoke calmly, his large pale hands folded over his wrestler's chest.

" 'I read another meaning in the legend of that sword,' he announced quietly. All the viziers turned to him, and the quiet of old Aquila's meditation room grew quieter still—an impossible silence, as though someone had banished all sound from the premises. I remember Mardonius's face, paler than the king's hands, than the white cerements in which his young brothers had been wrapped not a month before."

"Wait, Terrance!" Brenn interrupted. "You mean *you* were—"

"I left that room in the employ of King Albright of Palerna," Terrance said. "But that is another story. As is the story of the sword Libra itself—a murky tale of revenge and discord that began in a time when the mountains spewed fire.

"For now, our concerns are more simple: the words of a king to an upstart duke. Albright smiled coldly, a little sadly. 'I fear you have drawn justice and the balance of power from the rightful place in which they have resided for hundreds of years,' he said. 'I fear that if your brothers' wounds could cry out, they might well call your name.'

"Mardonius raised the sword again, this time with violent intent. But three of the viziers restrained him, and the rest of those in the room swarmed upon him and disarmed him.

"*Libra potestatis sum.* 'I am the balance of power.' Within another fortnight, rivulets of blood ran in those ancient engraved letters. For Mardonius, thinking that the king had indeed seen into the heart of his crime, confessed fratricide to all in his ancestral castle, and was beheaded in a somber ceremony within that very room of meditation. Beheaded by that very sword.''

⤝⤝⤝ X ⤞⤞⤞

"It gives me the shivers just thinking on it, sir," Brenn said after a long pause in which the wizard leaned back on the steps, then slowly and painfully rose to his feet.

"Would it had shivered Aurum a little more," Terrance observed bitterly. "Perhaps he'd be alive today.

"Together we walked down from the Notches, down from where young Aurum had received his own kingly vision. We spent the night in the foothills, in a flimsy little tent that suffered the misery of cold and wind and that second-rate Alanyan hocus-pocus man. Aurum gave me a dozen reasons why his case and that of Mardonius were completely different. I remember well: they were the same reasons folks always give when they Lock on a divination.

"But even if you're *given* something of the future—a situation, a place, a view out a window—even the best of oracles cannot show you how you will come to that place and that view, or what it will mean when you get there. It could not show Mardonius that his brief moment of triumph was not the end of the story, and Mardonius was smarter than some. Perhaps even smarter than Aurum.

"For there in the foothills, the young prince was filled with excitement. It seemed that the rainbows we had all seen rising from the steam of the oracle had been a part of his vision—rays of multicolored light springing gloriously from his sleeping body, which lay enclosed in a beautiful prism.

"At least that's what he saw. He was sure that the vision meant that luck and promise would rise from him, and that his reign would be long and prosperous. He even managed to bring in something about a pot of gold.

"Of course, the Alanyan charlatan agreed with Aurum's every word. And though I warned the boy against false confidence, against the belief that somehow his reign was charmed, he refused to listen to me, heading north the next morning convinced that no matter what happened or seemed to be happening, the crown he would inherit would sit secure atop his head."

"Poor Aurum," Brenn stated, not knowing enough about the prince or his vision to care much either way, but seeing that the memory affected Terrance profoundly. The old wizard sat down again, cupped his chin in his hands, and turned to look out over the sea. His eyes reddened, and a shadow of great regret and sorrow passed over his face.

"I suppose he didn't understand his vision at all," Brenn offered cautiously after a long silence had passed between him and the wizard.

Terrance nodded. He looked dreadfully old at that moment, the noonday sun shadowing the lines in his face until it looked weathered beyond imagining, as though it had grown from the bark of an ancient tree.

"What, my little friend, do *you* think that vision meant?" Terrance asked, collecting himself and looking straight into Brenn's eyes, wrestling with his age and weariness and at last recovering.

"I—I—what should *I* know of visions?" Brenn exclaimed. "I can't even foresee elves when I conjure with poetry."

Terrance chuckled, though the mirth never reached his eyes.

"What *would* you say, lad?" he asked again, his voice almost a whisper. "How would you read that vision?"

"Well, you said Aurum was sleeping in a prism. Maybe it wasn't sleep at all. Maybe the light he saw, and all those wonderful colors—maybe that was the good thoughts and the good stories people would have about him later. I mean, after he was gone and all."

"I believe some of that poetry rubbed off on you, Brennart," the wizard said, regarding his apprentice with a keen seriousness that made Brenn just a little uneasy.

"You mean I'm right, Terrance? That I read the vision correctly?"

"How in blazes should I know, lad?" the wizard asked merrily. "I couldn't even figure out what Mardonius's sword was saying."

"But you're the wizard, Terrance."

"Which carries no leverage, child. As I said nearly two score years before you were born, only the king can say when the story ends. So our guesses are neither here nor there.

"Time to go to town, Brenn. Follow me, if you care to divine some more."

With that Terrance labored to his feet once again and, his fingers clutching Brenn's robe, pulled his surprised apprentice toward the top of the half-finished stairwell.

"Wait! Wait, sir!" Brenn protested. But the wizard was hearing none of it. The tugging became more insistent. Brenn sat down in a desperate attempt to keep from being dragged up a stairway to nowhere, but Terrance kept pulling.

"But that doesn't go—" Brenn whined, bumping against two steps as a surprisingly strong Terrance yanked him to his feet again.

"Never you mind where it *doesn't* go!" the wizard commanded through clenched teeth. "It *does* go into town, where there are more oracles than you can imagine."

Brenn followed Terrance reluctantly up the stairwell, sure by now that he was in a madman's clutches. It was when the two of them reached the topmost step that his fears fell away, only to be replaced at once by new ones.

Off to the west, glinting under the early afternoon sun, the city of Maraven looked . . . different.

Everything was cleaner, better maintained than Brenn remembered or imagined. All along Cove Road the storefronts, once dingy and weather-beaten, seemed almost new, sporting fresh coats of paint and bedecked with ribbons and wreaths. For a moment Brenn wondered if somehow there was a holiday he had forgotten, something in mid-March that smacked of joy and celebration.

The midday sun had burnt away the morning clouds, evidently, and you could look down Cove Road all the way to Grospoint, where a hundred banners, each of a merchant or knight or provincial baron, fluttered in a light breeze, lifting slowly on the wind and then sinking again, as though they were beckoning any who looked on from afar.

Nor did the prospects dim as he looked south into Wall Town.

There in the midst of the roughest borough in the town, where Brenn had been brought up—or brought up himself—things had taken dramatic turns for the better. Though the buildings still crowded together and leaned over street and alley, there was a clean, quaint charm about them now, no longer the stifling closeness the boy associated with home.

"Beautiful view from up here, isn't there?" Terrance's voice was muted, echoing, as though he were speaking through walls.

Brenn nodded, all resistance gone from his thoughts. "I never saw Wall Town like this, sir," he marveled. "Look at those courtyards! And the fountains! All that water rising is like . . ."

"Quicksilver?" the wizard offered.

"That's it! Quicksilver! Or liquid glass! I've never seen the old haunts so clean and lovely and so . . . so *purified*. Perhaps it's only the vantage point."

"Exactly. We're looking into another time."

"I beg your pardon?"

"What you see below you, Brenn, is Maraven at a time other than our own."

"Is this a vision, sir?" Brenn was giddy with the view. Or giddy with the height—he was not certain.

"You might call it that," Terrance mused. "That is, unless you're used to such scenery."

"When was this? I mean, when did Maraven look this way?"

Terrance snorted. "Do not assume *was* and *did*. It's another time—not past, necessarily, or future, though it might well be either. Perhaps it's *might have been* or *could be* or *never was*."

"If you haven't the answer to *that*, Terrance, then what in the name of all the gods can you make of the vision?"

"Perhaps none. And if I saw something down there—let's say an accident—what should I do about it?"

Brenn sat on the topmost step, scratched his head.

"I *think* I follow you, Terrance. Say a cart overturns on a drover coming down this very Cove Road. Did it happen a hundred years ago, or will it happen a hundred hence? Did it happen at all? Was it supposed to happen because, hard as it may be to believe, something good is to come of it? Oh, all these prospects are baffling and aggravating, and it makes me almost dizzy to ponder them! I expect I'm not cut out for *serious* thinking.''

Suddenly a shadow passed over master and apprentice. Brenn looked above him, expecting a wheeling bird or a thick rack of clouds. Instead, he saw that the stairs had extended themselves, spiraling around behind him and ascending to a narrow, shimmering landing on which a large door rested. It looked familiar somehow: thick, no doubt heavy, rough hewn of an especially sturdy-looking oak. It sat on a film of glittering air, as though it were afloat on a layer of extraordinarily clear ice.

Most striking of all, it seem to lead to nowhere. Behind it lay an expanse of cloudless sky, as though while the boy had nodded the same ghostly builders who had erected the stairwell the gods knew when had come back and finished it, with no concern for its use or destination.

Brenn rubbed his eyes, but the landing and the door were still there. He tugged at Terrance's robe.

"I know, lad," the wizard murmured. "If you stay here long enough, the door avails itself."

"Where does it lead to, Terrance?"

"It leads back home," the wizard answered cryptically, and, not pausing for further questions, set foot on the first of the transparent stairs.

Brenn gasped, reached out his hand to stop his master, then considered the height and the possible fall and thought better of it. Soon Terrance was four, five, six steps above him: if you turned your head and squinted just right, it seemed as though the wizard was standing on nothing.

Terrance turned in the air and beckoned to him.

"I'm—I'm sorry, sir, but that stairway doesn't seem to be all that sturdy to me."

"It'll hold as many as want to venture upon it," Terrance promised, and beckoned again.

"I'm afraid I don't *want* to venture on it," Brenn observed, holding his left foot cautiously above the glassy surface of the step, as though he were testing unbearably cold waters.

"If you'll do so, Brennart, you'll never have a need for divination," the wizard urged, setting his hand to the latch of the hovering door.

"What if—what if I fall?"

"Look at me!" Terrance coaxed assuringly and beckoned once more, this time a little impatiently.

"Yes, but you're a wizard. The gods know what feats *you're* capable of. All that levitation and such. Things that simple folk like myself can't begin to manage."

"So I'm wicked. Is that it?" Terrance asked coldly, still poised at the doorway.

"Of course not, sir. Gruff you've been on occasion, but *never* cruel."

"That's the way it sounds, though," Terrance insisted. "You believe that I, a learned man, would lure my student into a disastrous, perhaps a deadly fall. What is that but wickedness?"

"Oh, but you wouldn't *mean* to, sir," Brenn explained, drawing his foot back from the transparent step and leaning against the solidity of the old, familiar landing he had seen dozens of times from the rooftop.

"Then I'm stupid or addled? I'm ignorant enough to assume that you'll have the same success as I on the stairs in front of you, when in fact I could be wrong?"

"No. No . . . I'm not going to win debating points against you, sir. We both know that. It's just that something tells me that this stone landing my feet are resting on is as far as *this* apprentice needs to climb."

"The 'something' telling you that is your own cowardice," Terrance taunted, an ironic smile spreading over his face. Stung, Brenn stepped forward, nearly placing his foot atop the first of the shimmering steps. Then again he stepped back, thinking better of venturing out on a dare.

So he would have stood, perhaps forever, if Terrance had not begun to stare at him and laugh.

"What are you laughing at?" Brenn shouted, forgetting the respect due his master, a wizard, an older man. Forgetting also where he stood, it seemed, for in his anger the boy took an unwitting step onto the first of the stairs.

"I was just wondering what the old phrase 'guts of a burglar' must mean after all." Terrance chuckled, and folded his arms.

"It means something along these lines, you old fart!" Brenn

exclaimed, and took a second and a third step up the stairwell. Terrance hovered above him, hand on the door, still far away but somehow no longer unreachable.

"Rage will get you only half the way here," the wizard remarked. "Sooner or later, there has to be more going for you than the simple desire to throttle me . . ."

Brenn continued to pursue in anger, taking another step and then another. He realized he was ascending the steps almost as quickly and as casually as he did the ones he climbed every night from the second floor to his bedroom in the attic. His anger disappeared.

Brenn would have continued, his eyes fixed on the wizard and refusing to look below him, until he reached the landing and passed through the door to "home" or nowhere, had Terrance not opened the door and turned his back, preparing to pass through the portal and leave his apprentice alone on the roof in the open air, at a great and dizzying height.

Terrance must have moved quickly, descending the steps in a rush and grasping one of the boy's flailing wrists. The instant Terrance broke his eyes away from his apprentice, Brenn sank through the stairwell quickly, dramatically, as though it had turned into water beneath him. Everything that followed happened suddenly and violently. Brenn was never sure he was even conscious in the minutes that followed, or whether some abrupt, clumsy movement had knocked him out in the journey that followed.

It seemed in that flurry of tugging and dragging and stumbling and climbing that somehow he followed Terrance up the steps and onto the landing. They had passed through the door together, and Brenn had held his breath, expecting a landscape of stars or a whirlpool of cloud and lightning.

The boy found his feet planted firmly on the floor downstairs, for when he stood up, he found himself beside the converted door that formed the surface of the solar table. It looked familiar somehow: thick, no doubt heavy, rough hewn of an especially sturdy-looking oak.

That's where I'd seen it, Brenn marveled. *So it is still a door of sorts, after all*. Then he remembered nothing else for a while, waking up to find himself lying faceup on the door—or table—a glass of Umbrian wine under his nose and the wizard propping up his head with a look of amused concern.

"I am sorry, lad. Sorry for the haste and the goading," Terrance said, though it looked to Brenn as though the sorriness was as thin and fragile as the steps he had hurtled through not minutes before. "I expected too much of you too quickly."

"I suppose I like solid ground beneath me," Brenn joked weakly.

"Natheless," Terrance observed, encouragement in his voice, "you took half of the stairs by yourself. It may be enough."

"Enough for what?"

"Enough for what comes next. Or does not come next, if it's not enough. Come along."

Wizard leading apprentice, the two of them stepped out of the solar into the world outside.

The surroundings of Cove Road and Hardwater Cove, the weathered eaves of the wizard's house and the half-toppled end of the East Wall—all of these were by now as familiar to Brenn as any back alley in Maraven. After all, he had lived with Terrance for almost four months now. And yet, no matter how well he knew them—black beach and tattered stairwell and broken-down gate—there was a different feel about them all here in the afternoon sunlight, as though they had all been caught by the brush of a painter. The color was different—thicker, perhaps—and the everyday movement of water and dust and blades of grass had almost stilled, and the air was thick also, and tinted amber. It was as though the breeze from the sea had a notion to cease altogether, and only some faintly remembered law of nature prevented it from doing so.

Brenn stepped into the full sunlight and looked about. Out around the Palern Reef, the waves breaking on the coral turned over slowly, like dark, rippling oil. Out on the sea a flock of gulls moved nowhere, their long wings stationary in some sort of strange, arrested glide.

Were it not for the warmth of the spring air, Brenn would have believed that the world had frozen.

"All right, Terrance," he scolded, sure that the wizard would produce some mirror or smoking vial or scroll of illusion—

something that would reveal all of this stillness to be some sort of magical joke. "You've had your fun, I'll wager."

"Oh, but the fun is only beginning, Prentice," Terrance said, smiling crookedly and loping off down Cove Road toward the center of Maraven. The air blurred behind him as if he were trailing smoke, and soon he dwindled into a gray cloak, a broad-brimmed hat, and a pair of spindly legs, skimming over Cove Road and past the cattle market, until Brenn almost lost him among pens and slaughterhouses.

It was all the boy could do to catch up with his sprinting master. With adventure on his mind, it seemed that Terrance could marshal surprising energy. A good mile from the house —about half the way to the edge of Grospoint—Brenn finally overtook the wizard, and the two of them slowed to a walk. Brenn panted and heaved, gulping in the unsavory stockyard air that dizzied him and turned his stomach. Terrance, on the other hand, was not even winded. From his robe he drew a book, a folio-sized volume that took both hands to open and maneuver. Oblivious to everything, from the almost unnoticeable movement of farmer and yard worker to the rather obvious coaxing of his apprentice, the wizard wetted his index finger and dramatically turned the first page of the book.

"What are you doing, Terrance?" Brenn asked, teetering at the edge of patience.

"I'm reading, lad," Terrance responded absently. "I would have hoped that the book would make that evident."

"Reading . . . what? Something about divining?"

"I am reading *The Tempest*, boy," Terrance replied, lifting his eyes from the page for only a brief flicker before plunging back into a text that Brenn could not imagine was all that interesting. "An English play. It won't be written until some years after you and I are gone. It's unearthly good, though. Things like this show up when you pass through the door, and you can't take them out again with you. So here is the right place to enjoy them, I reckon. I don't quite understand why, but I'm smart enough to know that if you can't find beautiful things elsewhere, you take time to relish them where you *can* find them."

"What *is* going on here, Terrance?" Brenn shouted. A few paces away from him a drover, almost frozen in his languorous walk from foul-smelling abattoir to the Sign of the Mallet, the stockyard's fouler-smelling pub, began a movement with his hand. After what would seem like ten minutes to Brenn, the hand would brush by the drover's jaw, as he waved away what he thought was a mosquito nestling and whining at his ear.

"What is going on is everyday business and your master reading," Terrance proclaimed. "You have . . . almost all the time in the world. Use it wisely, and I shall join you after I find out what happens in this wonderful shipwreck.

"Meanwhile, why don't you study the bird formations over-head. There are some geese in a nice little chevron out over Lake Teal. They're almost stationary, and if you're sharp-eyed enough, you can probably learn everything there is to know about the future just from looking at them."

At that moment, something white and blue-green glimmered at the corner of Brenn's eye. Thinking *goose*, he jumped back, dodging what he thought might well be a painful collision. Then he noticed that the winged and bejeweled thing was only about the size of his hand. With an uncanny quickness, made all the more odd because it was one of the few things that seemed to be moving around him on this sluggish spring day, the creature dodged his hand and fluttered to arm's length from him, where it hovered and regarded him intelligently.

It was a tiny winged woman, with glistening oiled feathers like that of a gull or pelican. She was a pretty, delicate thing, all shining and blue-green and graceful. She seemed as surprised by Brenn as he was by her. As he turned to look at her directly she moved, again to the corner of his vision so that even though he saw full well her color and outline, the transparent wings that kept her airborne and the white waves of her hair, he saw neither eyes nor facial features—she was that quick.

"What—"

"Siren," Terrance answered, a little impatiently, his nose buried back in the book. "The air around here is full of them, but you only see them full on when you've passed through the door. They're uncannily swift, you know, and they live in those seaside rocks you and your cronies think you know so well."

Terrance lifted his head, this time regarding the boy directly.

"Sirens are the ones that cause shipwrecks with their infernal whispering. The old stories say that they sit on the rocks and serenade the ships to destruction, but it doesn't quite work that way. What happens is they get up in a helmsman's ear and coax and wheedle and sing, and even if he can't understand their words he's so distracted by the infernal whine that he's likely to run the ship aground or onto whatever reef or shoal avails itself. In the Mare Nostrum west of here there's a lot more of these sirens than there are in the Sea of Shadows, but we're particularly blessed here in Maraven with a large, menacing swarm of them.''

Having pronounced on the subject of sirens, the wizard plunged back into his reading, his look of impatience changing at once to that of wonderment and amusement.

''How could he know?'' Terrance mused. ''What *history* he will have!''

Brenn stood above his master for a while, awaiting further instructions. It soon became clear, though, that the boy was left to his own devices, and that Terrance was lost to him for an hour, if hours meant anything on this strange, collapsing afternoon.

Left to his own devices, Brenn looked around for something to explore. For the world was different than he remembered it, and though he didn't know the *why*s he was bent on seeing some of the *what*s.

Something blue and green and white-winged flashed across the street ahead of him. The boy turned his back on the browsing wizard and took off after the siren.

$\prec\!\prec\!\prec$ **XI** $\succ\!\succ\!\succ$

After running several streets over, Brenn found himself out of the stockyard district and into the strip of old, well-established shops that acted as a border between the streets he had just left and the shabbier, noisier, and more bustling storefronts of Grospoint. Slowing to a trot, the boy passed a rider, a short, bearded fellow atop a huge bay stallion, dressed in the red leather armor of Dragmond's Watch.

The horse's legs were churning languidly, spanning great distances with long, impossibly slow strides. For all appearances, the beast was at full gallop. Yet Brenn passed him easily and soon left him far behind, a ruddy shape between narrowing rows of houses.

"Marvelous!" the boy exclaimed, stopping in amazement in front of a bakery. Someone, it seems, had slowed down the world. Or speeded up Brenn and Terrance.

Whichever it was, the evidence was all around him. Townspeople crept from shop to shop, plodded full tilt across road and alley. It was as though the city were submerged in amber water, everything taking place at a tenth its usual speed.

"I am faster than any living thing—on air or land or sea," Brenn proclaimed in wonder. "Well, except for all those sirens. And maybe Terrance. I guess I am supposed to receive instruction from this, though I'll be damned if I can figure out just what it is that the master expects me to learn."

He leaned against the storefront, pondering. A siren flitted through the open window of the bakery, pinching off the brown, fragrant crust of a roll and devouring it right beneath the nose of the proprietress, who batted her eyelids once and yet saw nothing, as the little winged woman pinched more and more, then soared with bread-laden arms to a nearby roof.

After some months of abstinence, theft reoccurred to the apprentice. Now would be the most handy of times for his old handiwork, he figured. Pickpocketing was like cherrypicking, and shoplifting a leisurely stroll through the market.

Brenn reached into the window, withdrew a loaf of bread, and was two streets away on a carefree saunter by the time it began to register with the old woman in the bakery that one of the loaves was missing. He had reached the outskirts of Grospoint by the time she had taken her quickest mental inventory, in three seconds counting in her memory the number of loaves she had baked that morning, how many had been purchased, how many lay cooling on the windowsill, and how many on the shelves behind her. By the time her suspicions flashed to her own apprentice, a dull-witted fat boy of seventeen, Brenn had eaten the loaf and was hungrily eyeing a greengrocer's shop on the Street of the Chemists.

Duval's Alley looked different in this slower, syrupy light. Three storefronts down Brenn saw his old companion Squab, in the midst of cutting the purse of a wide-faced young farm boy. The process inched along, and Brenn had time to approach Squab from behind and watch at his leisure as the laborious theft unfolded. As Squab completed the lift, opening his sleeve and slipping the purse in up to his pudgy elbow, Brenn drew his own knife and, cutting a hole in the same sleeve, caught the stolen purse as it dropped through the slit.

Minutes later, as Squab began to curse his tailor, Brenn stood back at the greengrocer's, laughing and watching friends, foes, and the faintly familiar pass by.

In turn, there were few who noticed Brennart. The squadron of Dragmond's Watch, formidably armed with sword and crossbow, marched right in front of the grocer's shop, their prisoner in a black mask, shackled between the burliest of their number. The guardsmen were blind to Brenn's presence, and when the boy reached out and flicked the ear of the small Watch lieutenant, a boy from the Teal Front named Amiens, the self-important little officer brushed his ear and cursed the early squinchflies.

Brenn's old friend Dirk had crept under a dairyman's booth where, concealed amid jars of milk and strong-smelling cheeses, he waited for the Watch to pass. Dirk was not sure, but he thought he noticed the air darken as squadron and prisoner filed by the grocer's booth on the way to the wharf and the street's end: from all he could see, covered by table and canvas and lying in the faintly sour, inviting coolness, it could have been a cloud or a bird overhead. Indeed, he would not have even noticed the strange dappling of shadow had it not seemed particularly sad and fitting on that occasion.

The Goniph, resplendent in his sapphire-studded nose ring, an ornament he saved for special occasions, leaned against a gallows erected overnight by the wharf where the Street of the Chemists ended. As he watched Dragmond's guardsmen approach, his old acquaintance and rival in tow, his unnaturally sharp eye picked up a flurry of shadows by the greengrocer's storefront. The cloth spread over the counter darkened and lightened and darkened again. A single tomato blurred and vanished.

"Sirens," he muttered ironically. "Don't even respect a condemned man."

Meanwhile, Brenn bit into the tomato with a special eagerness and delight. Thievery was never this easy before, he noted. Terrance's little portal might be just the trick to make a lad's fortune after all: if he was bound by that foolish writ to become a magician, it certainly wouldn't hurt to be a rich one.

The prospects of great fortune raced like the flitting sirens through Brenn's thoughts. He had just settled on a wonderful image of wealth——the attic stuffed to its elf-infested rafters with jewelry and gems——when a strong hand rested on his shoulder.

Brenn nearly swallowed an entire tomato whole. Spitting seeds and pulp onto himself and over the grocer's counter, he turned to face the bright green eyes of his master Terrance.

"I see you've put the time well to use, Prentice," the wizard said evenly, patting the boy on the shoulder affectionately.

"This is not what you think, Terrance," Brenn started to explain, backing into the grocer's counter. The wizard looked at him curiously, then with a look of mischief snatched up a tomato of his own and bit into it with gusto.

"Why yes it is, Brenn!" he exclaimed, chunks of the vegetable tumbling from his lips and staining his beard. "It's a tomato, and a right good one if you ask me! I could do with another!"

He reached out again, rifled the counter, and, clutching a tomato and a head of lettuce, loped off toward the dairyman's booth.

"Come on, Brennart!" he called over his shoulder. "Let's steal some cheese to go with this!"

Dumbstruck, the boy watched Terrance clamber over the booth, clutch a cheese the size of a dog's head, and burst through the back curtains of the establishment on a beeline to the butcher's. "And sausage, while we're at it!" he shouted gleefully.

Embarrassed, Brenn chased after his master. Halfway to the wharf the wizard stopped, sat down in the street, and began to eat his spoils. Brenn stood by him in perplexed silence as the crowd by the storefronts turned and inched northward, stepping around them and noticing little more than a curious gray presence about the cobblestones.

"Terrance. Terrance, you can't do this," the boy coaxed, tugging at the wizard's robe. Terrance looked up at him, a sausage link dangling from his mouth.

"Why not?" he mumbled. Then, swallowing dramatically, he continued more clearly. "You're quite an ingenious lad, Prentice. Why, here I am an old man who's known of this portal for a dozen years, and it seems I have lacked the sense to employ it in the fashion that it no doubt was *meant* to be employed."

"Sir?"

"No doubt the maker had grown weary of *paying* for produce, and saw in his new invention . . . a way to steal supper. Perhaps next we can break windows and run away, or start fires underneath Watchmen's boots!"

"But, Terrance! It just isn't . . . isn't *right*."

The wizard looked at him with mock outrage and plate-sized eyes, scrambled to his feet, and took off northward toward the wharf, this time moving at a more leisurely gait. Brenn followed, finding his voice trailing off into mutterings, into rambling attempts to explain himself.

Somehow all of this had something to do with divination, the boy figured. Terrance had a knack of teaching by foolishness, Brenn had come to understand, though he could never anticipate the form that foolishness would take. And then, when the lesson needed explaining, when the apprentice had stepped out onto the ledge and stood with foot suspended over the bottomless pit of his own stupidity, he would look for the wizard and find that he was on his own.

Well, so be it, thought Brenn, striding right between two younger boys involved in a shoving match, then ducking and passing beneath the belly of a trotting horse, accustomed by now to the new, particular stillness of Maraven.

Perhaps I can figure this business.

He and Terrance were like the diviners, Brenn decided, moving swiftly from point to point, so eager to get to the end of the story that they were left out of the story itself. For whatever they did, it seemed that nobody was taking notice, intent on the everyday business of living.

As they darted from point to point like the jagged fingers of spring lightning, or even more quickly like the nearly invisible winged sirens, it seemed that they *missed* the point entirely.

"It's like the end of the story is just a point in another story," Brenn whispered to himself, his short legs churning to keep up with Terrance's longer strides. "It's like . . . like no story ever ends."

Together, master and apprentice passed the last of the shops and joined in the crowd milling about the makeshift scaffold at the street's end.

It seemed that another of the king's theatrical events was about to take place, there on the Street of the Chemists.

Dragmond was ever fond of public display. On occasion these scaffolds were built without an hour's notice, in Grospoint or in the boatyards of Ships, on occasion even in Wall Town. Then some poor soul was seized and masked and dragged up its steps by Watchmen, where he was unveiled before the assembled crowd.

Sometimes the guards fed the prisoner and sent him on his way, with the proclamation that this was how the king provided for his people. On these occasions the crowd applauded Dragmond's generosity and kindness, though the poor among them never forgot that for every man fed in this ceremony, twenty starved, out of sight in the hulls of Ships or the hovels of Wall Town. For, as the saying among the poor went, King Dragmond sounded a trumpet before he gave alms.

More often, though, it was the expected hanging, or the occasional beheading when political crimes were involved. A criminal was seized, the scaffold raised, and execution carried out with the warning that the king's law was not broken lightly. All well and good, said many in the crowd, but a humble man couldn't know what the king's law was day by day. Folks had been hanged for robbery, true, but there was also the strange charge of "conspiracy to commit conspiracy," and recently two fifteen-year-old boys had been killed for being "of dangerous age"—a charge not even the lawyers could decipher.

Whatever the circumstances, it had become something of a sport in Maraven. One display was as arbitrary as the next, all revolving around what the king thought or felt at the moment. So whenever a Watchman hooded or masked some poor soul and dragged him or her toward makeshift scaffolding, money changed hands among the cynics and avid gamblers. Odds favored the hanging, of course, but a lucky bettor might chance a penny or two on the hopes of a beheading or even the off chance of a feeding.

On this occasion, the suspense was over almost immediately. The Watch lieutenant, still brushing his ear for imagined squinch-flies, lifted the mask from the head of Duval, and those around the scaffold sighed in recognition.

It was obvious that only one fate awaited the city's most famous cutpurse. Sure enough, the lieutenant produced a rope, and all around Brenn and Terrance the afternoon glittered and rustled with the movement of money among those watching.

"Ignore the wagering, Brenn," Terrance whispered, his hand resting heavily on the boy's shoulder. "Watch the scaffold."

"It's Duval, Terrance!" Brenn urged. "I mean, I don't know him well, but that isn't the point, is it? Couldn't we—"

"By no means," Terrance declared flatly. "We cannot."

"I don't see why," Brenn protested. "After all . . ."

" 'If you can steal a tomato, surely you can save a life,' " the wizard interrupted. "That's what you were going to say, isn't it?"

"No! Well . . . yes, something like it," the boy confessed.

"It's too large, Brenn," Terrance sighed, shedding his merriment as a burly Watchman began slipping the noose over Duval's neck. "Too large, and too . . . *volatile* to allow, I suppose. Or at least that's how I have it figured."

"*Volatile*," Brenn repeated. "I know that word from alchemy, now."

Terrance nodded. The two of them glanced again toward the scaffold, where little to nothing had moved. It was almost like an effigiary there—one of those Parthian stationary plays where the actors stay still in a posed scene for hours, their position on stage and the shifting sunlight supposed to illustrate some veiled moral truth from the ancient Parthian scriptures.

Brenn had always hated effigiaries because nothing moved or happened. He had stood at the foot of the stage and longed to leap up among the frozen Parthian actors—to tweak the nose of one and kick another's backside, anything to recover movement and breathing and all the signs of life.

The resemblance only angered him more. Quickly he moved for the stage. Terrance grasped his arm, but with a slippery, weaving motion he had picked up in his burglary days, Brenn freed himself from the wizard's clutch and leapt toward the steps of the scaffold.

The air solidified, tightened, and flexed in front of him. It was as though Brenn had run against a canvas of a thick yet transparent weave: though it was not hard enough to injure the boy as he hurled himself against it, the air gave way only so far, and Brenn's outstretched hand reached only about halfway up the steps to the scaffold.

Straining against this unnatural barrier and with rising frustration, Brenn watched the execution unfold. By now the noose had descended over Duval's head, brushing against a dark cowlick of hair, no doubt unsettled by the mask the cutpurse had been wearing. The unkempt shock of hair waved with a terrible, slow deliberateness.

It was as though if your eyes were sharp enough, you would have had time to number every hair.

"Brennart," Terrance called softly behind the boy. Brenn lowered his shoulder and battered against the clear wall, which bent once more, but did not break.

Again the wizard called, this time a little more loudly and insistently. "Brennart! Let it go."

Angry, at the edge of tears, the boy backed down the steps of the scaffold. He turned to Terrance and tried to explain the anger, but he was neither collected enough nor wise enough to put words to his feelings.

"I don't *know*, Terrance!" Brenn exclaimed, and swallowed laboriously. "It's not even that I like Duval all that much. He's a mean, calculating sort with a wide streak of assassin in him. It's just . . . just . . ."

"Over in Zephyr," Terrance murmured, his eyes fixed on the gibbet, "the direction a hanged man's body turns in the wind is supposed to reveal secrets of the future. It's done around here, too, with beheadings. They say you can tell whether or not a witness is lying by the direction his body falls when you behead him."

"That's barbaric, Terrance!" Brennart exclaimed.

"But it gives you the future," the wizard replied. "That's what you want with all this stargazing and net burrowing, isn't it? You want to comb beaches like some Teal Front matron or make sense of pigeon droppings like a Wall Town mountebank."

"I didn't say that!" Brenn protested, suddenly sick of prophecy and omen.

"Let's be gone, then," Terrance ordered. "We've seen enough."

Brenn hesitated at the foot of the scaffold, motionless until the wizard shook him.

"Do as I say, boy! I may clown and caper and stumble around the house, but that is because the house is a place to clown and caper and stumble . . ."

"I *know* that!"

"Don't interrupt!" Terrance thundered. All around master and apprentice, people in the crowd heard, or thought they heard, a high whine on the air. With excruciating slowness, they began to turn toward the source of the sound.

His hands digging into Brenn's shoulders, Terrance spun the boy around, stared intently into his apprentice's distraught eyes.

"Let's be gone," he ordered, more quietly and yet more urgently.

≺≺≺ XII ≻≻≻

Alone on the scaffold, hair tousled and warmed by the Maravenian sunlight, squinting at the brightness that rose from everything when the mask was lifted, regaining his sight and his bearings as the Watch lieutenant read the charges, Duval the cutpurse recalled the last month—an adventure of plots and guesswork and more plots that had led him up the steps to the gallows, where he now stood awaiting an even greater adventure, though few among those below him had any idea.

The crowd was thick around the scaffolding, and curious. Children gawked from atop the shoulders of their fathers, and an enterprising vendor or two had set up stands in the midst of the milling people. A hint of a smile flickered on his lips as he saw one of his Urchins—a lovely little girl of ten or eleven— lift the purse of a farmer who stared openmouthed at the spectacle on the platform.

It had begun with those Urchins, as it always began. He had managed to sneak one of them—a resourceful eight-year-old boy by the name of Talpa—into the topmost room of the Kestrel Tower, where the Great Witch held vigil.

Duval had sent the boy in broad daylight, through the browned tower gardens and straight by the well-armed Watchmen at the double iron doors that marked the principal entrance to the quarters of the king. Perhaps it had been Talpa's size that had led the Watch to believe he posed no threat, or perhaps it was the sheer matter-of-fact brassiness with which the boy walked into the tower. Whatever the case, Talpa walked by Watch and courtier and servant, all the way to the topmost room, which he claimed held neither jewels nor exotic items, neither money nor books nor crystal. The room was empty, he claimed, except for a circle of candles, one of which he brought back as a kind of simpleminded proof. As though carrying a candle proved that he was not lying about the other things.

Duval had Talpa whipped, of course—on suspicion of lying and on confirmed stupidity, for the boy confessed he had not poked through the room for false paneling and hidden compartments. It was a fact that no witchmistress of a king would sit long in a room without jewels, the Second Master maintained.

It was only later when, short a light in his study, Duval thought of the candle and plucked it from the pile of refuse where he had discarded it. When he touched flame to the wick, Duval knew that Talpa had spoken the truth, or at least some of it. For as soon as the flame settled, in its heart he saw the front of a pub on Hadrach Road, far to the east of Grospoint, but bearing a sign he remembered from his younger, flagon-tipping days. Sign of the Mongoose, with the small, almost reptilian rodent perched on its hind legs beneath an arching snake.

A good pub. Good company and beer. But what was its image about in the middle of the candle?

Duval looked closer, and the vision in the center of the fire melted into the front room, to a corner table, to a man facedown in beer and bread and a week of leavings, to . . .

A garden in blue light, loud with the cooings of a thousand doves, and a dozen winged women alighting gracefully among vines and branches, each naked and bearing a bottle of wine in her arms.

Winged women? Blue gardens and wine?

Quickly he thought of the upstairs at the Mongoose, of the three bedrooms cramped with cots and rush pallets, and then, suddenly and inexplicably, he looked upon the walls of one of them—scarred by dagger and charcoal, stained by tossed beer and piss and no telling what else.

There lay another, asleep and snoring, his head draped over the side of the cot on which he rested. Duval looked at him more closely . . .

. . . and suddenly there were fields impossibly green before the dazed eyes of the cutpurse, and sunlight racing through all the colors. A feeling of great sadness arose on the landscape, as Duval knew he watched it through another's eyes, through the eyes of one who remembered it only—who knew that the fields before him no longer existed or never were to begin with . . .

"Dreams!" Duval hissed. "I have heard of such things as this!"

So, by accident, he had found the workings of Ravenna's candles.

Never one to pass up a handy accident, Duval spied on the sprawling city. With glee he observed the daydreams of bankers and the worries of merchants. In the dozings of Watch captains he discovered which shipments were guarded and where those guards were posted.

He watched the bedchambers and dreams of young women, for no man should be all work.

Even now on the scaffold, the shadow of the rope swinging lazily over his face, the cutpurse smiled to remember the soft naked dreams of the women.

All the while he watched, Duval had grown in wealth and power. The candle shrank slowly to a mounded puddle of wax on the center of his table, and it was with some surprise that he noticed this and realized his time of advantage was running out.

Near the last of the candle, on a bright midday when the Goniph snored among his pillows deep in the bowels of Wall Town, the ambitious Duval looked into the dreams of his superior. Of course he saw nothing much: the Goniph was far too guarded to give away secrets, even in dreams.

Yet all dreams have a center that cannot be controlled, even for a man forever on watch. Perhaps especially for that man.

After almost an hour of spying, the candle spitting and gutting dangerously low, its wick almost drowning in wax, Duval was about to give up. *One more time*, he thought, and peered closely into the landscape of the First Master's dreams.

Where he saw, in a purple, damaged light, a column of horsemen approaching an overturned wagon.

Duval could not tell where the dream was taking place. Somewhere in the Corbinwood, perhaps, for though the light was tinted and distorted, there were trees everywhere, their branches as thickly interwoven as the reeds of basketry. Moreover, the Corbinwood was all the forest he knew.

Wherever the forest, no matter how thick, the riders moved among the trees as though the horses were fog or vapor, drifting slowly over that clearing where the wagon lay on its side.

He knew the face of the leader from the posters: Namid, Baron of West Aldor. Perhaps the most inventive of Zephyrian cavalry commanders. Certainly the most daring. At the wagon the baron dismounted, handed the reins of his horse to another rider. Drew a strongbox from the wagon bed and opened it.

The light of reflected gold spread over his face.

"Good," Duval breathed as the candle flame flickered and went out. "Good," he breathed again. Though he had no idea where the gold had come from, what it was doing in the wagon, how the Goniph knew its whereabouts, and why Namid figured in the dreams of a Maravenian thief, he knew that the mere mention of their names together—Goniph and Namid, Namid and Goniph—would set Dragmond's hounds to sniffing. General Helmar and two thousand Watch were down near the Corbinwood, they said, and no doubt the king would have him rooting in every clearing for Namid or for the wagon.

If indeed it was the Corbinwood.

If indeed there was anything to this dream. For whatever there was would no doubt be treason.

Duval asked the Urchin Larentia what she had heard of the matter. She had never heard of Baron Namid, but promised she would ask her brother Sandro. Sandro had heard of neither Namid nor Zephyr, though he remembered hearing something of West Aldor among the boatwrights in Ships. In pursuit of this rumor, the boy asked Wildon and Eamon.

Soon the questions spread like circles around a stone dropped into water. And the Watch came for Duval.

In the midst of a dozen burly Watchmen, he was ushered by moonlight to the old Maraven Keep in the heart of Ships—a squat, sturdy building the locals called the Locker. For two nights he sat back against the old walls of sweating stone, by daylight reading the shadowed graffiti by the light that slipped through the narrow windows twenty feet or so above him.

"*Mors vincit omnia*," the walls said. And obscurely—and thereby more unnervingly—the walls spoke poetry.

> "*This ae night, this ae night,
> Fire and sleet and candlelight.*"

Still, the food was not unpleasant, nor were the guards, and Duval's thoughts raced over how he would bargain when the time for bargaining came.

On the third day, as closely as he could tell from the dark of the Locker, counting the meals, the gray lights, and the changing shifts of guardsmen, he had his first visitor.

It was the Goniph, of course, who stood in the cell door, flanked by the Watch. The torchlight behind him made it look as though he stepped from a furnace into the cool dark of the cell. Dismissing the guards, the big man stooped, passed through the doorway, and closed the door behind him, leaving the two of them alone.

Then the First Master turned to Duval, his features dark with concern.

"Are you kept well here, lad?" the Goniph asked.

Duval kept hush. He looked straight into the eyes of the First Master, his face expressionless.

"As well as can be expected, sir," he replied. "Prisoner of the Crown and all."

All the while he was thinking, exulting. *He does not know, the tub of guts does not know, thanks be to the gods.*

The Goniph crouched by him, laying a red, meaty hand on Duval's shoulder.

"Don't be alarmed, son," he whispered. "You'll be free of this place anon."

"You mean—" Duval began, but hushed when the First Master looked at him curiously.

He does not know. Duval shrank against the wall, sighed almost inaudibly.

"The king is carrying the banner for law and decency again," the Goniph explained, his eyes on the thick cell door. "Makes for less grumbling on the Teal Front and out in the countryside, not to mention in his own bewitched bed. There's no telling what he'd do to you, given the reins."

Duval nodded, thinking of the beautiful dark-haired woman, of the lit candle.

"But two of your guards are mine," the big man whispered. "There's always enough gold in my coffers to buy Watchmen. They'll be in your escort to the scaffold . . ."

"The scaffold!" Duval interrupted, his voice rising in alarm.

"Did you think it would be bread or kisses?" the Goniph whispered ironically. "Don't be alarmed. For the hangman's mine, too. A Zephyrian. From West Aldor."

His last words dropped like light from the high, inaccessible windows of the Locker.

"What does all of this mean, sir?" Duval asked, catching himself looking toward the door when the First Master looked, lowering his voice and leaning into the hushed exchange of words. Some turnabout, this was, when the man he would have sold to the king was his key out of prison, the unraveling strand in the noose.

"It means," the Goniph pronounced, "that you can brave it like the most desperate bandit. Romance your death, lad! Spit in their faces and scoff at their questions! Hero it among the heroes. For I have hired these three for a purpose. A purpose veiled now, to be unveiled on the day Dragmond has appointed to yank you by rope into the cloudy beyond."

Duval leaned back, for the first time sharing the master's smile. A new adventure was beginning. He sensed it, as he always sensed such things, in the delicate ends of his fingers.

"May the gods rest you until that hour," the Goniph breathed, a warm, surpassing tenderness crossing over his face.

For once Duval felt warm in the cell. Felt a belonging to the guild, to a large, embracing brotherhood. He smiled again and closed his eyes, resting the back of his head against the cold wall of the Locker cell. He heard the door open, shut again, as the Goniph left the room. There was silence all around him, and then, as though it had been fooled by the comings and goings into thinking it was at last alone, a rat rustled in the farthest, darkest corner of the cell.

So there was to be a rescue, Duval mused excitedly. He would have to play things wisely, then. No bargaining with the names of Zephyr and Namid. No charge of treason to the ears of the Watch.

Those, perhaps, would be useful later. Perhaps not at all. No matter the choices, a future in which to make them had suddenly opened.

He rested and dreamt until the day of the rope, in the early spring of his thirty-third year. Duval was old enough to be wise, or at least to have taken the first steps toward wisdom. However, he had chosen a life of thievery instead, and his wisdom took the form of considering options, of wielding the prospects.

At first, anything but death drew his interest in the walk to the scaffold: the feel of the coarse black canvas on his face and the moist air rising through the eye slit in the mask, the strange play of light off the bronzed dome of the Burghers' Hall, the whiff of barley malt borne on a westward wind that, to his sensitive nose, meant a brewer's ship had passed through the Palern Reef and was heading to port.

I should remember the sounds and the sights and, oh, all of this, he told himself. *What a story it will make in Zephyr*.

"Lovely day for swinging the ankles," he joked to the guard. Who did not joke back.

Wrong guard, I reckon, the thief observed. *Too bad for him. I'll wager the Goniph pays better than Dragmond*.

He approached the steps, his eyes flickering through the crowd for a sign of untoward movement, a hint that the rescue was under way. A small child raced in front of the guardsmen, tearing at the peel of an orange with his fingers. A pigeon strutted between the vending carts of two bakers, its gray metallic head bobbing in a search for crumbs.

He ascended the steps, and the masked hangman lifted the mask of his supposed victim. A gasp surged through the crowd. Duval winked at his executioner and turned to face the milling onlookers.

Sure enough, there was the Goniph not far away, his eyes intent on something remote out by the Kestrel Tower.

Good. He was in place and on the lookout.

A clever plan, this seemed. Nowhere was there evidence of commotion. No swords were drawn, no hoofbeats on the cobblestones that would signal the delivering rush of horsemen.

Wouldn't it be grand, Duval thought, *if I were rescued by Zephyrian cavalry?*

He chuckled to himself. The hangman slipped the noose over his head, tightened it.

Odd. By now shouldn't something have happened? A small bead of sweat itched at his upper lip.

Some sort of gray, dodging light in the midst of the crowd resolved itself into a tall, bearded man and a boy strangely familiar, then blurred into haze and shimmer again.

"How strange," Duval whispered to the hangman. "Looks like the boy that the Goniph lost over the winter—the one I saw in the market when . . ."

"Don't tense up, boy," the hangman murmured. "It's better for all if you don't tense up."

Obediently, Duval slumped his shoulders, tried to relax. Tried to place the hangman's voice among the dozens he had heard at market, near the shops of Grospoint or even in the guild hall. Failing at that, he tried to place the accent and, shaken a little, found he had failed at that, too. He tasted salt. His left eye stung sharply.

The voice of the hangman was homeless. But of course that could mean anything. A voice merchant, perhaps, who had cleansed the man's words in Aldor before he had come to Maraven on his secret mission of deliverance. Perhaps it was even simpler than that—that the man had purged himself of accent, shaping the "ye" by which the traveling Zephyrian was identified into the "you" a man heard everywhere, and carefully watching each turn of a phrase for the way of talking that said to the ear "West Aldor" or "Transumbre" or "Grasslands."

Yes, Zephyr would be interesting to see. Duval had not . . .

Where *was* the rescue? The lieutenant had read through all the charges now, and still no man moved except to shift his weight, or rub his nose, or once to hoist a child to his shoulders so the little moppet could see a man's neck break. Duval's shirt clung wetly to his back and his unruly forelock was pasted to his temple.

His gaze skittered over the crowd—the green and red and blue, the banners of market day and a woman's white cap, *which was not a rescue*, and a stirring off to his left that was a juggler. *Where is Goniph now, what's keeping him, something is wrong, terrible terrible and he's going to let me die and then . . . then . . .*

Duval's sigh exploded, desperately, as the swirl of gray now at the edge of the crowd began again to resolve itself, to take on shape and substance, and surely that would be . . .

The strange old man, the boy, their backs to Duval, walking away . . . away . . .

"Who *are* they?" he whispered to the faceless and voiceless man behind him.

And the trapdoor snapped from beneath his feet.

* * *

"It was dreadful there," Brenn breathed when the sound of the body dropping and the outcry of the crowd reached him from up the street. "Terrible dreadful and blank. What was he looking at, Terrance? Duval, I mean."

"The future?" Terrance asked, steering the boy away from the spectacle. "Or maybe nothing in particular."

They both stood silent for a somber moment, then turned eastward and home through the darkening streets of the city.

By daylight Ravenna could not see well. Oh, her eyes were as good as any, and the sun removed the shadow so that the outlines and details of things were clearer, though this always surprised her since she had chosen the colorless night in which to observe and divine.

For divining had taken the place of eyes. In the heart of the candles lay the most important sights—the dreams and thoughts and the future. It was a more inviting landscape, in which all mystery became clear after the Lock, in which the truth rode up to meet you.

That was what she told herself. But in the last few months, since the green star had become auspicious, the sunlight hurt her eyes.

Perhaps it was only because she seldom saw the brighter light of the day anymore. Still, Ravenna thought, it *had* to be something more subtle than that.

"There must be a Power set against me," she murmured from the topmost window of the Kestrel Tower, shielding her eyes and gazing over the causeway into Grospoint, where the crowd around the scaffolding began to disperse. The execution of the cutpurse Duval had been carried out, and the onlookers were turning back to whatever had amused them before.

"When I learn the name of that Power," Ravenna pronounced, "the sun will no longer burn, and I shall take back the day from my enemies."

In the midst of the Street of the Chemists, a gray swirl of shadows caught her eye. At first she thought it was sirens, but the thing moved too slowly, too regularly.

Nonetheless, it was immeasurably faster than the strolling

marketers, than the Watch as they marched away from the scaffolding. She reached for the spyglass that lay at her hand on the sill, lifted it, and peered into it at the gray disturbance. Surging down the Street of the Chemists, then east onto Cove Road, the shadow dipped between leaning buildings, in and out of the shades of overhanging awnings only to lose itself finally, somewhere in the ominous dark of the stockyards.

"Ah," Ravenna whispered, a hint of uneasiness in the desolate music of her voice as she lowered the glass and turned to her ring of candles. "Something I cannot decipher. At least not yet."

All was light on Hardwater Cove. The Street of the Bookbinders and old Hadrach Road were sunlit and unruffled. Nor did the candles, their flames transparent in the full sun, illumine much more than the day itself.

"Another time, then," Ravenna conceded, stepping into the circle and scanning the populous Maravenian coast through the burning eyes of her candles. "A time when . . ."

Frozen by the flame of one particular taper, caught up by the strangeness of the vision, the dark woman brushed her hair back absently.

For the candle showed her the scaffold, the body of Duval the Cutpurse turning in the windless air, still propelled by the force of his last frantic convulsion, though it had been a good ten minutes ago.

Clockwise, Ravenna thought. *He turns clockwise. Threat to the Crown.* But it was not the turning of the body that had drawn her.

Frozen on the sightless black pupil of the thief's eye were tiny thin gray lines, detectable only by the unnaturally sharp vision of a woman accustomed to stargazing and geomancy.

As was often the case when she looked for things, Ravenna's senses had been fueled and intensified by acumen, the Alanyan potion extracted from sunflowers at noon, when their faces absorb the most light. The potion heightens perception, sometimes at the cost of memory.

This time Ravenna risked that cost. About her neck, suspended from a golden chain, three crystal vials hung, each of a different shape and size, each banded with two rings of gold. She raised the green vial, draining it of its contents, then wavered a little as she folded her hands over her breast, closing her eyes as the acumen settled. Then raising the spyglass to the candle, she looked through drug and crystal and fire, into the eyes of the dead man.

"Terrance," she hissed. "Terrance and . . . and a boy. Does the old fool have an apprentice? Again? What can he teach *this* one beyond sleight of hand? Or . . . something about . . . about claridad."

The laugh she had begun faded as she struggled to recollect. She shook her head, looked more closely into the glazing eye of Duval. The boy looked . . . familiar.

But who?

And of dangerous age.

There was something about that phrase . . . she did not remember now. Struggle as she might against the acumen, the drug had turned unlucky that night, mastering her memory until she fought for her intentions, for her bearings.

For one brief, nightmarish moment, she had trouble with her own name.

In a breath it passed, and she found herself at the window. The night air was cool on her face, and she found herself looking across the causeway to the Street of the Chemists, where the Watch dismantled the afternoon's gibbet.

Something about the spot disturbed her. About the spot and about her old rival Terrance, whom she had thought conveniently addled and out of the way.

Ravenna shook her blue-black hair. It glistened in the starlight.

She knew the echo of acumen. This had happened once, twice before, when she asked too much of the potion, when the strange illumination it brought her would cloud over, and she would waken obscure and terrified, knowing that something she had dropped in the shadows lay just beyond her grasp now, beyond retrieval and memory.

It had happened again. For reasons she could not remember, Terrance would bear watching.

She would, however, remember to watch.

⤙⤙⤙ **XIII** ⤚⤚⤚

From his stronghold deep in a network of tunnels under Wall Town, the Goniph watched everything, knew everything.

Reclining on a dozen cushions some hundred feet below a guard tower, directly under the headquarters of the Wall Town battalion of Dragmond's Watch, the First Master of the Maravenian Thieves' Guild held court. The pomp of this court was gossip, its ritual an elaborate system of accounting: money poured in from burglary and theft, from swindles and pickpocketing, marked cards, loaded dice, and shell games, and only the Goniph knew all the numbers.

The long night hours at his trade dwindled into rest and food and drink and talk. It was morning now, and his aching feet elevated and a glass of wine in his hand, the Goniph looked like a statue of an ancient god of vineyards. He was handsome in the very qualities farmers call handsome in a bull: he was stout, sleek, and confident, and he wore a nose ring well. Around him lay the booty of the past several nights: a strongbox filled with bronze Umbrian coins, two silver Alanyan samovars and a plentiful supply of dark tea, four necklaces and a tiara from a coach on the road too late through Grospoint.

The big man sipped from the wine glass, frowned, and inspected a piece of cheese with the same scrutiny that a jeweler gives a diamond. Satisfied, he dropped the morsel into his mouth. His sapphire and topaz rings clicked together as he waved impatiently at his two prized apprentices, urging them to continue with the story.

"That makes two more squadrons the king's moved to the Teal Front," Dirk observed from his pallet on the floor of the chamber, wrapping his bony little arms around his bony little knees. "I'd reckon he has three hundred men down there by now."

Seated beside the thief, Faye inspected the blade of her knife and, listening idly, nodded in agreement with her fellow apprentice.

The Goniph strained to a sitting position and grunted as he reached out a meaty hand to rub his swollen feet.

"Then," he decreed, after a long painful sigh, "we won't do business on the Teal Front for a while."

"Surely not so!" Dirk exclaimed, only his eyes and voice registering surprise. "After all, unless things have changed, the Teal Front is our chief . . ."

"Things *have* changed, Dirk," Faye interrupted. "Remember what happened on the Street of the Chemists last week."

"Grospoint is no longer Duval's Alley," the Goniph agreed, reclining once more. "Or the Blue-Eyed Haven, or the Country of the Urchins. Or whatever name Duval called it by to claim it as his territory."

"Duval was good, Goniph," Faye reminded her master. "His hand was fast and his eye bright, and the children he fostered . . . well . . ."

"Always the children, isn't it, Faye?" the Goniph asked. "We shall miss him, my dear. I shall miss him beyond your knowing."

Faye and Dirk glanced briefly at each other, guessing at what came next.

"I suppose . . ." Faye ventured finally, leaning forward as her brown curls tumbled from the slouch hat she wore nowadays, "I suppose there will be no new Second Master for a while."

A smile touched the edge of Goniph's lips. He knitted his brow and nodded.

"In honor of a Second Master whose successor will be hard to find," he announced.

The girl was smart, and Dirk not much slower. It would be hard hiding strategy from them.

All the more reason he would enjoy doing it.

"We have to . . . absent ourselves for a while," the Goniph explained. "Not only from felicity, but from sight. Buoyed by his success, Dragmond may decide to clear the city of refuse. And as you know, I am considered by some to be the largest piece of jetsam in the vicinity."

Dirk and Faye laughed politely, their thoughts racing. They

both knew the Goniph had an understanding with Dragmond himself, and that when the unusual happened—a burglary, say, in a rich merchant's house in the Teal Front, or the arrest of some high-ranking personage in the guild—it was because someone had struck a deal.

It seemed that the master was troubled now beyond Duval's death, somewhere in the intricate machinery of his plotting, close to his heart. In their understanding of the elaborate, unspoken ways of city politics, the apprentices believed that the king had overstepped his bounds. No doubt he had needed a trophy from the underworld. But when that happened, he would speak to the First Master, who would allow the occasional pickpocket or second-story man to be "taken in for questioning" or to "help the Watch with their inquiries," as the polite phrasing went.

But never another master. And never to an end such as this.

They wondered what the king owed the Goniph now.

Which was just what the Goniph wanted them to wonder.

That night the Goniph met with King Dragmond, quietly and secretly in the cellars of the Hall of Poisoners, the King of Maraven and Palerna with the king of the streets.

The hall was a small, abandoned stone building at the border of Ships and Grospoint, perched ironically at the corner of Light Street and Starboard Alley.

Usually business was brief, perfunctory: the two men despised each other cordially, and spent as little time as possible in their projects of civic improvement. On the floor above them, a squadron of Watchmen patroled and hovered, waiting only for a signal from the king to descend into the cellar and effect an arrest that would thunder through the streets and alleys of Maraven.

Somehow the Goniph did not fear this possibility. He did not fear being taken, for he played well on the imaginings of those who used him. Many in the guard supposed that Light Street swarmed with assassins while master met king, and there were stories that if the big man were ever harmed or arrested that Grospoint would fall victim to an army of a million rats, called from the tunnels and the sewers by the Goniph's distress.

Thus, in treacherous balance, the two men met when the new moon came and the sky was dark.

Dragmond steepled his fingers, leaned back in a mahogany chair. His black beard trimmed elegantly, he looked like a god in a Parthan effigiary, his blue eyes brilliant and haloed as he watched the Goniph's every gesture and examined every word.

What the Goniph had heard—that the king was intelligent, not so intelligent, observant, or lost to the world—he set aside for each meeting. For at each meeting Dragmond seemed different, as though shifting stars or tides or seasons changed his countenance, his character, his cause.

Nonetheless, the Goniph was always cautious. And especially this night.

"'Tis rare that *I* ask favors of *you*," the handsome, bearded king began, his hands falling to the arms of the chair, where his fingers, ringless and pale and oddly fragile-looking for the hands of an exceptional swordsman, drummed noiselessly upon the brown-black wood.

The Goniph nodded politely, his thoughts seething with memories of dozens of "favors," at the insult hanging in the damp cellar air.

The king must be drugged with acumen not to remember how much he owed the Thieves' Guild. There was the Zephyrian Conspiracy of six years back, when Namid's father, Count Macaire, had planned to invade the Gray Strand. A thousand horsemen had gathered in the Corbinwood, and another thousand traveled the eastern coast of the Gray Sea disguised as an Alanyan caravan—their troopers bound to the horses and covered with blankets and silks so that entire battalions looked like pack animals laden with merchandise. Had the two cavalries joined, it could have spelled embarrassment for Maraven, and perhaps even more, for old Macaire had borne a thirty-year grudge against the crowned heads of Palerna, every morning staring at and praying to an ancient parchment map of the subcontinent in which everything between the Boniluce and the Eastmark had been carefully burned away by coals, leaving a hole in the map where Palerna once had been. By the time of the planned invasion, he looked at the stars through the hole in the map and claimed to see into the future.

Though their captain was mad, the Zephyrian cavalry was the

best in the world, and their presence on the Gray Strand could have been desperate indeed for all Maraven. The Zephyrians were thwarted, though, when one of the old count's principal agents had boasted of his importance to a harlot, who had expressed her interest in things military. Of course, the girl was an agent herself and took the news straight to her master, the Goniph.

"If the master could learn from the news," she had said. And the Goniph had learned from it nicely, taking it straight to the king, who had sent his best commander west along the coast of the Gray Sea with three thousand cavalry and six thousand foot soldiers. A few skirmishes, won easily by the brilliant General Goran, were just enough to give old Macaire second thoughts and hold the Gray Strand for Palerna.

The Goniph smiled to himself at the memory. It had been a heady time in Maraven, and the intelligence he had set at the foot of the king had assured that the Watch would turn their eyes from Hadrach Road for six months. That, too, was a heady time, during which the merchants waded through road agents and bandits, cargoes growing smaller and smaller from Hadrach to Stormpoint to the Maravenian Gate. When they had reached town many of them had only what they wore on their backs, and some wore very little. Meanwhile, the coffers and treasuries under Wall Town bulged with jewelry and spice and gold.

Now Macaire's oldest son, Namid, was the Count of West Aldor. More ruthless than his father and more violent. Also more calculating, he made things difficult for the caravan robbers along the Gray Strand. You had to pay the new count handily to assure he wouldn't follow your people into Palerna. But there was good arising from this bother and inconvenience. If the time came for a war between Zephyr and Palerna, you could have friends in both camps, providing you kept each secret from the other.

Rumors had it that the ground was opening all along the coasts of Palerna, and the highwaymen were riding into the crevasses and fissures, trailing mist and fog from the flanks of their horses.

That had been the first of it—the business arrangement between thief and king. Then three years ago there was Duke Galliard of Aquila, the king's own cousin in some way or another, who had plotted to overthrow Dragmond and institute a government of merchants in Maraven "until the rightful king arose."

The Goniph had been fond of young Galliard, who was a just and decent boy, and yet managed to stay interesting, since he had a little of the lively thief in him. Nevertheless, the First Master was not foolish enough to support a band of magistrates whose first official act would be no doubt to dangle him from a gibbet. Instead, he had turned in the names of the conspiring merchants, covered for young Galliard, and watched with a gloomy satisfaction as the businessmen swung on the causeway.

The Goniph had gained from those names, also—an unexpected restationing of three squadrons of the Watch to the East Wall to defend against an Alanyan invasion that was never going to come in the first place. That movement left three streets unprotected on the Teal Front, and the Thieves' Guild had three nights of it until the outcry of rich folks became too shrill for Dragmond to ignore.

"But over the past week I have . . . extended myself for you," Dragmond intoned, having forgotten Macaire and the harlot, Galliard and the merchants, the Goniph's New Year's present of a hundred songbirds for the gardens of Kestrel Tower. Such was the gratitude of kings, the big man told himself, nodding because he had to nod.

"Have taken the troublemaker from your midst," the king continued, "and disposed of him."

The Goniph nodded again dutifully, tugged at his nose ring, and looked toward the ceiling. The ancient oak beams were well fitted and well preserved. *Peace and architecture are sisters*, the Goniph observed, his thoughts playing lazily as the king droned on.

Black wings brushed the edge of his mind. Black wings or the thought of black wings. Crows or ravens or a hundred starlings flickering over the carcass of an animal.

The Goniph shook his head, dove back into the words of the king.

". . . dangerous age. Are you listening, man?"

"Of course, sire," the Goniph answered, stalling and bluffing until he could recover the conversation. "The dangerous age is . . . I cannot find the words for it . . ."

"What words do you need? The dangerous age is fifteen!"

Baffled, the big thief shifted his weight on the creaking stool where he sat. Upstairs was strangely silent, the occasional sound of a Watchman crossing the floor the only reminder that the king and the Goniph were not the only two in the house.

The air of the cellar carried a whiff of a gamblers' den, the Goniph thought. Hard and burnt with speculation.

What was the word? *Volatile*.

"It's as simple as fifteen, Goniph," the king emphasized, his fingers drumming more loudly on the dark armrest.

The First Master cleared his throat, but then kept silent, peered at Dragmond, and thought, *The man looks too much like a king to be a good one.*

"The fifteen-year-olds I cannot reach in this city are the ones *you* can reach," Dragmond pronounced mysteriously, his hands folding together delicately in his lap.

Goniph looked puzzled.

"Never mind the reason, Goniph," he said with a smile. "Rest assured that all of them—'rich man, poor man, beggar man, thief' doesn't it go?—rest assured that none of them will be harmed—only inquired of."

A long silence followed, in which the king sat serenely, staring at nothing, it seemed, while the thoughts of the Goniph doubled upon each other, tangling in possibility and conjecture.

None will be harmed? he thought. *I wonder if the two lads he hanged a fortnight past for "being of dangerous age" went to the gibbet with that promise. Fifteen . . . fifteen. Why fifteen? A sum of Ravenna's conjury, no doubt. The art of fatic numbers or a fool's astrology—something to do with witchery and mirrors.*

"I fear I know of no other fifteen-year-olds," the Goniph asserted, shifting his weight uncomfortably again. The lamplight dipped in the windowless room, and for a moment the shadows of the beams above the two men lengthened and sank to the floor as if the Hall of Poisoners were set to topple around them.

"I have heard of three in your ranks," Dragmond prodded.

"I can tell you of these, and perhaps their names will help you to remember others. Fifteen is a common age among thieves, it seems."

And he gave the Goniph the names: Larentia and Eamon, two of Duval's Urchins, and Iliyas, a pickpocket from Wall Town. The Goniph knew the Wall Town boy well, had heard of the other two. As the king recited the names the big man looked up into the beams and shadows, thinking of scaffolding and rope and the terribly sad dreams of the young.

Sad, because where he came from, those dreams often ended in scaffolding and rope.

"I could have done for Duval myself," he muttered, scarcely aware that he was speaking aloud.

"So you could have, my friend," King Dragmond pressed. "And therefore my question is a simple one: Why didn't you?"

The First Master of the Thieves' Guild squirmed. It was because he was fond of Duval. He had known the lad since he had to stand on tiptoe to reach a tall man's purse, and somehow it had seemed more simple to step back—to let things unfold as they naturally unfolded when an unlettered rogue met the letter of the law. As long as he did not ponder it, the Goniph could rest easy, telling himself that Duval had stepped once too carelessly, had fallen into the hands of a severe and merciless king.

He could tell himself that and rest easy awhile . . . but then he would awake in midafternoon, sweating and distracted, having dreamt of shadows and gibbets. And recently of enormous, black-winged birds.

"Larentia, you say? Was that other name Iliyas? Never heard of them. The other is dead, I believe."

Dragmond smiled wickedly, shook his head in disbelief.

"All three are dead, unless you bring them forth. If I offer a gold coin for the head of each, offer it loudly in a city like Maraven, in a place like Wall Town, those heads will be brought dripping to my doorstep by the end of the afternoon.

"Far better that *no* harm should come to them, is it not? Far better that I should gather them, ask them what I need to ask, then release them—safe in some distant country where their silence is assured. Jaleel, perhaps, or the Notches. Or even in northern Aquila."

Perhaps Dragmond meant what he said, the Goniph told himself. After all, he *had* been true to his word when it came to Duval and the short rope on the Street of the Chemists. He was swift and efficient with his promises of death, this king. Galliard's merchants came to mind, then Duval again, his blue eyes brightening in the slanting light of the Locker.

The three young thieves would have no chance when the word was proclaimed. And the Goniph knew the king would do it. No doubt as they spoke the speech had been drafted in the loftiest regions of Kestrel Tower—charges, descriptions, and rewards to be shouted in streets by criers in red armor, to be posted on shop front and guild hall throughout the Maravenian districts.

Why, even the girls who *looked* like Larentia were unsafe from this time forward.

So the Goniph told himself that he did these things for the welfare of the good folk around him—the poor and the hardworking, as well as the decent sort who, by accident of birth or circumstance, had fallen outside of the law. Faye was thirteen and too young, he told himself. And Dirk, though sixteen and close enough to the dangerous age to be imperiled by searches and roundups, was so small that even the most sharp-eyed of bounty hunters or assassins would swear that the boy was not even twelve.

At least his own and his best were safe, the Goniph conceded philosophically. The First Master assented, and quietly, as though there still were something unjust in all of this, he gave to the king an address in Grospoint and one in Ships, and finally that of a gambling den in Wall Town—the place where young Iliyas gamed and bargained and dreamt. The big man dwindled a little in the rising shadows of the cellar as he gave name and place and directions, and the king, whose memory was good, took note of everything.

"You realize, First Master," Dragmond concluded formally, rising from the mahogany chair. A door opened at the head of the stairs above them, and light cascaded into the cellar, banishing shadows of beam and chair, driving the rats into corners more remote. "You realize that these three may not be the ones to . . . help me with my inquiry."

"They are, however, the only three I know," the Goniph protested.

"I understand," the king replied. "I shall be back for others if I need them."

The Goniph drew a silk handkerchief from his sleeve, wiped the sweat and the grime from his face, then cast aside the handkerchief, which spread and billowed as it dropped to the cellar floor.

Laboriously he ascended the steps, snuffed the candle in his large hand, and stepped onto Starboard Alley from the side entrance of the Hall of Poisoners.

And when the king comes back, he thought, *I shall have to have others for him.*

There was Brenn, he recollected, searching deep in his distracted memory. *The one we lost to the wizard. If he's not seaweed or a fiddler crab by now . . . well, he's lost to me, as I figure it.*

And after all, it may save one of my own.

‹‹‹ XIV ›››

It was the summer of the alienados, the hot winds from the south that every decade or so rushed out of the Notches and onto the Plains of Palerna, gathering speed and heat in the lowlands and leaving the country scarcely habitable behind them. The grain fields were scorched and the livestock smothered, standing upright in the pastures. In the wake of the alienados came hundreds of peasants, who at best lived on the edge of privation and now were ruined entirely. Packing whatever they could salvage from the wreckage of their homes, they journeyed north toward Maraven and survival.

It was a landscape from the legends out on those plains, as though some malign and terribly powerful giant had chosen this summer, these roads, on which to buffet a helpless people. The wind drove them pitilessly, hurling branches, undergrowth, even small trees, all of which tumbled by them as they flocked along the South and Hadrach roads. Small children who were too large for their mothers to carry walked beside the women, bent against the wind and tied to parents or to each other by ropes, since rumors had passed through the column of peasants that three unmoored children had vanished entirely, carried the gods knew where by the fierce and malevolent wind. The more ingenious among the peasants cut loose their horses or mules or oxen from the carts and fixed blankets to the wagon beds like enormous sails. Coasting over the plains at the front of the wind, they sped toward Maraven, their hearts lightened by the prospect of food and water and protective walls.

They yearned for Maraven on the long road, for Maraven was lucky, standing as it did on the edge of Lake Teal. There the anger and the heat and the dryness fell from the alienados and the winds became less fierce. Even in Maraven, though, there were rumors that the shores of Lake Teal boiled in the midday wind. The more experienced stablemasters boarded up the liveries, for horses had been known to go blind in the alienado, staring witlessly into the rushing wind until their eyes milked over and they stumbled and death was a welcome release.

Worst of all, though, was the madness that came in the wake of the wind. Especially where people were enclosed and bunched together, the madness spread like heat over iron. So the Palernan peasants discovered as they staggered through the East Gate into Wall Town. Half-mad themselves with joy that the drought and the ceaselessly burning journey were behind them, the refugees looked up to see the city folk leaping from rooftops, tumbling to their deaths from windows, gibbering on street corners. Then, since they were not the ones gone mad, they took up residence in the deserted rooms of the dead.

So it was through late June and all of July, and on the second of August the alienado stopped as suddenly as it had begun six weeks before. Finally the inhabitants of the city, from refugee and addled Wall Towner to those boarded into the mansions along the Teal Front, began to open their dwellings to air and light.

And then, for a fortnight, there was not a breeze to be found.

The coastal air hung humid on the city, and then when the inhabitants thought that surely there was nothing worse, that when this terrible calm broke they could go back to living and planning for futures and thinking of something besides the weather, it was then that the plague returned. The incidents had been few during the cold winter months and through most of the spring, and many people had come to believe that the Death was going and soon would be gone for good.

When it returned, it returned with a fury. The king called out the Watch with their sweet-smelling handkerchiefs, and the young men in leather armor went through Wall Town filling their carts. They formed barricades at the south end of the causeway, and a squadron of crack bowmen kept those infected to the south of the Needle's Eye.

It was in late August when Dame Sorrow, the legendary old woman who carried the cloak of Death, was first spotted in Maraven. She was standing, or so the distraught visionary told anyone who would listen, in the smoke of a healer's torch, holding out the cloak and weeping for the dead and for those about to die. That same day an Aquilan girl who suffered from the falling sickness saw Dame Sorrow in the shimmer of heat off the stones in the Street of the Bookbinders, and an Umbrian seller of wines, looking through his dark cellar for a special vintage, saw her sad black eyes and gaunt visage in the glass of a wine bottle where lamplight reflected in the amber wine itself. Soon the Grand Dame was everywhere, spotted in Ships and in Grospoint, and finally an Alanyan visionary—a dwarfish, brilliant man recently employed by the king himself—saw her climb in the smoke from a baker's chimney and unfurl the cloak of Death over all of the city.

It was a time, Terrance reflected, sitting in starlight on the roof of his half-built tower, that he was glad to be an unwelcome presence.

In the years after King Aurum's demise, Terrance had learned in no uncertain terms that his advice was no longer needed in Kestrel Tower. Gradually he moved from place to place in the city, always eastward until he could go no farther east and still remain in Maraven. For seven years he had lived alone in the half-built tower, and on some winter nights when the weather and the robbers and even the Watch itself made travel abroad unsafe, the wizard sat at home by the fire, talking to his old dog Bracken and the mice and grannars that nested in the darker notches of the solar.

They had been lonely evenings, to be sure, far from the sound of human voice and the learning and politics of the tower . . . but they had been safe. At last Terrance had found a way out of the maze of palace intrigue, and no longer did courtiers lurk behind him with real and imaginary knives. Home was humble, and his room a spare one, but Bracken was an amiable enough companion, who neither plotted nor disagreed. Ravenna considered the old man beneath official notice, and in the Maraven of Dragmond beneath notice meant *in less danger*. He was reasonably safe from the city itself: his dwelling too far away and much too shoddy-looking to attract anything more than an occasional amateur thief, easily scared off by a moving light or a polite *boof* from the lazy dog on the hearth.

From that distance there had been less of the king and less of the plague, and Terrance had welcomed both absences.

Before the boy had come to stay, Terrance had stubbed his toe in dark corners where the light he summoned with his magic had once made even the most shadowy parts of the room clear and distinct and greenly lit. The wizard had once raised winds almost as swift and high as last week's alienado, but by last November they scarcely stirred dust on the floor.

When Terrance had told Brenn that the best magic was often the least, he had been telling the truth. But no magic at all makes a wizard rusty, and a magic unused will eventually atrophy and fade entirely, so that when you need it you will find it no longer there. The presence of the boy Brenn had wearied him at first, asking him to draw on unexercised powers so that he could teach the lad, and of course to undo the damage that the boy's own efforts at conjury had caused.

Through the winter Terrance had felt older than he had ever felt before, and it had only been with the first stirrings of spring that he had shed some of that weariness, realizing that seventy was not that decrepit an age at all, especially for a wizard, and that if he intended to be useful in the good century he had remaining, it was best to get under way.

Hence the springtime, when he had taught the boy about divining.

But now it was summer, and the calling was more serious. He had to ready the boy for the last of the first lessons—or the first of the last, depending on what happened in the months to come. He also had to ready himself, to summon the strength for the teaching and also for the things that would come afterward —things that would demand even more of him because they had nothing to do with the glamour and hocus-pocus of the craft, but instead with the deep test of wisdom that was its backbone and source.

Terrance chuckled a little sadly at the prospect. He lay back on the roof and locked his fingers behind his head. A thousand stars floated overhead, the moon so near that he could extinguish her with poetry if he chose to do so.

" 'If the Sun and Moon should doubt,' " he began, then thought better of it. It would only be one night, after all, that he would blacken the moon—one phase, if his powers were at full strength and all focused on the moon and her disappearance. Much more trying things were ahead of him.

"Brennart!" he called, and again more loudly. After a brief wait he heard the boy's footsteps behind him, descending the stairway out of the air and sky. The wizard scrambled to his feet and turned to face his apprentice.

"Damn it, Brenn!" Terrance snapped. "How many times do I have to tell you that it's not a secret passage?"

"I believe that's only the sixth time, sir," the boy replied confidently, prepared to use charm and jests to smooth the edges of his master. "I expect there will be more to come."

Sometimes Terrance found it hard to notice the kind of changes that are supposed to be obvious in a boy of fifteen—that the lad is growing like a weed, his voice is deepening, and a stray hair or two has peeked out onto an otherwise smooth chin, promising the beard of a decade later. He would look up, and something would be slightly different—a crack in the tenor as the apprentice sang lessons through the house, or Brenn's being at last able to reach a high shelf without benefit of a stool or the back of a chair. But he could not figure how it had happened: it was as though Brenn's manhood was sneaking up on the both of them in a series of long and secretive bounds.

"There will be *no* more following secret passages, if you know what's best for you!" the wizard exclaimed, drawing his thoughts out of memory and reflection into the here and now. He sighed inwardly, knowing there was no way that Brenn would listen to him if the boy had made up his mind.

"Get yourself downstairs, boy," Terrance ordered. "And do it the normal, respectable way, if you'd be so kind: no vanishments and apparitions. I'm an old man and tiring quickly of cleaning up your ethereal messes. Time for bed, and close your eyes at once tonight. No whiling away until the wee hours with speculation or with listening for elves in the woodwork. Tomorrow's the big day after all."

Having planted the seeds of curiosity, he sat back down on the rooftop, his eyes on the amber moon.

"What's going on tomorrow, Terrance?" Brenn asked, trying his best to appear casual about the matter. For it angered him to play into the wizard's cagey hands, when Terrance stood apart from him like a philosopher, saying ambiguous things and asking questions he could not begin to answer because he didn't understand them in the first place.

"Tomorrow we begin the fourth art," Terrance declared, his eyes fixed on the moon and on the clouds that passed over her. "The fourth discipline of magic."

"Which is?" the boy asked eagerly.

"Healing and restoring. It demands a rested student. One with an iron nerve."

"Oh," Brenn said, a note of disappointment in his voice.

After all, the boy was young. And no amount of magic or street smarts or even native high spirits would be sufficient for tomorrow, the wizard feared.

For he had seen Dame Sorrow that afternoon, rising from a cup of tea, her dark eyes fathomless and without hope. In the deep, expressionless mist of her face he saw that she had come from Wall Town.

And that tomorrow his path lay there, amid pestilence and

death and the terrible fever that rose like the shimmer of heat off Hadrach Road. Though the good he could do was little, the time in which to do it was nigh.

"I did not promise a lark," Terrance declared to the boy, and smiled sadly.

"But, Terrance!"

"Do you want to see it in black and white?"

Quickly the wizard produced the scroll from his sleeve. It was the writ, of course. Brenn sighed at the prospect of more clauses and effects.

"I expect that once again I have signed away more than I'd bargained for," he muttered, and Terrance nodded.

"Read, if you would, clause sixteen, boy."

"Which is always the clause in question!" Brenn whined. As he took up the writ, a faint green light guided his eyes to the passage:

> *Under no circumstances should the apprentice come to believe that the aforesaid apprenticeship is a lark or merriment. Moments in which time staggers and elves are conjured may charm the green and unlearned, but this is serious business we are about. The apprentice should also go to bed now.*

Brenn swallowed angrily, looked up at Terrance.

"May I keep this writ, sir? To . . . to study it further?"

"Absolutely not!" the wizard snapped. Then softly, more reasonably, "Not yet, at least. For one thing, you'd keep yourself up past the contracted bedtime."

He reached out for the scroll, which Brenn dutifully handed him.

"Go to bed now," Terrance ordered, not unkindly. And Brenn, as he was learning to do almost by reflex, turned away and obeyed.

As the boy descended the ladder into the attic, the wizard stood and, walking to the northern side of the house, looked out over the glistening dark waters of the Sea of Shadows. From east to west he scanned the horizon, taking in nothing but moonlight and starlight and dark water and black sand. Far to the northwest he saw a pale light gleaming close to the horizon. He knew its source, knew it stood at a giddy height in Kestrel Tower and that only his great distance from the home of the king made it seem like the light almost touched the edge of the inky waters.

"Up late again, Ravenna?" he whispered glumly into the salty night air. Below him a startled elf squawked in the maple leaves, then scurried down the branch into the green light of the guest room. "She's always been a watcher, that Ravenna," Terrance called playfully down to the elf, who poked its head back out the window and squinted up into the dark, its face as bunched and wrinkled as a hairy fist.

"If she did not spend so much time watching and waiting for her fears, they would not come to pass," he added cryptically. He held the writ up to the amber moonlight and watched with mild curiosity as the ink swirled and the words changed.

Not even Terrance the Mage was altogether sure what it would say next.

The elf stared long and hard at the outlandish creature above it: the tall, bearded man holding paper up to light. Then, satisfied that further watching would bring no satisfaction, the ugly little creature drew its head back into the coolness of the room, nestled itself in a notch between two maple branches, and fell solidly to sleep.

By midmorning the sun was uncomfortably hot, and vapors rose from Cove Road ahead of them.

Terrance had shed four layers of garments before they left the house, and two more before they reached the Street of the Bookbinders. He had handed them both back to Brenn: a gray silk overshirt and an embroidered vest out of which a pigeon fluttered. Brenn accepted the clothing dumbly, marveling at just how much apparel the wizard managed to wear on a single occasion.

I'll wager he's thin as a rail and the rest is fabric and filling, the boy thought as he bunched the garments into a pack on his back. Soon he regretted even their negligible weight, for the sun became hotter still, and the pack and his own clothes were almost unbearable. What little breeze approached them came from inland—a torrid afterbreath of the alienado that dried up the sweat on Brenn's neck at its touch, leaving him more uncomfortable than before.

"It's like being a jug in a kiln," he muttered angrily, shifting the pack on his shoulders and thinking of lemon-water and surf. Terrance walked swiftly ahead of him on the hot stones, stooped willfully against the cruel, still weather.

"Are you sure you have it all, lad?" he called behind him, inattentive to Brenn's sweating and puffing and swearing.

"Even more sure than I was the last time you asked!" Brenn snapped. "The bittersweet, the camphor, the leeches, the gods know what else! Did you pack something to do away with sunstroke?"

Terrance said nothing, but his strides lengthened. He shed still another robe as he stalked comically westward into the rising stink of the slaughterhouses like a monstrous, melancholy crane. Brenn followed behind his master, scarcely stopping to pick up the discarded cloak before he picked up the pace again, his short legs windmilling in a desperate attempt to keep up with the wizard ahead of him, who turned down an alley and was lost from sight, emerging on the Boulevard of Candles and heading southward into Wall Town, into the roughest district of a rough city.

Where Dame Sorrow waited and held the cloak of Death.

In Wall Town each morning they dragged the dead out into the streets.

Brenn thought it was eerie as the shadows shortened and noon approached, for in front of him in the white unforgiving light of midday the corpses lay side by side on the Boulevard of Waters, as if somebody had thought that an orderly arrangement of death might somehow stop its random progress.

Gasping to recover his breath after the long run, the boy came to a stop behind Terrance, trying his best to keep the old man between him and the arrayed bodies. Even from a distance he saw the ravagement. Saw also the scarved and gloved members of the Thieves' Guild, who rifled the pockets of the dead and raced away at the wizard's approach.

Terrance, without even looking at his apprentice, reached out his hand and asked for lethe. Slowly, nervously, the boy approached his master.

Brenn knew it from talk and legend: the soft yellow fruit the size of a bean, tasting, they said, of honeyed apples. The lethe deadened the jaws and the roof of the mouth as you chewed and swallowed it, and Brenn had heard that the dullness passed through you and out of you until you felt like the king famous in legend for his golden touch—that the things you handled or even brushed against were somehow numbed in turn.

But more importantly, those things ceased to matter. The world around you receded and receded until it did not seem to exist at all. That is what the Goniph said, who had seen this stuff used to excess by small, hidden societies in the underworld of the city of Partha. Nasty stuff, he had told his apprentices, because aside from the oblivion it offered, the lethe was absolutely worthless, even damaging. You would yearn for the bliss of a painless stupor, and a hundred wrong things could happen while you lay about, and lolled, and forgot everything.

And yet when Terrance took the berries and handed them to a dying man sprawled in the midst of the dead ones, Brenn saw another use. The man took them gladly, ate of them, and smiled as his head sank to the hard stones of the street.

"Terrance?" Brenn began, his voice shaken and hushed by the sights and sounds about him. "I thought . . . Terrance, I thought you had brought me here to learn about healing."

Grimly the wizard looked at him, closing his fist around what remained of the lethe fruit. The man at his feet breathed deeply, unevenly. Now Brenn noticed the dark sores welling under the surface of the poor fellow's skin. No doubt they would erupt that afternoon.

Then it would not be long.

"Why, Brenn!" Terrance exclaimed quietly and ironically. "As we stand here, you are learning the greatest lesson of healing."

"But this lethe business and oblivion is only biding the time!" the boy urged, hoping that Terrance would do something—would lift the fevers or the sores, would turn back the Death and leave the man something more than these last sunlit hours of sleep and nothing.

Terrance moved on, however, administering lethe to yet

another—a woman holding a dead child in her arms. Then the wizard sat, propped his back against a building, drew himself into a ball, and rested his chin on his knees. His green eyes stared desolately across the bright street.

"There's nothing else?" Brenn asked in desperation, standing over him.

Terrance shook his head. "Not for those," he declared bitterly. "Not yet. Perhaps never."

The two of them walked up the rows of the dead, back toward the Street of the Bookbinders. Brenn was tempted to do what the Watchmen did, to bring out handkerchief and clove to sweeten the smell and taste of the air. Perhaps it would ward off the infection, for people said that the Death took wing when the victim died, that it soared invisibly through the air like a vulture or bat in search of new warmth and new life, and that only the sweet smell of spices could turn it away.

Then again, Terrance walked unmasked among these forsaken creatures. He breathed the air they breathed, touched them, and handed them the lethe. Sometimes he dropped the fruit directly into their mouths, his fingers brushing against their lips in the process.

And could that man's apprentice draw out handkerchief and clove, cower in charm and poem and warding? He wanted to.

Several of the suffering mumbled the plague chant as Brenn and Terrance passed. On their lips it sounded dry and harsh, but expectant with a sort of desperate joy.

> *"Physic himself must fade.*
> *All things to end are made,*
> *The plague full swift goes by;*
> *I am sick, I must die."*

Brenn wanted to cover his ears as he passed them. But that, too, seemed like a form of mask. So bravely he looked in their eyes and listened while his knees wavered and his heart raced away. He listened, then followed the wizard.

Terrance stopped for a moment beside a child—a girl of six or seven who sat among the dying. The wizard looked into her eyes, peered into her open mouth, felt her pulse.

"Thank the gods!" he breathed, and curious, Brenn drew nearer.

She was a small thing, and weak, but not yet taken with the final stages of the disease—the black boils and high fever and the hysteria that meant the end was approaching.

"Then physic will aid this one?" Brenn asked hopefully, forgetting his earlier squeamishness and fear as he crouched beside the sluggish child.

"Yes," Terrance observed, and Brenn thought that he gathered a note of dread in his master's voice. "Yes. This is the one to be healed."

And there on the street the wizard Terrance set his hand upon the brow of the little girl, and closed his eyes and thought of ice. Ice somewhere to the north. North of the Sea of Shadows, of the Mare Nostrum, north even of Europe and the places where the people herded reindeer and there was nothing but ice.

Then, the fever in the girl's blood subsiding, the old man thought of reversals. Of brown leaves rising like birds and alighting on branches, where they fixed themselves and greened before the startled eyes of young birds, which climbed back into nests and into eggshells. The sun moved overhead in his imaginings, coursing west to east, and the candles lengthened like shoots from impossible white plants. Terrance looked into the flames of those imagined candles. Looked and looked again, until he felt the burning in his hands.

With alarm Brenn saw the boils arise on his master's forearms, terrible black knots the size of thumbs. The wizard flushed and cried out, and the child in his arms broke into a sweat and began to sob. Gently, wearily, Terrance set the crying girl on a ragged blanket and, standing unsteadily, staggered onto the Street of the Bookbinders, where he sank to his knees and, with a sort of numb curiosity, held out his forearms and watched the boils shrink and fade.

"You've . . . you've done it, Terrance!" Brenn cried out jubilantly. "By the gods, you've saved that child and overcome the plague and now . . ."

"Now we go home," Terrance interrupted. He squinted, looked up into the afternoon sky. "I can't do any more, Brennart. I'm exhausted."

"You mean we must leave the rest of them?" Brenn gasped. "But, Terrance! There are hundreds of them and . . ."

"And one more like that one would kill me. That is, until I marshal my strength. Two weeks, perhaps. Maybe only ten days, if the food is good and I sleep well. Enough time for that very child to catch it again. Enough time for a hundred to die."

Brenn reeled at the prospect. Angrily kicking a stone up the street, he watched it clatter against an ox cart bulging with the weight of blanket-covered bodies. Sullenly he stood above the wizard, his thoughts muddled and feverish.

"Then we can do nothing more?"

"Nothing now," the wizard conceded. "Every now and then I can do this, but healing is the job of a king, after all."

"A king?" Brennart asked, helping the wizard to his feet.

"That very man who sits in Kestrel Tower," Terrance snapped. "Whose anointing gives him powers of restoration beyond those of man, physician, or wizard. You may ask what Dragmond does with that charge, but I'd be damned if I could tell you. He's afraid of the Death, I'd wager. I know that he's hemmed himself in with Watchmen and made sure that nobody with more than a head cold crosses over the causeway."

"The king is a bastard then," Brenn pronounced through clenched teeth. "A bastard unworthy of his crown. If I were king I'd be among 'em, and the touch of my hand would bring them peace."

"Oh, it's never that easy," Terrance corrected, grabbing the boy by the arm and turning him onto Cove Road and homeward. "Peace is like that heat mirage on the road ahead of us. Even for kings. But *intention* is the heart of peace."

Terrance turned to the boy, a melancholy look on his face.

"We fumble and stagger so much," he said, "that sometimes intention is everything."

So they went, wizard and apprentice, eastward toward home and safety and rest. Brenn thought of intentions, of Terrance's touch on the girl, of the thieves' gloved touch on the robes of the dead before wizard and healing arrived.

And Dame Sorrow arose from the rocks behind them, the dark cloak wavering in her bare and damaged hands.

‹‹‹ XV ›››

Brenn squinted and pondered above the scroll.

Sometimes the writing seemed to make sense—or almost to make sense. Spells and bodings and alchemical formulas seem to dance just on the edge of his understanding, and he was sure he could get to them if it wasn't for those damnably big words that all those ancient sorcerers and mages and alchemists were bent on using.

Sullen, the boy leaned against the hard back of his chair and looked across the solar to the hearthside, where Bracken lay spread-eagled on his back, snoring cheerfully and dreaming no doubt of grannars or cheese.

"You're lucky," Brenn muttered bitterly. "You can do *your* job without reading up for it."

Bracken paddled the air in his sleep and sneezed.

It was a February evening in the winter of Brenn's sixteenth year, and he felt farther from this magic business than he had that November night that seemed almost a century ago, when the green light had covered him and the library door wouldn't open. Everything seemed one step removed now, as though for a year and a half he had moved through this world in layers of thick mist. It was not just Faye and Dirk and the Goniph whom he missed, though he'd talked to none of them in over a year. But it was more that things weren't . . . working as Brenn expected they would.

His spells sputtered, his alchemy splashed and exploded, and he couldn't even forecast the weather, much less anything more personal. Healing, of course, was out of the question: Terrance would hardly trust a complete bumbler with such important duties.

Idly Brenn dipped his quill in the inkwell, his thoughts returning hauntingly to that time before all this foolishness commenced—when he was a happy-go-lucky thief with little to worry about beyond the complexities of a lock.

"And no philosophical double-talk!" he whispered passionately, dropping the quill on the oaken table. Bracken stirred by the fire and belched happily, and a scuffling sound in the darkest corner of the room, followed by a soft, high-pitched squeal and the sound of breaking glass, told Brenn that the house was still not free of the elves he had stirred up almost a year ago to the day.

"I have left fresh bread on the kitchen table," he said aloud, his eyes still fixed to the obscure words on the vellum. "Why don't you just take it now? I mean, we *all* know that no matter where I try to hide it, we'll end up with half of it for breakfast and the other half gnawed away overnight. Just take your share and leave us alone!"

"No, thank you. I'll gnaw away my part in the morning," a voice behind him replied merrily.

Terrance was standing in the doorway.

Of late the old man had taken to moving more quietly, more stealthily than Brenn had ever expected. At first it was downright bizarre: Brenn had found the old man sitting among jars on a pantry shelf, curled up peacefully in the notch of the guest-room tree, and lying back on this very table, staring up at the solar windows and chanting:

> *But living where the Sun*
> *Doth all things wake, and where all mix and tyre*
> *Themselves and others, I consent and run*
> *To ev'ry myre,*
> *And by this world's ill-guiding light*
> *Erre more than I can do by night.*

Brenn remembered all the words to that chant as though they had been burnt upon his skin. That night he had tried them out himself, alone on his rush mattress in the starlit attic, and nothing, of course, had happened.

Except that he still remembered them. That magic or no, they were words that stood for what he was passing through.

Terrance's sudden appearances had grown more and more unsettling. It was now as though the wizard was keeping track of him, sneaking about the house to watch him from every secret vantage point. *Wanting* to be discovered so that the times when he was not alert Brenn might think he was watching anyway.

Brenn hated it when Terrance did not trust him, especially when that mistrust made all the sense in the world. That is why he spoke harshly to the wizard who had appeared innocently but unexpectedly in the solar doorway.

"Damn it, Terrance! I'm liable to drop dead from the starts you give me! *Then* what would you do for a menial?"

Terrance's expression did not change. The peculiar half smile seemed fixed to his face as he entered the room. His eyes were as unreadable as the scroll in front of Brenn.

"Menial?" he asked. "Is that what you think you are around here? A menial?"

"Well, maybe not a *menial*, Terrance, but definitely not apprentice either. Perhaps 'employee' might be a nicer word."

"Like 'counselor' or 'enterpriser'? Those were the names we wanted to go by the first night we met—do you recall?"

"So?" Brenn asked defensively, leaning over the document in front of him as though he were protecting it from the wizard's eyes.

"As *I* recall," Terrance continued, "we haven't used those names since. It's the way we have between us, boy. We start with the rules and the niceties, and we end up honest."

"This is roundabout, Terrance. What are you driving at with all this summing up?"

"That it's time you should know a little more, lad. About Pytho in the belt of the Forest Lord. About candles by night and the doublings of watches by day. About . . . about your dangerous age."

Curious, Brenn turned from the table. The solar was silent. In the corner the elves ceased their quarreling, and Bracken rolled over on his side and hushed, eyes open and alert.

Even the fire ceased to snap and pop.

Terrance nodded, as sober as Brenn had ever seen him, even by Duval's scaffold or among the dead by the Boulevard of Waters.

"It is time you should know a little more," the wizard repeated, and seated himself across from Brenn at the oaken table.

"There was a time," the wizard began, leaning forward, framed by the firelight, "when I lived in Kestrel Tower myself.

"Oh, I was no . . . dignitary, mind you. Just a counselor—an instructor and tutor to the Crown Prince Aurum."

"Who later became King Aurum," Brenn said, watching Bracken turn peacefully at the fireside, his thick legs again churning. Dreaming of rabbits, no doubt, or something he ran to ground long ago, in a time when he could cross the floor of any house without feeling compelled to stop for food and a nap.

"Yes," Terrance snapped. "Don't interrupt. *And* pay attention."

Reluctantly Brenn looked into the eyes of the wizard. Who leaned back in his chair and continued.

"It was a good profession. Counseling, that is. Especially when your charge was a prince such as Aurum. A good-hearted lad, trusting and playful and not especially bright. Very much like Bracken over there and, unfortunately, about just as qualified to be king.

"But necessity and lineage would have it that way. Only legitimate child of the king and all. And somewhere in his possession, with all that good humor and inattention and leanings toward dice and women, there might have been the makings of a good monarch."

Terrance's face softened, saddened. Or so Brenn supposed. Perhaps it was only a trick of the light.

"Well, makings of a king or no makings, Brenn, we never had time to find out. But that part comes later. Let's say for now that he didn't incline much to scholarship, unlike his brother Dragmond."

"Brother? But I thought you said—"

"Don't interrupt," snapped the wizard. "Indeed, if you'll recall I said 'only *legitimate* child of the king.' Which is what Aurum was, all right. Heir to the throne of Palerna and all.

"But while the good Queen Elena was carrying the child, to the castle came the unsettling news that Myrra, a wealthy girl down on the Teal Front, was also pregnant by the king. Of course Albright denied it—it is the kind of rumor that now and again touches the monarchy, and almost everyone around me was sure that Myrra's family had put her up to the business.

"For I was in Albright's court even then," Terrance explained, reaching beneath the table and producing two glasses and an old leather-covered decanter. On that leather surface a map of the world was burnt. Brenn looked closely at it as the wizard poured a familiar amber liquid into both of the glasses: all the countries and provinces he knew were there, from native Palerna to Alanya, where Ricardo came from, and onward and farther away. For the first time he saw the boot of Italia descending into the Mare Nostrum as though a cavalry officer had stepped into the top of Europe and dropped through.

England was there, and France, and fabled Egypt. There was also Cathay, and Ultima Thule, where they nurse the infants on marrow in hanging cradles. There was also Tapobrane, home of the amphisbaena, and Eldorado far on the other side of the decanter. Brenn turned the bottle slowly in his hand, feeling the leather and the shape of the world.

"Enough of your pondering, lad!" Terrance snapped, and Brenn's thoughts tumbled back to the solar and the table and the slanted light. And the story the wizard was bent on telling, for the gods knew what veiled reason.

"As I was saying before you sailed away on your global adventure," Terrance resumed, "I was in the court of Albright when Elena was alive and before either of the sons. No more than a minor enchanter among many pedants and jugglers and hangers-on."

"I trust you were above their tricks and foolishness, though," Brenn observed, hiding a smile.

Terrance snorted. "No better than some," he confessed, holding a half-filled glass to the light. "But a damned sight better than most, I'll wager. And many of those others were intolerably loud for Albright to ignore the poor child Myrra.

"Now, she *did* come from a bad family. Wealthy but bad. Retemancers and tide readers and a cousin or two in the Assassins' Guild, back when that kind of thing still went on in Maraven."

"Still does, Terrance."

"I beg your pardon?" The wizard set down the glass.

"There's still an Assassins' Guild in Maraven," Brenn explained casually.

Terrance's eyes widened, and the boy laughed merrily.

"Come now, Terrance. You've taught me that just because you don't see something doesn't mean it isn't there."

"That's neither here nor there," the wizard sputtered. "It's enough to say that unfortunate little Myrra's family was not the kind of people to parley with kings, no matter how much wealth they had set aside.

"Natheless, Albright couldn't altogether *disown* the child she was carrying. He was shamefaced about it, but he admitted to all of us—Queen Elena included—that Myrra's child was his and, as such, would be brought to live in Kestrel Tower, to grow up side by side with the child Elena was carrying."

"I'll bet Queen Elena didn't like that news," Brenn observed innocently, his gaze back on the brown globe of the decanter. Terrance shot a quick glance at the boy, expecting irony or cruel humor in his face, but found none.

What a strange child, the wizard thought, peering over the glasses at the boy brought to him by fortune and design. *Knows so little of the heart, and yet I'm sure he could lead me straight into that den of assassins of which he talks so cheerily.*

Quietly he answered the boy.

"Queen Elena was . . . quite distraught at those ill tidings. Though I am sure it was not the news, but the events that followed that killed her."

"Killed?" Brenn leaned forward. He loved a good story with murk and conspiracy and possible homicides. Especially if there might be some truth in it.

Terrance leaned over the table, bringing his face within inches of Brenn's. The boy leaned back, put off by the wizard's caution and sense of the dramatic.

"I told you of Myrra's family," Terrance whispered. "The sorcerers and diviners and conjurors for generations back. You'd think they were Alanyans or Parthan mystics or Egyptians instead of home-grown Palernans, but there you have it. The worst of them was among the youngest: Myrra's sister Ravenna. Exquisite and brilliant, as though the gods had given her beauty and brains to make up for her complete and total lack of mercy and human kindness.''

"Ravenna? The same one who is mistress to the king?"

Terrance nodded grimly. "The same. And if anything, her evil has grown with her cleverness and with the passage of years.

"At that time, though, she was less subtle. Within weeks of the birth of Elena's child, a dozen ravens perched atop Kestrel Tower—one for each region of the stars, the diviners claimed. I remember the birds clearly: unnaturally large they were, with wingspans as wide as a man's full reach. They glittered blue-black with that eerie metallic blackness that you usually find only in enameled ebony or on the backs of insects. They would catch you with a tilt of the head and the sidelong glance of a bird that seems to dart right through you, and all of a sudden you would feel a wrenching in your bowels—mostly just uncomfortable, but sometimes downright painful.

"Once a guard tried to startle the birds, to frighten them away. They found his body in the Kestrel gardens, where even the thick vines and shrubberies could not break his fall from the top of the tower. A gardener saw it all, claimed that one of the birds simply . . . *stared* the man over the precipice, if you can imagine that.

"After the guardsman's death it became difficult to ignore the ravens. The birds took to perching at the sills of the queen's chambers, beating their enormous wings against the windows and startling Elena and her ladies in waiting. Finally one of the ravens hurled itself at the window, breaking through the expensive glass and the lead, then flapping insanely through the rooms of the chambers and out the very way it had entered, leaving chaos and terror behind it.

"Ravenna was after Queen Elena's child, though she claimed years later she had nothing to do with the birds. It was no accident that the visitors were ravens, and I am sure she knew that nobody—nobody, that is, except for Aurum, when he heard the story years later—believed her innocence."

"Why would she do that?" Brenn asked. "I mean, so obviously? Almost all the genuine crime I know takes place in whispers and under cloaks. Ravenna and ravens—it takes no philosopher to see *those* connections. The bird is even on her sails when she rides on Lake Teal, for the gods' sake!''

"Perhaps . . ." Terrance ventured, "she wanted us all to see her failure.''

Brenn frowned. ''I don't understand.''

Terrance smiled. ''You wouldn't. For an aspiring thief, you have a way to go in the realm of guile.''

Bracken stirred and whined, then stirred again and slumbered. Brenn marveled at how quiet it was outside the window. Even the rush of the tide onto the shore was muffled, as if someone had picked up the wizard's tower and moved it far inland.

''You're as green among deceivers as Aurum was, lad,'' Terrance said. And then, mysteriously: ''And no wonder.''

Brenn frowned again, but Terrance was back on the story.

''Suppose this. Suppose that Ravenna wanted us all to see her plots against Elena and the unborn child, so that when the plot failed or seemed to fail, we would all think she was done with it. Thinking, no doubt, that the combined strength of Albright's alchemists and bards and wizards and diviners had been too much for the sorceress from the Teal Front, that after one brief, dramatic attempt at the child she had given up. For the good may be complex or simple, but evil is always complex, approaching its desire down side roads and through tunnels. Imagine this, if you will.''

Brenn leaned back in his chair. Over the past year and three months, he had become quite skilled at imagining.

''This was . . . oh, forty years ago. Back then, the town of Maraven knew nothing of the plague but by hearsay. We'd heard of it in Italy and in France. Rumors had reached us of its spread into easternmost Alanya at the port of Rabia. But so far there had been no incidents in Palerna or Aquila—we thought our region was safe.

''Natheless, the physicians and scholars mulled over it long and hard. They consulted the auguries and the astrolabe. Some blamed it on celestial will, others on national destiny.''

Terrance smiled, picking up the glass again, this time by its stem. He swirled its amber contents until a drop or two tumbled over the lip of the glass and onto the table, where it rested and shimmered, catching the firelight.

"Fortunately," Terrance observed, "there were some of us who relied less on the flight patterns of birds than we did on accounts from plague-infested regions.

"What we discovered was this: the Death gained its footing in the port towns, in Marseille and Genoa and Rabia. And though we knew no more then—indeed, know no more now—as to the form it takes when it comes into port, we did know that into port was where it came.

"Which was why no foreign sailor was allowed to disembark, and the ships from the known plague-ridden regions were forced to anchor out of harbor and their goods were brought in by Maravenian fishing boats.

"It was the oddest sight when that happened, Brenn: our sailors wrapped like preserved Egyptians in thick, camphor-smelling cloth, and the smudge pots smoking on the decks of their boats to ward off the Death if the Death came by air. It was like something out of a legend, that flotilla setting out from shore, the white, mummied men on board dwindling and dwindling into the distance and the smoke. They would come back later, their boats heavily laden, and for a fortnight each would sit in a quarantine—crouched wide-eyed under torchlight in the old Gaunt Warehouse in Grospoint—waiting for the fevers and the boils and the nausea. But the Death never came, Brenn. It never came.

"Not, that is, until the women were confined."

Terrance stopped again, his eyes focused on the solar windows. Outside a cloud passed overhead, and for a moment the windows faded into the walls as the shadow overtook them. Brenn followed the wizard's gaze, his eyes resting on the andiron-sized hole in the middle window, still unattended though the elf who had done the damage had long since been deposited on the black sands of the cove. Terrance sighed and continued.

"Indeed, Ravenna left town but a month before the birth of the baby Aurum. She dropped from sight, which naturally made Albright's advisors terribly nervous and uneasy. For she could have been anywhere, hiring assassins or raising an army, or conjuring up a new menace for the queen and her unborn child.

"Then, on a starry May night not unlike many others—perhaps a bit clearer, a bit starrier—Queen Elena went into labor, and those in Kestrel Tower settled back for the arrival of the next King or Queen of Palerna. It was not all celebration, though: the midwives were saying that the birth promised to be a difficult one.

"It was then that they spotted Ravenna once more, a passenger in a coach racing westward from Stormpoint toward the city. The lookouts knew her by the crest on the door of the carriage —black raven on a field argent, as the heralds say. Through the East Gate she rushed, no doubt by this very tower, the coach trembling and rattling as it took the bends in Cove Road at dangerous speed. I have heard that she lost a footman when the coach sideswiped an apple vendor's empty cart left by the roadside for the night. The man somersaulted into a storefront and broke his back. They found him dead the next morning.

"The Watch on duty stopped the coach at the southern end of the causeway, as they stopped any coach from crossing on any night. This time, of course, they were more firm, for they knew the crest.

"I don't recall many of the particulars. All three were younger guards—one, if I recall correctly, scarcely a year in King Albright's service. It was this one who stepped past the foaming black horses, parted the curtains on the coach window, and, looking into the dark interior, saw the white skin flashing and the black hair glimmer. Saw Ravenna's bright eyes and heard that melodic voice—low, breathy, and sinuous.

" 'I have traveled four nights without rest bearing a gift for the child,' she announced, and the young guard recoiled. He told me later—that July, I believe it was, or not long before he was taken ill—that it was something in the air of the coach that unsettled him, something poised and malicious and hotly attentive, which smelled of spice and faintly of the sea, but beneath that something dark and soured that made him step back. He would have stepped too far away, he claimed, and Ravenna might have passed through and on to Kestrel Tower, where she could have conjured up the gods know what to gain entry.

"But her horses were ruined, having traveled from Stormpoint at a gallop, and the quick soothing hands of the other two Watchmen held them back. Ravenna's coachman, a man dressed in a sickly, bandaged white robe, lashed out with a whip at one of the Watch, but the brave man ignored the sting of the leather thong, grabbed it, and pulled the coachman down to the cobbled causeway.

" 'I expect the queen ain't holding audience,' he pronounced, 'being near birthin' and all.' From within the coach there came a hissing sound, a seething of a hundred snakes or of a fiery hot brand being immersed in water.

" 'Tell her, then, that the Lady Ravenna sends regards from far-off Rabia and also from Her Majesty's own doorstep,' the dark woman said. Slowly and painfully, her coachman ascended to the driver's seat, and with the horses staggering, blowing, he turned the vehicle around and headed south toward the Teal Front and home.

"My young witness claimed that the high laughter that came from the coach interior was barely human, rising in shrillness and desolation until it became almost a shriek, lingering in the unclean, spice-smelling air for a long time after the coach passed from sight."

Terrance paused, looked pensively into the firelight. Bracken rose and rumbled, then trotted out of the solar toward the kitchen, his claws clicking on the wooden floor.

"That's . . . quite a story, sir. Raises the hair on my neck just to hear it, and I don't expect from the point you've left off that it's even halfway over."

Terrance smiled and nodded. "Not even half," he murmured in agreement.

"And on some other night I should dearly like to hear the end of it," Brenn said politely. "But not this night, unless we really must. The story has nothing to do with why I'm so miserable at magic and conjury—at anything out of the ordinary I try. Indeed, the story doesn't have much to do with me at all. I'm tired— tired of the hour and the long day of chores and of studies that get me absolutely nowhere. If it's not too rude, I'd as soon climb the steps to my attic and to my bed."

"Not yet," Terrance insisted, a strange, urgent note of command in his voice. "Not until you hear just a little more. For the story has more to do with you than you could ever suppose.

"You see, Brenn," Terrance said, pausing dramatically and leaning forward, his white hair brilliant in the dying firelight. "That boy King Albright and Queen Elena awaited in the heights of Kestrel Tower on the starry May night when Ravenna rode south through Maraven laughing and plotting her terrible revenge—that child, Prince Aurum . . . was your father."

⋘ XVI ⋙

Brenn swallowed hard.

"My father?" he asked, expecting the wizard to laugh, or that the whole situation—the firelight, the story, Terrance seated across from him at the table—would vanish in a moment and he would find himself upstairs, groggy, lying on the rush mattress and looking up at the stars through the trapdoor in the ceiling . . . and yet he knew it was no joke, no dream. Something deep in him—beneath words, beneath thoughts, as hard to pin down as quicksilver under his finger—told him it was the truth.

Throughout his rough and comfortless childhood, Brenn had felt that somehow he was . . . more than what he seemed to be. That the calling of thievery that fit so many so well seemed like a borrowed cloak on his shoulders. Once he had confided this to Faye, one time when they huddled together in a half-assembled hull in South Ships, waiting for the Watch to pass. Brenn told her of his feeling that he was born to historic things, and she listened—seriously, he thought. And when he was through she nodded, as though she had taken every word into account, and her brilliant smile flashed through the shadows cast by the skeletal ship.

"Yes, Brenn, you were born to better things," she whispered. "And I . . . well, I reckon I'm Queen of Palerna!"

They had both laughed softly, crouched there in rags and lampblack.

Yet he had always felt as though he were waiting for the words he had heard this very night. That in some way, someone older and wiser and no doubt smarter would come along and show him how he fit in some grand and important story. At times he had believed it so strongly that Terrance's words would not have surprised him at all.

This, however, was not one of those times. He swallowed hard again and looked up at the wizard.

"If . . . if what you are saying is so, sir . . . Tell me . . . tell me about my father."

Terrance turned in his chair. Brenn saw him now in profile, framed in the brown-orange light of the low fire.

"I knew Aurum as well as any of them, lad," the wizard explained. "Knew him indeed from the moment he squalled out his first breath, when the physician slapped him and the midwife turned desperately to try to save his mother, who was not long in the leaving."

"You mean Queen Elena . . ."

"Died in childbed," Terrance confirmed, his eyes still fixed on something deep in the shadows of the room. "And they brought in the wet nurse nearly at once, and opened the windows to the chambers. It was as though the thought of Elena vanished from the earth with her last breath."

Brenn's thoughts turned sadly to the grandmother he never knew. He would have thought such of thieves—indeed, he had seen such things happen underneath Wall Town in the honeycombed lair of the guild, especially when the child in question was a boy.

Somehow, though, he had thought the royal family would have behaved otherwise. More kindly, perhaps, or with more ceremony. Especially now, when he had discovered his own noble blood.

"Do not think harshly of Albright, lad," Terrance corrected. "There is no way we can know what went on in his thoughts and his heart, on that night or on any night that followed. The gods know he was never the same: quiet, his sorrows hidden in his duty like a bird hides its head beneath its wing at night. Perhaps he considered the death of Elena a punishment for his own . . . indiscretions. Who knows?

"At any rate, Albright never remarried: that is certain. Nor was he cold by nature, for he treated both boys with respect and compassion and downright warmth.''

"Both?" Brenn asked. Then quickly it occurred to him. "Oh, yes. Dragmond."

Terrance nodded. "And I suppose you see how Dragmond fits into the story."

"Myrra's child?" Brenn asked, and the wizard nodded again.

"Born scarcely a week after Elena's funeral. The last of the guests had scarcely left Kestrel Tower, and we had only begun the process of returning the realm to business as usual.

"A raven brought the message. With a rolled scrap of parchment tied to its leg, the bird soared through the open windows of Elena's chambers, startling two of the maids who were about the sad business of gathering the dead queen's belongings. Your grandfather was in the nursery, sitting in melancholy watch over your sleeping father, when the news came from upstairs that bats and dragons had invaded the topmost floors of the tower."

"Bats and dragons?"

Terrance smiled. "Made us all laugh in that gloomiest of times. One of the maids was Alanyan, you see, and subject to prophecy.

"Only three weeks before she had been cleaning fish in the kitchen, and had seen in the entrails of a haddock ominous signs that Maraven would be invaded. The servants' quarters—or at least the Parthans and Alanyans among them—had sent up alarms and had taken to hiding the silver and stockpiling foods in preparation for siege. Finally your grandfather had to gather together his entire staff and tell them in the most forceful of terms that no invader, neither by land nor sea, could enter Palerna, much less Maraven, without his knowing.

"He soothed the servants with that lecture. Soothed us all. Which is why we were even more shocked to discover he was wrong.''

"Maraven was invaded?" Brenn asked, leaning forward intently. "'Tis a story I've never heard."

"Invaded in a way," Terrance explained. "Listen." Turning his eyes back to Brenn, he continued the tale.

"The note tied to the leg of the raven said simply that Myrra's child had been born. No mention of when, of the gender of the child, nor of its health or its mother's condition. I was with the king when he received the note. He took it and read it, then turned the parchment over in his hand and looked at the other side, as though somewhere upon it more words were encoded, or as though the watermark of the parchment hid some clue of the message's design and meaning.

"We stood there together for minutes that ran into centuries. Then he asked me to summon his other two advisors, and for the three of us to meet him in the throne room at once."

Terrance sighed.

"Miloud the alchemist, Katriel the bard—neither of them long for the world. I was the youngest of the three. When we were assembled, King Albright told us the strange, murky tale of Myrra and Dragmond. Told us the story, and called for our advice."

"It had been an evening's boating on Lake Teal. Wine and music and fireworks flashing over the waters and the edge of the Corbinwood beyond.

"Old Gauderic, Myrra's father, was nobody's darling, that was certain. He claimed to be a spicer and nothing but a spicer—his ships back and forth from Calse and Random, and from the more exotic Indies. Albright had it on good authority that spice was not the half of the old man's wares—that many darker things such as acumen and nepenthe and weapons and even slaves found their way into his holds.

"Whatever it was, old Gauderic had money and power, and Albright always said that under some circumstances one must dine with the king of assassins or the Atheling of Zephyr. We were never told what those circumstances were, though you can believe that Albright compromised not a thing. He would never have granted anything to a man of Gauderic's notoriety simply as gratitude for dinner and wine.

"Whatever the circumstances, the night was whiled away in banqueting and bargaining, old Gauderic promising a hundred things for the king's special favors, that Albright might look the other way when the wagons came up Hadrach Road, heavy with poisons and nepenthe. And the last thing he promised was his daughter Ravenna."

"Ravenna?" Brenn asked. "But I thought—"

"And thought correctly, no doubt," Terrance said. "That night beneath a hundred paper lanterns and a hundred mirrored ornaments catching and fracturing the lamplight on Gauderic's barge, the old criminal said to the king, 'Take Ravenna, for a year or a season or a night. She makes your dreams possible.' And the dark girl danced on board in a strange, submerged light.

"No doubt King Albright was tired, and no doubt the wine had taken its effect. No doubt the number of lanterns and mirrors doubled and tripled in the nodding hours of early morning, because Albright claimed he remembered nothing after the night turned."

"Wait," Brenn interrupted. "Where were the Watchmen?"

"On watch. Where else?" Terrance smiled ironically. "At one minute they stood on the decks of the barge, no doubt enjoying the music and the smells of incense and the merchant's daughter dancing to the sound of the Umbrian flute and the drum and the last thing they remembered was the music and midnight approaching, red Panthera floating above them in the Sign of Labyrinthus and the moon only a sliver over the Corbinwood. And then . . . then it was daylight, the sun two hours up, and all of them still at their posts, blinking stupidly at one another, and the king nowhere to be found.

"Of course, Albright was below deck. He awoke from fitful sleep, finding himself lying on a bed prepared weeks before by the plotting Gauderic, his naked limbs entwined with those of the dark Myrra, Gauderic's youngest daughter. Her hair, shimmering like black silk in the fragrant light of the pluvian candles, was draped over his neck, and somewhere above him, the king heard the soft music of Alanyan fertility lutes."

Brenn flushed. Somehow imagining the scene seemed like trespassing, Albright being his newfound grandfather. He changed the subject.

"Why—why not Ravenna, Terrance? Why wasn't Ravenna in the bed with him, like Gauderic had promised?"

"You would have to ask her," Terrance claimed. "I have thought of a dozen reasons, none of which ever quite explained it to my satisfaction. It remains as mysterious as Albright's agreement to the whole messy business of that evening, out of which only one thing definite came—the child Dragmond.''

Terrance stood and walked to the fire. Carefully he laid two small logs on the low flame, which rose and growled over the fresh dry wood.

"As I said, it was forty years ago," the wizard said, his white beard glowing in the renewed firelight. "I am not altogether sure I remember the details of that night. I am old, it was long ago, and it was wild with illusions to begin with."

Brenn did not believe him. He was sure that Terrance was holding something back. He had seen that look too often on the faces of new gamblers trying desperately to hide the fact that they had been dealt a wonderful or terrible hand of cards. Terrance was good enough at this game that Brenn could not tell whether the hand in question was good or ill.

Or perhaps Terrance was not sure himself.

Whatever the case, the wizard had guesses as to the mystery and perhaps more than guesses, but he was silent for now.

"The child came not long after Ravenna's message," Terrance said. "Ravenna herself brought the baby, whose mother had died of the plague. For Myrra, you see, was the Death's first victim in Maraven."

"The first?" Brenn asked incredulously. "How do you know?"

"I have heard of no others before her," Terrance declared flatly. "And it would make sense, anyway, for I am sure that Ravenna brought the plague to our city."

A long silence filled the solar, into which Bracken walked lazily, carrying some table scrap in his mouth and muttering contentedly as he circled in front of the fire and settled down to sleep.

"You can't be sure of that, Terrance," Brenn said, aghast at the wizard's monstrous accusation. "I can see that you hate the woman, and I can see that you'll put nothing past her malice and her hatred. But you can't be sure she brought the plague here. Surely it would have taken *her* among its first victims if she set about to carry it. But whatever the case, nobody knows—not even the physicians—how the Death travels."

"I cannot prove it, Brenn," Terrance conceded. "And perhaps I never shall. But I know it as surely as the pattern of the tides or that the cry of a gull somewhere out on the foggy morning sea means that there is a gull out there somewhere. It is as simple and obvious as that."

"Then set about to prove it!" Brenn said eagerly. "Take your proof to Dragmond. The plague is his chief worry as king—everyone says he's done nothing about it, and they say it's made his throne uneasy. Surely if he knew—"

Terrance waved his long, gnarled hand.

"You don't understand, lad. First of all, I have no inarguable evidence. And even if I did . . . well, you don't understand."

Brenn snorted and leaned back in his chair. Over by the fireplace, Terrance bent down, ran an absent hand over the back of Bracken's head, and rose again stiffly, his eyes on the solar window.

"Albright had no choice but to acknowledge Dragmond. The king was too honorable and much too just to do otherwise. And I do think he even came to love his bastard son, though that was hardly an easy task.

"Dragmond was already his name, even before the king had seen him. 'World of the dragon,' or 'World of the snake,' the name meant, depending on whom you asked or who translated. Not an inviting name for your second son. And second son the boy was, growing up side by side with Prince Aurum, only a month his junior. 'The young prince,' he was called by the servants, no doubt instead of less polite names that occurred to them.

"When the boys were of age, I was supposed to become tutor to them both, but Ravenna raged and furied until she was given sole charge of her nephew. It was odd to take the crown prince through his lessons, while up the hall in the chambers of the young prince, incense smoke rose from under the doors, and the sound of the flute, and readings in Parthan and in more exotic tongues. And the cries of animals."

"Sounds like necromancy," Brenn observed.

Terrance chuckled. "What would you know of necromancy, lad?" Then, more seriously, "However it was that Ravenna taught the young prince, it seemed to work. Dragmond was a quicker study than your father, more apt toward books and broadsword, a better horseman, and far more skilled at games of chess and chance.''

"What remained, then, to Aur—to my father?" Brenn asked uncomfortably. "How did he show worthiness for the crown?"

"By accidents of birth, mainly," Terrance replied bluntly, his beard billowing between his fingers as he rested his chin in his hands. "He was a month the senior and on the right side of the sheets.''

There was another long silence, in which Terrance stared intently at his uncomfortable apprentice.

"That isn't good enough for you, is it?" he asked, and slowly Brenn shook his head.

"I suppose that since I've just now found my father," the boy said, "I'd have liked him to be more . . . excellent in one thing or another. And it isn't just that, Terrance. If Dragmond was all that much better than Aurum, Aurum's being king first . . . well, father or no father, it just doesn't seem fair.''

"The very thought that occurred to Aurum," Terrance said with a smile. "Time and again he would ponder it, each time Dragmond bested him at archery or dice, or in the translation of Old Umbrian tablets—for like yourself, Prince Aurum was not the quickest and most skillful with philosophy and literature.''

Brenn lowered his eyes and nodded.

"He pondered it constantly anon," Terrance continued, "and oft he asked me if it would be fitting for him to step aside when the time came, to hand over the crown to Dragmond, who would no doubt wear it with more talent and ability. I don't think he ever understood that the very impulse that led him to that thought was what made him a better king than Dragmond could ever have imagined being, or than Ravenna could have imagined for him.

"For you see, fairness was an idea beyond Dragmond's understanding. As were sympathy and compassion and even justice. It seemed when that woman trained his body and his mind she had taken his heart as her payment. Had Dragmond been the crown prince, and Aurum a month and a law shy of inheritance,

Dragmond would never have given his brother a thought—indeed, when he came to the throne, he would have seen to it that Aurum was out of the way, quickly and finally.''

''I don't understand,'' Brenn said, and Terrance nodded wearily.

''It's compassion, lad. It's as simple as that. Do you remember my telling you that it lay within Dragmond's power as king to heal the whole lot of those plague victims in Wall Town? Ten for every one a humble wizard could bring back—that's what he could do, if his mind and heart were set to the task. Someone will say this centuries from now, when this occurs again, as it will always occur again and need to be said.''

Terrance closed his eyes, intoned:

''How small, of all that human hearts endure,
That part which laws or kings can cause or cure!

''But Dragmond would have done that part, had he cared a whit for the people he ruled,'' the wizard concluded. ''Instead, you have seen the Watch on the causeway, armed with crossbow and pike. The world will end before Dragmond heals one of those poor souls. Had Aurum been king, he would have been down among them every day, taking on their fever and boils and their heaviness of heart.

''Albright was two years dead,'' Terrance continued, ''and your father was two years king, of course. He had put down one rebellion from Dragmond early on—or General Helmar had done the job for him, true to his promise to Albright that whatever the circumstances, his loyalty would remain constant to the throne of Palerna. Lesser men would have hanged the rebel from a gibbet on the causeway, but your father was not a lesser man: he welcomed the traitor back into his castle, confident that kindness would win him over.''

''Why, that seems like suicide!'' Brenn exclaimed.

''Indeed, it almost was. In fact, it might well have been. But it was your father's way—compassion to its uttermost. For that was Aurum's greatest virtue—his capacity for kindness. Why, he even showed it in his womanizing!''

Terrance frowned at Brenn. "Nor should you judge him for that, lad. That's the very way you came into being."

"So I had figured," Brenn said. "Go on."

The wizard settled back into his chair, eyes on the ceiling as he remembered.

"Ravenna and Dragmond nearly drove me crazy with demands and with slander. I announced to Aurum that enough was enough, that I would set in motion the long spell that would turn them both into fiddler crabs—just punishment, I thought, for fiddling with the politics of the realm.

"Aurum only laughed at the notion. As king, he could command me, and he did so, telling me that not a hair on the head of either nuisance should be transformed or otherwise harmed. Nor did he ever believe that the crenels and gargoyles that fell from the tower stonework, narrowly missing him time and again, were anything more than the architecture wearing out, and that all those arrows sailing through the windows of the king's private chambers were misfired from the archery range some two hundred feet below."

"I think my father passed straight from trust into foolishness," Brenn observed. "But you were going to tell me how I came about."

"Indeed," Terrance replied. "I am coming to that. You have waited a long time to hear this story. Abide with me a few minutes more: it is late, and I shall be brief.

"Though he acted on trust, there was an instinct below trust that protected the young King Aurum. At night he took to wandering, took to . . . various liaisons. On some level he knew that the castle was no longer safe, despite all claims that Dragmond and Ravenna meant him no harm.

"Yet it was not only an instinct for survival that propelled him out into the streets of the city at night, recklessly in search of trysts and rendezvous with dozens of Maravenian girls. If it had been survival alone, he would have never come to Wall Town, where he and your mother were on the night you were conceived."

Brenn nodded, eager for this part of the story to be over. Though he barely remembered his mother and had known his father not at all, there was something he felt he should not know about this, something too intimate, almost . . . bridal in this midnight meeting of father and mother. Terrance sensed the boy's discomfort and was mercifully brief.

"So you came to pass, lad. The fruit of a night's romp in Wall Town. It's nothing to be ashamed of: I would imagine there was great sport and enjoyment at your conception, which is more than many a lawful child could say. And what is more, it puts you in line for the Crown of Palerna."

Brenn crowed aloud at the notion. He closed his eyes and imagined himself crowned and sceptered, seated awkwardly on a sapphire throne, a huge and wondrous map of Palerna spread under his feet like a rug. Ministers attended him, courtiers carried shoes in on pillows—a different pair for each room—and a trio of incomparably beautiful young women fanned him with ostrich feathers, fed him grapes and cheeses, and poured a glistening red wine for him into a faceted crystal cup.

It was all too ridiculous. Brenn laughed again and opened his eyes, only to look straight into the serious face of the wizard.

"W-wait . . ." he said, his laughter dying abruptly. "You are entirely serious about this, aren't you, Terrance?"

"Entirely," Terrance said. "Not long after the last night he spent with your mother, Aurum left the city for the west and the Gray Strand in an attempt to firm up his claim on the region. Old Macaire, the Count of West Aldor, was raiding all along the south coast of the Gray Sea, and there was talk that many a peasant had allied with him out of fear.

"The struggle did not take long. Helmar commanded one wing of your father's army, and Dragmond the other. Together in a masterpiece of Helmar's tactics, they trapped the main body of Macaire's cavalry between them and, though the casualties were great, destroyed the Zephyrians to a man. You have heard the rest: how on the brink of his greatest victory the young king was carried off by harpies, never to be seen again, and there on the battlefield, the severed head of the Zephyrian Macaire lying at his feet, Dragmond picked up the crown of his half brother, dropped from a terrible height onto the black sands of the coastline, and placed that crown on his head. And perhaps you have heard how, strangely, as though Ravenna had foreseen it all, the air above Kestrel Tower burst and sparkled with fireworks from the moment that Dragmond crowned himself on into the depth of that historic night.''

Brenn nodded. ''Everyone's heard that story, Terrance. But this inheritance talk has gone far enough, I believe. I'm no more a king than . . . than *Bracken* over there.''

He gestured to the dog who, hearing his name, looked up from his comfortable spot by the fire and belched.

''On the contrary, Brennart,'' the wizard replied. ''You are every bit a king because you are in line for it. That, my lad, is the single and formidable fact. It is your duty to take the crown. Your time of freedom and choosing is nearly over.''

''But—'' Brenn started to protest, but Terrance shook his head and pushed one of the filled glasses toward the boy.

''Lethe water,'' the wizard explained. ''From this night on, your dreams are dangerous.''

Unceremoniously Terrance drained the other glass and stood from the table.

''Drink that,'' he said, and to Brenn it no longer seemed altogether that much of an order—more like a suggestion, or perhaps even a request. ''Drink it, and sleep well. You shall hear more of this tomorrow.''

''One more thing, Terrance. How did you know?'' Brenn asked. ''I mean, how did you know I was the one in the first place? If what you are saying is true, then King Aurum might well have had a dozen offspring, each of which could serve as well—''

''But none with your touch, lad,'' Terrance interrupted, standing above the boy. ''None with the power in your hands. And your eyes.''

Somehow Brenn knew the wizard was not talking about thievery. Slowly, as if this moment had been written down long before and the two of them only now playing out the words and the movements, he extended his hands toward Terrance.

''Show me,'' Brenn urged, surprised at the note of command in his own voice. Terrance took Brenn's left hand and held it, palm up, in the dim light of the solar. Quickly the wizard passed his own hand over it, and suddenly a long blue scar began to glow on the boy's index finger.

It was shaped like a sword or a dagger, pointing toward his palm, his wrist, his heart.

"It itches when it rains," Brenn said quietly, his thought chaotic, confused.

"Aurum complained of the same malady," Terrance said, smiling. "And Albright before him. And I have heard that Albright's father did, as well. That's how the king knows the weather in Palerna."

"And why the fishermen blame the monarch if a sudden storm catches them out at sea?" Brenn asked, and smiled when Terrance nodded. "I always thought that was a folk tale."

"It is," Terrance pronounced. "It is also true." He yawned and stretched.

"The eyes, Terrance," Brenn whispered. "What's this about my eyes?"

"The eyes that can read the Leaves of Morrigan," the wizard intoned, his sharp features shadowy in the faint light of the candle.

"Leaves of Morrigan? What are they?"

"They are the key to this whole muddled business," the wizard answered sadly. "And I do not know what they are."

A grannar slipped from the white swirl of his beard and dropped clumsily to the table, where it scrambled to its feet, then stood on its haunches, sniffing the air with alert and alarmed curiosity. Then like something propelled in a high wind, it shot off the table and into the darkness, leaving the two of them— master and apprentice—facing each other over candlelight.

"Drink it," Terrance said again, and turned, and walked out of the room. Brenn stared into the palm of his hand, then shifted his gaze and regarded the glass for a long time. He wished he could set it aside—the glass, that is, though possibly the scar, too. However, he figured that to do so would no doubt be foolish. Slowly, reluctantly, he picked up the glass and drank its amber contents, then sat by the fire in wonderment and confusion.

He was only beginning to believe the wizard's story by the time sleep caught up with him. Terrance found the boy facedown on the solar table early the next morning, snoring blissfully after a long, dreamless night.

⊰⊰⊰ XVII ⊱⊱⊱

He drank a glass of the lethe the next night, then another on the night that followed. During the days all study of magic was suspended, as Terrance told the boy how the shape of his duties had changed. No longer was he expected to conjure or concoct or even to read about such things, not that Terrance had ever seemed to expect much magical or scholarly from him in the first place.

Instead, if anything, it was worse.

Now, all of a sudden, the days became packed with history and politics, geography and statecraft—everything from books and from books about books, until Brennart practically reeled at the prospects of more study. He sat moping over scrolls in the library, books in the solar, volumes in the kitchen, and a folio or two reserved in the attic before bedtime. Within a week he decided that another invasion of elves would be welcome, or even an explosion or two—anything to add excitement to all this infernal reading.

Throughout the next three weeks, Terrance hovered over the boy. At times Brenn would be reading something long and terribly boring about the sewer system of Maraven, and a shadow would pass over the page. Then a long, bony hand would descend from above him, and a finger would point to an obscure or difficult word on the page.

"The word is 'conduit,' " Terrance would say. Or " 'sicario': it's a warm-water lizard that winters in the more recessed tunnels. Large ones are man-eaters."

Brenn remembered bits and snatches of the more glamorous and gory subjects. But engineering eluded him, as did diplomacy and especially military strategy. When Terrance would set beans and pebbles on the solar table to map out the campaigns of Alexander or Caesar or Armel of Umbria, or even the more recent campaigns of General Helmar, Brenn would become dizzy and hot, platoons and flank maneuvers and supply routes blending in his mind like so much ink on a page.

All those people, their lives in the hands of generals. It made him sick to imagine.

It had been so simple not so long ago, when he had been only the hands of the operation. The most intricate lock was easy when you knew that it was your job and your job alone to open it, and you didn't have to worry about another thing. It could be tumblers, latches, even the door of one of those places in Wall Town where poisonous needles were part of the system of locks—whatever it was, it was honestly easy when nothing but the lock mattered, nothing but getting in and out.

"I was good at in and out," Brenn said softly to himself, sitting in the library, reading again his writ of apprenticeship beneath a dim hurricane lamp. It was getting on to midnight and Terrance had long since retired.

Tomorrow was geography of trade routes, basic economics, and again the hated military strategy. As if to mock him, clause sixteen of the writ now read:

> *The aforesaid apprentice will pursue all studies, whether magical or nonmagical, with diligence and enthusiasm. So be it for military science, too.*

"But I guess those days are over," he repeated, rolling up the scroll and putting it in his pocket. Rubbing his eyes wearily, he looked to the base of the lamp, where the nightly glass of lethe water sat. "Being a king seems to mean that you're in for good."

Suddenly there was a noise from the solar—the sound of breaking glass. Brenn dashed to the library fireplace, picked up the poker damaged that eventful night six seasons ago, and scrambled out into the hallway.

"Elves again, damn it!" he muttered. "I'm never going to live down that conjury!"

Quickly he moved through the corridor and into the solar, where the scene in front of him was hardly what he expected. Terrance's chair lay capsized by the mahogany table, in the center of a pile of broken glass. A fist-sized stone rested on the chair back, a white scrap of paper tied to it with string. The firelight glinted off the glass on the floor, as though someone had crept in and strewn diamonds among the rushes.

"Damn!" Brenn exclaimed again. "Can't keep the little monsters away from the windows!"

But it was not elves, of course, as the boy found out. Brenn rushed to the chair, picked up the paper, detached it from the string and stone, and began to read.

> *Brenn,*
>
> *We know you got good werke here wyth the wizzard, but we need you in Wall Town. The Watch hath took Faye and put her in the gaol. Tha saye she is dangerouse age.*
>
> *Squab*

Leaping onto the solar table, Brenn stood on tiptoe and looked out the hole in the window. Cove Road was deserted: for as far as he could see toward town, practically to where the squat buildings of the slaughterhouses stood black against the horizon, nothing moved on the street.

Sitting on the table, Brenn read the scrawled note again in disbelief. He took it to the fireside and read it a third time, his back to the hearth and the full light of the flames resting on the scrawled, scarcely literate letters of his old comrade.

"Squab's writing, of a certain," Brenn said to the approaching Bracken, whose curiosity had roused him from sleep and sent him waddling out of the kitchen to the source of the noise and commotion. "Such as it be."

Bracken snorted, sniffed at the broken glass, and backed away.

Brenn walked briskly to the door of the solar and grabbed his cloak off a peg. It was March now, and getting on toward spring, but the nights were still brisk in Maraven, and he'd be needing something warm on his shoulders.

Carefully, quietly, so as not to wake his master, the boy climbed onto the solar table and reached for the bottom pane of the center window—once broken by an elf-hurled andiron and now broken again by the rock Squab had hurled.

Dropping the note and slipping the poker into his belt, where it hung like the crooked sword of a fool, Brenn pulled himself up to the moonlit opening. Terrance would be angry, but after all, Faye was in trouble. Brenn had known her almost as long as he could remember. She had been his chief companion in the guild. And lately, most curiously, he had wakened from dreams about her—dreams in which he no longer looked at Faye as a partner or cohort, as the tactical prodigy who arranged the way their tight little band could ransack a house quietly and quickly.

Instead, he had dreamt of the way her brown hair curled at her shoulders. Dreamt of her gray eyes and the softness of her skin when it was not sooty with lampblack and the grime of the street.

"Maybe it's just because I've been shut up with wizards and elves and dogs," he said to himself, smiling with unusual embarrassment. Nonetheless, whatever his thoughts of her, Faye was his friend and had been so for years. If she called for help, he would be no friend if he did not answer.

Pulling himself nimbly up to the sill of the window, Brenn started to climb through the opening. His head emerged into what seemed like impenetrable dark, then his eyes adjusted, and the stars seemed to come out. Somewhere inland along the wall he heard the gurgling sound of a pigeon stirring in its sleep, and rising, drowning out the faint sounds of the city to the west, there came to his ears the continual, regular rush of the tides.

Parts of this could be pleasant. A stroll was what he needed. A walk along the beach in the March moonlight, away from books and writs and lamps and wizards. After he had seen to Faye's safety he could come back refreshed, could start anew with military science and all the rest of it . . .

Then it occurred to Brenn that he might not be returning. He could drop back out of sight and never have to think about being king—about *being in for good*.

"Good-bye, Terrance," he whispered with a mixture of excitement and relief. Then he started the climb through the window. But his shoulders would not fit through the opening. He shifted and turned, trying to discover an angle by which he could pass through to the outside. But no matter the shape into which he contorted himself, the hole in the window was much too narrow.

"Last year I slipped through with no problem!" Brenn insisted. "I *know* I did!" Drawing his head back inside, he seated himself on the solar table and tried to work out the difficulty.

His shoulders, it seemed, had widened considerably in the brief time he had been with Terrance.

"You'd not have thought it, the way he fed me," Brenn muttered, and opened the mahogany door that formed the top of the solar table.

The journey was brief and black, like it always was. And then, not two seconds after it seemed as though he had gone blind, as though he was trapped somewhere beyond his own senses, he found himself perched atop the unfinished stairway, high above the roof of the house.

Brenn sighed and sat there for a moment, then descended the steps, walked to where the trunk of the maple rose along the tower wall, and climbed down it until he reached the second floor, where he dangled by his fingers outside the guest-room window, and dropped twelve feet to the sand below him, where he landed softly and slid toward the rising tide before he recovered his footing.

He ascended the porous rock that marked the limits of the beach, scrambled over a low stone wall, and found himself standing on Cove Road. The house was dark behind him—as dark as that night six seasons ago, when he and Faye had stood at the library doorway, picking a damaged lock.

"Six seasons? It seems more like six years," Brenn marveled. Quietly he slipped around to that side of the house, in the deep shadows of the East Wall where the library door stood, scratched and weathered except for the spanking new lock on the door— smooth, oily brass, a large, triangular keyhole, and a doorknob carved in the shape of a turtle's head.

Brenn saw none of this, of course. As always, it was too dark outside the door. Instead, he passed his hand over it lightly and deftly, his thief's touch taking in the surface of the wood, the polished knob . . .

The folded piece of paper wedged in the keyhole.

"What's this with notes this eve?" Brenn asked. "Have to look at this by light." He pocketed the paper. Idly he tried the latch, and to his surprise the door opened.

"Silly old man," the boy muttered. "You talk of danger on the streets and danger from Ravenna, and yet you go to bed and leave the house wide open."

Quickly he reached inside and gave the knob the quick turn the locksmith had shown them. The door locked as he closed it behind him, and having secured his master's house one last time, Brenn stepped back into the road and into the dim starlight.

He had turned left onto Hadrach Road and was almost to Wall Town before he removed the paper from his pocket. Sidling over to a pub window, where lamplight from inside the establishment tumbled out onto the street, he held up the paper, squinted, and read, his lips moving silently with Terrance's words.

> *Brennart,*
>
> *By now you'll know that the library door is open, unlocked. It hath remained so for a monthe, because there shoulde alway be a door open somewhere—a way in or out.*
> *I praye that you are reading this from safely inside the library.*

Brenn crumpled the note and sighed.

"I'm sorry, Terrance. Terribly sorry," he whispered. And pulling his cloak a little more tightly about his shoulders, steadying the bent fireplace poker in his right hand, darted through shadows into the heart of Wall Town. Where Faye was in some kind of danger.

Behind him, out of sight and half a city eastward, the hurricane lamp on the library table guttered and went out, its last light reflecting sadly on the open book, the quill and inkwell, and the wine glass filled with golden lethe water.

Wall Town was not the way he remembered it.

Something had narrowed the roads, had dusted and darkened the alleys. Buildings leaned against one another precariously, even dangerously, as if the next strong wind could topple an entire row of buildings.

The night around Brenn was loud and menacing. The sounds from the pubs cascaded into the streets, the laughter and the bristling oaths mixing with the clatter of glass and metal. Behind and beyond those sounds lay the irregular rush and lapping of the Sea of Shadows against the shore. And always, in the fabric of the air around him, there lay the faint hum of violence about to break—a noise you did not hear so much as feel on the back of your neck.

"Zephyrian bees," the Goniph had always called it—that faint intimation of skirmish and weaponry and murder. A good thief could sense the bees in a crowd. A better thief could locate them swarming in the disgruntled drunk, in the wronged lover who saw his rival across a room clouded with lamplit smoke, in the Parthan actor who had blustered through two hours of gin and posturing, and now, as midnight approached, was readying himself to crash a bottle on the bar and show the nearest unfortunate soul that the play was over—that madness was deadly and close to home.

Brenn had almost forgotten the sound of the bees, but the two men staggering from the Dragao had the bees in their voices and movements, though the argument was trivial—something about fishing rights near the mouth of the Eastmark, and whose were the waters in Hadrach Shallows.

Brenn stepped alertly to the other side of the street, the odor of whiskey and smoke following him. Safely beyond reach of either man, at a reasonably safe distance from hurled bottles and all but the most skillfully thrown knife, the boy turned just in time to see one of the men draw a dagger and leap upon the other.

From this distance it seemed almost quiet. There was a ripple of cloak and shadow beneath the light of the pub, and the two combatants steadied themselves against each other. For a moment they stood almost motionless, as though they were embracing or preparing themselves for some graceful feat of gymnastics. Then one, perhaps the man holding the dagger, whooped mirthlessly, and both of them tumbled to the street, the blade flickering viciously between them,

"Hoy, you there!" Brenn began, and started back across the street. He stopped himself halfway to the struggling men, surprised at his own stupidity.

Where have you been? he asked himself incredulously. *This is not Terrance's library!*

One of the men turned at the sound of Brenn's approach, his wide, stupid face squinting into the darkness. It was a second, perhaps two, but it was long enough. Suddenly the eyes widened as the knife slipped deftly into the man's ribs. It was a wet, grating sound, as though someone had nestled the blade into sand.

"Thankee, lad!" the survivor called out, facing nowhere in particular as he staggered to his feet.

Brenn backed into the darkness, his thoughts swirling. Down the Boulevard of Moonlight the boy ran, looking back over his shoulder once.

Framed in the light from the pub window, the big fellow bent over and slowly, almost delicately, wiped the blade of the knife on the dead man's tunic.

Brenn kept running. In an alley to his left he heard a woman scream, heard the scream cut off neatly—by hand or knife or garrote, he could not tell.

At once he thought of Faye and came to a stop, drawing the poker from his belt and taking one tentative step into the alley. In the strangeness of the city and the night and the prospects of violence, Faye had slipped to the edge of his mind for a moment.

Frantically Brenn plumbed his memory for the sound of her voice. Straw and shell crackled under his feet, and he paused, clutching the iron poker tightly. Again the scream echoed in the alley.

Not Faye's, thank the gods! Brenn thought, and sighed deeply. *But whose, then?*

He swallowed deeply, crouched, and charged into the alley.

There is, in parts of Maraven, a strange occurrence that the old Umbrian sailors used to call the *galho* sound. The buildings throughout the city were tall and close together—ideal to baffle and deflect the sounds of tide and ships and even of voices as they reached the city off the Sea of Shadows. On occasion, on a night like this one where the winds were erratic and sometimes strong, the city streets would reflect and mirror and distort the sounds so that the voice you heard right beside you had its source several miles away. Like the spreading branch of the *galho* tree, sounds would fork and split and double back, until a baby crying in Grospoint was more likely to be heard by night fishermen along Lake Teal than by its very own mother in the next room.

It must have been right for *galho* sound that night, for the alley was completely empty and the street beyond it also deserted. Brenn stepped from the alley into the half-light of the street, then crossed over into another alley, now searching for the source of the voice, now stopping, now searching, until he suspected he had been fooled by that trick of the wind.

Nor was he sure of his whereabouts, either.

The alley opened into a small square, a dried-out, broken fountain in its center. The buildings around it were squat and faceless, indistinguishable from one another. Brenn walked to the fountain and up the steps surrounding it.

Four stone dolphins arched above a deep stone bowl. At one time—twenty years ago, Brenn guessed, by the litter and dust accumulated in the basin—the dolphins had belched water into the bowl in an endless sparkling cycle. But now the fountain was just another ruined thing in Wall Town.

In fact, Brenn thought disgustedly, it was not even a landmark. At night, especially when you have not been there in a year or so, even the most familiar city can turn on you, mock you with common fountains and voices from alleys and streets that look familiar enough to raise your hopes, to lure you into taking a path you are sure you have taken before. So you follow the street past buildings less and less remembered, sure that some other landmark will turn up, only to have that confidence dashed altogether as you find yourself on a strange, deserted street that as far as you know might have been lifted from the other side of the world and dropped here just to vex you. So the city becomes a maze to the outsider—even more frightening because there is nothing, really, at the heart of the maze.

"Well," Brenn muttered. "So much for my bearings."

He looked up into the chipped, mottled face of one of the stone dolphins.

"Squab said the Watch had her," Brenn told the statue. Then he paused, looked around, recognized how silly he looked. "But the Watch . . . *surely* they wouldn't do anything until daytime. Surely she's safe, if for only this evening."

He sat at the base of the fountain, scanned the unknown square around him.

"No choice but to wait until morning. Then there'll be light. And folks to ask directions of. And you can see the skyline then—you can find a lot of places just from towers and steeples.

"I warrant I can wait it out as good as the next man," Brenn concluded reluctantly, resting his head against the stone bowl.

Then from the alley behind him, he heard howls and snuffling.

"Raposa!" he hissed uneasily, scrambling down a narrowing alley to his right, praying ardently that the wild dogs had not caught his scent. They were worse than the wolves in the Aldor Mountains. Though he had never been far enough out of the city to see one, Brenn had always heard that the wolf was enormous but shy, would keep its distance from healthy, adult humans. But he had seen the raposa firsthand, and heard worse than he had seen: there were stories that the things had gnawed their way through walls to get at the sick or at children, and on a deserted street at night, three or four of them were not afraid of any human, no matter his size or bearing or armament.

The alley turned out to be a cul-de-sac, ending in a tall stone wall covered with dirt and offal. Whoever lived in the building simply dumped the nightsoil out the window, letting it settle and rise in the alley below them. The smell was horrible, but bad odors were the last thing on Brenn's mind at the moment.

For back up at the mouth of the alley, outlined in moonlight, three gaunt dog forms paced and sniffed, their heads lowered and the bones of the shoulders jutting like stunted wings over their swayed backs. They looked like skeletal hyenas—the same crippled, hopping movements. The same thick necks and huge jaws.

Damn! Brenn swore silently. He looked at the wall in front of him, hoping for loose stones, for footholds in the grime and fungus. Nothing availed itself.

So the boy turned, drew the poker from his belt, and backed to the wall. *Let them come*, he thought. For the first time that night he noticed how weary he was. *Let them come and let's get this over with. Faye is somewhere and needs me, and if I can't find her tonight, by the gods I'm getting some sleep out of this, at least, so I can find her tomorrow.*

He smiled. The poker felt heavy in his hands, but it felt good. *I wonder if this is what being a hero is all about*, he thought. *Fixing it so you can sleep undisturbed.*

Then it struck him that he'd never heard of a hero winning a name for himself by standing ankle deep in dung fighting wild dogs.

"But maybe the bards never told that part," Brenn whispered to himself, his smile spreading into a grin.

One of the raposa came part of the way up the alley and stopped. It sniffed, snorted, and ran back to the alley mouth, rejoining its two companions.

Brenn remained crouched against the wall. Fiercely he wished that Terrance was with him. The iron shaft of the poker was painful in his tight grip.

The raposa sniffed about the mouth of the alley, then turned and hobbled away. Brenn waited awhile, then moved slowly toward the mouth of the alley.

He stopped, reconsidered.

What if they were out there, scavenging? Waiting?

Cautiously he peeked into the moonlit square. There it was: the fountain, the dolphins, the squat black buildings. And nothing else.

Slowly the boy walked to the center of the square. The weariness surged back over him again, and for one moment as he crossed to the stone sculpture he fell asleep while walking, or so it seemed. The next thing he remembered, he was sitting in the stone bowl of the fountain.

Above him was a cloudy sky and the birdlike faces of the four dolphins looking back at him.

"Wonder what . . . ran them off?" Brenn asked drowsily,

wrapping his cloak more tightly about him, bunching one of its edges into a small, makeshift pillow. "The raposa . . . wonder what . . ."

He raised his head suddenly, disgustedly. The pillow beneath him smelled like an old outhouse.

"They couldn't smell me!" he exclaimed, laughing quietly to himself. "They lost my scent in the stink of that filthy alley."

As before, he could not be troubled by odors. Quickly his head sank back upon the cloak, and his eyes closed.

"Thank the gods . . . for sewage," he murmured, and fell asleep.

At the moment he began to dream, the candles in the top of Kestrel Tower began to waver and go out. A shriek rose from the topmost floor of the castle, and suddenly a dark eye scanned the slums of Wall Town, desperately, frantically seeking the dangerous arrival.

≺≺≺ **XVIII** ≻≻≻

It had been idle curiosity that led Ravenna to the discovery. She had dived into the boy's dreams quite by chance, noticing the tremors in the air somewhere deep in Wall Town—the tremors that always circled about a particularly powerful dream.

He was sleeping in a dry fountain, an oversize cloak across his face so that she could not see his features. That alone was enough to arouse Ravenna's interest. The boy was more unsettling because he was faceless: somehow, had she seen his eyes, even closed in sleep, she would have felt less mystified, more in command. But the dark cloak baffled and mocked her, and though she thought it was only coincidence—though indeed she started toward another candle—the riddle of the boy's face drew her back.

This accidental veiling left her no choice. She opened the phial on her pendant, drank deeply of the acumen, then cupped the flame of the candle in her hands, feeling suddenly and fiercely its uncomfortable warmth. She looked to the heart of the flame, at the cloaked figure in the stone bowl, and she said the words.

" 'By each spot the most unholy,' " she began, in what sounded almost like another tongue, and the flame of the candle bowed solemnly in response.

> *"By each spot the most unholy,*
> *In each nook most melancholy*
> *There the traveler meets, aghast,*
> *Sheeted Memories of the Past:*
> *Shrouded forms that start and sigh*
> *As they pass the wanderer by."*

It was then that she saw a sunlit street in the center of the flame. So vivid it was that Ravenna stopped, looked up from the candle to assure herself it was still night.

Yes. Blackness out the window. A rack of clouds over the moon. She nodded and smiled, returning to the dream of the boy.

It was time for the second charm.

" 'But yet, O dream,' " she murmured urgently,

> *"But yet, O dream, if thou wilt not depart*
> *In this rare subject from thy common right,*
> *But wilt thyself in such a seat delight*
> *Then take my shape, and play a lover's part."*

The dream opened: for a moment the flame cupped in her hands seemed to grow large, to swallow her thin fingers, her wrists, her forearms. In the matter of a breath Ravenna fell into light, floating softly and easily onto a wavering Street of the Bookbinders as though the air around her had liquefied.

The buildings about her swayed, as they always did in the dreams of others. Some of them vanished entirely when she turned her head. They were no longer there when she turned back to them.

Urgently, intently, Ravenna remembered the room at the top

of Kestrel Tower: not for a moment could it leave her mind entirely, or only the gods knew what might happen. She closed her eyes, and slowly a dark room filled with candles rose like an afterimage behind her eyelids.

"Good," she breathed, her eyes still closed. For three breaths longer she looked at the remembered room.

Finally she was satisfied. Whenever she closed her eyes, the room in the tower would be there—a refuge from the vapory world into which she had only now trespassed. It was safe now: no danger of the *croglath*, as the old Philokalian seers who lived in the dreams of the ancients had called it. For the *croglath* was the snare in the dreaming that entangled whoever was wandering there—a natural hazard like a whirlpool or quicksand that held the intruder in the dream until the dreamer awoke, leaving the visitor only a faint image in his recollection, which would vanish when he no longer remembered the dream.

She was safe from that now, she imagined, and as long as the boy dreamt and the candle stayed lit she could walk in the yellow warmth of his dreaming, learning the territory.

Across the square she floated, eyes fixed on the fountain. Four dolphins arched over the lip of the granite bowl at its center, their faces half eroded by time and the passage of water. Approaching the steps leading up to the fountain itself, she rose above the ground, adrift on the hot, indefinite currents of imagined air.

He was not in the fountain. The caped form she had seen from a distance had vanished. She swore a mild oath, shook her head.

Then recited the third of the chants.

> "Follow still, since so thy fates ordained!
> The sun must have his shade,
> Till both at once do fade,
> The sun still proved, the shadow still disdained."

He was on the hot road ahead of her, his retreating form blurred by the rising heat from the cobblestones. Faceless figures lined the roads like insubstantial pillars of fog or cloud. When the boy glanced at one or the other, it would take shape and features. For a moment it would stand teasingly at the edge of Ravenna's sight, almost resembling someone she would recognize or even know, if she could ever get close enough to see clearly through the rising heat and the wavering environs.

In front of her the boy ascended into a bright circlet of lights, blue and white and blue turning into white. Ravenna squinted, hungrily trying to discern the shapes in front of her. The more quickly she tried to move, the more quickly they retreated, so she slowed, reached to her pendant, drew up the bottle of acumen, and drained it.

Suddenly two of the shapes took on substance, weight, features. It was quick, temporary—the way a dark landscape resolves itself, taking shape and detail from a sudden flash of lightning.

In that moment Ravenna saw them: a girl, dark-haired, lovely in a difficult sort of way, her gray eyes bright and insistent.

Ravenna looked again. Then looked away. Something in the girl's countenance drew her eye, drew her memory.

In the girl's face Ravenna saw her own reflection, as it had appeared, fleetingly and mortally, in a long-ago Zephyrian pond.

As her tears rose, the Great Witch turned her head, gasping.

The other shape Ravenna knew, or thought she knew. A burly man, taurine and yet clever-looking, sporting rings of sapphire and opal, and a golden ring in his nose.

Where had she seen him? Heard of him? The Goniph . . . that was it. She anchored her gaze on the rings, on the thick neck, telling herself *Remember. Remember and tell Dragmond.*

For something about the boy's rambling movements on the lightstruck road was drawing her further into the dream. The Goniph and the girl dissolved behind the lad as his gaze passed by them fondly. Ravenna raced past the rising vapor where they once stood, reached for the boy . . .

Who was suddenly even farther away, racing up the road with renewed purpose, renewed direction. Ravenna gasped, struggled to keep him in sight. To her left she heard the erratic sound of waves, the creaking calls of gulls.

A tower lay ahead of them. Squat, half-finished, it was dark amid the surrounding light. Trees seemed to sprout from its midst, unfinished stairwells and scaffolding rose from its top, as though the salt wind had come and stripped its upper stories to a skeleton of wood and stone. The boy crouched in the red shadow of the tower, then crept slowly around its circumference, stopping finally at a half-hidden door where the tower abutted the wall.

Ravenna followed, gaining ground on the boy rapidly as his attention focused on the door in front of him. She stood over his shoulder, watched as his hands danced in the red darkness, about some nimble task.

Out of that darkness a faint light rose, growing, growing. Suddenly a long blue scar began to glow on the boy's index finger. A scar shaped like a sword or a dagger, pointing toward him.

Pointing beyond him, into the heart of the Great Witch herself.

She cried out, and the warmth and the light vanished, and she stood in the topmost room of Kestrel Tower, shaking uncontrollably, the candle before her extinguished.

She shrieked again, and yet again, as the candles scattered across the floor of the tower. They flew in all directions: some of them were still burning as they rolled into corners, others sailed end over end out the circular windows. A brass candelabrum tilted, rocked, and struck the stones with a clatter.

Ravenna stood above the damage and screamed until she found words.

"Dragmond!" she thundered, hands on her hips. Then, with a sweep of her black cape, she toppled and extinguished yet another row of lights.

Now her chambers were plunged into darkness. It took a moment for her eyes to adjust—a moment of complete blindness in which she ran against yet another candelabrum—a heavy one, wrought iron—and bounced it aside in her rage. Now the light seemed to return, faint and muted by a heavy rack of clouds that covered the moon, so that the room was submerged in shadowy waters—devoid of furniture and comfort, of everything, in fact, except for those guttering candles, the smells of burning beeswax and tallow, and a solitary lamp hanging from the hook by the door, its light low and blue.

"Dragmond!" the Great Witch thundered again, and collapsed dramatically by the window, her black cape billowing over her like a wave of dark smoke.

"Damn the winds and damn the dampness and damn most of all this drafty tower!" she hissed as her robes settled about her. Peering out from the folds of heavy cloth, she glared toward Wall Town, small and dark in the distance.

"I was so close!" Ravenna muttered. "A heartbeat more and I would have known for sure!"

But that heartbeat had not come.

At the rustle and creak of leather behind her, she spun to face the door. Her eyebrows arched and a terrible thin sneer crawled across her lips. In the doorway stood four of the Watchmen, their faces ashen, their swords drawn.

"Who summoned *you* here?" Ravenna shouted scornfully. "Go back down to the causeway and keep the sick off my estate!"

"*I* summoned them, Ravenna," a resonant voice replied from behind the men. Raggedly the Watchmen parted, and Dragmond, King of Palerna, walked into the room, his face stony and alarm in his eyes. "I thought . . . well, shrieks from the top of one's tower never bode well."

"Dismiss them!" Ravenna hissed. "Do you hear me, Dragmond?"

She glared at the king. Calmly, as though this were an everyday occurrence, Dragmond looked over his shoulder at the Watchmen and nodded almost unnoticeably. Quietly and in disarray, the soldiers backed out of the room, leaving the king and the Great Witch alone.

Dragmond looked around the chambers at the wreckage. He frowned, sniffed.

"What has happened here, Ravenna? Bad dreams or a high wind?"

Seething, the dark-haired woman rose and spun toward the eastern window. As always, Dragmond was astonished by her speed. It was as though he had closed his eyes and allowed Ravenna to move across the room, so that when he looked again, she seemed to have leapt undetected from the center of the room to the farthermost window, where she stood at the sill and pointed out toward the wall and toward the horizon, where a faint crimson cast to the black sky told him that sunrise was not that far off.

"Somewhere out there, Dragmond," Ravenna pronounced ominously, "the pretender to your throne sleeps peacefully."

In an instant the king was at the window, his pale eyes scanning the slowly brightening landscape below him.

"Where? Where, Ravenna?" he asked fervently. "Are you telling me you've seen him?"

"I've seen . . . yes, I've seen him. And he was lying . . . lying . . . I don't recall! Nothing but the *libra* on his finger! The rest is . . . is . . . damn the acumen!" With yet another sweep of her cape, the sorceress turned from the window, stormed to the center of the room, and dropped on her knees, fumbling in her robes for auguries, for talismans.

Dragmond remained by the window, watching the sun rise over Wall Town.

"Acumen aside, my dear," he coaxed quietly, shielding his eyes against the growing brightness. "Acumen aside, what do you remember?"

"A dream city. Maraven, but more . . . various. Peopled with thieves and the plague-stricken."

"Thieves?" Dragmond turned slowly to face the room. "Thieves?"

"Your comrade the Goniph was among them," Ravenna said distractedly. "Ah! Here it is!" Drawing a green crystal from a silk pouch she gazed into it intently.

Dragmond folded his arms and waited, his eyes intent on his scrying mistress.

"Nothing!" she exclaimed bitterly, lifting her eyes after a long, fruitless search. "No crystal can bring memory from the dead! Everything is in *croglath*!"

Dragmond frowned, puzzled at her mystery. These were the most frightening times to him—when Ravenna insisted on spells, on divinations, when she babbled the language of enchantment, setting layers of ether between herself and her senses.

To him, *croglath* was that place in her magic where Ravenna trapped herself, where it took hours, sometimes days of coaxing to lead her out.

"Please, Ravenna," he entreated. "Please. Not now. What do you remember? The boy's surroundings? What he was wearing? The direction in which he traveled?"

"Nothing," she replied desolately. "Nothing."

Dragmond nodded. He seemed calm in the face of this challenge. An onlooker might well think that the king was soothing his hysterical consort over some minor mishap—lost jewelry, perhaps, or broken crystal.

His chest, though, was knotted, and his warrior's heart racing. *Fourteen years*, he thought, bending over and righting a tall candelabrum. *And we always knew that Aurum was loose among the women, and that perhaps this moment could come to pass, where the unforeseen heir rises out of obscurity to press his claim.*

Our crimes are murky, and there is no bottom to them.

He did not show this to the Great Witch. Long ago Dragmond had learned that, to Ravenna, the weakness of others was like the scent of blood to a shark. He must appear iron, resolute, or face her threats, her accusations, her menacing weeks of silence.

If the pretender is among us now, he thought, *we have no time.*

Ravenna gathered herself slowly off the floor of the chamber. It would take a moment, Dragmond knew, but soon she would be whole. She would assemble again, composed and resourceful, free of the snares of her own imaginings.

She would be strong, her hand once again at the helm of Palerna.

Then Ravenna was on her feet, her face still covered by cascades of dark, straying hair. Painfully she arranged herself. She breathed deeply and looked into Dragmond's eyes, her gaze brilliantly dark and beautiful, no longer distracted.

"What shall we do?" breathed the king, his voice thick with desire. At a moment's glance the thought of pretenders, of threats to the throne, raced to the edge of his memory, and his consciousness, his being, was filled with *Ravenna Ravenna Ravenna*.

She smiled, and the air in the chambers plunged toward unbearable cold. Dragmond shivered as the sunlight caught the glaze of ice on the windowsill, the ice on the floor, the frost in Ravenna's hair.

"It is simple," the Great Witch announced. "It is also inevitable.

"You will meet this very morning with the Goniph, in whatever fashion the two of you are accustomed to meeting." She waved her hand carelessly, knowing Dragmond himself would see to the security, the secrecy, the silence. "You will see to it that the boy comes to us by midnight—if not through the Goniph, why . . . through whatever means you can invent. A king is clever, resourceful."

"I have talked to the First Master anon," Dragmond said. "Let us say that he is . . . calling in his sheep. But as for you, Ravenna? I cannot do this alone, no matter what the Goniph knows."

"No doubt," Ravenna observed ironically. "No doubt the balance of the next few hours rests in my hands. As it always does."

Scornfully she gazed at Dragmond, who shrank from her, his back to the wall now.

"What shall I do?" Ravenna asked, mocking the king's deep voice, his uncertainty. "Why, *I* shall sleep awhile, Dragmond. My part in this begins at twilight, outside the walls in the potter's field."

The king frowned, but he knew better than to ask.

With a sweep of her dark cape, Ravenna floated from the room. A mist followed in her wake—a gray swirl of condensed air and ice, settling on the path behind her like snow. Wrapping his own heavy cloak more tightly about his shoulders, Dragmond followed her, the steps of his booted feet crackling on the gelid floor.

As Ravenna passed through the door, the dim light from the hanging lamp ceased its flickering. The flame seemed to poise unnaturally in the shimmering air. Dragmond stood by the door for a moment, ice encrusting his moustache. He looked into the globe of the lamp, into the steady light.

Where the flame itself had frozen at the passing of the sorceress.

Brenn awoke, the dry sunlight of winter on his face, and four stone dolphins staring down on him like happy gargoyles.

He startled for a moment, reached down for the fireplace poker with which to defend himself, and found it tangled in his cloak, which had slipped off him in the early morning hours. With a powerful tug he attempted to free the makeshift weapon, to defend himself against the creatures he realized were harmless halfway through his motion, but not before he could call that motion back.

Like a cloud rushing in from the sea, the dark cloak surged over him. Brenn wrestled with it for a moment, tangling himself in the folds, and came up finally gasping for air, the sunlight of a Maravenian morning startling him almost as much as it had only a moment before, offering no warmth and hurting his eyes.

"How in the name of the gods did I manage to get . . ." he began, and remembered it all: the night, the note from Squab, his escape from Terrance's tower, the strange and frightening path through the streets of Wall Town.

His hope that daylight would restore his bearings.

So here he was, in the middle of a deserted square in the middle of a deserted fountain, with no earthly notion where in Maraven he was.

But finding his way was easy from here. Standing in the fountain, he peered over the lowest of the encircling buildings, his sharp eyes passing through cloud and air and distance . . .

To where the lights of Grospoint Tower, the tallest of the city's lighthouses, winked out in the face of the oncoming day.

"Well," Brenn said to himself with confidence. "That's north, I reckon. Unless they've moved the Grospoint Tower, which I doubt they did."

He smiled, a sense of his old freedom and balance returning. It was something what a new morning and a notion of north did for a boy. The prospects of the day ahead seemed downright promising. From where he stood at the top of the fountain, Brenn figured he'd have Faye safely back by nightfall.

And then?

He resolved not to think about it. The first thing to do was to get to the Goniph, to find out the particulars of Faye's arrest, and to get the First Master's help, if that help were needed.

Funny. He had dreamt of them both last night. Of the Goniph and of Faye, that is. Of the two of them sunlit on Cove Road, gazing at him admiringly as he passed by with his . . . *entourage*.

Yes, "entourage" was the word. He did not turn and look at

his followers. It would have been unroyal. But he knew they were following.

The journey had taken him to Terrance's tower. Just as he had done on the first night, with Faye beside him and Dirk perched high upon the roof, he had circled the tower and come to the library door, and had started to open the lock.

The old lock. Not the new one with messages inside.

For a moment the scar on his hand had glowed, as it had on that night in the solar, when Terrance explained his past, his inheritance.

Brenn shook his head, tried to recollect the rest. Maybe he could find a dreamwatcher—one of those Alanyan visionaries who sits by your bedside, reading your eyelids while you sleep, so that when you awaken and tell him what you have dreamt, he can fill in the gaps of your memory and then interpret the whole of it for you.

"Probably just means it's likely to rain," Brenn concluded with a laugh. He scrambled out of the fountain and down the steps to the square, surprised at the soreness in his knees and the back of his neck.

He would not miss the gloves he left lying in the basin of the fountain. They slipped his mind entirely, never to be remembered again, as happens too often to a boy bent on serious business, for whom the small things grow smaller in the shadows of great endeavor.

"Guess I'm not used to sleeping on stone anymore," he observed. Untangling the cloak, he wrapped it tightly about him, for the morning was brisk, and when he left the shelter of the square, he figured there might be a stout breeze coming off the sea from the way the clouds were moving.

One of those clouds passed over the sun, and Brenn shivered, though not entirely with the cold.

"Something about that dream," he mused, stepping back toward the alley that had brought him here last night. Above him in an open window he heard movement, then the beginnings of a loud conversation about breakfast and work.

He could not guess the particulars, for his mind was far away from the words of the upstairs residents.

Something like a cloud had passed through his dream. That

was all he remembered, except that it was a shadow unlike cloud or night, or the passing shade of a wind-shifted tree.

"The brush . . . of a dark wing," he said to himself, and passed through the alley, turning onto the first main thoroughfare toward the Goniph and Wall Town.

$$\prec\!\!\prec\!\!\prec \textbf{XIX} \succ\!\!\succ\!\!\succ$$

The upper chamber was dark except for a faint, green glow at its center. Ravenna knelt there beside the box—the small collection of rings and amulets and artifacts she bitterly called her "hope chest."

The girl's face had brought her here. The face from the pretender's dream—a dark face, not unlovely, that mirrored her own face fifty years before, in the warm days of her own apprenticeship in Zephyr.

It was the apple again that Ravenna held, there in her topmost chamber—the apple aglow with the strange, unearthly light of half a century past. It was still fresh in her hand, its scent deep and dusky, a bit leathery to the touch, but still firm and uncorrupted.

In the heart of that apple Ravenna kept her youth, for only to look on it brought back memory.

Memory, and the years of rage that followed.

Archimago had been what they had called him, though certainly he had another name. "Archimago," after all, was like a dozen other guild titles, for as the thieves called their First Master "the Goniph" and the bards "the Trovador," among magic users the lord of the guild was "Archimago" or "the Archimage."

Archimago carried only two apprentices at a time, for his magic was more subtle and difficult than that of the journeyman wizards around him. Only the most promising of students were worthy of the attentions of Archimago.

Of course, she had been one of the most promising. The elder daughter of Gauderic, that old corrupt son of a bitch who ran the black market out of his Teal Front villa, she had surprised everyone, who had grown to believe that the only magic in that family was done by false weights and lies and sleight of hand. At the age of eleven she had made a horse vanish at a bazaar in Jaleel, and of course such things did not go unnoticed by Archimago. Despite Gauderic's protests that "no daughter of mine should read beyond her raisings," she signed the writ with Archimago, her father's misgivings allayed considerably when the great wizard offered a thousand deniers to make up for ruining the girl with study. Old Gauderic saw the light, and Ravenna entered the Wizards' Guild.

She was one of the two. The other was a farm boy from the Palernan countryside, somewhere just south of the Corbinwood. He was an orphan who spoke with the broad drawl of the Rurals, as her family had always called such people scornfully.

Yet he was tall, green-eyed, and uncommonly brilliant. Ravenna was sure that he could not be a Rural—that some passing count or atheling must have fathered him in a haystack, passing on a noble heritage amid the squawks of the scattered barnyard fowl and the louder squawk of the tupped milkmaid.

And yet, strangely enough, she never heard the boy utter a word to suggest that he thought himself any more than simple, humble Terrance from the village of Keedwater. He seemed . . . well, not ashamed of such origins, as she surely would have been, but not quite proud of them, either, as so often befalls a boy who uses his humble beginnings to congratulate himself constantly when he has amounted to something.

No, Terrance was odd, strangely admirable. From the start he was concerned with the Benign Magics and the Benign Magics only, as though his purpose with Archimago was not to broaden his art or even deepen it but to find something peaceful at its center and rest in a quiet knowledge. He was completely unafraid of looking foolish, and as a result learned things more quickly than she did, only to store them away after the learning.

He chanted for nothing, divined no futures, performed no alchemy.

Ravenna, on the other hand, learned magic so that she might

wrestle the world. It was good, she figured, that Archimago did not stick on questions of Benign and Malign, that he did not balk at the darker knowledges of charm and curse, of dream-walking and blight and necromancy. It meant there was more to learn, more ways to govern things.

You did not have to rest like Terrance, who after long bouts of study would sit back serenely, choosing to do nothing, spending his time reading poetry or sitting in trees, or in genial conversation with visitors to the guild hall in Maraven, learning Italian or Umbrian or English in the process, as though such things would enable his spellcraft rather than take time away from it.

Still, as perplexing and futureless as her fellow apprentice seemed, she was drawn to Terrance. There was something attractive about the balance, the health with which he pursued this whole business. Of course, he'd never make an enchanter himself, for he lacked the aggression and the backbone.

But that did not make him . . . unattractive.

Her corrupt old father had told Ravenna that when all was said and done, she would find her body and eyes and her long dark hair to be her most powerful magics. It had angered her at first, as if her difficult and obscure studies stood for nothing next to her chiseled nose and her flawless white breasts. Nevertheless, she had found that sometimes, in the absence of magic, more natural allurements worked as well, if not better.

She knew that Terrance would not be immune to her beauty, when the time came. But at first, there were other, more profitable fronts on which to try those enchantments.

It surprised no one but Archimago. He was a challenge for feminine wiles, wrapping himself in his alembics and incantations high in a dead tree in the Zephyrian Corbinwood. Smoke enshrouded him at his labors, and he would blow it away with a hand-held smith's bellows. The apprentices would stand fifty feet below him, watching the cloud float out over the Boniluce, where it condensed and rained precious metals into the lake—sometimes silver, sometimes electrum, though never the elusive gold that the master sought.

Eventually, though, his thoughts strayed from the ill-starred search for gold and settled on the young girl he had taken on as apprentice. He liked the smell of her—like narcissus—the white curve of her neck, the gray eyes that through some trick of inheritance she could turn black at will.

Especially he liked it when she wore the thin tunic she had worn in the first days of her apprenticeship. For within six months she had virtually outgrown the garment, growing taller and taller until its hem brushed her at midthigh, even farther up her leg when she reached for a beaker or for a wire from atop a tall shelf that Archimago gradually moved upward so that she would have to reach and reach higher still.

Within a year Ravenna shared the master's bed.

It was where old Gauderic had told her she should end up. He said that older, scholarly men like Archimago were prone to look up from their books one day and discover a fondness for young girls.

That much was true.

Then, Gauderic had told his daughter, those same old men tend to go foolish over the girl in question, granting her every favor, every wish, every preference. It was where Ravenna would want to be, he said, because from the master's bed a girl could step into any post in any country, become guildmaster herself in no time. Or better still, the mistress to a king.

That much had *not* been true. At least not the way that Gauderic foretold it.

For where Archimago might have granted the girl special privileges over Terrance, might have opened new knowledge for her, assigned her unfairly the best and most lucrative tasks, he played no favorites in their studies. It was Terrance that was given the chance to study a month with the dryads, and though Ravenna was allowed to go with Archimago to Rabia where she learned the properties of gems, Terrance was the one who traveled south of the Notches into Umbria, and south of there into a country he never spoke of after returning.

Ravenna soon tired of this fairness. If the master insisted upon treating the two apprentices equally, except, of course, away from lessons, the girl decided that she would use her only advantage to turn the master against Terrance.

* * *

Ravenna stopped in the midst of remembering. Rolling the green claridad apple deftly in her hand, she smiled to herself.

Oh, the bed was a dangerous battleground. And early on she had learned to use it. Ask Terrance.

Ask the slow-witted king who sat in the hall below her, his thoughts on his endangered throne.

But Terrance had been first. First Terrance . . .

At fifteen Terrance had been subject to the scarcely controllable forces in the blood that rise up when a young man's thoughts turn to young women. After she made up her mind to seduce him, it was not an hour before Ravenna succeeded.

Of course, her next task was to make sure that Archimago knew.

She started with veiled clues, thinking that the subtlety of the master extended beyond his art. But Archimago missed the faint smell of her perfume in Terrance's quarters, the calculated torrid looks she gave the boy across the dinner table. He even missed the short white tunic draped conspicuously over Terrance's bed-post.

Finally she threw all subtlety out the window, luring Terrance into the master's chambers, dragging the ardent boy down onto Archimago's monstrous featherbed and keeping him there as minutes passed into an hour and and an hour moved quickly to two. Terrance was bewildered and exhausted and thanking his lucky stars for what had befallen him when the door to the chambers burst open and Archimago rushed in to find his apprentices entangled in each other, ready to enjoy each other once again.

"Terrance! Ravenna!" the master shouted, and the girl turned, feigning surprise and fear as she hid her malicious delight. For now it would happen, she was certain: the two men would puff and threaten and bristle like two cocks intent on the same hen, and the result would be that the innocent girl, victimized by the older male apprentice, would receive all attention when Archimago kicked the boy out.

She had never been more surprised when the wizard waved his hands excitedly toward the window and shouted joyously to both apprentices, "You can do *that* later! Hurry up! It's happened! By the gods, it's happened!"

Outside, an amber cloud condensed and rained gold into the clear, flowing streams of the Boniluce.

Terrance, of course, was the first to the window. Archimago was beside him at once, pointing and exclaiming.

Behind them the air turned blue and boiled with Ravenna's anger.

It was even less expected, what happened next. When her rage lifted, Ravenna discovered that she liked the boy. Or that at least she liked to dwell upon him.

Shamelessly she began to court him, dazzling the countryside with illusory dragons that flew by night, showering green light upon the master's dwelling for Terrance's entertainment. She arranged it so that flowers bloomed in his pathway, and where he put down his feet he would lift them to still more flowers.

Terrance, on the other hand, promised little in return.

"It's this necromancy business of yours, Ravenna," he would say, shaking his head as they sat side by side of an evening on a low-hanging claridad branch.

It was their special place. Ravenna nestled against the thin crook of his arm and they watched the sun set and the green claridad apples—inedible, but brightly luminous throughout the darkest of nights—begin to release the sunlight they had stored throughout the day.

"What's the difference?" she sighed, looking intently, obsessively at the boy beside her. "Curse or healing, poetry or charm . . . it's all the same, isn't it?"

"Why, of course not, Ravenna!" Terrance replied with a puzzled smile. "Why would anyone want to learn *all* of them, if they were all the same?"

"But you don't want to learn *all* of them, do you, Terrance?" she asked, catching his green eyes and slowly, alluringly darkening her gray ones until the young man thought he was about to fall into them, into a blackness unfathomable and unnavigable. "You have no interest in necromancy or blight, and what little you seem to have learned of charms and dreamwalking you'd as soon forget altogether."

"That's not quite true," Terrance replied. "I want to remember it—I want not to *use* it."

"That . . . squeamishness is beyond me, my dear," Ravenna taunted, running her finger slowly up the inside of Terrance's leg. "It is there to *be* used. So that you might vault beyond the others in power. Beyond Archimago even, if you study deeply and well enough."

"Why?" Terrance asked.

"I don't understand."

"Why should I want to be more powerful than Archimago? If I can do everything that I need, or that those who employ me need, I shall have done enough. It's more important to *enjoy* doing it. To feel right doing it. Let the powerful worry about who would vault over whom."

"But, Terrance," Ravenna urged. "Suppose your . . . employer has powerful needs?"

"If it involves consorting with the dead or invading someone's dreams, I shall refer them to you, Ravenna."

"You *are* irritating, Terrance," she said coldly, sliding away from him down the branch. A gap of darkness lay between them now. The mist rose up from the Boniluce below them and, dappled with night, made each appear like a distant, shadowy outline to the other. The faint glow of the claridad fruit illumined only itself, not its surroundings.

"Look," Terrance said. He reached out, bracing himself against the thick branch beneath him, and plucked two of the luminous green apples from a more distant, thinner limb.

"They . . . they grow from the same stem," Ravenna observed, her anger subsiding briefly.

"And . . . they are separate fruit. Distinct from each other," Terrance added, splitting the join and handing one of the claridads to the girl. "Ravenna, I simply have no interest in doing this for more power, or even in doing simply because I *can*. What it comes to, despite all this high-sounding stuff about knowledge and technique, is simply that some things are full well *wrong*, and so we should refrain from their doing."

"What a timid, common little thought that is, Terrance," Ravenna replied bitterly. "I am sad that you treat yourself so disrespectfully."

"It remains, natheless, how I choose to treat myself, Ravenna," the boy replied, slipping nimbly to the ground.

Ravenna followed him, intending another lecture. And yet she held her peace, hiding the apple into the folds of her robe, as the two of them descended from the tree and walked back toward the wizard's lodging through the thickening dark.

Though Ravenna tried many times to restore their closeness, though she entered his dreams and spun a dozen charms on him, though she put potions in his wine and amulets under his pillow, they had separated as surely as the two claridads he had divided that evening.

Ravenna glanced up from the green-glowing apple and closed her eyes, alone in the dark chamber at the top of Kestrel Tower. It was midday now, hours past the time she was accustomed to take to her bed. But she was busy. Drawn back suddenly out of the dream of her past at the shores of the Boniluce, she hovered for a moment in the present world, where she was no longer apprentice to Archimago but the Great Witch and mistress of King Dragmond.

"No," she said. "Not yet. I am not through until I remember the end."

Back to the glowing heart of the claridad fruit she looked, remembering . . .

When Danton, the Duke of Aquila, called upon Archimago, it was brief and businesslike.

His advisor in matters wizardly had fallen from the top of the Arbor Tower and been swept by a southward current into the Gray Sea, where he was lost and presumed drowned, leaving behind only the enormous pair of mechanical wings he had been testing for the festivities surrounding the marriage of his eldest son Julian and Rosamond, a princess from the distant and fabled Aquitaine. His heir now married, his house in order, the duke was shopping for another wizard.

As brief and as businesslike as the man who consulted him, Archimago recommended the apprentice Terrance.

He and Ravenna had no moment together of farewell beyond

Terrance's sad wave from the other side of the Boniluce. It was, of course, an apprentice's duty to go where the master assigned. They had both known that from the beginning: they had lived by that rule.

And yet, Ravenna thought, as she watched them ride off—Danton, his armored entourage, and the green-robed young man in their midst—she had always figured on doing the departing, on waving to a Terrance who remained behind.

She had stood there by the banks of the Boniluce for an hour, watching the horsemen dwindle on North Road—the road that would take them eventually to the caravan routes, and to Stormpoint, then up the coast to Maraven. Her anger rose as the horsemen became tiny figures at the edge of the horizon, as the figures became a cloud of dust and the dust dissolved into nothing, and her anger kept rising as the day turned to night and the lights flickered on in the master's dwelling behind her, and she climbed to the thick branch of the claridad tree one last time, alone with her ominous thoughts.

What her master had told her in the hours before Terrance's departure had set her heart against both of them forever.

"*Why?*" she had asked him angrily. "*Why*, Archimago?"

And he had smiled at her cruelly, and replied, "Because you came to my bed, girl."

She had stood dumbstruck at the door to the wizard's study, as he told her how the duke's son was newly married, how prophecies had bespoke of danger to his kingdom if he were ever unfaithful to Rosamond. She remembered the curtained window in Archimago's study, the warm night wind billowing it into the room as she tried to collect herself, diving through the words of the spells and the doctrines back as far as Gauderic's advice for some wisdom that would make this understandable.

Meanwhile Archimago told her the worst.

"What it comes down to, Ravenna," he confessed, "is something more basic than prophecies and young, susceptible kings. I believe and have always believed that whoever will do *anything* for power is precisely the one who should not have it. You have shown me all along that hunger, and you have been treated . . . accordingly."

So she thought in the top of the claridad tree, and when she screamed, venting the rage that would carry her fifty years to the floor of Kestrel Tower where she now lay, remembering all this, the branches of the tree she sat in curled in upon themselves and the claridad apples dropped lightless from the branches, rolled across the hard Zephyrian ground, and tumbled into the Boniluce, where they vanished downstream in the rising darkness.

It was the last of them, this green-glowing fruit that shone more brightly in her chambers now that the sun had passed the midheaven, starting its afternoon decline into the western hills behind her. It was funny, she thought, how the claridad apple kept its light after half a century, as if something unquenchable burned inside of it.

You would think that so much hatred would consume so little a thing.

For it could only be hatred, could it not, that would burn continually for fifty years?

She smiled icily, her eyes on the claridad.

Terrance's boy. The pretender is Terrance's boy. It will be the boy first, she decided. So Terrance can watch his destruction and know how a nurtured hope can vanish.

Then Terrance, of course. Who would be hardly worth her time. For he was old and weak, having long ago chosen to waste himself on gentler arts.

After all these years, she would have paid him back so completely that death would be only an afterthought.

Somewhere in all of this, the girl's turn would come. Her dark hair and gray eyes brought back the time in Zephyr where something was promised that never came to pass. But for other reasons, too. For the sheer delight in watching something that beautiful fade and wither and spoil.

Oh, yes, Ravenna had special gifts for the girl. And the time was coming to present them.

≺≺≺ XX ≻≻≻

Of course, the passwords had changed. It had been more than a year, after all. That was why Brennart felt particularly lucky that Dirk was manning the storefront.

For the years that the Goniph had been First Master, Euterpe's Palace, Emporium of Fine Musical Instruments, had run a busy commerce in Wall Town. For those who looked for the place, having heard its high-sounding name in the marketplaces of Hadrach or Jaleel, Marseille or Partha, it could be quite a disappointment to come across this ramshackle wooden building lying in the shadow of the guard tower between an abandoned building and a chandler's shop whose mad proprietor had recently taken to carving candles in the shape of hands, feet, and less polite features of anatomy.

Not the best of surroundings. But then, Euterpe's was not the best of places.

Certainly it was almost the last place to go for musical instruments. In its many years of business, Euterpe's had sold perhaps a dozen items in its inventory, most of which were pennywhistle souvenirs, bought by visitors who remembered the place for far different reasons.

For the three-stringed lyre by the door was a key of sorts, and if the right string was sounded at the right time and in the right combination, the mosaic lyre set in the floor of the establishment would open onto a stairwell leading down into the city's underground, into a tunnel complex surprisingly well lit and clean and free of rats and grannars.

This honeycomb of passages extended for miles in all directions—all the way from the cove to the Teal Front. And in the center of this intricate network, like a big white-bellied spider at the center of its web, the Goniph would recline, survey the booty, and wait for the rumors and news.

Above ground, in Euterpe's, Dirk was cautious at first. Though he was glad to see his old companion Brenn, he was not nearly as glad as he pretended.

"And how *is* the wizardry business?" Dirk asked cheerily, after the expected round of hand-shakings and back-thumpings. Brenn leaned against the door he had closed behind him, smiled, and sighed.

"Over. Over for good, I'll reckon, Dirk. And I'm no smarter than I was before, though I expect I'm a little wiser. *Now* I know better than to meddle in ensorcellment."

"Is that so?" Dirk replied neutrally.

He had no idea what to make of this taller, sturdier Brennart who had walked in on him while he was dozing. Size was not that important in itself—in fact, when you were Dirk's age, you figured everyone was growing but you—but what was more puzzling was Brenn's presence.

It was as though you could see his resources, Dirk concluded. And whether that was magic or book learning, or just getting away from Wall Town for a while, he couldn't tell, but there was something in his old friend that smacked of importance and purpose and altogether better things to do.

Dirk was pretty sure he didn't like it.

Soon enough the politeness wore thin. Having little left to say to each other, the two set about the business at hand. Down the dark, narrow stairwell Brenn walked, holding a candle, while Dirk stood above him at the head of the stairs. As the little thief had taken down the lyre and played the opening notes for his old companion, Brenn had seemed impatient, driven, not much for chatter.

And all those questions about Faye . . .

Well, best let the Goniph attend to all these mysteries.

For after all, Dirk thought as Brenn reached the bottom of the steps and followed the corridor out of sight, *big and wise don't matter to the Goniph.*

If it comes down to it, he'll eat the likes of you alive.

The Goniph was feasting on other delicacies at the moment. Reclining on his customary cushions, he was halfway through a roast goose and a tankard of beer when Brennart walked into his chambers.

The Goniph smiled, feigned surprise and joy. Though of course he had known of Brenn's approach for almost an hour. Brenn had forgotten how genuinely large the man was.

Spread over the floor of the chambers like a map of gluttony, the Goniph's playthings lay scattered around him.

A capsized chess set, its pieces carved in the shapes of hippogriffs, wyverns, and gnomes—a gift from an emir of Partha, where such creatures were said to live, along with the world's finest chess players.

Piles upon piles of coin from the various realms—silver Umbrian eagles and Parthian dromedaries, *denier de Provins* and Italian grossos. For a while the Goniph had collected coins, Brenn remembered, though he tired of it soon because there was an end to it, he said. Someday he could have all makes of coins, and then what good would the collection be?

Beside these lay a book of Parthian meditations and a miniature Venetian galley made of Cathayan teakwood that he was slowly but skillfully building in a wine bottle, for the Goniph had his softer side.

Of course, Lucia, the little Alanyan dancer, scarcely a third the Goniph's age or size, was at his side, carving the goose. No doubt she was the most expensive of the First Master's playthings.

It was the chamber of a king. If anything, it was more opulent than Brenn had remembered it.

"Why, Brennart!" the big man exclaimed, waving a meaty hand at the boy as though he had seen him in the midst of a crowd or at a great distance and was struggling for his attention. "How splendid of you to answer my invitation!"

"Invitation, sir?" Brenn asked. "I came because of Faye."

The two of them stared at each other across the wide chamber.

"Faye?" the Goniph asked, his big brow knotting. "What about Faye?"

"I received news, sir, from Squab. News that the Watch had seized her," Brenn replied stiffly, already suspecting a trick.

"Busy yourself . . . in other surroundings, Lucia," the Goniph said. The girl stood up and, gathering the half-finished meal, scurried from the room.

The Goniph watched Lucia leave, then turned, once more resting his eyes on Brenn.

"It was the only way to assure your return, Brennart," the big man explained, mock seriously. "Believe me, if it could have been otherwise, I would *not* have lied to you, of all people."

"I don't understand."

"Oh, it's quite simple, Brenn," the Goniph said, a trace of a mischievous smile passing over his countenance. Lying back on the pillows, he cupped his hands to his mouth and bellowed.

"Faye! Oh, Faye!"

He looked at Brenn slyly and winked.

"She'll be here shortly," he announced in a stage whisper, then began to laugh.

"I—I fail to see what's so funny in all of this, sir!" Brenn exclaimed angrily, his arms held rigidly to his sides, his fists clenched.

"Oh, come, come, Brennart!" the big man soothed, waving his enormous, ring-studded hand as though he were brushing away a fly or a squinchbug or some other inconsequential nuisance. "Did that wizard of yours teach you enchantment at the cost of your sense of humor?"

Brenn said nothing, wrestling down his anger and trying to collect himself.

The Goniph smiled again—this time more gently, indeed a little compassionately.

"There, there. Sometimes I do these things because I know the best place for one of my boys or girls. You were . . . my best apprentice at one time, Brenn. I suppose that's why I've let you follow this wizardry nonsense for as long as I have. And indeed, you may follow it again, if you've a mind to after tonight."

Brenn frowned. He was still angry, but despite himself, that mysterious "after tonight" had drawn his interest.

The Goniph folded his hands on his enormous stomach, lay back on the cushions, stared at the chamber ceiling, and continued.

"Do you remember the old Hall of Poisoners? Over at the border of Ships and—"

"Grospoint," Brenn interrupted. "Corner of Light Street and the Starboard Alley. I've been away from Wall Town for eighteen months, sir. That's not a lifetime, mind you."

The Goniph nodded. "Not a lifetime if you say so, I suppose," he said equivocally, his eyes still on the ceiling.

"Why the Hall of Poisoners?" Brenn asked. "As I remember, the old place was abandoned. There wasn't anything to *find* there, much less to steal."

A magpie sailed into the chamber through a dark side tunnel. For a moment, seeing the movement of wings in the corner of his eye, Brenn thought it was a bat. Instinctively he ducked, and the Goniph chuckled scornfully.

"Indeed, it has been lifetimes and lifetimes, Brenn," he declared. "For in less time than it takes for a boy to forget the difference between bird and bat, a band of robbers has set up a stronghold in the old hall. The cellar is filled with booty—gold bracelets, chests full of Parthian dromedaries. Sapphires, I have heard. It'll take four of my best prentices to give the place a just pillaging."

"And I am flattered, sir, that you have remembered me for the occasion," Brenn said, his eye on the door. "But I think I began by asking you Faye's whereabouts, and I don't believe I have yet been satisfied on that account."

The magpie, perched in the rafters of the chamber, plummeted suddenly toward the floor and, banking only a foot or so from the ground, swooped up and onto the Goniph's shoulder, staring at Brenn with eyes that were black, bright, and shallow.

Much as the Goniph himself stared, his smile fading and his face growing steely and unreadable.

"The old boy taught you to talk like a scholar, didn't he, lad? You 'think' we spoke of things, and you 'don't believe' you've been . . . what was it? 'Satisfied'?"

Brenn flushed, and the Goniph's smile returned. This time there was a certain coolness to it, as though somewhere under the charm and the intrigue the big man had been wounded.

"Those books are no good in the tunnels," the First Master

declared flatly, reaching behind him for something wedged among the pillows. Brenn tensed, then wondered why he had.

After all, the man before him had practically raised him, and from those mountainous cushions he was drawing . . . only a jar.

"But those books of meditations, Goniph. The ones you recite to us . . ."

"Have their proper place, lad," the big man interrupted. "Look," he said more quietly, more urgently. "I want you to look."

He held the jar up to the light. Brenn took a hesitant step nearer, to make out . . .

Crabs. Three small fiddlers hurling themselves against the glass sides of the container, a tangle of leg and claw and carapace. The glasswork was Belgian—thin, transparent, yet sturdy—so Brenn could see the every movement of the frantic little creatures, brought suddenly up to light from their imagined safety in the darkness of the Goniph's bedding.

Immediately one of the crabs—the largest one, about the size of an Umbrian silver eagle—stepped on the shell of another and vaulted toward the lip of the jar. Even from where he stood, Brenn could hear them, could hear the scrape of claw and chitin against the insides of the class.

The large crab wrestled itself halfway over the top of the jar, toward freedom and sure vanishing in the dark of the Goniph's tunnels, but another of the crabs, its fiddle claw grasping the legs of the creature above it, pulled down the topmost crab and vaulted over it toward the same freedom and air.

The Goniph watched and laughed as the process repeated itself a dozen times—crab vaulting over crab only to be pulled back down into the wavering, flailing chaos of legs and pincers. Brenn watched, too, in horrified fascination. He had seen this kind of thing before on the rock face surrounding Hardwater Cove; he knew that it was part of nature. But something about the glass and the light, the audience and the laughter, repelled him. Something that had seemed cruel but part of the surroundings took on a glint of evil there in the Goniph's chambers, and Brenn backed away from it, toward the door and toward . . .

Faye, who had entered the chamber silently behind him. Brenn backed straight into the girl, turned with a start.

The seasons had worked a wondrous change on Faye. The tall, willowy girl that had burgled villas and shoplifted jewelry was gone somewhere in memory and lost time. In the place of that girl stood a dark-haired, gray-eyed young woman, her face tanned by the sun and the wind, her body supple, blossomed in Brenn's eighteen months of absence.

Seeing his old friend—or the shadow of his old friend in the body of this woman—Brenn cried out with delight and hugged her. Slowly, almost reluctantly, Faye's arms circled him in return, and they stood there for quite a while in an embrace that was . . . a little more than brotherly.

And yet, in the midst of this happy reunion, the memory of the scrambling crabs crossed alarmingly through the boy's mind, and he broke the embrace, holding Faye at arm's length.

"F-Faye," he stammered. "Such a d-delight to see you!"

"Oh, how full of gentilesse he has become, has he not?" the Goniph observed ironically from behind Brenn. "All full of manners and fine phrases."

Faye smiled a little sadly, took Brenn by the shoulders, and turned him to face the First Master.

"I think," she said distantly, "that the First Master was instructing you."

"Just showing him Wall Town in miniature, my dear," the Goniph murmured, brushing another crab from the lip of the jar with his thick forefinger. "Showing him the endless . . . contest in which our resources are forged. I am sure it is an emblem you understand, Faye. Better than any Parthian effigiary, this jar of crabs."

"We struggle *with* each other, *among* each other," Faye said dutifully.

"And we are the stronger for it," the Goniph responded, completing the girl's thought, perhaps even her sentence.

"And when we climb too far," Brenn declared angrily, "our friends below us reach up, grab at us to pull us down, and climb over us. And if that doesn't work, rest assured that the Goniph is above us, more than ready to cast us back to the bottom with a flick of his mighty finger."

At once the boy regretted what he had said.

The First Master reddened. "You *have* been gone too long, Brennart," he said, his teeth clenched. "And if we had the time and the liberty, I . . . why, I would *show* you how wrong you are."

He sighed, stretched, composed himself.

"But the Hall of Poisoners awaits us, and a cache of riches the likes you'll never see in those bookish surroundings that have overeducated you and softened you—though in neither case past repair."

The big man smiled amiably, and Brenn sighed with relief. Thank the gods the Goniph carried no grudges!

"But as for now, Brenn, I am tired. A man my age needs sleep before endeavor, you know."

"It will be worse when you're old, sir," Brenn responded.

"A flattering jest," the Goniph said with a laugh. "I believe I see the remnants of my old Brenn beneath that bookish carapace. There's thief remaining in you, boy, and though you'll swear by the gods, if there be gods, and by your ancestors, if any of us knew them, that the sole reason you left that tower was to rescue sweet little Faye here like some storybook hero, I'd bet the contents of this chamber that it was thievery you yearned for and books you were glad to put behind you."

The big man gasped, left short of air by his torrent of words. Brenn, on the other hand, stood gaping, silent.

It was as though the First Master read his thoughts. For after all, the studies that lay ahead of him were daunting at best. Nor did they lead to anything better than a dangerous, no doubt fatal confrontation with Dragmond and Ravenna.

For Terrance might be able to cure elves and poor folks or conjure pigs out of stalls, but Ravenna was the Great Witch, who raised tempests and tremors and could make the sun wink out with a wave of her hand. And Dragmond had an army that came when he called. Those two were about important things —kingly business and great magic—so the best thing a fellow could do was leave himself as invisible and insignificant as possible. All the better not to get in the way.

And as Brenn looked at it, better a crab in a jar than the heir to a throne.

Taking another deep breath, the Goniph waved away his apprentices.

"Begone with you, Brennart!" he ordered. "Faye will show you where to rest your head and tell you what we know about the stash in the Hall of Poisoners. I figure that the best way a lad regains his sea legs is to stand on deck in the turbulence. 'Tis a philosophy that works for thieves, too, I wager."

The big man looked kindly at Faye and Brennart.

"You must be tired," he said softly. "The noontide approaches—time for all worthy folk to be abed. Look to the midnight, when the storming starts."

He followed them with his eyes as they left the room, stifled a laugh as Brennart tried to slip his arm through Faye's, and the girl moved politely but quickly away.

Charmers, they were.

He was going to miss them, he thought sadly. He could not guess at what Dragmond had in mind for the prentices: he expected it was no good, though the king had promised solemnly on his regal word of honor that no serious harm would come to any of the children.

Dragmond had always been a man of his word.

That, of course, was the only reason the Goniph had consented to hand over his four best—Faye, Brenn, Dirk, and Squab—to the king's custody.

Duval's death became more expensive daily. And yet the toll was still light.

For Brenn was right in one thing. If any crab in the tunnels of Wall Town climbed to a threatening height, the Goniph would stand above him, and with . . . what was it?

. . . *a flick of his mighty finger* . . .

He nodded. All of a sudden he was drowsy. Reaching down into the maze of pillows below him, he produced another circular piece of glass—the lid of the jar. His eyelids heavy, he replaced the lid snugly, knocking yet another crab to the bottom of the container as he did so. Then, setting the jar aside, he lay back on the pillows.

The Goniph was snoring as Lucia returned to the room. Quietly, deftly, she tidied the chambers around the huge, sprawling body.

She was a delicate girl, and uncomfortable around tidal creatures, so she left the Belgian jar where it lay, the lid clamped tightly on the struggling crabs, who grappled with each other until the air gave out.

The Goniph was sleeping deeply, still several hours away from his appointment at the Hall of Poisoners, when the boat skimmed along the ashen Aquilan coast, the mountains to its starboard, the fog and the wide sea to the port side. Beltran, the steersman, leaned forward nervously, soothing the oarsmen with soft, almost meaningless encouragements.

"Steady, boys," he urged, squinting through the descending mists, trying his best to ignore the dull pain rising in his stomach. "If the Corrante grabs us, don't lose your head over her. Keep at what you're doin' and leave steerage to the bowsman and me." He hoped they were listening, knew that if the long canoe slipped into the swift current they'd be up in the Bay of Ashes before they could right themselves, no matter how attentive his thick-necked, thick-headed oarsman.

It was twilight, and everyone on board seemed like shadows now, dark rowing forms scarcely visible beyond the hooded woman who sat back toward the stern.

Beltran looked beyond the woman. There were the oarsmen, then beyond them sat the Alanyan at the prow of the boat. It was as though Beltran looked into the recesses of a cavern, where the voice afore seemed almost disembodied, rising out of shifting dark.

He longed for the comfortable coast south of them all, for the Gray Strand across the wide, desolate water off to port. On the strand, navigation was easy. Even in fog like this you could steer by familiar markings: the old lighthouse, the Tower of Varthing, Atheling's Pier.

The markings shifted here, for the boats of the dead moved on the tides.

To his starboard, menacingly near, the Aquilan coast rose up into the mountains, leaving ash and cinder cones and rubble.

Like a fire pit, Beltran thought to himself. *Like hell, rather than a country where folks live.*

But they don't live here, he reminded himself with a grim chuckle. *'Tis the last thing they do in South Aquila.*

Manning the oars, doing most of the back-work, were two Aquilan sathers, mercenary swordsmen from the twin cities of Arbor and Origo, far to the green north of the duchy. They were skilled fighters, their swords the strange blades forged in Origo, toothed edges equipped with small metal reeds so that, flashed through the air by a skilled, unnaturally quick hand, the sword would shriek maniacally.

The Aquilans were fighters, not sailors.

Their backs were strong but their rowing was unsteady. It was as though the sathers had never been in a boat before, as though they had watched someone row from a shore or pier and said to themselves, *That looks easy enough. Passing a plank through the water.*

Beltran sniffed disgustedly, winced again with the indigestion. He wondered why Ravenna had chosen those two.

The bowsman beyond them was an Alanyan from Rabia, an easterner schooled in the Ruthic Shallows, but a Gray Sea sailor for only a year or so. He was down on his luck, and the Great Witch had brought him into service off a corpse boat. Beltran had insulted him once and was forced to wrestle a very quick knife from his hand.

In short, it was no ordinary escort for the woman in the stern. Then again, she was no ordinary passenger.

Ravenna had traveled from the tower in disguise. She was dressed like a monstrous beekeeper, the thin, gauzy black cloth that covered her from the top of her head to the top of her thick-soled boots having been fashioned to allow its wearer to see clearly while keeping out the drifting cinders and ash.

Perhaps keeping out the plague, too. For physicians claimed it could nurse on a body for days, flying like squinchbugs into the ears of the unwary a full week after the carrier died.

Ravenna pulled her hat down snugly. The ears. Now the physicians were saying that the Death came to you through your ears, like song.

She sat quietly in the boat and watched the Aquilan cost emerge from the fog, then recede again suddenly. It was like entering the landscape of someone else's dream. When the mists would lift or dissolve for a moment, Ravenna's eye could follow the tiers of graves halfway up into the foothills—dark terraces littered with white, with limestone and marble and coral statuary intermingled with humbler stones and mussel shells, shining like teeth in the dark mouth of a hungry leviathan.

Somewhere below the merchants' graveyard lay her destination—the potter's field. But to get there, she would have to pass over the black sands of the beach, where lay the numberless, tattered boats of the dead.

Where the corpse boats had been set adrift and had run aground, the coast was littered with skeletal hulls, salt-bleached wood half reclaimed by the black sand. Wind-eaten prows jutted from the shore like the bleached ribs of mermen or hafgygrs, and occasionally a human limb, bone-pale or merely bone, draped over the weathered side of a rowboat or coracle. Ravenna had heard it was worse up in the Bay of Ashes: that you could not take a step without tripping over wood or bone.

The Great Witch wrapped her cloak about her more tightly, staring feverishly at the black shore. Quickly and surely her plans were changing.

To travel over this wreckage in search of the potter's field would be too dangerous, even if the sathers were as good as their word and knew the shortest, most direct way to the huddled graves of the cwalu—the criminal dead who die remorseless and regretless, their flinty hearts sparked only by the necromancer's twisted words. Even in times when the plague abated, this beach was a hazard of traps and perils. Snakes prowled there, and flesh-eating lagartix lizards, and rats as long as your forearm.

No. What she needed to do, she could do from the canoe. Besides, she observed—as the Alanyan bowsman clutched his stomach and leaned against the prow, a puzzled look on his face—time was running short.

''Ship your oars!'' she called out to the Aquilans, who stared at her in disbelief.

Ravenna stared angrily back until they could almost see her eyes glitter beneath the gauzy black cloth. They set the oars in the bottom of the boat and shuddered as they turned to face the bow.

Good, she thought. *They are the two largest. So much body weight. It will take longer with them.*

She stood unsteadily and extended her arms. Beltran reached for her, afraid she would topple overboard, but a sudden sharp pain in his abdomen threw him back into the stern. The long canoe pitched violently, and Ravenna staggered.

The black waters rushed to meet her.

Immediately, though, she recovered her balance, and again stood unsteadily, bracing herself against the starboard side of the boat. Her crew was distracted: no longer attending to their oars, they sat dumbstruck, clutching themselves and staring at each other.

Left to itself, the craft immediately slipped into the Corrante—the swift, circling current that rode up into the Bay of Ashes. The Great Witch began the chant nervously, but her voice grew louder and more confident as she continued.

> "At the round earth's imagin'd corners, blow
> Your trumpets, and arise, arise
> From death, your numberlesse infinities
> Of soules, and to your scattred bodies goe . . .

Beltran tugged at the hem of her black robe.

"M'lady," he called, an unasked question in his voice.

"Agonia." She smiled icily, and began the chant again.

Agonia, Beltran thought in horror. *The poison of executioners.* Slow-acting but always fatal, so that the Hooded Ones could give the odorless, tasteless herb to their victims, then sit back while the poor souls dug their own graves and, their tasks completed, fell dead into them.

But why? Why strand herself in the Gray Sea? Great Witch she might be, but the Corrante recognized no power but its own and that of a stalwart oarsman.

Still, Ravenna continued:

> *"All whom the flood did, and fire shall o'erthrow,*
> *All whom warre, dearth, age, agues, tyrranies*
> *Despaire, law, chance, hath slaine . . ."*

She paused, spread wide her long, black-nailed fingers, and something began to move in the husks of the boats along the beach.

Chance, Beltran said to himself, and the mist seemed to encircle him more closely. *Chance hath slaine me*. For a moment he tried to stand in the stern, to lay hands on his poisoner and avenge them all, for the Alanyan had fallen in the bow, and the oarsmen now clutched their stomachs and moaned.

But his legs no longer worked. For a moment he felt a fuzzy, nettling pain in his right foot, as though it had only gone to sleep. Then he felt nothing at all, and the nothing crept from the knees to the thighs to the loins . . .

And Ravenna vanished, swallowed by a pale green mist, which swirled and roiled for a moment above the boat. Then the mist solidified into green-glowing hands that hovered armless and bodiless in the foggy air.

It was the last thing that Beltran the steersman remembered.

The hands kept moving, though. Moving after Beltran's eye went blank, when the Alanyan at the prow gasped and lay still, when the burly Aquilan oarsmen coughed up blood and black fluid, falling facedown across the midbench.

Ravenna waved, and chanted, and the cwalu stood in the beached boats as though they rose out of graves. Pale they were, some of them half-decayed, others skeletal, some with rope burns on their swollen necks, others with wide deep gashes below the ribs, yet others with terrible black pustules—the fingerprints of the Death—on their arms and necks. Slowly, as though at every step and movement the cwalu had to stop to seek their purpose, their direction, they began to guide their decrepit boats off the shore: some with oars, others paddling with boards, still others swimming alongside their crafts or even swimming alone, far from any boat.

They were joined by some who had risen from the inland graveyards. Out onto the beaches they clattered and stumbled, wrapped in shrouds and cerements, the black, sandy earth tumbling off of them as they waded into the oily waters.

Sniffing the air hungrily, as the Great Witch waved a glove above their heads. A glove her ministers had found at midday, lying in the basin of a dried-up fountain guarded by weathered stone dolphins.

Ravenna called softly, soothingly to her undead legions.

"Not yet, my children. Not yet, but soon."

Soon the boats could not move without colliding. The Gray Sea was thick with swollen bodies and skeletons, with faces and arms pale as grubs, as fish bellies. A skull breasted the waves of the sea like a coracle, setting its course for the Maravenian shore. Ravenna sat back down in the stern of the canoe, watching the water churn below her.

Her own powers astounded her. They rose from some grim, unfathomable chasm, and left her spent.

But by the gods, they made commotion.

Ravenna began to laugh quietly, raising her glowing hands toward the Aquilan coastline, which now almost surrounded her, the boat having ridden the Corrante clear into the Bay of Ashes.

"Beltran!" the Great Witch called, and her tears were triumphant, joyous as she watched the dead mill around her, looking up to her with dull, expectant eyes or black, empty sockets.

"Beltran! Arise! Back to Maraven!" she ordered.

At the stern of the boat, Beltran the steersman shuddered. Sluggishly, awkwardly, he raised his head and fumbled with the oar, as though each limb moved vaguely about its own remote purpose.

"Back to Maraven," Ravenna whispered serenely. In the waters around her the dead listened, clutched at one another like some strange new sea life, pulled one another along toward the mouth of the sea and the Needle's Eye and the docks of Ships and Grospoint. Their queen rode the waters among them, rode the switching Corrante, by the power of dead men's oars; rode the backs of the dead to Maraven to welcome the heir apparent.

≺≺≺ XXI ≻≻≻

Brenn's reception in the halls of the guild was a chilly one.

In what he called "the interest of fairness," the Goniph had spoken to all his best apprentices, urging them to accept their wayward brother back graciously, happily. Their former associate had passed through hard times, the First Master maintained, made the harder because he felt that he had fallen from some great wizardly height back into Wall Town.

"He had dreams of being . . . well, *better* than us," the big man confided to Squab sympathetically. "We should understand that Brenn is a dreamer. He may always fancy himself a little more gifted than the next boy: indeed, when I restore him to Second Apprentice it may not be good enough, what with having studied under a wizard and all."

The resentment on Squab's fat face told the Goniph that his words had struck home. And yet the boy followed instructions: he wrote the note and threw the stone through Terrance's solar window.

Good. Let Squab think the Second Apprenticeship is his by right. So what if his footfall is loud, if he stumbles his way around locks, if in fact he is worth little more than the vigia bird? He has a vicious and gossiping mouth. Nestles in suspicion like a badger in a tunnel. Those things are useful in their own right.

For it was important, in the Goniph's world of intrigues and darknesses, that every apprentice suspected and vied with the others.

Made them wily. Made them strong.

Squab had done just what the Goniph wished, mingling hard words with the lives of Faye and Dirk and Marco and the rest of the little thieves. "Sunday thief," they were calling Brenn days before he returned. "Sunday thief" and "sorcerer's apprentice." With no doubt other less flattering names that the Goniph would discourage if he heard them.

Nonetheless, he was a curious man, and he had heard plenty earlier that evening, his ear to the door of the Prentices' Quarters, where Faye and Brenn and the others prepared for the night's adventure.

Shortly after sunset, five of them assembled. Faye and Brenn and Dirk of course, joined shortly by Squab and little Marco, barely eleven but resourceful, eager, and promising. Sunset was the prentice time, an hour devoted to preparing for the business ahead, for smearing each other with lampblack, for wrapping rags about the shoes of those who would enter the halls and houses so that their footfalls would be silent, for feeding and stroking the vigia birds so the things would remember to return and whisper their secret reconnaissance to the ear of the trainer. A time for prayer and oath to the Four Lucks of the guild: to dark and silence, of course, and to the hidden lucks, the gullibility and the greed of the lawful.

Most of all, the prentice hour was a time of banter, where the young folk shored up their courage in insult and mimicry.

This evening appeared to be no different. And yet, as the Goniph spied through the keyhole, he knew that it was.

For in Wall Town the crabs were climbing, as the apprentices stared sullenly at one another across the wide, barracklike room. The banter was there, but the words were edged, were iron.

What he saw, he saw through the keyhole. And what he heard was this.

"Since when has the Hall of Poisoners been such a plum, Faye?" Brenn asked amiably, slipping on the dark boots he had left in his sea chest. The footwear pinched: he curled his feet to be more comfortable.

"Oh, for ages," the girl replied coldly, dressing in the corner modestly, behind a Cathayan screen she had stolen from a Venetian galley several years ago, when the differences between her bunkmates and herself had become embarrassingly apparent. "For ages. Since . . . right after you left."

"Six seasons, Faye! That's all!" Brenn repeated, this time with a rising impatience. "It's not as though that is a lifetime."

"Was for three of us," Dirk remarked tersely, his deft little hands sharpening the blade after which he had renamed himself. "Was for Larentia and Eamon and Iliyas."

"I don't understand," Brenn said.

" 'Dangerous age,' " Faye explained, stepping from behind the screen, now clad fully in black sailcloth, her face darkened with lampblack. Brenn caught her looking at him, but she averted her eyes at once.

"Or haven't you heard, Brenn?" she asked, spreading the fingers of her right hand and turning the palm up. From somewhere in the rafters, a vigia descended, alighting on her index finger. Alertly it cocked its white head, stared into Faye's eyes, and trilled softly.

Fay nodded, drew a thimble-sized piece of cloth from the top of her boot, and hooded the bird. Then, for the first time, she stared directly at her old friend, her gaze abstract and wounded.

"We're all o' dangerous age around here," she said. "That's why the master hides us."

"And a good thing he does," Squab interrupted, drawing on his black moleskin gloves dramatically, though everyone knew he would pick no locks, would dislodge no window glass. That instead, the Goniph would station him at the mouth of Starboard Alley, to call in case the Watch approached. "Good thing he does, on account of nobody else looks out for a thief in these hard times."

"That sounds familiar," Brenn said with a smile, thinking of the many times the First Master had reminded his charges just how grateful they should be.

You're coddled thieves, after all, he would say. *There are children who are Grospoint Urchins, who live daily from what they can dip out of yokels' pockets. There are children who live off of middens.*

"Where did you hear that, Brenn?" Squab asked. "Read it in some book?"

Brenn ignored his heavy colleague, began slowly to tie the black cape at his neck.

" 'Hoy there!" a voice cried from behind him, and from the corner of his eye, Brenn saw a shape hurtling toward him, glittering red on yellow on white. He ducked, raised his hand to shield his face, and watched startled as the copper cup hurtled over him and clattered harmlessly against the far wall.

Brenn looked around him in embarrassment. Dirk and Squab laughed malignly. Faye said nothing, going on about her quiet, solitary business, while little Marco watched the brewing conflict attentively.

"Eye and the hand are going, Brenn," Dirk taunted. "That's the real dangerous age, when you're not quick enough to catch something tossed at you from—from a friend. On account of you won't be able to catch something more deadly when it comes from the hands of an enemy."

Silently Brenn walked to the far wall and picked up the cup. It was a light, well-polished thing, dented in lip and side. At once he recognized the runes along its base as Umbrian.

"Why, this is the old cup you used to make so much of, Faye! What was it they called these?"

"Profeta cups," Faye said, suddenly alert. "What are you doing hurling around my belongings, Dirk?"

"How—how again did they work?" Brenn asked.

Marco craned his neck toward the copper vessel in Brenn's hand. "Work? D'you mean it's a magical cup, Faye?"

"Well, they say it is, Marco," Faye answered the little boy. She spoke kindly, softly, for Marco was a favorite among the apprentices, combining innocence and larceny in ways that none of the others recalled in themselves. Of course, he was the youngest of the pack by a good three years, and there was no apprentice—not even Brenn—who remembered that far back in their own lives easily. The past was a series of days like this, and the future lay in the bottom of a profeta cup.

The cup that Faye took up and handled protectively—much as one would handle a child that the other children had been bullying and tormenting. Then, with an eye on Marco, the girl lifted a carafe from the rickety communal table and poured a swallow of wine into the profeta.

"The Umbrians say *in vino veritas*," Faye explained to Marco. "That's the Latin for 'there is truth in wine.' We usually take that to mean that a drunk will say anything. The vintners say it to advertise their wares: I suppose they mean that wine is a more true thing to drink than beer or water.

"But the Umbrians had a different meaning for it entirely. They meant that wine can . . . prophesy. Can foretell, Marco."

Quickly Faye turned the cup upside down.

"The wine will run down the inside of the cup," she explained to the boy, who nodded curiously.

"It'll make a mess on the table," Marco added gravely. Despite themselves, all the apprentices smiled, except for Squab, who retreated to his bedside and fumbled through his belongings, no doubt taking some things along with him, no doubt hiding other things from the prying eyes and fingers he imagined each of his companions to have at the ready.

"Aye, Marco," Faye agreed. "But we're not concerned with that now. Instead, we're after the future. Because even though most of the wine is on the table, making the mess you're talking about, there's some left in the cup. Three drops, maybe, or four, clinging to the inside. It'll be clinging on a rune, Marco, because the cup is all engraved and marked on the inside with all the Umbrian symbols for this and that. What you're supposed to do next is look at what the wine covers—what runes, what signs and symbols. That tells you your future. Or so the Umbrians say."

Faye sat back triumphantly, no doubt proud of her explanation. She handed the cup to Marco, who looked inside it curiously.

"I see two drops," he said, and the rest of the apprentices, Brenn included, peered over his shoulder into the basin of the cup.

"What do they mean, Faye?" Dirk asked.

"Let's see," Faye said, squinting at the runes that shimmered beneath the red drops. "The Lapwing is one of them, I believe, and the Pelican is the other. Or that's how I see it. One of the drops kind of straddles two runes, doesn't it?"

"Kind of between the Lapwing," Dirk offered, "and . . . what is the other Faye?"

"The Sow," Faye pronounced ominously. "A bad sign. But I'm pretty sure it's on the Lapwing, which means one of us will have to deceive or decoy for the sake of the others. Happens often in a case like this."

She looked more closely at the cup, her voice gaining confidence as she spoke.

"You see, the Lapwing's a funny bird. She limps away from her nest to lure off predators, to keep the helpless young safe. She's a confidence artist, *that* bird is, and a wonderful omen for thieves."

"Faye?" Brenn asked, but his old friend was off and running with her divination. Marco sat wide-eyed, and Dirk and Squab nodded in rapt agreement with the girl's explanation.

"The Pelican's easy," Faye said. "Feeds her young with her blood."

"Feeds *his* young," Dirk corrected. "It's the male pelican that does the feeding."

Before Faye and Dirk could launch into an argument about the gender of omens, Brenn tried again.

"Faye?" he asked, this time a little less cautiously, a little more loudly.

"What?" Faye snapped, turning from Dirk and staring directly at Brenn, her eyes sparkling with anger.

"What if it's the Sow, Faye? That drop of wine you had trouble reading at first. What if it's . . . the Sow?"

"But it's not, Brenn," Faye declared, as assuredly as if her friend had asked if the sun were rising, not setting, outside. Dirk stared at Brenn in consternation, as though the question were mad to begin with.

"But what . . . what if it *was*?" Brenn insisted. "I mean, *hypothetically* speaking?"

His comrades all glared at him, angered by the long word.

"What's a hypothet, Brenn?" Marco asked.

"Something he learned at a wizard's knee, boy," Squab answered curtly. Dirk and Faye turned back to the cup. Brenn stood above them, flushed, embarrassed, as though he watched them through iron bars or a thick, transparent glass that shut out all sound and touch.

"You . . . didn't answer my question, Faye," he insisted, feeling his ears growing hotter still. No doubt his face was red by now—the deep scarlet of apples or sunsets or blood.

Faye refused to lift her head.

"It's an obvious Lapwing, Brenn," she said finally, swirling the drops in the cup and erasing the augury. "The Sow, when it comes up, is bad news. It's the Sow who eats her farrow, the Lady Huch in the old Umbrian story.''

Faye looked up at Brenn and smiled, having recovered entirely from interruption, from challenge.

"Of course, that would make no sense with the Pelican and everything, now would it? One good parent and one bad parent your only omens? It's the Lapwing, Brenn. That's all it could be.''

"I thought the Pelican foretold a storm,'' little Marco offered eagerly.

"Old wives' tale,'' Faye replied tersely. She stood up, walked to her bed, and slipped the cup into a grayed canvas sack between bed and wall.

Brenn shuddered. This was what Terrance had meant by the Lock—the absolute certainty of the diviner, the augurer, the visionary. The reading that shuts out all other readings.

What was it the wizard had said?

When you see the Lock settle in, rest assured that the one having visions is wrong in one dreadfully important way. That, or something like it. Whatever it was, it unsettled the boy, and the misgivings that had started with the Goniph that noon rose to an ominous suspicion as the children of the guild went through their final preparations for night and for the business at hand.

Faye applied the last of the lampblack on little Marco, as Dirk and Squab armed themselves with daggers and short swords. Dirk flipped one of the daggers, blade over hilt over blade over hilt, glittering wickedly in the lamplight of the chambers. Defiantly he looked at Brenn as he caught the knife and sheathed it.

Now in silence, the prentices filed out of the quarters, Faye's vigia bird settling jauntily onto her cap. Brenn sat on his bed, chin in hands.

Faye turned at the doorway.

"Brenn? Hurry up. You'll be late,'' she urged softly, a hint of disillusionment, of downright sadness in her voice.

"In a moment, Faye,'' Brenn answered weakly, and as the girl left the room, he reached into his sleeve and drew out the writ of apprenticeship. It seemed that he signed into Terrance's employ a lifetime ago, and already, after not even twenty-four hours in Wall Town, he felt out of place, evicted.

By this time at Terrance's tower, they would be preparing to retire. Perhaps a look at the stars accompanied by a long, windy discourse on astronomy by the wizard, who maintained that the *science* of stars was a damned sight better than all of this astrology business. Or perhaps a glass of Umbrian wine in the solar, and conversation about the sea routes or Terrance's eccentric friends in Partha or Alanya. Brenn missed it—the safety and fellowship and, most of all, the guidance.

It occurred to him as though it were the voice of an oracle. Clause sixteen—the shifting passage in the writ! Just what he would need in this district of misgiving and cloudy prophecy!

Eagerly he opened the scroll, his eyes racing indifferently over the page until he came to the clauses, the numbers. He stopped and began to read.

> *The apprentice should trust himself. As he did when he left the tower. Farewell.*

Disconsolately Brenn threw the scroll to the ground. Then, thinking better of it, he placed it carefully among his bunched belongings and, one of his boots yet unlaced, stumbled out the door after the others.

The rain began before they were out of Wall Town. It came down fiercely, then abated, then came down again, uncommonly warm for the season. Between downpours the air in the city was close, oppressively humid, and the thick black clothing with which the thieves had bundled themselves against night and detection was soon clinging to limb and back, as though each of them was bathed in sweat.

Twice Faye tried to send out the vigia bird in the direction of Ships. Once on the wing, the tiny creature could have seen all —the traffic on the midnight streets, the dangerous presence of Watchmen. As luck would have it, though, the air was too moist, too rain-heavy: each time the vigia returned at once and perched itself on Faye's shoulder, its feathers unkempt, its sullen head tucked at once under its wing.

So they were eyeless until they struck Cove Road somewhere in far Grospoint, where gazing off to his right, Brenn could see the causeway and its gibbets, dark in the fitful moonlight. Beyond that was only the wasteful expanses of the Gray Sea, and the occasional rush of the rains off the waters into the city.

"Damn!" Dirk breathed as the third wave of rain hit them, as the thieves ducked into a doorway to shelter themselves against the showers that were coming harder each time—each time more merciless, more relentless.

"It's the doing of them pelicans!" Marco exclaimed triumphantly. "Don't care what Faye says. A pelican means rain!"

Behind him Brenn chuckled. Faye, a doorway up from all her comrades but still within earshot, hid a smile in the darkness of her hood.

"Light Street up ahead, brothers!" she called back softly, her words lost and recovered in the clamor of rain on roof and awning. "Least it better be, or we're going out to sea with the tide."

As the rain lifted, the five of them turned left onto Light Street, headed back toward the heart of the town. Looking over his shoulder, Brenn squinted out over the Gray Sea, hoping to see some clearing behind them—the stars peeking out of the clouds, perhaps, or moonlight reflected off the distant water.

There was no such luck. The sea was dark in the distance, though twice lightning hurtled over the Bay of Ashes, and for a moment Brenn could make out the mountains of Aquila, the lofty white tombs of the necropolis, the beaches.

Then the light failed, and the surface of the waters sank back into darkness. For a moment—though it was surely impossible, defying belief and all common sense—Brenn thought he had seen boats on the water. Not just an isolated fishing boat or two, out foolishly late of an early March night and trapped in the sudden onrush of rain, but a whole flotilla, a hundred boats or more.

Surely it was an afterimage of lightning on the water—the kind of illusion that takes place when you look at a sudden bright light and then close your eyes. Brenn was turning to follow his comrades, was ready to forget it all for the excitement of the Hall of Poisoners and the treasure therein, when at a distance he saw something pale, phosphorescent—a strange light on the water and above it, fragmenting into a thousand steady, sickly points of luminescence far out on the churning sea. Some stood tall in the darkness, while shorter ones moved slowly, steadily from side to side—a strange movement, Brenn thought, on the rainswept waters offshore. Slowly but inexorably, the flickering lights approached the Maravenian shores.

Brenn shook his head. He turned to follow his friends.

Mirage, perhaps. Or a distant reflection of moonlight on the waters off to the north where the storm had broken and the clouds passed.

Or what the sailors called corposants—the strange and stormy descent of "fire" onto the masts and sails of a ship in turbulent waters.

He ran to catch up with Faye and the others, imagining unsettled things in the darkness of the streets.

Four blocks over and inland, where the Starboard Alley opened out into rainswept Light Street, a hulking form stood huddled in a blanket of sailcloth against the Hall of Poisoners.

As again the rain began to rise, the Goniph looked up the street toward the causeway and the harbor. Water raced in rivulets over the cobblestones, filling the gutter and the small conduit in the center of the street.

The prentices would be here soon. Faye would lead them, and she could find her way through pitch-black and any rain—through hurricane if she had to. Whatever came to pass that night, Faye would not be the one to fail him.

The Goniph was less sure about those who lay waiting in the cellar of the hall.

Surely Dragmond was as good as his word. Surely the prentices, gathered tonight in the king's wide net, would be free and on the streets by tomorrow evening, as Dragmond had promised, the questioning over and the business transacted.

For a leader could not lie to his people and stay a leader for long. At least, he could not promise them one thing and deliver another, could he?

The Goniph rested the back of his head against the stone wall of the hall. Rain coursed down the lip of his hood. It was like looking at the street from behind a waterfall. You almost had the impression that nobody could see you.

Of late, the death of Duval had been on the Goniph's mind. Three prentices he had lost because of it—Larentia and Eamon and Iliyas. He had dreamt of the three of them that very afternoon. Or of Iliyas and two faceless children—he had never seen Larentia and Eamon. The three of them grappled with one another in a glass jar—a jar held over a flame by a black-gloved hand.

And now, tonight, his best prentices, the most promising thieves in the guild, were being . . . what were the sugary words?

Taken in for questioning?

But surely the king was a man of his word. Could not promise one thing . . .

In the damaged light up the street, two gray forms darted from shadow to shadow. For a moment the Goniph thought it was more Watchmen—that the king, not satisfied with numbers, had called for more.

But then three others followed, and the big man recognized the stubby-legged gate of Squab, the tiny forms of Marco and Dirk.

On time, the Goniph thought uneasily, and again, unexplainably, Duval's expressionless face arose in his memory. He stood in the rain as Faye approached, as she caught sight of him and waved quickly, eagerly.

Surely a man of his word.

⫷⫷⫷ XXII ⫸⫸⫸

"It is time," the Goniph whispered when they had all gathered together, shaking the water from their cloaks as the rain lulled, the air thickened, and the streets around them fell into an almost unnatural silence. "By now the robbers have set about their own business—whatever cutthroat undertaking or road agency they have in mind. Regardless, think how sweet, how just it will be for them to return and find themselves . . . bereft of where-withal.''

The Goniph pushed back his hood and smiled wickedly, a rapturous, almost poetic note in his voice, as though the words he spoke had been savored and saved for this night and this place. ''Why, the first place they turn will be on each other.''

Brenn looked at Faye. He could not see her expression in the dark. Indeed, most faces were hidden, obscured by the night, the rain, and the lampblack.

The boy remembered how you had to trust the other prentices in the perilous blackness of the business at hand. Trust them, and go about your own part of the job, assured and assuring that everything fit—that the eyes and the arm and the fingers worked together as one body, even when the fingers were those of the lock-picker, the arms those of his companions, and the eyes those of a lookout on a rooftop or two streets away.

But something about this was disjointed, wrong. Perhaps it was the rain, obscuring vision and muffling sound, that brought confidence to the Goniph. Perhaps it was the something more that the First Master knew, as was often the case in any guild, and in this guild especially.

Whatever it was, some pieces were missing. The whole world of caution and plan and tactics that the Goniph had thrived on, and in which he had instructed them all, seemed suspended on this unnatural night.

The Goniph himself seemed Locked—Locked in a vision of how the business at hand would progress and turn out.

And when someone was Locked . . .

A light flickered yellow and red in the cup of Dirk's hands. He held the candle out, and Faye took it swiftly, shielding the flame against sudden breezes or downpours.

Suddenly a rich herbal smell hung on the air—green and orange and mint interwined, the sharp smell of an apothecary's shop.

''Here,'' Dirk whispered, and Brenn felt small, waxy leaves being slipped into his hand.

"Rue," the little thief murmured. "Plague bane. With the air's miasma and all."

"*This* week's charm," Faye observed scornfully, turning to look back up Light Street. But the Goniph's big hand rested on her shoulder, turning her about, pointing her at the cellar windows of the hall.

"There's the best way in," he hissed. "Don't even need your fingers—a sturdy short sword should pry loose the grating. It's old, after all, and been there years."

He leaned over Faye's shoulder, his face enormous and craggy in the dim candlelight.

"All five of you can slip through there," he ordered. "The last of you goes up to the front door and lets me in. Simple as that. We're back to Wall Town two hours before sunrise."

"Sir?" Brenn began cautiously, and the Goniph turned to face him.

"Yes, Brennart? You certainly seem to be full of questions and suggestions for a fellow so . . . out of practice."

"But this, sir, is my *first* question," Brenn continued uneasily. The big man's eyes narrowed, and the boy thought, *Careful. Above all, be careful now.*

"I was just wondering, sir. About the lookout. Whether the practice has changed since my long absence. When last I burgled a house, I recall at least two sets of eyes fixed on the nears and fars so the rest of us could work the place in peace and all. But perhaps things have streamlined in the guild over the last few months?"

"Oh, that's simple, Brennart," the Goniph began, and there were snakes in the tunnels of his voice—that sweet, level address that hides fang and drips venom, that tells you, *No more questions like this, boy, if you value your health.* "Oh, it's very simple and very easy."

He smiled at Brenn, then focused his gaze beyond the boy and onto the darkened windows of the hall.

"That was when you were green prentices, liable to break into a wizard's home when the wizard himself was there and stir up commotion for blocks about you."

Dirk laughed wickedly, and the Goniph paused, savoring the laughter.

"But of course you're older now, and wiser," he continued finally. "And I trust you've a version in all that book learning of what the rest of us have picked up in six seasons on the street. If you don't, Brenn, it won't matter much tonight, seeing as you have as fine a pack of housebreakers about you as I've had the pleasure to assemble."

A murmur of approval from Squab and Marco. Brenn shifted his weight uneasily from one foot to the other as the Goniph gathered words and reasons.

"Most important, Brenn," the big man urged, "is that I'll need all of you to carry out the booty. I mean, we'll have but twelve arms between us, and one look at that robbers' cellar will show you why I think it's few enough to go in with. There's also the question . . ."

"First Master?" Faye interrupted, her pretty, sharp-featured face almost invisible beneath her hood.

All conversation stopped. As though he knew and dreaded what would next come to pass, the Goniph gazed intently at Faye, his small eyes cold and glittering.

"Yes?"

"You aren't making much sense, sir," the girl observed shyly, and another warm shower began to descend over Maraven. "Did we grow up overnight, or something? I've never seen the time we didn't post the eyes."

"I was afraid of this," the Goniph said, raising his voice over the rush of the rain. "You're letting the boy turn your head, Faye, like he turned it before he left us for hocus and pocus. You're forgetting who's reared you, who's taught you."

The big man stepped into the street and, to the alarm of the prentices, raised his voice even more. Faye started to rush to him, to pull him back toward the shelter of the buildings, but Brenn grabbed her, held her back.

"Who, by the gods, is the First Master, anyway?" the Goniph roared. Down the street a cat yowled. There was a scuffling sound as some shadowy, unnameable thing stirred, then was silent again.

"You are," Brenn replied quietly, but with a boldness that surprised them all—perhaps himself the most. "You are First Master, Goniph, and I hold by your thoughts and your teaching.

But I'll be damned if I'm stepping into that hall without someone watching my back. You're the First Master, but I'd as soon go back to the wizard's tower and read books as get myself killed at your whim."

The rain was coming down harder now, rushing in rivulets over the cracks in the cobblestones, over the stones themselves. It poured over the eaves of the buildings on Light Street like a hundred cascades. Softly it poured down the mountainous man who stood motionless in the center of the street, his eyes downcast, his cloak pressed wet and dark against his body by the continual downpour.

"I suppose you can go back there, Brenn," the Goniph said. "Anytime, you can go back there. But these others—Faye and Dirk and Squab and little Marco—they've no wizard's tower and charm school to come prancing back to when they've botched up things in the real world of streets and knives and windows that are never quite open. Maraven is what they've got, lad—Maraven and Wall Town and nothing else. Nothing else but the Goniph."

"All the same, sir," Faye called out meekly. "I'd rather a lookout."

The big shoulders slumped. There was a long pause in which Goniph thought quickly, drastically.

Finally, he turned to his apprentices, opened his arms, and lumbered toward them, out of the rain and the fitful light of the street. He embraced Brenn and Faye, enfolding them entirely in his thick, wine-smelling cloak. He murmured to them, over and over, as a father soothes small children. Brenn didn't quite fit under the cloak or the comforting.

"Let's not fight, my little ones," the big man purred. "Anything but fighting at this late hour. You'll have your lookouts. Let's not fight."

The enormous voice, used to bellowing, shouting, and singing a harsh baritone in the tunnels under Wall Town, was now so soft that it seemed like the rain was speaking.

Brenn hugged the big man, taking in the smell of wine and of cinnamon, and beneath those smells the sturdy aroma of bread and wheat and flour. For all their differences, the Goniph *had* raised him, *had* taught him. He was all Brenn knew of Wall

Town: indeed, he *was* Wall Town in its extravagance and meanness and its curious honor.

Perhaps the Goniph was right after all: anything but fighting.

Awkwardly the First Master pushed away his two favorite apprentices. Back to the thoughts of the night and the business his mind raced, because it was there, in a world where people moved like chessmen at his beckon and bid, that he was more at home—not in the shadowy land of affections. He sprang to the time-honored tactics that quickened the group of children around him.

"Stay here, Squab. You're the eyes on the ground."

"But . . ."

"No arguments. Dirk, to the rooftop, as usual."

The little thief nodded and, crossing Light Street, scaled the outside of the Poisoners' Hall like a squat, leathery spider.

Good, the Goniph thought. *I'll handle them later. If the Watch doesn't collar them and they escape to the tunnels, Squab and Dirk are the two most likely to believe my version of what took place in the cellar.*

He looked back at Marco, who looked up at him eagerly.

Come along, child, the big man thought with a little sadness. *Hard lessons are in the offing.*

But after it's over, may the lot of us be free of that damnable Dragmond. At least for a while.

"Ah-ah. Too easy," Brenn whispered to Faye as the window to the cellar opened with a soft push.

The three of them—Brenn, Faye, and Marco—crouched and looked down into almost absolute darkness. Faye's candle, even held at arm's length and extended into the room, illumined no more than a few feet in front of them—a cellar that seemed empty except for a barrel or two, a couple of battered chairs.

"For the life of me, I can't see where you'd hide a treasure down here," Faye whispered. "Do you suppose the robbers have picked up and left?"

Brenn shook his head. "I expect it could be. Could be other things, though. The Goniph's our friend, but he's not quick with the whole story."

"Hush!" Faye urged. "Don't say things like that about the First Master."

"Why?" Brenn asked. "He's up at the entrance, waiting for one of us to open the door for him. He can't hear me."

"But *I* can," Faye insisted. "Whatever we do, you're not to speak ill of the Goniph."

"So you think he's told us the whole truth, Faye?"

"No," she replied, eyes lowered. "But the Goniph's is the best truth we have."

Brenn stared at his friend in puzzlement. He had forgotten how it was in Wall Town—how the lies built a shaky structure upon other lies until the only truth was the version you heard from those in the neighborhood, easily changed for another the next street over.

"Well," he sighed finally, "there's no way to tell until we're down there, is there?"

Feetfirst, Brenn slipped through the window and landed softly on the floor. Faye handed him the candle, and he set it securely on the seat of one of the chairs before he helped her and Marco into the cellar.

From floor level, the cellar was as empty and forbidding as it had seemed from the street. In the wavering light of the candle, Brenn noticed that the floor was swept, fresh rushes strewn. It seemed a little finicky for the likes of the robbers he knew.

Picking up the candle, he scanned the wide cellar of the Hall of Poisoners. Shelves filled with old clay bottles and dusty vials and flasks lined the far, windowless wall, and the candlelight broke over waves of glass and glaze like the sun on Lake Teal. It was hard to believe their contents were deadly poisons.

"Faye," Brenn offered nervously. "There's nothing about this room I like."

"It only gets worse from here, young man," a voice from nowhere observed. Startled, Brenn dropped the candle, and the cellar plunged once again into darkness. He heard nothing except the startled breathing of Marco and Faye behind him.

Then, behind the shelves of bottles, someone lit a lamp. Its light was dim and unhealthy, like a will-o'-the-wisp. The man holding the lamp was tall and blond. He wore a white leather armor, studded with silver, and motioning behind him, he smiled humorlessly at the prentices. Out of the confusing light of lamp upon bottle came three Watchmen, armed with swords and daggers.

"Lightborn!" Faye whispered. The three young thieves backed against the wall, their knives drawn.

Shortly after Dragmond ascended to the throne, the legend of the Pale Man had spread quickly through Maraven. Some said he was of noble lineage, of high station once in the court of some northern king, who fell from grace after a brief, ill-starred rebellion. Others said he was simply a murderer, having killed a count up in Arbor. The darkest stories were that he had killed his own children—three or four or, in some versions, five of them. Why he had come to Maraven and why King Dragmond had welcomed him were even greater mysteries.

The greatest mystery of all was the nature of what Lightborn did in Kestrel Tower. Some said it was intelligence, a sort of secret police that answered only to Dragmond and Ravenna. Others said he was a court enforcer—Dragmond's eyes and ears into the intrigues among his own courtiers. Most decided early on that he was nothing more than a glorified torturer, as boxes of strange machineries, of broken glass and of terrible caustic elixirs, came at his request from Jaleel and from points south and east. All the deliveries were supposedly secret, supposedly silent, but no caravan was secret or silent in Wall Town, and soon all Maraven knew that Captain Lightborn collected exotic things.

As his stay in Kestrel Tower continued, the Pale Man became less and less visible. Occasional appearances on Teal Front dwindled until rumors had it that Lightborn was ill, confined to his chambers. Rumors arose that he was dead, and that the white form that walked the battlements was his hungry ghost, cheated in transactions by the honorable King of Maraven and Palerna, stalking for revenge.

At least the last rumor was proven false that night in the Hall of Poisoners. For Captain Lightborn was very much alive, and there at the behest of Dragmond.

Slowly he walked to the center of the room, the Watchmen alert and poised behind him. His eyes were uncommonly pale, the color of shallow water, and his blond hair faded into white at the temples and at the widow's peak, so that in the lamplight he resembled an elegant Norseman—one of their *jarls*, perhaps, set down in seedy Maravenian surroundings.

"There are only three of you?" he asked. His voice was without accent, without inflection. Brenn thought for a moment that the words might as well have been written, because on the captain's lips they were homeless, belonging to no country or human circumstance.

"The Goniph had promised more. Five, I believe," Lightborn added tersely, leaning over the back of one of the cellar's simple chairs. Brenn and Faye looked at each other in astonishment. Marco huddled near the wall, too bewildered to follow the words of the captain.

"We don't know what you're talking about," Brenn declared.

"Of course you don't," the Pale Man answered. "That was the idea."

There was a noise at the top of the stairs—the sound of movement, of heavy boots upon wooden floors. A door opened above them, and the light of a lantern shone down into the cellar.

"And here he comes"—Lightborn smiled—"like the villain in a comedy. He makes his speech, he departs, and we are left to bury the wounded."

He stopped, pretended astonishment, and set his hand to his thin, white lips.

"Did I say, 'bury the wounded'?" he asked in mock horror. "My, what an embarrassing phrase. But somehow fitting, as you will see."

The Goniph descended the steps, behind him two more members of the Watch. Suddenly there were noises outside on the street: the movement and clatter and shouting of a dozen men.

"They'll find one in the Starboard Alley, another on the roof," the Goniph pronounced uneasily, scanning the room as if in search of something or someone more.

"He is not here, First Master," Lightborn said casually. "Surely you didn't expect him to . . . descend to a gathering such as this."

"He's been here before, damn it!" the Goniph snapped. "He's

always here when he wants something. Comes beggin', crown in hand, he does.''

A curved knife appeared in Lightborn's hand, so suddenly it seemed that he had drawn it from the air. He handled it deftly, eyed the Goniph, then pared his fingernails.

"My, my, First Master. This smacks of the insubordinate. I would have thought you'd had your fill of rebellion, what with Duval and everything.''

"What's this about Duval, Goniph?'' Faye asked in astonishment.

"A cutthroat's bluster, Faye. He's trying to fright you.''

"Oh, believe him, little Faye,'' Lightborn said, his courtier's smile widening until it became a grimace—the grin of a hunting shark. "I know *nothing* of Duval. After all, you are the price of my ignorance.''

"It's interrogation, Lightborn,'' the Goniph urged. "Interrogation only. 'Tis the agreement I made with Dragmond.'' His voice sounded weak and desperate. What he had suspected all along but never let himself examine was coming to pass now, and the horror of the moment deepened with the knowledge that he had seen this coming from miles away, had trusted the king because it was easier to trust the king than to stand up to him.

"I wasn't there at the agreement,'' Lightborn explained, an inhuman mirth in his eyes. He rolled the dagger in his hand, pointing it menacingly at the dazed First Master.

The Goniph backed slowly toward his prentices. He raised his hands in what seemed to be a gesture of surrender, then lowered one lazily, casually, to the back of the other chair. Brenn knew the gesture: he had seen the big man do this or something very like it in the dives of Wall Town, in the streets of Grospoint when bargaining turned to bickering and bickering to knives.

Zephyrian bees, the boy thought, and in the fitful light strained to catch the First Master's glance—the signal to fight, or flee, or do nothing for the moment.

The Goniph's eyes rested briefly on Marco, then flickered toward the window behind them. Brenn waited, his gaze intent on the big man, unsure if he had read the signals right.

"Marco!'' the Goniph bellowed, and hurled the chair toward

Lightborn. The Pale Man stepped aside nimbly, and the chair hurtled into two of the Watchmen, striking them at the knees and felling them. Quickly, as though it were part of some juggler's performance, Faye knelt, and the littlest thief sprinted up her back, grabbed the windowsill at the apex of his jump, lost his grip for a fraction of a second, then caught his balance and, with surprising strength, pulled himself toward the opening and freedom.

Suddenly Marco cried out softly and looked back over his shoulder at the white-handled knife buried hilt-deep in the small of his back. He groped at the sill, at the world outside, his fingers surprised and vague. Then he toppled to the cellar floor, where he lay still and lifeless.

Faye ran to him, pressed her hand softly to the side of his neck, and looked up at Lightborn in shock.

"You—you've killed Marco!"

"Unfortunate, isn't it?" the captain observed with mock seriousness. "Especially since he was the one of you not yet of age—the one I had liberty to spare. Well, such is the nature of business."

He motioned to the four Watchmen, two of whom were still gathering themselves from the floor. Deliberately the soldiers drew their swords and advanced cautiously toward the three thieves at the far end of the cellar. Carefully they spread out around the Goniph, understandably leery of four hundred pounds of anger.

"Get out of here, Brenn!" the Goniph muttered, drawing a wicked-looking Moorish scimitar he had won at dice.

"But . . ."

"Get out of here and take her with you!" he snapped.

Brenn nodded, his old instinct to obey the First Master drowning out the fear and the honor and the sorrow and everything else that rushed through his mind at the moment. Faye was dumbstruck, crouched over Marco like she was preparing to weep forever. With a leap that surprised himself, Brenn struck the side of the cellar wall with the sole of his right boot and vaulted to the window, slipping his legs through in one acrobatic movement, and rolling over onto his stomach, he reached back into the cellar, his arm dangling like a lifeline for Faye, who was shaking herself from her stupor. Quickly, resourcefully, sensing the grave situation, the girl grabbed his hand as behind her, the Goniph spun himself through the air, gathering in three of the Watchmen with his dark, enormous cape. Goniph and soldiers crashed into the table and splintered it, as Lightborn arced away from the flying debris and pointed toward Brenn, whose shoulders knotted as he lifted Faye through the window.

"Get *them!*" the Pale Man screamed. "Damn the rest of them! Bring me that one!"

Brenn looked back down into the darkness. He saw a hulking form thrashing and dodging, heard the sound of bones breaking, of metal against rock and flesh. Saw blades and arms cartwheeling in violent movements as though they lay at the center of some deadly dance. With a final tug that sent him toppling into the street, Brenn pulled Faye after him out into the air and the rain.

Quickly they raced up Light Street, ducking behind a capsized vendor's cart as a Watch squadron raced by with drawn swords, no doubt heading for the Hall of Poisoners. Faye was weeping still for Marco, her tears mingling with the drizzling rain. The footsteps faded down the street, and struggling to compose herself, she looked at Brenn.

"It's going to be like this all the way back to Wall Town," she said. "Dragmond's Inlaws are coming from all quarters."

"All the more reason to move quickly," Brenn urged.

"For *you* to move quickly," Faye corrected. "Three blocks over is the Anacreon. It's a new pub in Grospoint. Has a wooden statue of a poet strumming a lyre outside it. You know about lyres from Euterpe's, don't you?"

Brenn nodded stupidly.

"Just strum the lyre," Faye explained, "and the poet will do the rest. You'll be in the tunnels in no time."

Brenn smiled. "Terrance told me once to befriend all poets," he said. "It's good to know one of them will help us escape."

"Help *you* escape," Faye corrected again. "As for me, I'm off down Cove Road."

"Not alone, you aren't!" Brenn exclaimed, clutching her shoulders. "The Watch is everywhere by now. They're . . ."

"Looking for you," Faye said with a curious smile. "I don't

know what it is, Brenn, but the whole bunch of them must have you marked. Give me your cloak."

"I don't understand."

"Give me your cloak," Faye insisted. "It's warmer than this thin little rag of mine. I need a warm wrap more than you do. The seashore's cold of a morning."

"But you can't . . ."

"I have to. This wizard of yours is our only hope in the long run. You see, the Goniph was up to his ears in Dragmond and Ravenna, and if things fall out for the rest of the night the way they've been falling so far, then the king won't rest until he has you. You know that: you're not telling all."

Brenn fell silent as Faye wrapped his cloak around her shoulders.

"Three streets over," she urged. "Anacreon's. The lyre."

"Faye! I can't . . ."

"It's the prophecy, Brenn," she said, mustering a brave little laugh. "You see, I'm right about the Lapwing."

"Oh, you're always right, Faye," Brenn said, his own eyes filling with tears.

"Three streets over," she said again, and, scrambling out from under the vendor's cart, raced off up Light Street toward the shore, Cove Road, and the wizard.

He felt nothing until the third knife.

Nothing, that is, but the thrashing of limbs beneath him, the thin neck of a Watchman snapping like a breadstick in his enormous hands. And then the wound, and another after it, and a strong arm straining to pull back his chin, to expose the soft fleshy neck.

Still, the First Master struggled, and the pain sharpened in his back, in his side, once, twice, a third time in his shoulder. A warm stream trickled down his forearms, and the lights of the room dimmed and rose and dimmed again.

By now Faye and Brenn should be halfway up Light Street. If the gods were willing, they would meet no Watch on the way.

Something came crashing down onto the Goniph's head. The room went black, and he heard nothing.

He awoke in the darkness.

He could not move.

Someone lay still beside him—not Lucia, the little courtesan, but a man in armor.

Slowly, his eyes adjusting to the dense gloom of the cellar, the Goniph remembered where he was.

Slowly the room turned. The ceiling rocked above him. It receded, then suddenly vanished into a deeper darkness. His sides and chest and back ached with the white-hot pains of forty knife wounds.

He wanted to sleep, to give it all up. But the old Goniph, the one who had struggled to the top of the heap in the roughneck tunnels of Wall Town, would not give it up without a better fight.

There in the cellar, for the few minutes left him, the big man struggled to the edge of wakefulness.

Out of all the mistakes, this one had been worst. He had won Brenn and Faye some time, of course, but now as he felt the sticky and gaping wound in his side, he knew he had won it at mortal cost.

For a last time the Goniph thought of Brenn.

There was something about him they had wanted from the beginning. All of Dragmond's questions had led toward the little scholar, toward the book-smart lad and his whereabouts.

So you're something special, Brenn, he observed. *The top of the crab heap. Well, you pay for that specialness, boy. Best to scramble nameless in the jar and avoid all that infamy. Because when they know you, they ask things of you, promise things in return.*

And when they promise, they betray.

Softly as the light in the cellar window faded, the Goniph thought of his own namelessness. Somewhere, far back over years and miles, they had called him something else. He could not remember that name.

Just as well, he thought. *Has nothing to do with me anymore. Has nothing to do with . . . nothing . . . nothing.*

His pale eyes looked into nothing and lost their focus.

≺≺≺ XXIII ≻≻≻

At that moment the Great Witch entered King Dragmond's throne room. Shaking the rain from her shimmering black cloak, draping the cloak theatrically over the torch-encircled throne, she turned like a dancer to face the king, who stood at the window looking out over the causeway.

Dragmond turned to face her, a thinly disguised look of dread on his face.

"Why are you sitting up here like some damned functionary," Ravenna spat, "instead of defending your crown down in the city?"

"Despite your magic, m'lady," Dragmond retorted defensively, "a ruler cannot be all places at once. He should be first in the throne room, at the center of power from which all polity issues."

"Well, if you don't take it into your own hands, someone will *issue* your *polity* for you, nephew!" Ravenna observed ironically.

Dragmond cringed, as he always did when she called him *nephew*.

"It is in the hands of Captain Lightborn, Ravenna. Hands you have trusted in times past."

"To twist the arms of augurers, Dragmond. Not to support your throne."

He turned from her, looking angrily out the window.

"Where have *you* been while I was 'endangering the kingdom,' then? I shudder to think."

Dramatically Ravenna moved to the center of the room, her black dress dripping water behind her. In full torchlight she looked older, wearier, the king thought.

"Oh, but you would, Dragmond. You *would* shudder to think

where I had been. For it was at the necropolis on the blasted shores of Aquila, scarcely an hour west of here.''

''Placing flowers on Mother's tomb?'' the king observed bitterly. Ravenna stared at him with withering fury, and the stone wall around the window began to smoke and curdle.

Dragmond stepped gingerly away, moving resolutely toward the throne. Something in him he could not name, something below thought, was telling him to be seated, to rest in the bejeweled residence of Palerna's power.

She knew it, too. At the moment that Dragmond was seated Ravenna's anger faded. She stood in front of him, her thin pale arms moving aimlessly as though she had forgotten something in the throne room and come for it, only to have forgotten what it was she forgot in the first place.

''I—I have brought the cwalu to help you.''

''You have—*what*?'' the king exclaimed, leaning forward in the throne, but even in his astonishment taking care not to rise from it. In silence they looked at each other.

''How dare you?'' Dragmond hissed. ''Whatever you imagine, Great Witch, I am the King of Palerna, by the gods! You can augur and divine and enchant and raise what you damn well wish in your own chambers, up there among candles and visions. But once you haul your sorcery into the body politic you trouble my waters, and, my dear, you do not want to do that!''

''Then take those politics into your own hands, Dragmond,'' Ravenna replied icily. ''Go down to the Poisoners' Hall and see this through. Guide Lightborn's dagger into the pretender's throat if you have to, and twist it a time or two for the throne. For assurance. And for me.''

She smiled, held out her hand. The torches in the room bowed and fluttered. The harsh light softened, reddened. Cautiously Dragmond removed his glove.

They were staring at each other when Captain Lightborn dragged the fat little thief into the room.

''His name is Squab, Your Majesty,'' the Pale Man announced, hurling the boy toward the foot of the throne. ''And a sweet little pigeon he is. All that remains of my night of revel.''

"And the wizard's apprentice?" Dragmond asked triumphantly, still staring at Ravenna.

"Slipped away, alas," Lightborn admitted reluctantly.

Suddenly two pairs of eyes were upon him. The sharp, feverish eyes of raposas they were, he thought. Or of archers, their bows bent, looking down the shafts of nocked arrows.

And yet he showed no fear. Fear was what they fed upon, this king and this witch.

"This is no cause for alarm, sire," Lightborn said smoothly, giving the cowering Squab a kick. "For this pigeon knows a song few pigeons know. A song of tunnels and thieves in Wall Town."

"Is that so, Lightborn?" the king asked, giving Ravenna a sidelong glance. She stood there, her hands folded demurely in front of her like the statue of a child.

"He will sing that song for you, as he sang it for me."

"In return, we may give him his life," Dragmond prompted.

Lightborn smiled and nodded. "Such as it is," he agreed.

Ravenna stood rapt by the throne, her eyes on some far, indefinable region.

"The glorious lady has . . . peopled our city with the dead, Captain. I do not expect we shall need the Watch for the rest of our endeavors."

Lightborn raised his eyebrows, fingering the dagger at his belt. Quickly, almost indetectably, he lifted his hand from the hilt, and, drawing a white handkerchief from his sleeve, wiped the crosspiece and pommel. The handkerchief was gone almost before he noticed it, but Dragmond's sharp eye caught a hint of rusty red at its corner as the Pale Man hid it away.

The cwalu, then! the Pale Man thought giddily. *Then such things are possible!*

"The dead, sire?" he asked levelly, a feigned calm and amusement in his voice. "Why, most of my friends are dead! What . . . happy circumstance! Should I expect reunions?"

It was now Dragmond's turn to smile.

"Will you excuse us, Ravenna?" he asked.

The Great Witch looked at him in consternation, her disbelief turning quickly into anger. Nor would he look at her, but addressed her with his eyes fixed all the while on the boy Squab cringing in front of him.

"You can serve us best in conjury, my dear, in the upper reaches of the tower."

It was a calculated risk. For the sake of the throne she would neither say nor do anything that would undermine him in the presence of subordinates, especially a man as dangerous as Lightborn.

Ravenna shook her head as though she were trying to dispel voices. These were the hardest parts—when she nodded and bowed and did Dragmond's bidding like a dutiful little servant. But she needed him until the Leaves were found, when his ancestry and wit and above all his eyes would be useful.

Then they would see about service and conjury.

Gathering her robes around her, she swept from the room, the torchlight bending to follow her as she swept up the stairs to her uppermost chamber, dizzy with its candles and the old chaos of night. She would augur and rant up there, curse Dragmond for tricking her and casting her out of this night of victory. Meanwhile he could use her deeds of recent hours to his best advantage, sending the cwalu after the boy, as she no doubt intended.

For if legends were true, a walking corpse is the best of soldiers, having no way to tell of the crimes he is asked to commit, and nothing to risk when committing them.

But not all the cwalu had fallen at the point of a knife, or turned at the end of a rope. For the plague had taken many, and if they crossed the Needle's Eye and entered the city, no doubt they would bring it back with them.

Whatever the king was, he was no fool to dance with the Death.

"Who would you expect to meet, Captain?" Dragmond continued, his eyes following his mistress uncomfortably out the door. "Among the cwalu, I mean."

"Oh, the Goniph," Lightborn answered. "And one of his apprentices, a boy named Marco, I believe. Not to mention the Watchmen you sent with me. For of course, *they* were the ones who allowed the lad in question to escape."

"Of course," Dragmond replied ironically, leaning back in the throne, his mind pacing more assuredly over strategies, over options. "And I would suppose, like any good commander whose charges were in error, you are prepared to lead others in a venture that will . . . correct all mistakes?"

Skillfully the Pale Man masked all but the faintest trace of his frown. If the cwalu were there, the Death was among them. No fool, this Dragmond. He would take no royal chances with the plague, but send instead his hirelings and ministers.

But there was always rue, the captain thought. And rosewater, and vinegar, and myrrh and saffron. Whatever the preventive, Lightborn kept it near him.

And he would use them all.

"It will be my pleasure, sir," he replied reluctantly, bowing slightly at the hip in a smart military salute . . .

From where? Dragmond asked himself, his thoughts racing. *Do they salute like that in Aquila or Prussia or Umbria or where?*

Damn that you have to trust them when you don't even know where they're from!

He did not hear the sound of the coach as it clattered out the main gate of the tower, down onto the causeway and across the strait into Maraven.

The road behind her was swarming with people.

Faye looked over her shoulder as she walked briskly up Cove Road, headed toward the East Gate and Terrance's ramshackle tower. Onto the beach the legion came, in rowboats, in dinghies, in canoes, their small craft scraping against the gritty black sand of the cove.

Out of the boats they climbed, or crawled, or stumbled, then steadily made their way up into the black rocks. Slowly, as though something drew them back seaward and they were struggling against its pull, they climbed painfully on the road behind the girl and headed south through the slaughter yards, finding the narrowing streets that led straight into Wall Town.

Faye stopped, wrapped Brenn's heavy cloak around her, and watched them filter between buildings and into alleys. From where she stood, they looked like a ragtag lot—not the general fashion of men King Dragmond was accustomed to hire.

For the briefest of moments she thought Maraven was being invaded.

Aquila was known to be terribly uneasy, its rightful duke in forest exile. And Zephyr . . . well, Zephyr was always itching to get at Maraven. Rapidly Faye's mind raced over all the threats, from the robber guild the Goniph had spoken of to the distant menace of imperial Espana. All the time she knew otherwise, and before long she turned eastward, directing her steps once again toward the wizard's dwelling and the help she and Brenn hoped desperately would come.

She turned too late.

There, on the coastline in front of her, three ragged figures emerged from the water, staggering up the beach toward the high rocks and the road. Faye thought of hiding at first, of waiting until they passed by on their way toward the center of town. She changed her mind after a moment, when the men reached the road, climbed upon it, and stood there, as if they awaited someone or something.

"Well, it's surely not me!" Faye said aloud to nobody in particular. The sound of her own voice soothed her at first, but it faded quickly into the commotion in the distance behind her and the rush of the nearby tides.

She thought of Brenn, who by now would be down in the tunnels if the gods were kind.

"After all, I'm nothing more than a sneak thief from Wall Town," she said, steeling herself. "This lot are after a bigger catch."

Though what Brenn had to do with that was beyond her entirely.

Nonetheless, it was Brenn she was bound to rescue. With a deep breath, Faye trotted down Cove Road toward the three ragged men in the distance.

She slowed her steps as she approached them. Something about them was awkward, unnatural. They stood like puppets, controlled by hidden strings.

Even from this distance, her sharp eye noticed that the rags they wore were more tatters than rags, that seaweed draped all three of them, tangling in fingers and arms and in their bunched and matted hair. Through the mist she could see a faint flicker of scrimshaw at their ankles, at their wrists.

It was a few steps closer that she smelled them.

For the smell at first was salt and the night, and the strong, familiar smell of fish and weed and dead things adrift on the rising tide. But something below those smells was stronger still, arising unpleasantly and even vilely from the road ahead of the uneasy girl.

It grew stronger the closer she got: the smell of something corrupted far beyond death itself. Faye reeled with it, for the wind of it was worse than the midsummer slaughter yards or the tanneries, worse by far than the middens outside the west walls. For a moment the street seemed to fall away under her feet, and despite her struggle, she was toppling, head over heels into a greater dark . . .

Then, like a respite, like a blessing sent from the sea, the clouds opened above them and Cove Road was drenched with a warm downpour of rain. Faye blinked groggily as the road resumed beneath her. She covered her head, lowered her eyes, and kept walking.

They sniffed like dogs as she approached, a rooting, snuffling sound that rose above the rush of the rain. Faye shuddered. She dared not lift her eyes, but walked through them, holding her breath . . .

The hand that grasped at her was skeletal. The man that grasped her was dead.

Faye shouted, reeled, and pulled at the hand, struggling desperately to pry bone and tendon from her arm. The clawed grip of the man-thing held firm, and with all her strength the girl wrenched against it once, twice, a third time. Slowly, despite her struggle, the creature drew her toward itself, opened wide its shredded cloak to receive her.

And the smell rose again, rising over her like a gas, like a sickness. Lightning flickered out at sea, and for the briefest of moments Faye looked into the eyeless face, into the loose skin hanging from it, at the rotten black boils at the base of the torn ear.

She screamed, and tore at the fingers once more, propelled beyond her natural strength by surging fear. With the brittle sound of dry twigs snapping, the hideous fingers broke away, and the girl tumbled free into Cove Road. Another of the dead men lurched at her, arms outstretched. With a burglar's skill she tripped aside, gained footing, and ran hard, leaving her monstrous attackers lurching behind her.

There were more of them at the Street of the Bookbinders.

When they saw Faye their strides became purposeful, swift, as though some inaudible voice had set them running. The girl turned right, stumbled, and raced down the Street of the Book-binders. Now every step took her back into Wall Town, into the belly of a district even she barely knew, where the old streets sometimes narrowed to the point that only a child could continue to follow them, where three streets were named the Avenue of Rushes and ran together at a triangular fountain each side of which appeared the same, and where roads and alleys stopped altogether at the back of a house or the East Wall, doubled back on themselves, or circled around to their own beginnings.

Faye's streets were a place where thought and a map could get you lost forever.

Back and forth the girl went, guiding herself by instinct and by ear. For the snuffling sound was all about her now, as the dead men circled her eagerly. Sometimes the sound would diminish, and she would lose it altogether as she raced through an abandoned square, trying to recover her bearings, to recognize a building or street or landmark she could steer by. But then, when it seemed she was on the brink of familiar surroundings, when something about a door or a balcony or even the sign of a pub danced tauntingly at the edge of her memory, the sniffling would rise again from behind her, from a side alley, or even from rooftops, and she would lose herself again in the quiet, welcoming dark.

It took less than an hour, this wandering, though it seemed to have no end for the frightened girl. Finally she toppled onto a narrow brick stairway, her strength and resources exhausted. Gasping for air, she listened in terror to the snuffling and scraping that surrounded her, as steadily and tirelessly her pursuers closed in.

Frantically she looked for escapes as the first of the cwalu came into view in the mouth of an alley across the street from her. Standing upright, sniffing the air, the thing turned to face her, and with that horrifying swiftness that predators take on in the dreams of the prey, the man loped toward Faye, staggering over cobblestone and gutter.

Faye spun about and scrambled up the steps behind her, grabbing the latch of the door at the top of the stairs. It opened readily, to her complete and joyful surprise, and the girl tumbled into a room lit with glass lamps, shining in dark mahogany. The room was circular, as such rooms are supposed to be, and each of the portals was present and open.

"A chapel of the Four Winds!" Faye murmured, closing the door behind her. "Oh, let it be true what they say!"

Two centuries ago there had been no port city on the Sea of Shadows—neither Maraven nor Arbor, nor Random, nor even most decadent Rabia—where you could not find a shrine to the Four Winds. For the winds were the breath of life to the sailor, and whatever his other beliefs, each man who lived by the sea found time to pay homage to the Four when his ship was docked.

Though in some parts of the city the doctrine had changed, and the brightest and most learned felt it was better to build sturdier ships than to scrape and chant and meditate in the appeasement of winds, in parts of Maraven such as Ships and Wall Town the practice was still honored. The globe lamps in the chapels were kept constantly burning, the mahogany walls and portals and statuary were polished and buffed and oiled.

Legend had it that the chapels brought blessings on those who entered them. Poets would visit for the gifts of inspiration, visionaries because it was said that the future rode on the back of the winds. The walking corpses—the zombi and the cwalu of the frightening old stories—were said to fear the chapels, because the winds within them could blow the animating force out of the bodies of the undead. But most of all, the chapel portals were kept clear so that the winds might blow through them, and a sailor seated in the chapel, feeling a breeze rising from one of the walls, could know without fail the prevailing influence.

At one time Faye, who at thirteen had believed in nothing that slipped through her five senses, had asked the Goniph why they bothered.

"Imagine the time and the money that goes into keeping those places," she lectured, as only a thirteen-year-old could lecture those older and wiser. "Time and money better spent on the ills of the people, in making Wall Town something more than a brothel and gambling den for Maraven's rich. After all, I've heard sailors say that compared to the west coast of Europa or up on the Oceanus Germanicus, the winds aren't all that bad in our part of the world.''

And the Goniph had smiled, looked at her curiously, and asked her: ''Have you ever thought, Faye, that our winds are calmer because we fill lamps and polish and oil the wood?''

She remembered his words now, in the hour she spent at the shrine. Faye began to believe that the Goniph was right, if only that there was something to a thick oaken door and an iron bolt, for the cwalu drew no nearer than its threshold. Outside she could hear them pacing, shuffling, waiting. Once, through the western portal, she saw the moon break through the clouds as the night cleared for a moment, and before the rain resumed she saw five of them, sniffing and walking in circles on the deserted street.

''Where are the people, though?'' Faye asked herself. ''Am I the only live one awake at this time of night?'' Not a window held light.

Almost as though in answer, a heavy coach clattered up the street, riding through the milling dead and losing itself in the dark beyond them. Faye watched it pass by, noticed the dark wings inlaid in silver on its side.

''Well, then,'' she said, walking to the center of the room and standing on the huge mosaic compass inlaid in the floor. ''There are some folk that can pass through them without getting attacked. Or even tangled up, for that matter. It's good to know that they're not after the whole living lot of us.''

She sat, cupped her chin in her hands.

''But why me? And not . . . Brenn?''

She traced back the night's events, beginning at the Hall of Poisoners. Perhaps the trap set by Captain Lightborn—and by the king himself, it seemed—had nothing to do with dead men wandering the streets of Maraven.

That seemed unlikely. There was just too much intrigue and commotion all falling together on a single night for Faye to believe that coincidence had brought these things to pass at the same time.

She thought of the profeta cup—of the Pelican and the Sow and the Lapwing. She still puzzled over the odd arrangement of runic signs, of how they fit with one another, though she trusted that they did.

So it was with her pursuers.

If what she believed was true—if Lightborn and the army of dead men outside were in league with each other—then no doubt everyone was looking for Brenn.

"All the more reason to get to this wizard," Faye whispered. "But how?"

Dust skittered out of the western portal, raising the hem of her cloak. Even the flames in the lamps tilted eastward—a sure sign that the wind was up outdoors.

"Perhaps if I could get downwind of all this sniffing," Faye mused. "After all, that's what works with bloodhounds, isn't it?"

She paused, curled into a tight little ball, her arms wrapped about her knees. Slowly a smile broke across her face. She shook her head in disbelief as the west wind swirled around her.

"How could I be so dimwitted?" She laughed. "Blood-hounds!"

Had you been standing that night in the Street of Nails, the narrow avenue that ran by the eastern side of the chapel, you would have seen a stirring at the large portal in the wall. Usually passersby could look straight from the street into the heart of the chapel, where the lamplight shone tranquilly and invitingly, but not this night.

For something had entered and blocked the portal, eclipsing the lamps behind it, and after a moment of darkness and movement a small graceful form slipped out of the portal, dangled for a moment over the street, then dropped silently to the cobblestones below.

Laughing quietly to herself, Faye darted through alleys on the way back up to Cove Road and Terrance's tower. Meanwhile, behind her the cwalu still wandered about the chapel, drawn by the smell of Brenn's cloak, which Faye had dropped carefully in the center of the compass so that its scent could ride on any of the four winds.

That very compass had given the girl back her bearings. North and east she moved constantly—north and east untill she found herself on a side street that ended at the East Wall of Maraven. She scrambled to the top of the wall as the rains began again, silently thanking the Goniph for having trained her so well in the arts of climbing and scaling.

Then, as the rain swept the battlements, she followed the wall toward the sea and the half-finished tower. Though the rain grew more fierce by the minute, grew altogether blinding at times, there was still the wall beneath her feet, and if she put one foot in front of the other carefully, like an acrobat walking a rope bridge, that eventually she would find herself at the house of the wizard.

When Terrance answered the knock and found the girl leaning in his doorway, bent against the cascading rain, he knew it could be none but Faye. Given the circumstances, she was not as attractive as the hitch in Brenn's voice had always suggested when the boy had spoken of her in the past. In fact, she looked rather mousy and frail: her hair was plastered limply against her face, and she was so thoroughly soaked that she walked with an inch of standing water in her boots.

And yet to have taken on that water, she must have come through the storm and through other things worse—far worse.

So he told himself as he let her in.

"It's Brenn, Master Wizard," Faye announced, her teeth chattering, as the old man drew her into the solar and seated her by the warm blaze in the fireplace. "It's Brenn, and he's needing you in Wall Town."

⤛⤛⤛ XXIV ⤜⤜⤜

Not long after Terrance heard the news, things were desperate indeed in Wall Town.

It had begun smoothly. Following Faye's instructions, Brenn found his way to the new pub, strummed the lyre in the hands of the statue, and when the base of that statue had shifted, revealing a trapdoor in the very street itself, he had climbed down the ladder into the westernmost edges of the tunnel system that riddled half of Maraven.

The way home from there was torchlit and easy. Soon Brenn found himself in the apprentices' quarters, wrapped in a warm wool blanket, among friends, awaiting the return of his other comrades.

It was then that Ravenna's army arrived.

Theodor, one of the young apprentices who had come to Wall Town when his former master Duval had met his fate on the scaffold, rushed into the quarters, his tough little eyes wide and frightened.

"There's—there's a man in the corridor, Brennart, the likes o' which I've *never* seen!" the child exclaimed, grabbing Brenn's arm and tugging frantically.

Brenn smiled, tried to reassure the boy. For some reason the younger children had always taken to him, had always singled him out in times of crisis or trouble. At times it had been flattering, but more often it was only inconvenient.

On rare occasions it promised outright danger. This boy Theodor, whom he had met only hours before, now shivered in the corner of the apprentices' quarters, his bravado vanished entirely. Who knew what he had seen in the vast network of tunnels?

"Settle down, then, lad," Brenn urged, resting his hands on the boy's shoulders. "A man, you say. Why does he startle you so?"

The child turned to Brenn, fighting away tears.

"He smells something fierce, Brennart!"

"Well, Theodor," Brenn soothed. "Not all of us are . . . fragrant."

Randall and Nick, two journeyman thieves who had been playing cards in the quarters when Brenn arrived, laughed amiably, their eyes still on the cards in their hands.

"But, Brenn," the boy exclaimed in a hushed, awestruck voice. "The man *glowed*. Like . . . something they pull up from deep in the Sea of Shadows after a Storm has shook up the waters."

Brenn nodded, recalling the dim lights on the Gray Sea that evening.

"Like . . . St. Elmo's fire?" he asked.

Theodor nodded.

"*One* of them, you said?"

Theodor nodded again, dazed by the excitement and by his own importance.

"Then it's best we look into this, lad," Brenn decreed, drawing his dagger. He motioned for the others to follow.

The corridor outside the apprentices' quarters was clean and well lit. Though parts of the Wall Town tunnels were a shambles, the Goniph made certain that his charges kept their surroundings spotless: it helped them, he said, in learning to cover their tracks after burglaries. Whatever the case, Brenn was glad now that the tunnels in front of them were clear. His companions were tense, starting at shadows and echoes, and everyone knew that sharp metal and frayed nerves were a deadly combination.

Brenn and Theodor walked side by side, the child directing them back through the tangled network of passages toward the spot where he had seen the glowing invader. Randall and Nick followed behind them, short swords drawn and ready.

They had attended Brenn instinctively, all of them. Randall and Nick had set down their cards at once, had asked him what to do. Brenn marked it down to politics—to the fact that everyone knew he was important among the Goniph's prentices. But there were trespassers in the tunnels, and that meant that there was no time to question motives. Brenn was only glad that he had company if it came to blades.

But if it came to blades . . . and tactics . . . could he *order* Randall or Nick down a dark and possibly deadly corridor?

He smiled at himself. It probably wouldn't matter. They'd likely balk at *that* order, anyway.

He was still smiling when he smelled the invader.

The odor struck them in the corridor like something liquid, as though the air had condensed into something vile around them. It was far more corrupt than the beach rot Brenn had breathed in his nostrils since childhood, more even than the wind off the potter's field that would pass over Maraven sometimes in the summer. For something beyond bodily decay lay in that smell

—it was sick, as though it corrupted the very air upon which it rode.

"Get back!" Brenn hissed to those behind him, but instinctively Randall and Nick closed with the two in front of them, turning their backs to Brenn, forming a tight, protective circle around Theodor. Weakly Theodor drew his little knife. Brenn blindly reached his free hand to find the boy's shoulder, and felt him cease trembling at the bolstering touch.

Sluggishly, aimlessly, the intruder staggered around the corner and stood in an intersection of four corridors. His face was bloated and glowing, his hair matted and dull. He carried an arm-sized piece of driftwood in his right hand and swung it back and forth, slowly and menacingly.

Brenn had seen enough. There was no life in the gaze—nothing but listlessness and torment and a strange, ominous calm, as though, now dead, the body repeated the violent movements impressed on its bone and muscle through a violent life. Brenn grabbed Theodor by the arm, intending to beat a hasty retreat, but Nick edged between the two of them, breaking his grip on the boy.

Then a sound began in Brenn's ears, a *rrritritrit* he was sure was Zephyrian bees—the strange ringing in the mind's ear that precedes great violence. He stepped back, shook his head, but the *ritritrit* persisted, and Brenn soon realized that the sound was a real one, coming from somewhere in the tunnel itself.

Nick, however, had given up listening.

"However foul he is, there's but one of him," the big journeyman said, snatching Theodor's dagger and striding toward the creature ahead of him. He approached the creature in what the swordsmen call Florentine style—dagger in the left hand, sword in the right. He feinted once at the walking corpse, then again as the grisly creature raised its wooden club. Clumsily, as though it was relearning the more subtle movements of combat, the creature brought its weapon harmlessly to ground with a thunderous blow that missed the dodging Nick by a good yard.

Deftly, like a trained assassin, Nick spun about and caught the creature a swift, slashing blow on the left shoulder, severing the arm. A black, viscous fluid tumbled from the wound, but unaffected, the invader swung his club again, this time missing a startled Nick by only inches.

"Get 'em back the corridor, Brennart!" Nick shouted.

Brenn stepped forward. "I'm not leaving you here!" he cried.

Nick stepped back, looked over his shoulder, and winked at his three companions.

"If nothin' else, I can outrun 'im!" he declared confidently, sidestepping yet another crushing blow from his adversary.

"No need to run when we can stand together!" little Theodor piped, and started rashly toward the combat up the corridor, armed only with his doubled fists. Brenn lunged, grabbed the boy again, and, despite his railing protests, began to drag him out of danger.

It was then that two more of the creatures lumbered in from a side corridor. Tattered in clothing and skin, they were on Nick before he had time to react, covering him in a fierce, rotting embrace.

Propelled by a strength he did not know he had, Brenn yanked Theodor back up the tunnel. The boy's feet left the ground entirely, and for ten yards or so Brenn carried him along, buoyed by anger and fright and frustration, pushing an equally frightened Randall in front of him.

The things were unstoppable, it seemed. Lop off a limb—no doubt even a head—and they still kept coming, as relentless as the plague, as inevitable as death itself. Brenn gasped at the exertion, and felt his lungs fill with the stench from several corridors.

The things were unstoppable, and they were everywhere.

Now, nightmarishly, he had forgotten where they were in the tunnels. Panic-stricken, he looked at wide-eyed Randall in front of him, at the wriggling boy with more courage than sense whom he carried in the crook of his arm.

They were *his* charges. *He* had started this business of going to find the intruder, had led them out into the tunnels, into Nick's certain death and most likely the deaths of the rest of them.

Loudly, more insistently, the *ritritrit* continued at his ear. Sirens, maybe? For a moment he remembered the brief bright moments with Terrance in Maraven, when the world had slowed and the two of them strolled through the market . . .

Which was foolish to remember in a time when he needed to recall geography.

Desperately Brenn turned young Theodor about and shook the boy vigorously.

"Where are our quarters, damn it!" he shouted. Theodor blinked and, without hesitation, pointed right down a well-lit corridor.

"You just needed to ask, sir," the boy whimpered, but Brenn was past diplomacy. Dragging Theodor, pushing Randall ahead of him, he lumbered down the passageway, leaving the noise and the stench behind him. The heavy oaken door appeared before them now as they turned the corner, scratched with a hundred years of apprentice graffiti. Randall and Brenn reached it at the same time, tugged it open, and tumbled over each other into the quarters, young Theodor pulled along on top of them.

Brenn leapt to his feet, closed the door, locked it, and listened intently for sounds in the hall beyond it. Faint, in the distance, he heard the shuffling of feet, the wet sounds of someone or something making its way through the maze of passages. He heard for the first time the strange, snuffling sound of the trespassers. And beneath it all, that high-pitched, insistent *ritritrit* that he now knew was in the air rather than in his imaginings.

Winded, sweating from his exertion even in the clammy tunnels, Brenn backed away from the door. "Do you hear it?" he asked Randall, Theodor—asked nobody in particular.

Randall looked at him vacantly.

"Hear—hear *what*, Brenn?"

"That whine, that buzzing! Like an overgrown mosquito or squinchbug is loose in the place!"

"I . . . can't say I *do*, Brenn," Randall replied, fastening the other door. Now the three of them sat together in the middle of the chamber, staring nervously at one another as outside both doors a scraping and snuffling began. Clumsy hands tried the locks to no avail, and then what Brenn had feared the most ensued: the steady, dull beating of dead men's shoulders against the doors.

The battering became more forceful, more dogged.

"I believe they are beyond *hurting* themselves and going away, you know," Randall observed desperately, his eyes intent on Brenn as he awaited some kind of decision, some kind of strategy.

Brenn nodded distractedly as both doors shook on their hinges, absorbing powerful blows. Between the persistent pounding and the continual *ritritrit*, he was scarcely able to think, wishing desperately for the speed and elusiveness of the sirens, so he could open these doors and fly away, out of the chambers, the tunnels, out of the city itself . . .

Like the sirens.

Or like Terrance?

"Terrance?" he said aloud, glancing rapidly around the room.

Ritritrit throbbed the air at his ear.

Suddenly it occurred to Brenn that despite his own thick-headedness and the chaos of the moment, the rescue Faye had gone to bring might already be under way.

"Are you here, Terrance?" he asked, and one of the lamps in the chamber went out, extinguished by indetectable winds.

"Show me!" Brenn cried, raising his arms before his dumb-struck friends. "*Tell* me what to do!"

Ritritrit droned the air in reply.

"Are you all right, Brenn?" Theodor asked, starting for his distraught companion before he was held back by a more cautious Randall.

"As right as I can be," Brenn answered, "with these *rits* in my ear."

Then it dawned on him.

Falling to the floor, he burst into delighted laughter, then crawled on all fours past an astonished Theodor to his bedding, where fumbling among the linens he found the writ and raised it triumphantly into the air.

"It was *writ* all along!" he exclaimed, and opened the document hungrily, his eyes racing down the page until they fell upon clause sixteen, the last words of which were forming just as the boy began to read:

> As journeyman now, no longer governed by a writ of apprenticeship, the party of the first part must make decisions as well as journeys. Some of these he must make by himself. However, he might think about walk-

> *ing through the other door and leaving his companions*
> *behind, since the pursuers want nothing from them in*
> *the first place, and then trusting his heart, and not his*
> *eyes, and certainly not his fears, until he can get back*
> *to the party of the second part, who will meet him at*
> *precisely the place where the document was signed.*

Brenn's jaw dropped. The clause had changed, but it had changed into hard words, indeed. To walk through that door into the arms of the dead would be as foolish, as reckless . . .

As staying here and waiting for them.

Soberly Brenn looked at Theodor. The boy returned his gaze eagerly, trustingly, as though somewhere in all his muddling Brenn had discovered a secret, had found a map to a maze even more confusing than the one they sat trapped in now.

He had seen that look before, on the faces of the ill and the damaged when they awaited Terrance's words, his touch.

"I always thought that being selfless was the last thing I'd do," Brenn muttered to himself. "Wouldn't it just beat all if I were right?"

He stepped by Randall and Theodor, and before they could stop him, he opened the door.

The dead man in front of him had taken several steps back, preparing to rush against the door once again. Brenn's action had caught him by surprise—if the walking dead were surprised by anything—and in the moment's pause and indecision, Brenn stepped resolutely out the door, closing it behind him. He heard a scuffle begin inside the chambers: no doubt the prudent Randall was wrestling Theodor away from the latch and from an ill-starred attempted rescue.

Brenn breathed deeply, taking in the fetid air. He choked for a moment, then drew on all his bravery, all his character, and steeled himself.

For a moment it seemed that the cwalu waited for him at the end of the hall, confused by his recklessness, his resolution. They bunched together in a pale, ragged throng, dripping seaweed and ordure. Slack-jawed and mindless, they weaved on their feet, brushing against one another, against the walls of the corridor, staring at Brenn and around him and beyond him with dark, unfixed eyes.

Looking into the blank and aimless faces, Brenn swallowed hard. "So much for courage," he muttered as the fear rose again.

At that moment, as though some purpose or energy coursed through the lot of them like an eel's charge surges through a living body, they moved in unison toward the boy leaning fearfully against the door at the end of the hall.

"I reckon Dragmond won't take no for an answer," the boy jested weakly, clutching the writ tightly in his hand. The faces of the dead caught the torchlight and glowed off-white, the strange blue-green of the drowned, the blotched dappling of plague. Some of them were almost recognizable, familiar: Brenn's mind fastened on one face, then another.

"Oh, how do you stop your fearing?" he asked the corridor around him as the faces closed in.

Then Duval parted the milling corpses in front of him, moving resolutely and blankly toward his prey, rope in hand.

Despite his terror, a great wave of sorrow and woe passed through Brenn. Though he had never much cared for Duval, he remembered him without malice and remembered the gloom of his passing.

Instinctively Brenn blurted forth:

"By the gods, Duval! I hated to see them do this to you!"

It was as though a strange sigh and release stirred through the waves of the approaching cwalu. Duval stopped in his tracks, then toppled to the floor, a look of surpassing peace and calm and even sweetness upon his face. The air crackled about him, as though he were a mast in a storm at sea, and the corpses who followed him bent knee, steadied themselves, and lay down in the corridor slowly, clumsily, as though settling into a yearned-for and final slumber.

Over them the boy walked, sidestepping one and then another, reaching the ladder that led up into Euterpe's through the body-clogged corridor. Onto the surface of the city he climbed, into the shop, inhaling eagerly the fresh lacquer and sawdust smell of the lutemaker's shop, leaving below him the stench of dampness and carrion and loss.

They littered Cove Road in dozens. There were women among

them, one of whom clutched grotesquely a cornhusk doll soaked almost past recognition. Brenn stepped around them as best he could, thanking the gods for the clearing sky and the moon that was now setting behind him as the night passed on into its last hour.

Brenn looked about him, behind him, searching for whatever power had brought the dead men to rest. For the life of him, he could not figure it, yet something told him the answer lay in the words he had spoken to Duval.

Up the road he trotted, the streets astonishingly deserted all around him.

"Where are the people?" he asked himself again. "Has— has Dragmond killed them *all*?"

Before him spread a terrible vision, of everyone—of Faye and Dirk and Terrance, indeed, everyone he knew in the city and beyond it—lying dead and forsaken in their long beds, as the Great Witch danced in her upper chambers, and laughed, and rained plague upon Maraven, upon Palerna, upon the farthest reaches of the continent.

He doubled his pace, and soon his lungs were burning.

The sky darkened in front of him, as though yet another rack of clouds was rising off the far Sea of Shadows to the east, smothering the sunrise and bringing with it the horizontal rain and the waterspouts of the tempestuous storms of early spring.

"Let Terrance be free from harm!" he prayed into the rising clouds, which seemed to glisten, to sharpen at the edges, to take on substance and weight far beyond the vapor his science had told him they were. They roiled and rose like cyclones, like waterspouts, and they took on the shape of women, then birds, then women with the bodies of birds, shrieking and swooping westward along the Maravenian coast.

Brenn fell to his knees, to his face. He covered his head with his arms and thought of Terrance's story about Aurum, about the harpies who had taken him.

But the leathery clouds passed over in a rush, propelled by more than wind. Brenn looked over his shoulder and watched the things flash over Grospoint and veer sharply north, where they circled tightly about Kestrel Tower and then, surging back out into the Sea of Shadows, dissolved over the Palern Reef.

Back over the squat buildings of Ships Brenn looked, where the gibbous moon descended, seeming to settle on the Hall of Poisoners. He wondered if the Goniph had escaped, or Dirk and Squab.

"Oh, let *Faye* be free from harm!" he whispered passionately, as somewhere far to the east, beyond Maraven itself—perhaps somewhere on the Gray Strand—a great shape floated across the face of the moon, its black wings jagged and toothed like the tendoned wings of a bat. For a moment it arched, black and reptilian in outline, then vanished behind the tall houses of the city.

Not stopping to speculate, the boy turned and ran toward Terrance's tower, which he could see now ahead of him. Around him the buildings nodded and began to move slowly toward the coast, as though an earthquake shifted them at their utter foundations. Cove Road narrowed to a footpath in front of him, as the buildings themselves seemed bent on forcing it into the sea.

Yet he passed through it unscathed, for with every lurch and slide of the buildings seaward, the sea itself receded, and the road bent ahead of him like a wide, stony bow. And still the tower lay in front of him.

"Illusion!" the boy pronounced triumphantly. "The Great Witch is spinning her web, but it won't take!"

Through fire Brenn passed, and a wall of ice, and an absolute shimmering darkness that lay in the center of the road. As he passed through each of them, he found the road clear, intact, and unobstructed on the other side.

Now all that stood against him was his own fatigue. It had been a night of terror—a night so exhausting that he only wanted to lie down, in the middle of the road if need be, to steal the hour of sleep his spent body yearned for.

It seemed now that the road was actually calling his name. In soft, melodic tones—in Faye's voice, it seemed—it told him that sleep was permitted, was fine, was even what he should do. That if he trusted in his heart, as he had been told to trust, why then, he would lie down and rest.

For wasn't it the heart that was saying *no more*?

For a moment, not three streets from the wizard's dwelling, Brenn slowed and staggered as his knees gave way in weariness.

Falling to the cobblestones, he skittered along atop rock and gravel and shell, his eyes ablaze with fireworks and stars and his throat dry and prickling with the long night's running.

He lay there on the street, his bones and muscles telling him that, yes, this was right. After all, what was the wait of another hour, or even a few minutes, when the body cried out and the mind went blank?

On the edge of sleep—or of stupor, for he could no longer tell the difference, and things lurched by him with the swiftness and the freakishness of dreams—he saw Faye.

Her movement was swift as shadows or clouds. One moment she stood ahead of him, where Hadrach Road came up to join Cove Road from the south. She stood at the intersection, dark-haired and dark-robed, her long garments swept up in a western wind.

Brenn called to her, but a powerful gust blew his voice back to him, and she spun about, framed for an instant by purple damask, and vanished, a look of curiosity on her face.

The air around him bristled with heat lightning, and what started as low rumbling thunder rose past the pitch of drum and woodwind and brass until it shrieked angrily like a monstrous predatory bird. And within that cry Brenn made out the rage of a woman, the shape of words:

"Damn you, Terrance!"

"Got to get to Terrance's," he told himself painfully. "Find out about her. About him."

Perhaps the longest moment of the journey lay in getting to his feet on Cove Road. Brenn stood wearily, excruciatingly, and it seemed for a moment that the wind would blow him down again. But the wind changed, dwindling to a pleasant breeze out of the east, and he walked the last street over to the shadow of the wall, to the library door he had decided to enter, since somehow the front door no longer seemed appropriate.

As he had guessed, the door was unlocked.

As he had not guessed, Terrance was waiting. Seated beside a lamp in the library—the very lamp Brenn had left burning when he departed—the wizard looked up from a manuscript through glittering, thick spectacles.

"Welcome back, lad," he said quietly, warmly, as he reached for a glass of lethe.

Brenn opened his mouth to speak, but the darkness rushed in before the words rushed out. He toppled into a shelf, scattering volumes, and fell soundly asleep, his head resting on a Druid botany text.

⤙⤙⤙ **Epilogue** ⤚⤚⤚

It was compassion that made her leave, and it was pluck that kept her going.

No sooner had Terrance left than Faye's thoughts became unsettled, her imaginings dire.

Brennart, she trusted, would soon be in rescuing hands. The wizard bounded upstairs once her story was told, and there was unearthly calm about the house after only a few minutes, as if somewhere in its heights or recesses, something had settled in place.

"Good luck, Brenn," she breathed, confident that if there was luck hiding in this great city full of sorrow, that he was the boy to find it. "I'll find the Goniph for the both of us."

It had never quite left her mind, of course. She had seen the knives drawn behind her, seen the struggle begin as the big man barreled into the Watchmen to allow her and Brenn a chance to escape. He'd never been one for selflessness, this First Master: the odds were he wasn't too good at it.

She was sure they would laugh together, the Goniph and she, over the strange uneasiness she felt when she thought of him.

"Why, the damned old oliphant probably smothered the lot

of them when he fell across 'em,'' she said to herself with a nervous laugh as she stepped into the Maravenian night, closing the library door behind her.

There was something in her that did not believe that.

The dead still walked the streets as Faye moved north and west through the city. Even the empty streets showed eerie signs of their passing: wet rags in the gutters, an old, dirt-covered shoe in the middle of Front Street, a Parthian silver coin designed especially to cover the eyes of the dead, the open eye engraved on both of its sides still visible in the fitful light of the streets. Above all, though, was the smell of the potter's field, of the necropolis.

The smell seemed to be fading now, somewhere off to Faye's right as she moved through the center of town toward Light Street and the border of Ships and Grospoint. Fading, she decided, because the dead were moving, were assembling in Wall Town. She was on Light Street, six streets south of the Hall of Poisoners, when she saw the first of the bodies.

There were two of them, a woman and a man. Sprawled beneath a cobbler's awning, they lay side by side, their hands touching curiously, almost tenderly. It was as though sleep had surprised two lovers walking the street together, though the mud on the man's clothing and the necklace and cerements about the woman suggested that only hours ago they lay on the Aquilan shore—he in a humble grave, perhaps the potter's field, she in one of the loftier mausoleums.

Faye paused for a moment, struck by the oddity of the scene. She found herself wondering if the dead had thoughts, and if so, what these two had thought of what had brought them together, most likely for the first time. But the imagining dizzied her: she was a young woman of sharply practical thought, and at once it dawned on her that something had stopped them, had allowed them to rest here in the center of Maraven, ten miles from the resting place their next of kin had no doubt imagined would be the final one.

A street away from the hall, in an alley between the shops of two moneychangers, Faye saw another one, seated against a building, an oar in his hand. His feet were still dripping seawater and kelp. An enormous white cut coursed under his chin from ear to ear, and yet this man whose violent death had no doubt crowned a violent life sat in the alleyway serenely, peacefully, the smile on his face that of a visionary or a child.

"Something has stopped them," Faye whispered in wonder. "They are released." Then she crouched in the alley, drawing her knife, for directly ahead of her, in the entrance of the Hall of Poisoners, there was the sound of movement, coarse laughter, an explosive oath.

Two Watchmen backed out into the street, followed by four others, who struggled with a litter atop which lay an enormous body covered with canvas.

"Looks like he took four of us with him," one of the men observed.

"Natheless," another replied tersely, straining at the pole he carried, "I still wish this one had got away and they'd killed a lighter one instead."

"You don't get heavier than him," the Watch captain said, folding his arms as the men staggered by, the litter bowing beneath the ponderous weight of the dead man. "He was First Master of the guild."

Through to the other end of the alley Faye raced, biting her lip and holding back her tears. She refused to cry for the big villain. She would not cry, she said, and she remembered the time the Goniph tried to sell her to an Alanyan silk merchant, the time he left her on the third floor of a Teal Front burgher's house when they heard a large dog growling downstairs.

Why, just this night past, he had brought them to the Hall of Poisoners, intending to hand his apprentices over to Dragmond!

And yet this was the man who had fed her all the meals she remembered, who taught her letters and numbers, enough Parthian to burgle an effigiary company and enough Aquilan to pass for a dangerous swordswoman when being a swordswoman and a dangerous one was a matter of life and death.

He was mean and nurturing, cruel and gentle and fascinating, like the city that had spawned him.

Faye did not even hear the coach draw near. It was a beautiful vehicle, black with the faint silver outline of wings decorating its sides. Slowly the coach came to a halt beside the sobbing girl, its driver silent, his mind continents away.

The purple-damasked curtains on the coach windows parted, opened by pale, long fingers.

"You must be exhausted, my dear," the passenger said, her voice deep and melodious, with something beneath it that crackled like lightning far out on the Gray Sea. Faye looked up into the gray eyes of the dark-haired woman.

There is something I am supposed to know about . . . Faye started to think, but her thoughts broke against the gaze of the woman like waters against a reef. Instead, she could only nod and think of the depth of those eyes.

"How understandable," the gray-eyed woman whispered sympathetically. "It has been a long night for all of us, poor dear. For where are you bound?"

"Ma'am?" Faye muttered blankly.

"For where are you bound, my dear? Your old home's not fitting for the time being."

"No, ma'am."

"Indeed it isn't," the woman proclaimed cheerily. "So for now, why don't you step into this nice warm coach, and I shall have Beltran drive us to my lodgings . . ."

"I thank you, ma'am," Faye said, struggling to recover her sense as well as her manners. "But I cannot . . ."

"Nonsense. The city's a wreck, and I shan't stand on old courtesies when I see a young girl in need. You remind me of myself at your age, my dear, and that alone will delight my heart in providing for you."

Faye shook her head, blinked awkwardly. The young woman smiled at her, black eyes flashing, distant, as though they held many sights at once.

Eyes. But I thought they were . . .

"Come, dear. We haven't all day."

Suddenly the eyes of the woman went blank, cast over with a milky whiteness and rolled erratically in their sockets. Gone was the alluring face of a moment before, and in its stead something grotesque, tormented—a pale-eyed gargoyle for the cornice of a seaward building.

Faye stepped back and gasped.

"*Damn you, Terrance!*" the woman screamed, her fingers groping aimlessly at the hems of the purple curtain. And around them the sea began to boil and tumble, and lightning plunged from the sky.

The screams and the thunder that followed drew Watchmen from their tasks at the Hall of Poisoners. Bursting through the alley, swords drawn, they rushed to the coach of the Great Witch, torn between duty and fear.

They found Ravenna coiled in her coach, clutching at curtain and door, her rage subsiding. Quickly the Watchmen slipped to the side of the disheveled girl in the street, who looked at them blankly, stunned and silent.

"Take her," hissed the Great Witch, pointing a long, black-nailed finger at the girl. "For if all else has failed, I have her still!"

Quickly and quietly the Watchmen wrestled Faye into the coach. At Ravenna's touch the girl swooned and collapsed. The curtained windows closed about the two women, and the clatter of hoofbeat and wheel resumed. The driver was motionless, scarcely moving the reins, and it seemed that the horses traveled by their own sense of direction, north through Ships to the southernmost point of the causeway and north after that toward the Kestrel Tower, the cobblestones streaked by the dark shadows of gibbets.

Broad and cobbled and corduroyed, Hadrach Road went on to Stormpoint, and from there, of course, into the rich deceptive land of Alanya.

It was the road that he could not take.

Instead, Terrance turned the wagon onto the narrower way, little more than a glorified cattle path that stretched southwest along the borders of the Corbinwood. He looked over his shoulder one last time, straining for a glimpse of Maraven.

Behind him the city looked gray, mist-covered, as though it had risen from the sea.

In the bed of the wagon Brenn lay sleeping on a pallet of rushes and blankets, the dog Bracken curled warmly beside him. A snore arose from one of them, but they were lying so close together the wizard could not tell which.

Terrance had made the bed hurriedly, while Brennart lay dozing amid the capsized bookshelves. It was a last-minute detail, for though you might prepare the bed, the wagon, and even pack the trunks for days in advance, the horses and the rushes had to wait until the last minute so they would be fresh for a long day's travel.

He had never dreamt it would be this quick, though. The old girl in the tower was as shifty and shrewd as ever. No matter how streetwise the lad was, she'd have taken him within the night, and it wouldn't have been pleasant.

Calmly Terrance drew forth a small flask from the voluminous storehouse up his sleeve. He laughed quietly. Times were when he had drawn things out of those dark folds that surprised even him. Once, looking for keys, he had drawn out a sprig of pennyroyal he had placed there to ward off fleas, and once, looking for pen and inkwell, he had come across an ancient but lively mouse, and only later had he realized that he had stored the creature in its infancy only to find it two years later spry and well fed from its foraging among wrinkles and pockets and stitches.

But this was the flask he had wanted, and he'd found it at first try. Gratefully he opened it, tilted it to his lips, and swallowed.

For even an old fool was not fool enough to give all the gin to the elves.

Oh, he knew it was bad for him, and he had sense enough to set it aside for months, sometimes for years. Brenn had lectured him about it, and Aurum and Albright, and Archimago before all of them. *She* had even looked disapprovingly upon his yen for the juniper.

But by the gods, he had no other vices! He didn't ravish peasant girls or pick locks, much less hang children and roust up a band of zombies. Defiantly Terrance took yet another sip from the flask, then set eyes and attention to the road weaving ahead of him.

Perhaps he should have told Brenn about the girl. When Terrance had returned from the underground, she had taken off to no telling where. Terrance only assumed she was safe, but he thought there was a good chance. After all, the Goniph had raised her, and if the big man's charges learned anything, they learned to survive.

Brenn was a case in hand, back there entangled in blanket and dog, facedown in rushes. Terrance smiled at the slumbering lad and shook his head admiringly.

Couldn't say the young fellow was the quickest of studies.

Oh, he was smarter than Aurum by some, but it was probably a good thing that he was not called to scholarship. Nonetheless, though he seemed capable of only one thing at a time, when he set about that thing, he generally did not disappoint. For what he did have was a certain doggedness—a grit that made up for the missing gifts—and a willingness to learn, no matter how much he complained about it.

Brenn had done marvelously well in getting from Wall Town to the tower, even though near the end the wizard had to fight magic with magic to let the boy see that these dragons and harpies and fires on the street were illusions of the Great Witch, set on all sides to waylay him and prevent his escape.

It had been simple, Terrance thought with a chuckle. From her place in the coach, traveling the streets of Maraven, Ravenna had searched and scanned the cove, Teal Front, Wall Town—everywhere she thought the lad would be running or hiding. It was only a matter of time until she would have found him, and only a short time afterward, all the dark magic of Kestrel Tower would have converged on one small vulnerable spot in the city.

How inconvenient for her that momentarily her sight was . . . stolen.

Terrance laughed aloud, and something stirred and chittered in his robe.

"Well, I'm in for good now," he conceded. "I've pitched the gaff. I suppose the old girl knows I'm still one to reckon with.

"Oh, well," he murmured. "It had to happen anon. All her black arts hang by a thread, and there'll always be someone holding the shears above her. I guess the 'dangerous age' has gone up fifty years."

He clucked to the horse and shook the reins, remembering the night behind him. Remembering Faye.

Perhaps he should have told Brenn about the girl. But then . . . it was those *biological* things that generally ambushed a boy of sixteen. He could weather an army of dead and a wall of illusions, then find himself taken in by dark eyes and soft skin and the natural enchantments of romance.

Terrance took another drink from the flask.

He should know. A girl's ambush had almost taken him in once, and he still was paying for the *almost*.

And after all, there was a king asleep in the bed of the wagon, and a country's soul lay in the balance. There was no time for flirtations and courtships with a small world to save.

"But the best to you, Faye, my dear," the wizard murmured, flicking the reins and replacing the flask as the horses broke into a trot. "I mean you no harm. Indeed I hope you find better times and a suitor worthy your compassion and pluck."

Brenn awoke with a shout, sweating in the wagon bed, from a dream in which Faye's countenance took on the sadness and lines of Dame Sorrow, and then the boat in which she sailed floated slowly into the jaws of a black leviathan, while he stood on the shore and shouted and gestured and waved in vain.

Terrance turned on the wagon seat, looking down at him with deep concern. Brenn was pale and fevered.

"Wh-where are we, Terrance?"

"South of Maraven, five miles from the Corbinwood. Sleep now."

"We have to—"

"*You* don't have to do anything but sleep."

Brenn tried to rise onto his elbows, but his head swam and his faculties shifted.

"It was a long night," he said. He coughed and smiled weakly.

"All the more reason to sleep," Terrance said, and quietly, awkwardly, the old man began to sing.

> *"Lullay, lullay, lullay, lullay,*
> *The faucon hath bore my make away . . ."*

Despite himself, Brenn felt his eyes closing. Bracken turned and grumbled at his side, and the faint soreness about the boy's throat faded with oncoming sleep.

So they traveled together, wizard and journeyman, master and king, with the woods and the wide world ahead of them.